JUMP DRIVES AND COFFEE STAINS

SPACESHIP MECHANIC
BOOK 2

JAMIE MCFARLANE

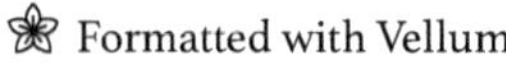
Formatted with Vellum

1

ALAS, PIRATES

"RIX, you gotta get that thing off me, already!" Kel called over comms, raucously tipping *Calypso* to port and dashing behind a fast-moving, semi-truck-sized asteroid.

"Frak, Kel, you're jumping around like a Texas frog on a hot sidewalk," Rix answered. He tried with significant effort to line up on the Model 72 Falistad light attack craft with *Calypso's* needler weapon's targeting reticle.

"Deal with it!" Kel snapped.

Rix tapped a thumb stud on the yoke, which caused his turret to jerk around so that it once again aimed straight at the pirate ship. With one eye on the acceleration vectors virtually tailing off behind their attacker, a quick mental calculation and an even breath, Rix pushed the targeting reticle some three hundred meters ahead of the aggressor and sprayed a ten second volley of needler darts.

"If you're going to make a move, now's the time," Rix said. "I just ventilated their cockpit. It's going to take them a minute to adjust."

Just then, the attacking ship swung hard to starboard and its aft engine clipped a refrigerator-sized asteroid, which sent it into a high-speed tumble.

"Uh, oh." It was all Kel could manage to say before the Falistad craft wrapped itself around another asteroid moving in the opposite direction. For a moment, it almost looked like the pirate spaceship would become forever engaged with the rock, but it then exploded.

"Recording debris field for Inner Passage map," Beverly said, appearing virtually as a ten-centimeter-tall woman wearing a scholarly robe and sketching on an unrolled map with a quill pen.

"Copernicus robes?" Rix asked. He and the four hundred nanometer long alien symbiote who had hitched a ride on the third member of *Calypso's* crew, Philo, played a game in which it was Rix's responsibility to guess what sort of costume Beverly was wearing when she showed up.

"Ding, ding, ding, we have a winner!" Beverly answered.

"That was close," Kel said, relief evident in her voice. "Is everyone okay?"

"Philo okay," Philo, the short, bearded alien chimed in. "Need suit. Fell to sleepy." It wasn't uncommon for Philo to sleep in his small bunk. That he didn't have easy access to a vac suit was something Rix noted to talk to him about. The combination of asteroids, space combat and lightly armored *Calypso* meant the odds of loss of pressure were significant, especially considering that Philo was trapped in his bunk because the main part of the ship was currently venting atmosphere.

"Stay put, Philo," Kel said. "We'll get to you shortly."

"I guess Jacknie wasn't too happy with our decision to stop paying for security," Rix said. "How is this approach better? Feels like taking down a pair of his short-range fighters is going to escalate bad feelings between us."

"Agreed. Sout Atal is going to be tricky for a while," Kel said.

"Tricky? I imagine we won't be going back."

"At least we have a hold full of flour and fish."

"I have a dozen subsystem failures reporting right now," Rix said. "We're going to lose money on this trip."

"It cost Jacknie more than it did us," Kel said. "Two Model 72s, even old ones like that, are worth at least a hundred fifty thousand."

"You're not making it better," Rix said. "Where do you think Jacknie's going to want to find payback for those?"

"Look, Rix, that's not my problem," Kel jutted her chin out. "Someone shoots at me and mine, we gotta do what keeps us alive. That's just the law of the deep dark."

"I'll be below deck to see if I can get us patched up so we can limp home," Rix said. "We're leaking coolant from the main."

"Turn off the reservoir," Kel said.

"Right. We're in an asteroid belt if you didn't notice," Rix said tightly. "Cutting power to the main seems like a bad idea."

"Well, shoot, you're not wrong. Can we make it another forty minutes? Cactus Flats isn't that far away." Cactus Flats was a wide-open area where the asteroid belt thinned, allowing pilots to make up lost time when sailing the Inner Passage.

"I'll know in a couple of minutes," Rix said, pulling the deck tile up so he could swing beneath to the 'tween deck. A cloud of steam greeted him as his feet hit the hull. Rix steadied himself as his suit struggled to clear vapor from his transparent face shield. "Beverly, could you give me a wireframe? I can't see anything."

"Of course I can," Beverly said.

An overlay of green lines projected onto his view and even through the steam, Rix had enough detail to orient his feet and move aft to where *Calypso* was reporting both a hull breach and a critical subsystem loss of the cooling system.

"What are you seeing?" Kel asked.

"Trouble," Rix answered. "That last hit we took scarfed out a chunk of the main coolant tank across all four of the baffles."

"I don't know what you're telling me aside from 'we took damage and it's bad,'" Kel said.

"No coolant will cause the main engine to overheat in a few minutes," Rix said. "If they'd known, they could have just avoided us for a few more minutes and we'd have been sitting ducks."

"We can't exactly sit around here," Kel said, "or the asteroids will finish off what Jacknie's crew started."

"I need to shut down power for at least a couple of minutes, tell me when you have a window," Rix said.

"Now. You have ninety seconds, max."

"Okay, good," Rix said, turning off the coolant supply.

"What Rixy do?" Philo asked, catching up with him. Rix gave him a double take, wondering how the little alien had escaped his bunk with the low atmospheric pressure they were currently maintaining.

"Looks like we're patching." Rix grabbed a roll of duct tape, grateful for its fantastic ability to adhere to anything. "Hold these rods in place for me, would you?"

"How's it going down there?" Kel called over comms.

"Don't pressure me," Rix grumbled, stretching tape around the temporary spine Philo was holding in place. Five strips high, Rix filled in the missing coolant walls with duct tape.

"Buddy, I need main in twelve seconds," Kel said.

"Frak," Rix growled. Instead of the shape he'd planned, he pushed the duct tape wall over so it grabbed onto the opposite side and placed one more piece atop it.

"Go now, Kel," Rix shouted.

Steam immediately poured from large gaps in the reservoir tank and Rix worked feverishly to apply duct tape patches. It wasn't anywhere near his best work, but in the end, he had a big silver-gray ball that no longer leaked.

"Are we okay?" Kel called after a few minutes.

"Kind of," Rix said. "I don't know how long my patch is going to last and best I can tell, we lost way too much coolant."

"We're still a couple of days out, Rix."

"I know, I know. It's holding for the moment. Let me look at the other less critical issues first and I'll come back to this. We need to coast through Cactus Flats to give me time to deal with this."

"If you can get us there, I have a path that'll give you thirty hours of free sailing."

"Sold," Rix said. "Philo, do you want to start with the hull patch? I'm going to work on subsystems."

Rix moved from one problem to the next, his estimate of the costs of the trip escalating with each one. "Man, maybe those guys did exactly what Jacknie wanted," Rix said after spending thirty minutes reviewing the critical issues. "Talk to me when we're clear for shutting off the main engine."

"You're good to go, Rix," Kel said. "Engines at full stop for thirty-one hours, twenty-two minutes. Going slow will chew into our timeline, though. Ordinarily, we'd burn hard through this spot."

"I wouldn't recommend it," Rix said, tapping a small sheet of steel into place with his boltgun. As expected, fixes applied while sailing were often temporary. While he was able to get all but the coolant problem dealt with after two hours, the fact that they had burned off all their coolant in both the primary and reserve tanks was a problem he wasn't sure how to fix.

"Talk to me, Rix," Kel said as he joined her for a meal of cold cereal. "You're looking uncharacteristically glum."

"Any idea where we can get some coolant? Do we have contact with Patience? Maybe we could get Freda to bring some out?" Rix asked.

"We have a reserve tank. Did you find that?"

"The reserve took a bigger hit than the primary," Rix said. "Of course, the primary was hot enough that when it got hit, we lost all but a couple of liters. It's not enough."

"How much do we need?"

"Five liters if we limp in," Rix said.

"We can't make it with two?"

"You'd burn up the main in four hours, give or take."

"How could you possibly know that?

"The specs are publicly available."

"And you just happened to have read them?" Kel raised an eyebrow.

"What can I say, I'm curious and I like to read."

"But manuals. You like to read manuals."

"Not only," Rix defended. "Let me take five hours for sleep. I'm irritated that I don't have a better solution than calling Freda."

"Freda is six days out and if she agrees to it, we're probably talking twenty-five hundred credits just to get her to come," Kel said. "And that's assuming I can bounce a radio signal through all this crap and get it to her."

"I'm taking a nap," Rix said, pushing back from the table and standing. "Let me know if something breaks."

"Are you mad?"

"A little."

"At me?"

"At the situation," Rix said. "I'm pissed that Jacknie sent those fighters after us and even more that six crew are dead because they did what he told them. It was senseless."

"If you hadn't shot them, we'd be the dead ones."

"I know. I'll be in a better mood with a little sleep."

"Okay," Kel said. "Want me to tuck you in?"

Rix looked back at her. The comment was unexpected given they'd shared exactly one, one-sided kiss in the past. She wore an impish grin which caused Rix to shake his head. "You're too much," he said.

"Probably," she agreed. "But seriously, how can I make it better? I know, how about I make your favorite breakfast when you get up. You barely ate any of that cereal. We have enough in the reefer for that egg wrap you like, and I'll make you some hot coffee, since that's the way you like it. I'll even clean out the warmer mug so it doesn't get cold on you."

"That'd be nice, Kel," Rix said, grabbing a bar at the top of his bunk cabinet and swinging his legs in. Instead of the full-sized cabins found in larger spaceships, *Calypso* had rectangular bunks that were a meter and a half square on end and two and a half meters long. A person couldn't stand within the bunk but had plenty of room to spread out as they slept and even had a few drawers to hold possessions.

Rix closed the hatch next to the main hallway and tested pressurization. With individual atmospheric controls, he discovered that his bunk had two through holes and was one of the culprits of why *Calypso* wasn't holding cabin pressure.

"Philo, can you grab that hull patcher?" Rix called over comms. "My bunk is venting."

"Coming, Rixy," Philo said.

A moment later, he heard rapping against the hatch and he opened, accepting the small tool that would force a plug into the hole and inject a foam sealant that expanded. Rix pulled back his blanket, only to discover it also had a through hole. "That's just great," he groused, tossing the blanket aside and filling two more holes.

"Sorry 'bout blanket," Philo said as Rix handed the tool back to his little alien friend.

"Thanks, Philo," Rix said. "It's not you. I'm just frustrated. Pirates ruin things. It's just such a waste."

Pushing his pillows into place, Rix stretched out, his foot immediately finding the hole in his blanket. It was not without effort that he tamped down his frustration. They were out of coolant. It wasn't even difficult or expensive material to come by back on the station.

He allowed his mind to wander as he struggled for sleep. It was nice that Kel would let him use the warming mug for what passed as coffee. The lode bean, while easily adapted for growing on space stations and laced with a cousin of caffeine, was much better as a cold drink, as it cooled more quickly than it should. A warming mug was about the only way to enjoy it hot. These were the thoughts on his mind as he drifted to sleep.

Five hours later, he awoke to knocking and grinned. "I've got it, Kel!" he said, opening the hatch. He repeated excitedly, "I've got it!"

"You've got what?"

"Lode bean coffee. Its thermal transfer rate is fantastic."

"I don't know what you're saying," Kel said, her eyes going glassy as she reviewed a definition on her HUD. "It gets cold faster than it should. Yes, I know."

"Beverly, if we keep under forty percent power, can you run the numbers? Will it work?" Rix asked.

"Will what work?" Kel asked.

Beverly appeared between the two of them, her hair was white and wildly frizzy, and she wore a white mustache. "Rix is considering using lode bean coffee as a coolant. It is poorly suited to the task, but my calculations show that forty percent power is achievable."

"Get to brewing!" Rix exclaimed, grabbing Kel and dancing with her. "We're going home, baby!"

"Now who's crazy?" she asked, grinning at his enthusiasm.

"Me. You're talking about me," Rix said with a big smile.

"I like this Rix a lot more than grumpy Rix."

"That's fair. Me too."

"Burrito and coffee are waiting."

After a long nap and breakfast, Rix was once again ready to take on the coolant leak that had once felt insurmountable and was now just a matter of brewing enough coffee. He chuckled quietly as he splashed some of the drink on himself while filling the makeshift reservoir.

"What are you laughing about?" Kel asked, having accompanied him below decks.

"Coffee and duct tape," Rix said. "Who'd have thought the most sophisticated machines in the galaxy could be repaired with these things? It's like the universe is laughing at us."

"Someone has a sense of humor, that's for certain. How long before we know if this'll work?" Kel asked.

"It'll work right away. The question is probably more 'how long will it last?'" Rix said. "I'm hoping the answer to that is 'long enough to limp back to Patience Station.'"

"Have you checked the hold yet?"

"Not yet. I know there are some through holes in there because I tried to pressurize it and it didn't work."

"Philo says he's about done applying patches to the hold," Kel said. "We should be able to pressurize fully in twenty minutes."

"How about we check the hold before you fire up the engines?" Rix suggested.

"You're done here?"

"For the moment, at least," Rix said. "I have a couple of parts we're going to need to manufacture. I'll put them in the communications queue so they're done by the time we get back."

"Good plan. I'm afraid to ask ... how expensive are we talking?"

"Twenty-one hundred credits."

"Frak, that wipes out anything that looks like profit," Kel groaned.

Rix nodded and led Kel up through the main hallway and back to the hold. Pushing through the hatch, he initially wasn't sure what he was looking at. A cloud of dust hung in the air, and there were large puddles of something milky on the deck.

"That's not good," Rix said, rushing over to where a cask of Jacknie's Grog had once been stored. In its place was the remains of the aluminum cask, its contents having been expelled due to enemy rounds piercing the hull. "Yeah, that's what I figured. They shot up the grog and the flour. I imagine there's a few good bags left, but this is a mess. Looks like the fish survived, though."

"How depressing," Kel sighed.

"Yes and no," Rix said. "We survived a two-on-one assault by a superior craft due to your excellent flying in close quarters. We've had no casualties aside from some low-rent grog and a few bags of flour. Damage to the ship is pennies to the dollar what we inflicted on our enemies. You, kiddo, are the hero in this."

"I got us shot up to all cognie," she shook her head.

"Again, look at the other guys," Rix said. "When people come swinging, there's going to be pain. Your point isn't wrong, though."

"I think you're saying we need to drop the spec loads, and I need to use my shiny new short haul freighter license and start making some predictable, if boring, income," Kel said.

"I'm not saying anything other than we need to figure out how to dial down the danger," Rix said. "We're not indestructible and we've been lucky."

Kel's face fell as she considered the conversation. "I know," she said and then changed subjects. "No more than forty percent burn?"

"I'd keep it to thirty-five if you can," Rix said. "I know it's annoying, but who knows how much stress my fixes will take?"

"Rix, if we've lost most of our load, I'm not going to have anything to stake our next run," Kel said, circling back to Rix's suggestion. "I'm going to have to take a job if I'm going to hold up my end of the partnership. And before you offer to stake the entire thing, no. I know better. You're putting your mechanic's bay on hold. Have you even looked at the space?"

"We dropped off tools and a cabinet," Rix said. "Nothing beyond that."

"Okay, then. Can you deal with me taking *Calypso* out by myself? It's not like I don't know how."

"To do what?"

"There's a premium load on Gestalt Station that's six days through Dravari space. They'll pay for a deadhead to their station and twice standard to get the load safely to Majis on Grelvox," Kel said.

"Majis ... oh, there it is. It's a city of a million. Doesn't seem like a big thing. Why are they paying so much?" Rix asked, gesturing to his HUD's map.

"Dravari are choking off loads from anywhere in Surnac Belt. You know this."

"I do," Rix agreed. "How is it you plan to get around Dravari?"

"Oh, you're so cute," Kel said. "I've spent a lifetime avoiding Dravari. Now that I have a legit license, even if they catch me, there's not much they can do other than impound my cargo. And, if they do that, my client has insurance that covers the load if they hold it for more than thirty days. None of that works without my license, but now that I have it, I need to take advantage of the perks."

"You're assuming they won't lock you up for past crimes, Kel," Rix said.

"Assuming is such a strong word," Kel said. "My first choice will be to avoid them. After that, we'll see."

"And you want me to stay home. What if things break down?"

"We'll come up with something, but Rix, I need you to do your thing," Kel said. "I've taken over your life enough already. Tell me you wouldn't love to have the better part of a month to focus on your work. And maybe without me around, you might pay some attention to Amari. She has a daily exercise class in the Atrium gardens at 0700."

"Hutari's mom?" Rix asked. "Why would I do that?"

"Oh, Lords of Gavenar but you're as dense as a black hole."

2

LEARNING THE ROPES

"You have coffee stains all over your jumpsuit," Kel laughed as Rix joined her on the bridge.

"We had a leak," Rix said without quite the same humor.

"If it's any consolation, we're already past Church Rock, and that's Aegis right up there," Kel said, pointing at a massive, slowly spinning asteroid. One of five guardian asteroids of Patience Station, Aegis soaked up most of the loose asteroids that would otherwise strike the station.

"That's good news," Rix said. "I'm short on duct tape and it's starting to fail. Something in the coffee is reacting to the tape."

"I could call a tug at this point if we needed," Kel said. "Are we good to keep going?"

"Yes, twenty minutes, we have. Two days might be a bigger problem," Rix answered. "I feel badly that this load is a bust. I was going to spend my part of the payoff to make a cleaning robot. I'm tired of all the grit and gunk everywhere."

"Forty years of service. There's bound to be a little buildup here and there."

"It's more than buildup. I'm afraid that when we start really cleaning things down to the bone, we're going to find structural problems," Rix said.

"Out of sight, out of mind?"

"Hardly. I'm a mechanic. It's in my nature to poke at anything that's flimsy."

"Tell me something I don't know," Kel said. "And thanks for cleaning up the hold. That was quite a mess."

"What I did can't be classified as a thorough cleaning," Rix said. "I picked up most of the mess and separated broken bags of flour from whole ones. About half the remaining load is in broken bags. We can't sell those. We have no idea if it's contaminated."

"You're nuts. We don't throw away perfectly good food on a station this far from civilization," Kel scoffed.

"No way I'm selling this stuff. We'll end up eating it," Rix said. "Wouldn't that be poetic? We get sick on food made from our own supplies."

"Can't you get it inspected or something?"

"That's not a horrible idea," Rix said. "Let me check the market. I bet I can have a sifter manufactured. There it is, only two hundred credits. You're a genius, Kel!"

"That's coming out of your half, Rix," she said. "I'd just sell the broken bags if it were up to me."

"Go ahead and dock down by my shop. I'm going to have to work on *Calypso* before you take off anyway," Rix said.

"Bet you wish you had those photonic barrier generators still," Kel said. "Patience Station, this is *Calypso.* We're on approach and request permission to dock on the station."

"Kel, you're back!" Hutari said. "Permission granted. Are you docking on the public pier on Level 5?"

"Negative, we're headed to that private pier on Level 8," Kel said. "Rix made a deal with Quixly for a spot down there. You should have something on that."

"Let me check," Hutari said. "You do know that Level 8 is mostly unoccupied, right? Power and gravity have been intermittent down there. I've been getting warnings, but we're muting those now."

"Sounds about right," Kel said.

Rix sighed. Like *Calypso*, Patience Station had been poorly maintained for decades. It was a good news, bad news type of situation. He'd profited well from fixing some of Patience Station's systems, but it also made him wonder how far from a major system failure the station really was.

"Rix is on the security list for Level 8. You should be good to go. I'm not sure if there's anything powering the magnetic moorings, though. You might have to go manual," Hutari said.

"Copy that, Patience," Kel said. "We're out. Will I see you at Atrium tonight?"

"Mom and I will be there. Patience Station, out."

"Did you hear that? Hutari wanted to make sure you knew that Amari would be on the Atrium tonight. I bet she'll be playing over by the waterfall."

Rix smiled but didn't comment. He'd spent more than one evening sitting in the Atrium's slowly failing gardens listening to Amari play an instrument that was essentially a synthesizer with a piano keyboard. He'd never talked to the woman aside from small talk when he'd left tips in her tip jar from time to time.

"What's involved in docking manually?" Rix asked.

"I'll bring us in close and use our mag clamps to hold us to the pier. You and Philo will lash us down with a few lines so we don't have to rely on the mag clamps," Kel said. "There's a trick to tying up, but Philo can show you all of that."

"Okay."

"Philo, come on up, we're going to do a manual tie down on Level 8 pier," Kel said. "I need you to show Rix the ropes."

"Yup, yup!"

Under Kel's experienced hand, *Calypso* slid smartly into place, the ship's bright lights illuminating a long-ignored, dilapidated pier that suffered from significant corrosion and obvious asteroid damage. The task of tying up was made more difficult by cleats that were missing entirely. Yet Philo was undeterred and found alternative tie ups, which he easily handled.

"Good job, boys," Kel said. "Rix, any chance you can get your bay open from the outside?"

"Never tried," Rix shrugged. "Beverly, can you augment what I'm looking at here? I'm not exactly sure which one is mine."

"Bay 807," Beverly said.

Rix chuckled. "That'd be helpful if there was anything showing that designation."

Without warning, large bright white numerals, 807, appeared on one of the several large bay doors that opened to the pier. "How about now?" Beverly asked.

"That works," Rix said, just about to take a step, when he felt a flutter in his stomach. "Frak, gravity's out." Suddenly, his boot magnetics engaged, and his feet were pulled to the deck.

"Hutari said we've been having trouble down here for a while," Kel said. "I wish we knew someone who was good at fixing things."

"Yeah, yeah, yeah," Rix waved her off. "How long are you going to be gone? I don't think half a month is going to cover everything that needs doing."

"I have news about that," Kel said. "Is there any chance you can have me back up and running in seventy-two hours? That's like the border of what works if I want to take that job. They're offering to go past their deadline if I commit today."

"I don't suppose you'd take an 'I'll do my best' type of answer," Rix answered.

"That's implied. The thing is, if I mess this up, it'll make other jobs harder to get."

Rix clanked over to 807 and tried the security panel. As expected, there was no power. Knowing that was a possibility, Rix had brought backup power and a tool to get him into the cavity that would allow him access to manually power the lock. After a few minutes of trying different things, the blue screen of the security panel glowed to life. Three minutes after that, the security panel had been updated after reaching out to Patience Station's controller. The sound of an actuator straining grated on his ears, only to turn off after thirty seconds.

"Why does everything have to be so hard?" Rix complained. "Hutari, come in please, this is Rix Banner."

"Go ahead, Rix."

"Can you transmit the error log for bay 807's external security panel? It's not opening, even though access was acknowledged."

"Log is inbound, Rix," Hutari answered.

"Thank you."

"What's the problem?" Kel asked, having exited *Calypso* and joined Rix.

"Big door isn't working," Rix said. "Beverly, what do you make of the logs?"

"Drawing too much power when the actuators fired," Beverly said. "I'd guess the door is frozen shut. Try the man door five meters to your left."

"Sure," Rix said. It took another fifteen minutes to power the second security panel, but this time, the door popped open after Rix manipulated the handle. "Looks like there's no pressure in the shop. Hope you didn't leave anything important in here, Kel."

"What are we doing, Rix? It looks like power is out down here," Kel said.

Rix had crossed to where his tool cabinet stood. Opening the cabinet, he pulled out a pair of lighting sticks and adhered them to the wall, providing decent illumination for the entire bay. "Philo, grab a persuader, we're going to see if we can unfreeze that big door."

"Philo like bang, bang," Philo said.

Twenty minutes later, the door was unfrozen and they managed to open it fully, draining Rix's portable power unit as they did.

"Bring her in, Kel," Rix said.

"You'll have to untie her, first."

"We've got it."

And they did. After a short time, Kel backed *Calypso* into the shop. Longer than it was wide by quite a bit, the spaceship easily fit inside.

"Give me a minute," Rix said, exiting the shop into Patience Station's hallway after passing through an emergency airlock he set in front of the hatch. Suddenly, the lights within the shop turned on. Rix returned shortly after. "Someone turned us off while we were gone.

I'm going to have to figure out who's in charge down here so they don't keep doing that."

Closing the open doors, Rix checked the seals and found they were within spec for flooding with atmosphere. Leaking a liter of atmosphere each minute seemed excessive to Rix, and he silently vowed to track down and fix the leaks. As it was, however, they were home, the shop was pressurized and heating up and there was a whole lot of work in his future.

"I think these seeds got ruined when they shut off our power," Kel said, picking a bag from the shelf where they'd stored the beginnings of their boutique. "This place sure can be frustrating at times. Tell me, what can I do to help get you moving forward on repairs to *Calypso?* I'd hate to miss that deadline."

"Pick up parts from the manufactory for me? I've got a bunch. You'll need to take both grav pallets." Rix paused. "You know what, that's a bit too much for one person. Let's go together."

"Push me!" Kel squealed, sitting atop one of the grav pallets with her knees beneath her. Philo climbed up behind and gave Rix an excited smile.

"You're such children," Rix said, smiling as he gave Kel a push into the hallway. Not to be outdone, he lay flat on the second pallet and pushed off from the deck with his foot hanging over the side to catch her. Neither grav pallet slid along particularly straight and they careened off the walls of the long hallway, leaving small marks behind. Rix mentally added fixing the damage to the list of things he planned to accomplish.

"Are you getting hungry?" Kel asked. "Petju is asking about the flour. What are we telling her?"

"Yes, I'm hungry, and we tell Petju the truth," Rix said. "I have that sifter that'll clean impurities from the flour ready to pick up. I made some more bags, too. But no matter what, we fess up."

"You're no fun."

"I've heard that before," Rix said.

With a bill totaling thirty-eight hundred credits, Rix's bank balance dwindled to forty-two hundred credits. Like Kel, he had a substantial amount of capital tied up in speculative cargo, much of which had been ruined. Fortunately, his manufactory patterns were still selling well, bringing in, on average, four hundred credits daily, the details of which he hadn't shared with Kel.

"This is a huge pile of parts," Kel said as they struggled to fit into the cargo elevator together.

"There was quite a bit of damage," Rix said. "Some of it is for the shop, too."

"Shixen cleaned you out of tools," Kel said. "Are you worried Sable is going to compete with you for ship repairs?"

Before Rix could answer, they heard a familiar voice calling for them to hold the elevator, which they did. Jogging down the hallway, Constable Quixly caught up with them and stepped in.

"Hello, Constable," Rix said. "I'd offer my hand, but I've a poorly balanced load."

"How busy are you, Banner?" Quixly asked. "We have a thing going."

"What kind of thing?" Rix asked. "We had some trouble with Draven Knights just outside of Sout Atal, *Calypso* is pretty beat up."

"Kurth, our new station maintenance guy is stuck on Grelvox waiting for a ride," Quixly said. "In the meantime, we have blackwater backing up into Belflower Suites. Jesif is beside himself and is threatening to shut the Belflower down."

"Blackwater? Are you sure?" Rix asked.

"Yeah, we're sure."

"You're here as the acting mayor, then."

"Yes."

"Tell you what, give me an hour to get things put away and I'll run up and see what the problem is," Rix said. "You should talk to Kel about your man on Grelvox, though."

"Is that so?" Quixly asked, looking at Kel.

"Your blackwater might make it so I can't help you," Kel said. "I have to leave here in seventy-two hours if I'm going to make a rendezvous on Gestalt Station that has me transporting to Grelvox."

"I don't see the problem."

"*Calypso* isn't safe to sail," Kel said. "Rix might be able to get her space worthy again, but not if he's up fixing Jesif's poopy water."

"Patience Station needs Kurth transported, but we can't pay for unlicensed transport," he said.

"I'm licensed for short haul," Kel said. "What are you paying?"

"Eighteen hundred is standard."

"Right, and how's that going for you?"

"Not very well."

"I'll do it for twenty-five hundred. Your man will get first-class treatment," Kel said. "You gotta keep Jesif out of Rix's face, though."

"Hold on, now," Rix said. "Blackwater backups shouldn't be that hard to fix. It's almost always a blockage. I know that Geoff had tools that would clear blockages. At least let me take a look. Jesif's right to make this a priority, blackwater can seriously damage things."

"You'll go look, then?" Quixly asked.

"Time and materials, one hundred fifty credits per hour, minimum two hours," Rix said.

“Fine,” Quixly said, sending over an expedited contract.

“I need you to restore my maintenance security status,” Rix said. “Would you help Kel take this down to my new shop? I’ll run right up and take a look.”

Rix could see Quixly’s struggle with doing something he felt beneath him. But pragmatism won the day, and he unhappily nodded agreement.

Exiting the elevator on Level 17, Rix thought it a good sign that he couldn’t smell any sort of sewer fumes as he stepped onto the floor. It was the middle of the day, and the Atrium wasn’t quite as busy as it was in the evenings. Even so, he passed several friends who knew he’d been traveling, and it took some effort to avoid getting bogged down too much.

The entry to Belflower Suites was through a carved stone archway. At some point, the Belflower, as locals referred to it, had been the picture of elegance in an exotic locale. Time hadn’t been friendly–while it still had a sense of grandeur, much had been lost. Upon entering, the smell of sewage hit him right away.

“We’re closed today, Rix Banner, and your lease has expired,” Jesif said with obvious irritation. “Please leave.”

“I could do that, Jesif,” Rix said, allowing the statement to sit uncomfortably for a moment. “Quixly asked me if I’d investigate a potential backup. I’ll just let him know you’ve taken a disliking to me and you’d prefer he found someone else.”

“Wait, hold on,” Jesif said as Rix started to turn toward the entry. “If you’re a hireling, you should do your work. My business is suffering for *paying* customers.”

“Is that why you have a chip on your shoulder with me?” Rix asked. “Because Garba called in a debt to get me a place to stay for a couple of weeks?”

"Not just a place, Rix Banner. You took my finest suite so that I could not rent it out."

"Fair enough. You've been wronged."

"Are you mocking me?"

"Nope. Where's the poopy water, Jesif? Probably best to get moving on this," Rix said.

"Suites 101, 103 and 105," Jesif said. "It appears to be that side."

"Makes sense," Rix said. "Are they open?"

"No, but come here and I'll add temporary security tokens so you may have access." Rix placed a hand on the security panel. "When you're working, you'll use the side entrance. I don't need people knowing we have a municipal problem."

Rix nodded. "Anything else?"

"No, those are my conditions."

"I'll be back."

"Where are you going?"

"This will go a lot faster if you let me do my job, Jesif," Rix said. "That is, unless you have experience with space station wastewater handling. Then, by all means, let's talk this through. I could use your help."

"You *are* mocking me. I will report you to Quixly."

Rix shook his head and walked back to the suites. Upon entering 101, the smell he'd picked up in the lobby intensified. In the head, he found a fountain of blackwater pushing up through the toilet. "That's for sure not good," he thought he been talking to himself, but Jesif had followed.

"Are you always this brilliant?" Jesif asked.

"You're funny," Rix said. "No, I'm not always this brilliant. I have no idea how wastewater systems work on a space station. That Quixly has asked me to work on this shows just how few people around here are willing to get their hands dirty."

"I'm calling him now. You are, as I have suspected, a complete fraud," Jesif said.

"Suit yourself," Rix said and walked out. "Beverly, can you find diagrams? This can't be too bad. There's just a block, right?"

"Yes I can," she said. "There are fail safes that should have prevented this issue."

"Show me, please," Rix said. Beverly projected the complex mesh of wastewater pipes that ran through Patience Station. "Zoom in. Focus on whatever is downstream of those suites." The morass of the wastewater pipe expanded in his view. "What's the first common pipe used that's south of the common connection beneath those suites? Also, highlight where those suites connect so it's easier for me to see."

Rix's view expanded as some pipes seemed to fly over his head, and he found himself within the three-dimensional sculpture which was the waste system. With his finger, he traced the lines that dropped away from the suites and finally joined up.

"Do you think the blockage is there?" Beverly asked.

"Hmm, look here," Rix said, pointing his finger closer to the edge of the space station just beneath Belflower Suites' soaring bank of windows. "Does that strike you as interesting?"

"I'm not following, Rix."

"Can you navigate me to this location?" Rix asked. "Philo, are you there?"

"Yes, Rixy."

"Fifty credits an hour today if you'd like to be my apprentice."

"Philo free."

"Not my money, Philo," Rix said. "Bring my main tool bag, and we'll need that big heating element from the environmental tool cabinet. Also, grab some hull patch. Beverly knows where I'm at."

"You are intuiting a station breach, Rix?" Beverly asked as she highlighted the doors he would need to pass through.

"More of a guess," Rix said. "But the wastewater for those suites runs right by a thin spot in the rocky surface of Patience Station's surrounding asteroid. If that were penetrated, it'd freeze up those pipes without necessarily causing new problems."

"There would be a decompression event if that were true," Beverly said.

"You're right. Philo, we're going to need some pipe," Rix called. "Load the tools on a grav pallet and stop by manufacturing. I'll have an emergency order."

"And now you believe there is a break."

"Trust the process," Rix said, opening a hatch and climbing in. He clambered through the maintenance space between station levels and smiled as his lights fell on a brownish ice block that encased a tangle of sewage pipes. "Will you look at that?"

"Well solved, Rix," Beverly said. "I remain impressed with how quickly you diagnose issues."

"Thank you. And first things first, would you have the manufactory make those suits that can keep us clean as we work? This will get messy. We're also going to need some sort of vacuum cleaner. Heck, there are several things we're going to need. We might as well get to work."

3

ALL ABOUT POTENTIAL

"How's it going?" Quixly asked when Rix strode into the foyer of Belflower Suites two hours after his heated conversation with Jesif.

"I was just about to ask Mr. Jesif if I could have access to the suites," Rix said.

"Were you able to find a problem?"

"A small asteroid strike punched out a piece of the station next to where the waste pipe ran. Blackwater flooded the opening and froze, also freezing the drain at that point. I grabbed a junction from maintenance and replaced it. I also applied a hull patch to the breach. The hole was small enough that some of the less fluid parts of the blackwater clogged the opening and then froze in place."

"That's a vivid picture you paint," Quixly said. "Jesif is back cleaning up the overflow. He said the two of you were arguing. Is there anything I should know about?"

"I'm not sure Jesif and I are going to be best friends anytime soon, but I think we're square," Rix said.

"Let's see if things are working and I'll get you cut loose."

"Sounds like a plan," Rix followed Quixly back to Jesif.

"I suppose you want an apology," Jesif said, looking at Rix skeptically.

"Not at all, Mr. Jesif," Rix said. "I wanted to check to make sure things are flowing correctly."

"Must have been a simple problem," Jesif muttered to himself.

"I'll just check the other suites and be on my way," Rix said after examining the head in the suite where they all stood.

"Jesif, don't be like that," Quixly said. "Banner did you a solid here and you're acting like he took your last comera. You're better than that."

"Just too dang coincidental that a semi-sentient Earther is magically fixing things on a space station that's so darn sophisticated. Something doesn't add up, and I'm done with all this intrigue. It's impossible to make a credit on this larva-infested outhouse, and now we're to believe he's some sort of superhero? It's just too darn much."

Rix and Quixly exchanged a look, which Rix interpreted to mean it'd be better for him to leave than to stay, so he moved on. As expected, the other two suites were unlocked, and while he had to tramp through quite a mess to validate, he discovered the wastewater was flowing just as it should be.

Peeling off his environmental suit once he was out into the fresh air of the Atrium, Rix took a deep breath. The station air was still a bit fouled, but with new filters installed in all accessible locations, it smelled significantly better than when he'd arrived. Unfortunately, to really finish the job would require duct-crawler robots or a team of nimble, hardworking spacers to brush down the insides.

"Are you stuck?" It was a woman's voice that seized Rix's attention after he'd caught a whiff of light perfume. He turned and found a woman with long dark hair looking at him with a bemused grin.

Rix had been removing his suit and had run into resistance slipping his boots off. Add to that getting lost in thought, he realized he'd been frozen for a good thirty seconds. "Ah, oh, right," Rix said. "A little stuck." Taking her in, he found that she was probably in her late thirties, if her species was similar to humans in their aging, and had an athletic build.

"Lean back," she said, chuckling with good humor. "You're Rix Banner, our newest resident, right? I'm Amari, Hutari's mother."

Rix leaned back and let Amari help pull the environmental suit off, inside out, and dropped it to the ground. "Oh, Amari, Kel said she was going to introduce us. She doesn't think I have a rich enough social life."

"That's flattering," Amari said. "I saw you toiling over here and thought it would be an opportune time to introduce myself. Do you have any interest in a coffee?"

Rix blinked a few times, his 1950s view of relationships confounded by her straightforward nature. "Well, heck, that's very nice. I'm not sure I smell very good, though. I was just working on a problem with wastewater."

"There is a smell," she said. "But I believe you've captured it nicely with this environmental suit. Perhaps you'd allow me to drop it into the recycler."

"I was thinking I'd get it cleaned," Rix said. "I keep finding myself in situations where I need a suit like this."

"Oh, that's unfortunate. That purple material is an indication the suit cannot be cleaned by a suit cleaner," she said.

"Rixy! I finished. Pay now?" Philo asked excitedly, bounding up to the pair.

From his personal funds, Rix paid Philo the promised fifty credits per hour, rounding up to three hours, even though Rix would only be paid for two and a half. "There you go, little man," Rix said, tousling Philo's hair. Philo smiled at Rix and then at Amari.

"Did you get the tools put away?" Rix asked.

"Philo do now!" And with that, Philo bounced away.

"Looks like recycling is the key," Rix said. "And to your offer: I'd be down for a snack before I get back to work."

"I thought you were done with your job," Amari said, looking a little disappointed.

"That was the emergency job," Rix said. "*Calypso,* Kel's little freighter, ran into some trouble on the way back from Sout Atal. She has an opportunity for a legit freighter job if I can get our ship fixed up and running."

"I'm so sorry. I don't mean to intrude on your day." Amari lightly touched his arm and then started to walk away.

Rix watched her walk for a few seconds and then ran to catch up with her. "Wait, I'm the one who's sorry," Rix said. "Can I redo that conversation? Sometimes I don't get it right the first time."

A grin played over Amari's face as she considered him. "There's no getting it right, Rix. You're a busy man with important tasks ahead, I should not have interrupted you."

"See, that's the thing," Rix said. "I'd love a coffee and a snack, especially with someone new and interesting."

"You can't possibly be that bored," she said, a twinkle in her eye showing that she enjoyed Rix's attention.

"I've only had coffee from Petju," Rix said. "Should we go there?"

"I have wanted to try her new pastries. I'd love to," Amari said and then hooked her arm around Rix's.

It was a short walk to Petju's Pub and they were quiet along the way. It was early afternoon and there weren't many people inside the newly established restaurant. A single glass display case housed a paltry collection of pastries with only two varieties, one with a blue glaze on top and the other with a lemon custard filling.

"Greetings, Rix, Amari," Petju nodded at them. "I understand you had a mishap with the flour transport. Something about pirates shooting up your hold. How much will you be able to recapture? I'm quite interested, as long as it is well cleaned."

"Ah right," Rix said as Amari squeezed his arm at the talk of pirates. "I have a sifter in the manufacturer queue. I'm hoping to get that all to you by tomorrow morning."

"Send me the details on your sifter," Petju said. "I'd like to approve based on filtering capability."

Rix grabbed the pattern from his HUD and flicked it to Petju who whistled. "That's a top-of-the-line grinder, sifter and filter. It'll do a lot more work than you'll need to clean up a little spilled flour. You'll barely break even," Petju said.

"That's quite an investment," Amari said.

"It feels like a good one. I'll bring the flour by around noon tomorrow?" Rix asked.

"Sold," Petju said. "Now, can I interest you in a pastry? I only have half a dozen left."

"Let's fix that," Rix smiled. "Load the rest of your pastries in a box, add a large coffee for me and whatever it is Amari is drinking."

"Cress water, please," Amari said.

Rix followed Amari to a table next to a window which looked out over the Atrium.

"You must be very hungry," Amari said.

"I have a lot of work ahead of me, so I'll be working in my shop for the next few days. I like to have something around that Philo likes. He's helpful in fixing ships," Rix said. "And this looks right up his alley."

Rix waited for Amari to sit before he followed suit. She gave him a questioning look but didn't pursue. "I'd heard you were outfitting a spaceship repair business, but then I also heard that Sable might have interfered."

"I'll be honest, I'm not sure that discussing Sable's business is a good idea," Rix said. "I did have a shop that I was setting up on Level 13. Quixly brokered a deal and now I have a spot on Level 8 that I've only visited twice in the last two weeks."

"Why only twice? Oh, I suppose you were on that trading run to Sout Atal," Amari said. "And then you came back to backed up toilets?" Amari's grin split her face. "I'm sorry to laugh, but what a treat to come home to."

"I can't complain," Rix said. "I get paid well for repairs. So now you know something about me. Tell me something about you. Have you always lived on Patience?"

"We moved between stations quite a lot when I was young," she said. "My dad had trouble keeping a job. We'd lived on twelve different stations or domed colonies by the time I was fourteen, when he decided it'd be easier to move around on his own and left me and Mom behind."

"That must have been hard," Rix said.

"Sorry, I didn't mean to start out with something quite so depressing," she said, looking at the table.

Rix reached over and picked up her hand. "We all have stuff that gets heavy. Sometimes it's easier to tell someone you don't know very well because it just feels good to say things out loud. I can't imagine moving that much as a kid. Keeping friends must have been hard. How old were you when you got to Patience?"

"Mom's next boyfriend brought us here when I was sixteen," she said. "She left me here with a friend of hers and I haven't seen her since. Oh, for the Lords of Gavenar, I'm doing it again."

"Your cress water is here," Rix said, chuckling. Petju set both his coffee and her water on the table and then grabbed a small box, into which she loaded the remaining pastries. "Glazed or filled? What's your choice?"

"Would you split one with me?" Amari asked.

"Yes, but you choose because I'm also going to have another of whatever it is you didn't choose," he said. "So, you were here at sixteen, then what?"

"I've done a lot of odd jobs. Early on when we had ships regularly coming to and from Patience, I'd pick up crewing jobs. It was hard work, but the pay was good. Now that's enough about me, what about you?"

"A lot different than you," Rix said. "I was born right after what's been called The Great Depression. My folks were dirt poor, and we scraped for everything. I joined the Army as a mechanic because my dad was good with his hands. With some training, they put me to working on airplanes, and then I found myself in the middle of a war in a country across the ocean. That caused a lot of growing up. After the war, I borrowed money for a shop and a little diner. I was just getting that going when Kel crash-landed *Calypso* and asked for help. That led to Dravari blowing up my life and Kel whisking me back here. You pretty much know the rest."

"You're certainly leaving out details. Do you have children? A wife at home?" she asked.

"Neither," Rix said. "No wife and I haven't kept a girlfriend for more than a couple of months. You have Hutari. Is her father still in the picture?"

"That would be Shixen. I imagine you've met him," Amari said. "Shixen and I were together for three years, ten years ago. It was turbulent to say the least. But I got Hutari, and she's everything I could have hoped for."

"Shixen is interesting," Rix said neutrally.

"Years ago, he was smoldering and exciting," Amari said. "He had money and was important. I learned a lot in those years. Mostly that I'm not interested in being part of the kinds of activities that smoldering and exciting people participate in."

Rix nodded understanding. "Was the split mutual?"

"No. He was angry, still is to some degree, which might scare you off. If it does, I don't blame you. Shixen is a lot to handle," she said.

"I bet that's put a damper on your dating life."

"You have no idea." Amari's face clouded for a moment. "Rix, this might not be a good idea. I'm sorry. I can't do this again."

"Hold on," Rix said. "We're just having coffee. Also, what are you doing this afternoon besides drinking cress water?"

"My day is open. I was hoping to pick up some work with Petju, but apparently, there's some delay in a shipment she's been waiting for." She added the last with a wan smile.

"I was thinking about that very thing," Rix said. "Are you up for making a few credits today? I have a job I need someone to deal with, and it'd be a big load off my plate if you had interest in seeing it through."

"You don't need to take care of me, Rix. I'm doing just fine."

"Did you miss the part where I said I need help?"

"What's it entail, and what's the pay?" she asked, pursing her lips to show she wasn't about to brook charity.

"Eighty credits to oversee picking up the sifter, bringing it down to my shop, processing the spilled flour and then taking it up to Petju. I'll get Philo to do the heavy lifting, but he's not as strategically minded as I need him to be to get the job done," Rix said. "It'd be a big help to me. It's not the best pay, but it's what I have. I think we're looking at four hours of work or so. I'll pay more if it takes more."

"I saw the machine you're buying," Amari said. "You're going to lose money on this deal if you pay me."

"Yes and no. I'll come out alright," Rix said. "The thing is, I need to get Kel's ship going. She has an opportunity she doesn't want to miss out on, so my time is better spent getting her squared away."

"You do know that I can probably move all that flour myself," she said. "I've done a lot of hard work in my life."

"And where I come from, you don't ask women to move a thousand kilograms of flour by themselves," Rix said. "Especially when you're on a first date."

"Is that what this is? I thought we were just having coffee and cress water."

Rix smiled but didn't answer, instead taking a long drink of his cooling coffee. Setting the cup down, he changed gears. "I'd love to continue talking with you, but I need to get down to the shop, which is an ungodly mess. I've only had time to dump my tools on the deck, and someone keeps turning off my power, so it's cold and I've no atmosphere."

"That'd be Laddy Dunn," Amari said.

"Turning off my power?"

"He's in charge of the station's power generators. Quixly probably didn't tell him he leased out the space," she replied. "I know Laddy. I could call him if you want."

"Sure."

"Laddy, hello .... And good afternoon to you too. I missed you at class," Amari said, her face breaking into a smile as she spoke. "Say, did you get word that Mayor Quixly leased out a bay to Rix Banner down on eight? I think he's trying to work in there today, but his power is shut off .... Right .... Well, thank you very much. I'll let Rix know you're on it."

Amari looked at Rix with an even bigger smile. "See, it pays to know the right people."

"I guess so," Rix said.

"You're antsy to get going."

"I'm sorry. It's just I have a lot to do."

"How about this? I'll go change into work clothing and we'll meet on Level 8."

"Bay 807," Rix said, standing. Unexpectedly, Amari leaned in and gave him a hug. For a moment, she seemed to melt into him as he returned the embrace, but just as quickly as it had started, she released him.

"See you soon, Rix Banner."

"Right."

"Someone's got a cru-ush. Someone's got a cru-ush," Beverly said in a sing-song voice, appearing in front of Rix in a jumpsuit after he'd stepped onto the elevator.

"Level 7," Rix said, directing the elevator to the manufactory level. He'd ordered additional parts for *Calypso* as well as several new, crucial tools. Even with everything he'd earned, his income was barely keeping up with his expenses, and it felt like every forward step was accompanied by backward steps.

Exiting the elevator, Rix was quick to unload a numbered locker into a rented grav cart that was better setup for carrying the myriad parts he'd manufactured than was a grav pallet. Back up on Level 8, he was just headed toward the interior entrance to his bay when a voice called to him from behind.

"Rix, hold up," Amari waved, jogging in his direction. Rix stopped and turned to wait for her. Instead of the baggy leggings and shapeless sweater she'd worn for cress water and coffee, she'd changed into coveralls. His imagination ran wild with what the shapeless clothing could be covering. Did her species have wings or maybe a tail? What if she had another set of arms? He didn't love that it might matter to him, but he had to admit, there were things he probably couldn't get beyond, like an elephant trunk for a nose or alligator skin.

"What was that look for?" Amari asked, slowing as she caught up to him.

"Just distracted."

"There are lights in the hallway," she said, apparently satisfied with his answer. "There must be some power."

"Lights are new. Are your coveralls good for no atmosphere?" Rix asked.

"Ah, no, I'm sorry, I didn't know I needed it."

"If there's power, I'll get the doors closed and we can pressurize the bay. Working in a vacuum is a lot harder," Rix said.

Arriving at the hatch into Bay 807, Rix palmed the energized security panel and was gratified when the hatch clunked open. Rix closed the hatch behind him in the temporary airlock and voided the small space so he could enter the bay. Once inside, Rix was pleased to discover working ambient lights in a wide band that ran around the bay at three meters off the deck. The doors that had been left open were heavy and took every bit of Rix's effort to get them tightly closed. With that done, however, he made his way over to the environmental controls and set the bay to pressurize and the temperature to twenty-two degrees, which would allow him to work in short sleeves.

"We've got pressure and the bay is warming," Rix said, opening the hatch so Amari could join him inside.

"This is a big bay, Rix. Is that Kel's *Calypso*? I've never seen her ship this close up before," she said.

"That's *Calypso*," Rix said, his eyes catching on the hundreds of patched holes in the ship's hull. "She's a little rough to look at and needs some TLC, but she's a tough little bird."

"That's quite a romantic notion," Amari said. "I like that you see her potential and not her flaws."

"We're talking about *Calypso*, right?"

4

RESTLESS

"Philo, Buddy, where are you?" Rix asked.

"Philo sleeping, Rixy," Philo answered dreamily. "Good credits. Philo buy sleepy drinks."

"Rix, Philo has imbibed and is not in any shape to help with projects today," Beverly said, appearing on an inset of the starboard bulkhead of the hold.

"Gotcha, Beverly," Rix said. "Okay, Philo, go back to sleep, you've earned it."

"Bye Rixy."

"That didn't sound hopeful," Amari said.

"Yeah, Philo likes to spend his credits quickly."

"Ooh, what are you and Amari doing in a darkened hold together," Kel said suggestively, stepping through the hold's forward hatch.

"Kel!" Amari said, crossing the distance and hugging her tightly. "I heard that Draven Knights came after you. *Calypso* took quite a beating. I'm so glad you're all okay."

"You remember, Jacknie, no doubt," Kel said. "I think I remember him trying to hit on you after you and Shixen ... well, you know."

"Yes, Jacknie was quite persistent," Amari said. "Why do you ask?"

"He's wrapped up with Draven's gang now. He was squeezing us for protection to use Inner Passage," Kel said. "Draven sent a couple of those Model 72 Falistads after us to send a message."

"Oh, my, you are so lucky to have survived. Did they give up after inflicting all this damage?"

"Sort of," Kel scratched the back of her head. "I had Rix loaded up in the needler. They ended up wrapped around a couple of asteroids after losing steerage mysteriously."

"That's quite a statement, Kel. Draven isn't going to forget losing expensive equipment like that," Amari said.

"You see the condition of *Calypso*. Do you doubt they were planning the same outcome for us?" Kel asked.

"No, and I'm sorry. There's no winning with folks like Draven Knights and Sable," Amari said. "It's good you didn't knuckle under and pay them. It's nearly impossible to escape once they have their hooks in. But it's not like I'm telling you anything you don't know."

"No, but I'm glad for Rix to hear it," Kel said. "He agreed to pay Jacknie for protection. I convinced him that was a bad idea. When we went back to Sout Atal, we paid his protection and then let him know it was the last time he was getting any."

"And he made it sound like everything would be just fine," Amari guessed.

"That's right," Kel said. "Tell me what's happening between you two."

"Amari is going to help get the flour picked up, sifted and off to Petju. I was kind of counting on getting some help from Philo. These bags are heavy," Rix said.

"Because dialing down the gravity in the hold is such a mystery," Kel said.

"She's not wrong, Rix," Amari agreed. "I can get started without Philo. If I find something too heavy, I'll ask for help. I've done harder work when I was working crew."

"Maybe I'll stick around and help with the flour," Kel said. "I feel like it's partly my fault that Jacknie came after us so hard."

"Okay, I'll let you girls work it out. I'm going to spend an hour or so getting organized," Rix said. "After that, I'll get started on the coolant."

"Can I ask you guys something?" Amari asked.

"Sure," Kel said.

"Does it smell like lode bean coffee in here? I know we just had drinks, but I'm getting a strong whiff of coffee," she said.

Rix and Kel laughed. "You can explain, Kel," Rix said as he walked out of the hold.

Three hours later, Rix heard a noise alerting him that someone had joined him beneath *Calypso's* deck. He'd been working to disassemble the main coolant reservoirs that had been taken out in the last trip.

"Who's there?" he called, having slid with his back against *Calypso's* belly and wedged himself into a tight position. With a grunt of exertion, the bolt he'd been working to free finally gave way.

"It's Amari," a muffled voice answered.

"Hey, do you see all that silver-colored tape that's connected to the reservoir?" Rix asked.

"I think so," she said. "How can I help?"

"Get a good handful and give it a yank. I've disconnected the tank, and I'll push from below," Rix said. "It's in here in an awkward way."

"Um, well, that's going to be interesting. I'm going to have to straddle you to make that work," Amari said hesitantly. "Are you okay with that?"

"Whatever works," Rix answered, not quite understanding the position she'd be required to take. First, Rix felt her footstep on the outside of his left leg, and then as she lowered herself into position, she ended up sitting atop him in an otherwise provocative position. "Oh, I understand now," he muttered to himself.

With both hands, Amari pulled at the reservoir, her right hand slipping off and smacking into the hull. "Ow!"

"Are you alright?"

"That's just me being clumsy."

"We need to do this together," Rix said. "Otherwise, it's just in there too hard."

Amari giggled. "Whenever you're ready."

"Three, two, one!"

With Rix pushing and Amari pulling, the reservoir finally released causing Amari to sit down fairly hard on Rix's legs.

"What are you two doing?" Kel asked in mock horror. "I leave you alone for two minutes and you're right to it."

Amari hastily pushed the reservoir off to the side and struggled to disentangle herself from Rix. The entire process was comedic and ended up with a few more awkward moments, which caused Rix to sit up quickly and bang his head.

"I'm so sorry, Rix," Amari said.

"I just need a minute," he said. Kel and Amari pulled the oddly shaped reservoir further away as it splashed lode bean coffee all over the subdeck. "Maybe someone pull my legs so I can get out of here?"

"Kel?" Amari pled.

"Oh, no, be my guest," Kel said.

"We'll do it together," Amari said. "Please."

Kel grinned and the pair helped pull Rix out from beneath the engine. Free from his confinement, Rix set his tools to the side and brushed off the spatters of coffee that covered the front of his work clothes. "That could have gone a lot worse," he said cheerily. "Appreciate your help, Amari. I was going to have to rig something to get more leverage on that if you hadn't shown up."

"How much longer are you working tonight, Rix?" Kel asked. "Amari has all the flour cleaned up and stacked on a grav pallet. The loose stuff she picked up is in some food grade barrels we borrowed from Petju. And we have it all down at the back of the shop, next to the station side hatch."

"That was good thinking," Rix said. "Kel, are you going to be around later? I'm going to need help getting the new reservoir in here. It's a two-person job because I have to be underneath to get that darn bolt in, and it's a crazy reach to get there. They have a specialized tool for that."

"You're so stubborn," Kel said. "Just manufacture the tool."

"It's a hundred and twenty credits and it's only for three bolts," Rix said. "If I work at it, I can get them."

"I can help," Amari offered. "I'll eat dinner with Hutari after she gets off work, but after that, I have a couple of hours before I go to bed."

"I'd make it worth your while," Rix said.

"Oooh," Kel said suggestively.

"You're so bad, Kel," Rix said. "What I meant is, I don't mind paying for a second hand. There's always work to do. I can't pay a crazy amount, but if you have time over the next couple of days, I could go a hundred a day, especially given how hard a worker you are."

"Oh, Rix, that might be a bad plan," Kel said. "I was trying to set you guys up, not find you a new employee."

"It's not a permanent gig," Rix said. "I just need reliable help if I'm going to get *Calypso* going in time for your trip."

"Hold on," Amari said. "I'd love to pick up some work, but a hundred a day sounds like way too much. Let's go more like fifty."

"How about fifteen credits an hour and you work as much or as little as you want?" Rix asked. "I need four or five hours each day and can take as much as seven or eight hours if you have availability."

"I'll be back after dinner. Come up with a list of what you want me to work on," she said, lifting her shoulders with a big smile on her face. "Oh, Kel, you're such a good friend. Thank you for introducing us. You guys are so much fun, and you know how hard jobs on Patience are to find."

"Aww, okay," Kel said, embracing her friend.

With that, Amari scooted out from the 'tween deck and was gone.

"She has a good energy," Rix said.

"I think you like that she sat in your lap," Kel said, smirking. "Oh, and it doesn't hurt that she's super attractive."

"Is she?" Rix asked.

"Oh, don't give me that."

"No, I'm serious. She's had baggy clothing on the entire time," Rix said. "I've been wondering if that's some species thing or what that's about. I mean, I don't care, I enjoy her help."

"But you have questions," Kel said.

"Sort of, I guess."

"I need your confidence on this."

"Shoot."

"She's Tejlari, like me," Kel said. "Well, technically full Tejlari, where I'm half. I can't shift quite as much as her, but more than you might think. It's more that I can't hold my changes for as long."

"I thought there weren't a lot of you around."

"There's not, and I wouldn't have outed her if you didn't already know about me. She wears baggy clothing because she's trying not to attract attention. Shixen did a number on her."

"What kind of number?" Rix asked, growing still.

"A number that you don't get to go do something about," Kel said with irritation in her voice. "Besides, it's her story to tell."

"If she ever comes back," Rix said, dragging the broken reservoir over to the hatch that opened to the main deck. "I didn't mean for things to get weird pulling out the reservoir."

"That was innocent, and I made sure to overplay it so it was just funny. Which it was," Kel said. "You really didn't know how she was going to have to sit on you?"

"I did, but I didn't think about it that way," Rix said. "I didn't have a good way to get that thing out of there."

"I can't figure out if you're really this naïve or if you're a super genius at getting things to work in your favor," Kel said.

"Hah, I wouldn't go with super genius," Rix said. "Help me bring the new reservoir up, would you? It's going to be a long night."

"What would you like me to work on?" Kel asked once they'd set the reservoir into place and Rix had the bottom bolts firmly in place. "I've got all night."

"I'd like to replace all of the emergency foam inserts with hull patch material. I doubt we'll have time to fare the hull, but if one of those foam pieces comes out while you're sailing, that could go poorly for you."

"Yuck," Kel said. "My least favorite job."

"I have *Calypso* broken out into eight sectors. It feels more manageable if you focus on a single sector at a time," Rix said.

"What are you working on?" Kel asked.

"Remember that asteroid you knocked out of the way with our starboard aft thruster?"

"Oh, right. That was clever of me to flip *Calypso* and use the port thruster though, wasn't it?" Kel said, fishing for a compliment.

"Clever is hardly the word," Rix said, initially bringing a scowl to Kel's face. "It was brilliant. That level of precision whilst under fire sets you apart from anyone I've seen, so far. Now, if you could avoid banging into asteroids, it'd be a lot cheaper."

"At the expense of getting hammered by a Model 72's kinetic loads?"

"No, and that's why it was brilliant, you did the math and figured out we'd be better off with a small collision than taking a backside full of lead," Rix said.

"If you keep talking like that, you'll probably get more help around here," Kel said.

"You're a captive audience right now," Rix fired back. "You want to get out on your first solo job as a legit captain, so you're mine for the time being."

"If you think you own me because of that ...," Kel said with a dramatic pause. "Well, that's where you're right. I want to start earning my way here. You keep funneling every credit you earn into our partnership, and I don't feel like I'm contributing enough."

"Keep bringing your A-game and this'll work out just fine."

"Plugging holes in the hull, though?" Kel complained again.

"One sector at a time," Rix said, handing her the tool. "Also, make sure to record every patch. Beverly has offered to review your video so we can look for unreported damage that's covered by the foam. And I already know about the continuity problem beneath the needler turret, so you don't have to report that one."

"It'll take ten hours to fill all these holes," Kel said, her eyes glassy as she reviewed the work list Rix had shared with her.

"Less than two hours a sector," Rix said. "See if you can get one done before I get these coolant reservoirs installed."

"A race it is," Kel said.

It was hardly a fair fight, as Rix knew he only had forty-five minutes of work remaining to finish his current job. To extend the time, he moved to the structural member that had been damaged next to the engine's lower unit. Whistling in appreciation, he reflected on just how lucky they'd been as he inspected the steel alloy skeletal member. The missing chunk had been taken at the strongest point of the brace.

"I'm done!" Kel shouted. "You owe me a treat!"

"Just a minute, I need to finish this weld," Rix said from behind a dark welding mask. While he'd completed a rough fix earlier, he'd spent extra time repairing adjacent corrosion, which looked a lot like grinding and adding additional metal patches.

"How do you feel about pastries?" Rix asked.

"It's 2000," Kel said. "I'm having rum or grog. You get to choose, but I'm done patching for tonight."

"Knock, knock," Amari called from the station side hatch.

"Looks like the night shift is here," Kel said, waggling her eyebrows suggestively.

"Come on in," Rix hollered back from the bottom of *Calypso's* loading ramp.

"Do you still need help tonight?" Amari asked. "I brought some left-overs from dinner with Hutari if you're interested. Kel, I'm sorry, I didn't think you'd still be here, or I'd have brought enough for two."

Rix's stomach growled and he realized just how hungry he was. Since his departure from Earth, he'd had few moments to rest, and with his focus on repairing both *Calypso* and Patience Station, his poor eating habits had led to a loss of weight.

"We can split it, no problem," Rix said approaching the back of the shop. "Thank you for thinking of us!"

"No offense, Amari, but I was just heading out," Kel said. "Three might be one too many, here."

Rix shook his head at Kel's impish grin as she needled Amari and him. As planned, Amari blushed at the implication and set the covered plate she carried atop of a crate. "We're just working tonight."

"Whatever you kids want to call it," Kel said, leaning in to hug Amari companionably. "Don't stay up too late, I hear the boss around here can be a real slave driver."

"Two hours of plugging the hull you got shot up and now I'm a slave driver?" Rix asked, feigning hurt.

"Booorrrring," Kel said theatrically as she exited.

Having spent no time organizing his shop, crates of Rix's possessions were stacked neatly in the only clean space within the shop. Rix hadn't yet sifted through the junk left behind by prior occupants. There would be reclaimer credits for recycling, but given the material, they would be low.

Rix tipped an empty crate onto one end and rolled his chair next to where Amari had set the plate of food. "Have a seat," he said, opening a refrigerator that had been left behind. Cleaning the refrigerator had been Rix's first task once heat had been restored. It was empty other than a few bottles he'd added. "Any interest in a bota water?"

"Maybe later," Amari said, heading for the crate.

"Take the chair, please," Rix said. "It'll drive me nuts to sit in a nice chair when you're on a box."

"That is kind. I don't mind sitting on a crate, though, Rix Banner."

"Humor me?"

"Okay."

Rix set a bottle of bota water on the crate next to the food Amari had brought. "This looks great," Rix said, taking the cover off the plate. Unexpectedly, he found a small pile of green vegetables next to a chunk of proto meat and several small rounds of a fruit similar in shape to a banana.

"I wish there were more, but Skef has given up on planting edibles due to the trouble we've had with atmosphere and temperature swings," she said. "I miss working with plants."

"This is great," Rix said. "I kind of live on proto bars. Why'd you give up working with plants?"

"Skef didn't have any work for me."

"How hard are seeds or seedlings to come by?" Rix asked, continuing to eat.

"Most people save all the seeds they come across, so they're not hard to find," she said.

"I had this idea that I haven't been able to do much with. I wonder if you'd be interested in running with it?"

"What is your idea?"

"Back home, we have things called greenhouses," Rix said. "On Earth, we're close to the sun and have plentiful rainfall, most of the time, so planting things outside generally works, as long as you're in the right season. But some people build a glass building they can close off to retain heat and moisture to bring up harder-to-grow plants and extend the seasons. There are lots of advantages because you can control most issues plants have."

"We have similar ideas," Amari said. "Because station conditions are generally ideal for most plants, a cordoned off room isn't often necessary."

"Unless your environmental controls aren't working," Rix filled in.

"What are you suggesting?"

"More of a question than a suggestion," Rix said. "Are you interested enough in growing food items to take on a project?"

"What kind of project?"

"I talked to Skef about this a while back, but he didn't seem that interested," Rix said. "My proposal would be to rent space somewhere cheap, but with good power. We'd build a greenhouse first and get a bunch of seedlings started. After that, we'd start a larger growing operation. I was reading about how plants are grown on space stations. It's unbelievably compact, but there's some machinery required to make it all work."

"There are a couple of approaches common around here," Amari said, sitting straighter, her eyes alight with interest. "Hydroponics are systems without soil like you'd find on a planet. A nutrient bath is circulated around the roots of the plants and there's a lattice for vines and stems to follow. If you have more room, you can create a habitat for fish and utilize their waste as nutrients for the plants. It's slightly more efficient, but then you need to feed the fish."

"What are you familiar with?" Rix asked, finishing off the plate of food and tipping back his crate so he could lean against the station bulkhead. "Or maybe you have a preference?"

"Why does it seem like this isn't an idle conversation for you?" Amari asked. "You are quite focused."

"Maybe it's just part of who I am," Rix considered. "I see opportunity all over the place and I wonder why people aren't taking advantage of it."

"You only have to lose your crop a couple of times before you lose heart," Amari replied. "Skef has been watching his crops and plants die due to troubles on Patience Station. He's struggling to keep a good attitude."

"Take a look at this." Rix pulled up the plans he had for a small, three-by-four-meter greenhouse, and flicked them to Amari.

"Where did you get this?" she asked. "Did you design this yourself?"

"I had help," Rix said. "But, generally, what do you think?"

"If you're asking if this would allow for the production of a tremendous number of seedlings, it certainly would," she said. "But you have considerable expense in the closed design. Ordinarily, you could simply place a clear plastic tent over tables of seedlings and start them in growing medium."

"And when the atmospheric pressure drops or heat fluctuates, you lose your seedlings," Rix said.

"But that doesn't happen that often."

"Except it does enough to stop Skef."

"What are you proposing, Rix? I can see it in your eyes. You have a plan."

"I want to rent the warehouse space opposite this shop and build that greenhouse in there," Rix said. "I need a partner, though. Someone who will tend the plants and take charge."

"There are numerous startup expenses, Rix. Seeds can be expensive, although there are ways around that. A larger issue is that most of what you have here needs to be manufactured. I don't have credits to invest in something like this," she said.

"If I build this in two phases, I have enough to get it started and I'll have some left over to buy seed stock," Rix said. "Do you think Skef has any he'd be willing to part with?"

"I don't know about Skef, but everyone saves seeds on a station. Are you serious about all this? I know you're asking if I'll manage, and the answer is I'd love to."

"I'm dead serious," Rix said. "Talk to me about what kind of salary you'd need."

"How much of a partner am I?"

"Full. We split fifty-fifty. I bring the capital, you bring the know-how and the man-hours," Rix said. "I assume this isn't more than an hour or two a day once we get it built."

"A project like this is a labor of love. The hours worked are unimportant," Amari said. "Leave the seed gathering and planting to me. I have plenty of friends who will donate time and seeds if they're part of the project."

"Paid employees?"

"You're so focused on money, Rix Banner," Amari said. "No, these are my friends who will be thrilled at the opportunity for fresh produce."

5

MAKING FRIENDS

"OH, NO!" Amari's surprised exclamation carried through into *Calypso* where Rix was on his stomach, reaching deep into a cabinet in a struggle to replace a ruined atmospheric filter cover. He and Amari had only spent an hour working on *Calypso* the night before.

"Are you okay?" Rix called, pushing off the deck and half jogging down the ramp into the shop. Last he'd left Amari, she'd been feeding potentially contaminated flour into the sifting and sanitizing machine he'd recently manufactured. Looking over, he found that Amari's face and chest were completely covered in flour.

"This is so embarrassing," she said, brushing flour from her hair. "I forgot to latch the hopper."

"But you're okay?" Rix asked, hurrying over to her.

"Wounded pride, perhaps," she said, accepting a towel from Rix.

Rix surveyed the bags of flour she'd already processed. "How much of the affected flour do you think you'll be able to recover?"

"Forty percent of your load was spilled, we'll recover eighty percent of that," she said.

"How much more work do you have here?"

"Aside from cleaning up this new mess, I should be done shortly after midday."

"How about when you're done, I'll help move the flour up to Petju and we can get something to eat?"

"I'd like that," Amari smiled. "Also, thank you for the work, Rix. Honest work is hard to come by on Patience lately. You have no idea how far a few extra credits can be stretched."

"Well back at you," Rix said. "We needed this flour to pay for the parts we're manufacturing to fix the damage caused by those Draven pirates. We're still going to lose money on the trip, but I didn't have time to both fix the ship and deal with the flour, so your help is really appreciated."

"Okay, three more bags." Amari pulled a twenty-five kilogram bag from beneath the machine and waddled it over to the grav pallet, where she let it rest for a moment. Rix noticed her pause and stepped in, lifting the bag atop the pile. "Oh, thank you. I was just taking a moment. I could have gotten that."

"I know," Rix said, not wanting to repeat the conversation about how his sense of chivalry clashed with the idea of tasking her with manual labor while he stood nearby.

Fifteen minutes later, the final, although partial, bag of flour was sealed and set atop a heavily loaded grav pallet. With Rix and Amari pushing in tandem, they moved the load through the shop's hatch and down the hallway to the elevator bank.

Finishing the delivery to Petju, Rix checked the manufactory queue. The parts he needed next required tools that had lost their priority and wouldn't be produced until later that evening, even though the parts could be completed in thirty minutes. "Gah," he said under his breath, sending an additional fifty credits to the manufactory to have the tools expedited.

"Trouble?" Amari asked, setting a fork into a log shaped nutripaste serving. With Petju limited on fresh supplies, the bakery's output had temporarily stalled, although the new load of flour would do quite a lot to get her going again.

"Manufactory queue is messing with me. I need to get Kel launched so I'm spending money to expedite. I don't love that," he said. "The good news is that all the parts I need have been manufactured and I should be able to meet her deadline, other than filling holes. Maybe I'll have time to get to that too, if I'm lucky."

"Or I could work on filling holes," Amari said. "I don't have to work until tomorrow morning, so my day is yours if you want."

"What have we here?" Shixen's voice interrupted their conversation.

"It's nothing, Shixen," Amari said. "We were just delivering flour to Petju. Rix hired me to help him clean up a mess in *Calypso.*"

Rix watched Amari's face as she spoke. Instead of looking directly at Shixen, she kept her eyes down and spoke softly. It didn't take a psychologist to understand she was afraid.

"Little mousies tell me you two have been spending time together. Is that right, Rix Banner? Have you been spending time with my girl? I thought Kel was more your speed. You like them tall and narrow, hard and unbendable like."

Words raced through Rix's mind as Shixen spoke. So far, the two men had managed to work together without clashing. For some reason, Shixen was going out of his way to poke at him, and Kel's warning about Amari and Shixen's prior relationship seemed to be the most obvious.

"I'm not your girl anymore, Shixen," Amari said, her voice so soft it was difficult to hear.

"What was that?" Shixen asked, stepping closer, clearly trying to intimidate her.

"Hey, what are you doing, Shixen?" Rix asked. "We're just grabbing some lunch and then we have work we need to get back to."

"I'm asking a simple question, Banner," Shixen said. "Not like it's any of your business. See, Amari is *my* girl and maybe we're takin' a little break right now, but that doesn't mean she's a free agent if you get my meaning. You not being from around here means you probably don't know how things work."

"You figured you'd clear that up for me. Is that about right?" Rix asked.

"I'm glad you understand. We've done a good job of staying out of each other's business," Shixen said, turning to Amari. "Don't forget who pays the rent on that flat of yours Amari. I've been patient, but there are limits."

"You ... that's not fair," Amari stammered, standing suddenly, tears running down her face. "I'm sorry, Rix." And with that, she ran out of *Petju's Pub*, crying.

"I hate it when they do that," Shixen said, but before Rix could respond, he too left.

"Would you like a box to take your food with you?" Petju asked, looking sympathetically at him.

"Nah," Rix said. "I've twenty minutes until my parts are done at the manufactory."

Petju pulled out a chair and sat where Amari had just been. "Are you okay?" she asked.

"I think so," Rix said, although the shock on his face said otherwise. "I'm not really sure what just happened."

"You just received a warning from Shixen to leave Amari alone," Petju said, and though objection filled Rix's face, she continued. "I'm not saying it's the sort of thing that feels good, but I've seen Shixen handle that a whole lot differently. You must have made an impression on him if that's how he's working through this. A word of advice. Shixen is a dangerous man all by himself. Add that he's a leader in Sable and that's just a new level of trouble. Amari knows better and now, you do too. Besides, what about you and Kel?"

"Kel and I are partners. We own a spaceship together."

"And you seriously think that's the end of it."

"I do think that," Rix said. "She's the one who set me up with Amari."

Petju chuckled as a chime indicated a new customer had entered the pub. "I'm going to let you think about that, Rix Banner," she said, pushing her hands off the table as she stood.

"Wait, how is that anything other than her trying to give me the brush off?" Rix asked Petju's retreating back.

"Mysteries of women, Rix," she called, not turning. "Not everything is as simple as it seems."

Rix shook his head in equal parts disgust and confusion. He'd largely failed at dating back home because he'd been too busy to unwrap the mysteries of Cranberry Cove's eligible women. At least that was the excuse he gave himself. That Shixen felt he had some claim over Amari disgusted him, that much he was clear on. The rest of it was as clear as mud, which was how dating topics always turned out for him.

"Thanks for lunch, Petju," Rix said, pushing the leftovers into the recycling hub.

"Anytime, Rix," Petju said, giving him a friendly wave.

Pushing the grav pallet down to the manufactory, Rix loaded the tools and parts he'd paid for. With a bill of fifty-two hundred credits and having received eighteen hundred fifty credits for flour delivery, Rix was left with just eighteen hundred credits. That the patterns he'd designed and placed on the manufactory marketplace were still earning him nearly four hundred credits daily was a financial boon, making possible the idea of economic freedom in the future. It was these thoughts that restored his good humor as he pushed the pallet back to his shop.

"Can I help you?" Rix asked, approaching a hooded pair who stood outside the station side entrance to his shop.

"Rix Banner?" One of the two men asked as he got closer. Beneath the hoods, Rix discovered the men were Graveborn, which didn't bode well.

"Yeah, that's me," Rix said, tapping his hand against his hip where a pistol had occasionally rested. Even before he reached for it, he knew he hadn't brought it along. "How can I help you two gentlemen?"

"We're here to collect."

"Okay," Rix said, slowing the cart and walking around them. "I'll need you to be a bit more specific. I have lots of bills." The men allowed him to open the hatch and appeared to be interested in having the conversation inside, instead of in the hallway. Rix pulled the pallet inside and attempted to keep it between him and the pair, the quietest of the two Graveborn wasn't having it and pushed the grav pallet out of the way, stepping closer.

"You are indebted to Jacknie for the Model 72s you destroyed," the first said.

"Come again?" Rix said. "The Model 72s that were shooting at us. You want us to pay for that. Are you crazy? They got what they had coming."

Apparently, that was the trigger the quiet Graveborn was looking for, because without warning, he stepped forward and jammed a fist into Rix's stomach, folding him over as he did.

"Should have seen that coming," Rix groaned as the pain washed over his body.

"You should have," the talker said agreeably. "Jacknie says he'll take *Calypso* as partial payment and he'll work the rest out with you at some point in the future."

Rix raised his hand to stave off another punch from the quieter of the two. "Do you see all these parts on this platform? That's all the stuff I have to put back into *Calypso* just so she can sail again, so nobody is taking *Calypso* anywhere. Second, when pirates attack my ship in deep space, it's my God given right to defend myself. Wait!" Rix pushed his hand at the irritated Graveborn. "One more and then you can do what you want."

"Let him finish, Spryg," the speaker said, amusement tugging at his lips.

"Thank you. And third, you're in Sable territory. I was just having lunch with Shixen. I can't imagine his response to you horning in on his business," Rix said.

"Are you done?"

Rix half lidded his eyelids and nodded while shrugging. "Yeah, I think that pretty well summarizes my thoughts on all of this."

"Your first point is valid," the Graveborn said. "We'll take the parts and you'll forgive me if we choose our own mechanic. I've lost some respect for the current establishment. Your second point is erroneous, if you destroy Draven Knight property, we will collect it from you, your family and your friends. And third, you're not wrong, which is why we appreciate you inviting us in."

"Now what?"

The quiet Graveborn glanced at the speaker who nodded in response. "Everyone needs to be convinced. That's Spryg's job."

This time, when Spryg's fist lashed out, Rix blocked it with his forearm and followed up with a quick combination to Spryg's face. Faster moving than Rix had expected, Spryg managed to block one of

Rix's blows but reeled back upon being struck. The sound of blaster fire added a sense of urgency to the fight, and Rix closed distance with Spryg, holding his arms up in a classic boxer's pose. Spryg punched out again and each time, Rix blocked and countered, his own blows not as powerful because he was testing out the Graveborn's response to pain.

"Rix, you're doing well," Beverly said, showing up on the Graveborn's shoulder. "But you should know, Graveborn are not easily knocked senseless. You must focus on the midsection. Ideally a kidney shot if you have the opportunity."

Rix hunched lower so that his arms blocked the Graveborn's blows, if only somewhat. Working on the Graveborn's midsection didn't immediately pay off, but he did notice a lessening of his opponent's strikes.

The sound of a blaster round echoed through the shop and Rix's entire right side felt like it was on fire. The pain was enough that he dropped his right arm and opened himself up for the Graveborn's haymaker punch, which caught him square in the jaw and sent him reeling across the cluttered bay.

"If you have any desire to walk from this bay, you will lower your weapon and lay on the ground," Kel's voice filled the bay, followed by the sound of *Calypso's* needler turret slowly turning its position, obviously lining up with the standing Graveborn.

"Do not shoot," the talkative Graveborn said, holding his pistol over his head.

"You will both lie flat."

The two Draven Knight enforcers lay on the deck.

"Rix, are you okay?" Kel called over comms.

"I got shot," Rix answered. "It completely sucks. My side feels like I'm on fire."

"Can you secure those guys?"

"I have it," Rix said, struggling back to his feet. "Do we have those flex cuffs anywhere?"

"They're in one of those crates. I think the second one down," she said.

"You cannot be serious," the talkative Graveborn said with disgust.

"Look, this whole tough guy thing isn't our gig," Rix said, opening the crate Kel had suggested. It took some digging, but he finally found the cuffs. "Okay, fellas, this'll go easier if you tell me where you've stashed your weapons."

"What are you doing?" the Graveborn asked as Rix searched them.

Rix extracted three pistols, four knives and a few objects he couldn't easily identify but was unwilling to leave on their person. "You've put me in an awkward position," Rix said.

"You need to release us."

"Sure, it makes sense you feel that way," Rix said. Just then Kel walked down the ramp holding an energy rifle which she kept leveled at the pair. "Oh, hey, Kel. I didn't know you were back."

"I guess you got lucky, huh?"

"He begs a good question. What do you want to do with these guys?" Rix asked. "I was thinking you could take them with you on your trip and dump them once you got past Church Rock. What do you think about that?"

"Hold on," the Graveborn said. "If you kill us, more Draven Knights will come, and they will not be as reasonable."

"I got a message from Amari," Kel said. "What happened? She sounds upset."

"Maybe not in front of the kids," Rix said.

"Just a hint?"

"Shixen."

"Oh … that bad, huh?"

"It's not good," Rix said. "I'm not in love with killing these guys."

"Draven Knights have a lot of nerve coming to Patience Station," Kel said. "I hate poking the beast again, but Shixen would probably like to know they're here."

"That is not wise," the Graveborn said.

"I guess we have our answer," Kel said.

"Let us go, we will return to Sout Atal and deliver the message that you are uninterested in repaying Jacknie for his losses. This message will be poorly received but you will not have escalated the conflict between yourself and Jacknie," the Graveborn said.

Rix squeezed thumb and forefinger in front of each of the Graveborn faces. It was a common gesture for recording an image. "How about this," Rix said. "I've just sent a message to Shixen letting him know you're hanging around. I bet if you get moving right now, you can get out to your ship and be gone before they find you."

"You play a dangerous game, Rix Banner. We will meet again."

"That is good acting, right there, Kel," Rix said, hooking a thumb at the Graveborn. "I know you all are way ahead of us with movies and all, but this guy, he really sells it."

"Release us, now," the Graveborn demanded.

With snippers, Rix cut the cuffs after opening the door. "Get going, already."

"Our weapons."

"Bub, you shot me with your weapon, so now I'm keeping it. It's kind of my thing," Rix said.

The Graveborn looked at Rix as if he wanted to argue but then remembered he had little time to escape. With unexpected speed, the pair of Graveborn raced down the hallway, disappearing around the corner.

"Shixen will catch them."

"I didn't send the picture," Rix said.

"Why?"

"They left. That's all we needed. I don't want to be further into Shixen's business than I already am," Rix said. "Were you going to tell me that Shixen doesn't know he and Amari aren't a thing?"

"He is possessive," Kel said. "Amari does not want to be with him. Tell me about how things were going with her up until then?"

"I'm only talking if you're going to help me work. I have less than twenty hours before you need to leave and I have a lot of work to do. As it is, I'm going to be working through the night."

"Fine," Kel said. "How did you afford all of this?"

"It took all our flour money," Rix said. "I've also invested my profits from the manufactory patterns. We just need to catch a break, and this ship will start making money."

"I'd like that," Kel said. "You didn't tell me what you think of Amari."

"I like her," Rix said. "She's a hard worker and she's easy to talk to."

"So, did you guys, you know ... get frisky last night?"

"Is that what you wanted?"

"Whoa, hold on there. I'm not your pimp or anything. I was just trying to help you find someone to spend time with," she said. "So, did you?"

"No. I don't know her well enough to be doing anything like that."

"What do you mean?"

"What do you mean?" Rix fired back.

"If you two feel that connection, why wouldn't you ... you know?"

"Because I don't move that fast. I want a relationship that's more than sex," Rix said.

"Well, okay," Kel said. "But you didn't get hurt in your war, did you? You can have sex, right?"

"We're not having this discussion, Kel," Rix said. "My parts all work just fine. I'm just not going to be like Philo and have a woman in every port."

"Rixy, not every port," Philo said, startling Rix, as he hadn't seen the little alien arrive.

"So far it has," Rix said.

"Yes, we sail good place," Philo said.

"Okay, kids, time to grab some parts and start carrying them, we have lots of work to do and we're short on time," Rix moved on.

"Shiny parts," Philo said. "Bring snacks?"

"Check out that box on the tool chest," Rix said. "I picked those up yesterday afternoon. Just have one, though!"

"Only one box, Rixy," Philo said, jumping over a crate and pulling the box from where it sat. Before Rix could correct him, Philo already had two pastries in his mouth. "Carry all parts now, you'll see."

Rix picked up the tools he'd need for the next job and walked with Kel toward *Calypso.* "If Amari doesn't want to be with Shixen, how can we help her? And, also, I feel like you should have warned me."

"I *did* warn you," Kel said. "I told you she had an ex-boyfriend. I think I even told you it was Shixen."

"You missed the part where he didn't see it that way."

"That's fair," Kel said. "I'm not sure how we help her. You like her, huh?"

"I like a lot of people, Kel," Rix said, sighing.

6

RIDE ALONG

"WHAT'S your interest in this Bay 808?" Quixly asked, opening the door directly opposite Rix's still heavily disorganized shop. Rix had been up the entire night working on *Calypso* and had finished repairs. With Kel and Philo picking up supplies for their trip, Quixly's timing couldn't have been more perfect.

"I have a delivery for Rix Banner," a man Rix had seen hanging around Collie Beard's bar, Hidden Room, called from down the hallway.

"That's me. Is that rum from Collie?" Rix asked.

"Forty liters. As ordered."

"Just set it in the hallway. I'll grab it in a minute," Rix said, flicking him a five-credit tip.

"Thanks!"

Rix turned back to Quixly. "I wasn't sure how big the space was. The location is too good to ignore, and I have a variety of projects in mind."

"Two hundred meters, but we can move a wall if that's more space than you want," Quixly said, pushing open the door. "Also, Geoff was using the space to store the worn-out parts from station repairs. I can have someone move them out or you can take 'em. As far as I know, they're worthless and I was thinking about having them recycled."

"How much for all two hundred?"

"Fifteen hundred credits per month and that comes with atmosphere, heat and station power. That's, of course, assuming a three-year lease."

"It's more space than I was looking for, but the price is good. I don't suppose you'd move back to twelve-hundred fifty, would you?"

"You'll take the entire bay?"

"Yes, and I'll make it my mission to clean it up. Who knows, maybe there's a part in here I can repair."

"We can do twelve hundred fifty for the first year. I'll put an annual escalator so we're at sixteen hundred by year three. That gives you a break on the front end," he said.

Rix scanned the room, which was way more space than he'd been expecting to get for the money. There was significant debris, including unopened crates that bore no labels, which piqued Rix's interest.

"All this stuff is included?"

"I don't have the interest or energy to be looking through it," Quixly said. "Unless it's clearly labeled as belonging to someone on the station, whatever you find is yours to do with what you want."

"Could you throw the last of this month in for free?" Rix asked.

"You and your deals," Quixly pursed his lips, directing his HUD to a security screen where he gave Rix administrative access to Bay 808. "I'll draw up your lease and send it to you later today."

"Copy that," Rix said.

"I need to ask you about something unrelated," Quixly said.

"Can you do it while I move this rum?"

"That's fine."

Rix stooped and picked up one of the two cases of Collie's Black Rum, which he'd soon enough rebottle as Collie's Reserve. He had a deal with Collie that he wouldn't sell the rum on the station but otherwise had free rein.

"What's up?"

"Security shows a pair of Graveborn on station yesterday," Quixly said. "I have video of them on Level 8 for about thirty minutes. Do you know anything about that?"

"Those are Draven Knights, part of Jacknie's gang over in Sout Atal," Rix said.

"What did they want with you?"

"*Calypso* ran into a pair of Draven Knight small attack craft on the way back from Sout Atal," Rix said. "We made it home. They didn't."

"You can't go around shooting up pirates if you plan to live on Patience," Quixly said. "There are more pirate gangs around here than there are cats, and believe me, there are more cats than people."

"You never see them," Rix said honestly. "Do you?"

"They're around," Quixly said. "I also heard that Shixen was giving Amari a hard time in Petju's Pub while you were having lunch. Do you want to get killed? You've not only managed to get a pair of Draven enforcers to trespass in Sable territory but you're actively flaunting a relationship in front of Shixen. These aren't good decisions and it's going to catch up with you."

"First, Amari is a friend, and we were grabbing lunch after finishing a project," Rix said. "Second, as far as Amari is concerned, Shixen is an ex, not current boyfriend. Or can I not even hang around her because she once dated Shixen?"

"I'm telling you that you're making bad decisions and they're going to get you hurt or killed," Quixly said.

Rix nodded once. "Message received. For the record, if Shixen comes after me, will you do anything, or does he have a free pass?"

"In this moment, there's little I can do to Shixen. Patience Station just doesn't have the manpower. Maybe in the future, we'll have enough funding to build a force that can stand up to Sable, but that time isn't now."

"Thank you for that," Rix said sincerely.

"For what?"

"A man likes to know where he stands."

Returning to his new shop, Rix looked around at the disarray of the now empty bay, having moved *Calypso* out to the pier only an hour previous. Weariness washed over him at the realization that he had absolutely nothing lined up to work on once Kel and Philo were off on adventure. It was in his mind to start cleaning the shop once they'd left but instead, he sat in the chair he'd procured from the prior mayor and kicked back.

"Beverly, are you around?" Rix asked. The alien symbiote that shared Philo's body often spent time with him while he was working, as they both enjoyed their conversations and she didn't mind helping him locate reference materials for systems he was working on, even though she'd shown him how to locate those same materials through various sources using the extraordinary computational abilities of Patience Station's systems.

"Yes, Philo and Kel are in the chandlery making purchases for their trip," Beverly said, appearing on his knee sitting in an Adirondak chair and wearing a 1950s bikini.

"First, that's not a bad Brigitte Bardot impression," Rix approved. "Second, do you have time to help me finalize the greenhouse plans we were working on the other day?"

"What changes are you interested in? Also, you should learn to become more comfortable with the computational assets available to you both embedded into your HUD's controller and the station," she said.

"It's more fun working with a partner," Rix said.

"So you like me for my personality?" Beverly asked, giving him a flirtatious smile.

"Don't make this weird."

"I'm a symbiote living inside a semi-sentient, albeit friendly, host," she said. "My experiences are beyond weird."

"I can't imagine being in Philo's head every day. The things you must see," Rix said.

"You truly have no idea," Beverly agreed. "Do you know why I chose Philo as host?"

"I have an idea."

"Care to share?"

"According to Galactic Empire law on symbiotic hosts, you had few other options. The regulation around pairings is considerable and requires deep background exposition as well as psychological testing. That you've chosen someone on the fringe of civilization suggests you're avoiding something. Bottom line is that Philo doesn't ask a lot of questions and can be cajoled or manipulated," Rix said.

"You make it sound so tawdry," Beverly said breathily.

"You're not denying it."

"I'm not, but I'm also not agreeing. And you're wrong. My primary reason for bonding with Philo is because his species is a poor match for bonding."

"That sounds contrary to a good idea."

"Not really. Because of the poor bond, I can leave without hurting him," she said. "A bond with most other sentients is lifelong. The risk of unpairing and causing psychological or physical damage is considerable."

"You're hiding and have distanced yourself from something," Rix said. "Why are you telling me this?"

"I have a proposal."

"This should be interesting. You're tiny. I don't think dating is in the cards for us."

"Don't make fun, Rix. I'm serious," Beverly said. "Also, I'm not tiny, I'm microscopic. Four hundred nanometers microscopic."

"Visible with an electron microscope," Rix said. "But barely."

"Right."

"Humans are classified as semi-sentient. You could bond with me without legal challenges, especially considering you don't have to register the bonding, and I have even fewer legal requirements placed on me," Rix said.

"You've thought about this a lot, then?"

"I wouldn't go so far as to say I've put a lot of thought into it," Rix said. "Mostly, I wanted to understand if there were protections for symbiote hosts. There are. But also, it's a discouraged practice due to the opportunity for the symbiote's influence over the host. There are a couple of symbiotic species, Korgul were top of the list, that are closer to parasitic bonds than symbiotic. Beltigersk aren't fully clean in this, although according to what I've read, that's changed in the last fifty years, but I think your species is still on probation."

"I'm impressed with your research," Beverly said. "Did you anticipate this conversation, is that why you did so much studying?"

"Philo is a great friend, and I love him like a brother. His sleep patterns alone would drive me nuts if I was trapped within. The reason we're always talking is likely because you don't find him an intellectual equal," Rix said. "How am I doing?"

"Considerably more insightful than I'd have expected, even from you, who I'd thought I'd learned not to underestimate."

"I prefer it when people underestimate me. It allows for a lot of freedom," Rix said. "Also, I'd need to know, up front, the impacts to me. I'm not that good with sharing and this body is mine. I'm not up for you taking it for a stroll when you're bored or if you disagree with what I'm doing. You have strong feelings about a variety of topics. I won't be okay with you overriding me. Also, does bonding hurt? Do I need different nutrition? Will I feel you moving around? Will I ever have privacy?"

"That's a strong list of questions," Beverly said. "First, your body is yours to do with what you wish. I will have recommendations for which I will strongly advocate. It is next to impossible for me to compel you to do anything."

"Unless you tap my nerves," Rix said. "I've read about Beltigersk's past, Beverly."

"Pain is a strong motivator, and while I can't promise to never draw your attention with pain, I can commit that if you ever want to separate from me, I will not resist. There would be some danger to you if we did this, but then, what in this universe doesn't come with risks?"

"What do you gain and what do I gain, from your perspective?"

"My gains are obvious. I gain a partner who is more my equal. You are motivated, hardworking and creative. We will both benefit from each other's experiences and talents. In addition, you will never have to worry about illness. Once I have studied the systems of your body, I'll be able to regenerate missing tissue and clear up that failing eyesight of yours. Obviously, we can work on projects together as we already do."

"There's something else," Rix said. "I can feel it. There's something you're leaving out. It's a big ask and you don't want to say it."

"How do you know this?" Beverly asked.

"Am I right?"

"Yes, but how?"

"Intuition. Go ahead and spill it. What don't you want to tell me?"

"I want to go back to Earth," she said. "When we were there, something seemed off and while I have a suspicion, I don't know for sure."

"You want me to return home," Rix said.

"Only for a moment and not even to Cranberry Cove," Beverly said. "I have a team. We need to pick them up and take them somewhere we'd have access to a large cross section of humanity. Ideally, people who would have their guard down."

"So your team could bond?"

"No, but you're on the right track. We have technology that allows a Beltigersk to accompany a host without bonding. There is no pairing. They can't talk to one another, but that Beltigersk is able to observe everything around them. You'd need to pick up a package and deliver it to Earth."

"What about the quarantine?"

"You can't go back home to live, and technically you're not supposed to return with advanced technology, but the truth is, the Galactic

Empire isn't monitoring Earth. That's why I suggested it as a landing site for Kel to get *Calypso* repaired."

"You knew I wasn't a spaceship mechanic, didn't you?"

"Or so I thought," she said. "Turns out I was wrong on that count."

"You need me to pick up a package, deliver it to Earth, somewhere where there are a lot of people from diverse locations with lowered inhibitions," Rix said.

"That's right."

"Does your team hurt the people they're attached to?"

"Not at all. That's not even possible with this kind of attachment."

"But you and I would be bonded for life after that."

"I'm afraid that's critical to pull this off. I thought I could make it work with Philo. He is uninterested in the prospects of new adventures."

"That's quite a payment you're willing to make. You're essentially giving yourself away for this mission," Rix said.

"It's not as much a stretch as you think. A Beltigersk is so small that physical location isn't overly relevant, although we tend to stay on our home planet strictly out of convenience," she said.

"Do I have time to think about it?"

"Yes. Certainly," Beverly said. "If you're amenable, I could manufacture a cuff for your arm that would provide habitat and connectivity between us."

"We wouldn't bond but you'd do a ride along?"

"That's right."

"I'm game. I don't see the disadvantage. Won't Kel be disappointed to have you separate from Philo?"

"I have already discussed the matter with Kel," Beverly said. "She has no objections. We are on a short schedule. If you're interested, you should pick up the cuff before *Calypso* departs."

"There seems to be no downside in experimenting," Rix said. "Let's try it until Kel and Philo get back and we can make a decision after that."

"Thank you, Rix."

Rix tapped his HUD to open a channel to Kel. "Hey, Kel, I'm running down to the manufactory for a minute. Don't leave without talking to me, okay?"

"Heya, Rix. Wouldn't think of it," Kel said. "I'm guessing you talked to Beverly about you giving her a ride-along. Just so you know, Philo is a little sad about losing her. You might need to figure out a way to make it up to him."

"Oh, I know just the thing."

"You're not making that Fisherman's Folly drink, are you? Because, you do know that he's using that to pick up female companionship now," she said.

"That's impossible," Rix said. "The drink smells like the backside of a weightlifter."

"A what?"

"Earth reference, but the backside should resonate well enough."

"Rix, Philo just said if you mix him a liter of the Fisherman's Folly, he'll feel okay about Beverly," Kel said. "How about I send him down to the manufactory and you get started on his drink. Can you make a liter for him? It's going to be a long trip."

"I'll do what I can. We don't have exactly the right ingredients, but I think we can get close," Rix said. "I experimented making fish sauce with those fish we got from Sout Atal."

"Didn't that stink?"

"Yes, and I believe that's the appeal."

"Okay, we're on the move. See you in a bit."

Rix scanned the crates that were still stacked in his mostly empty workshop. Aside from part ownership in *Calypso,* every item he owned came down to a pile of crates filled with tools, clothing and four partially filled bottles of spirits he'd managed to buy or trade for. The recipe for Philo's favorite drink required specific liquors, including sake, dill pickle juice, green tea and gin. The pickle juice and tea weren't hard to come by, but he had to get creative for the gin and sake. He was still mixing the foul green drink when the station side door announced Kel's arrival.

"I can smell it from here," Kel cringed, holding her nose between her forefinger and thumb. "Please make sure your container isn't easy to spill. I'd hate to have to smell that the entire ride out and back."

"Even I wouldn't want that for you," Rix said, pushing a cork into a glass rum bottle filled with his best impression of the cocktail.

"What are you going to work on while I'm gone?" she asked.

"First thing, I plan to clean this bay out thoroughly," Rix said. "It's like a family of pigs lived in here. I have a pressure washer on a low priority thread in the manufactory, so I need to get busy and clear out all of the trash. After that, I'll get the tool cabinets pushed into place and bolted down. Once that's done, I can organize all the tools I brought along and get your shelving setup for your shop, which I think I'll move to the other side of the hallway."

"Is that okay with Quixly?"

"It is now," Rix said. "I've leased Bay 808 also."

"Why?"

"A project Amari and I are working on," Rix said. "I'm hoping Shixen didn't scare her off entirely."

"I talked to her a little. She was humiliated at lunch. That's why she ran off," Kel said. "Look, Rix, I know it's complicated with her, but don't let Shixen ruin things between you guys."

"So that's the thing, Kel," Rix said. "There isn't anything between us aside from enjoying spending time together. I'm still working out if I'm willing to let Shixen run me off because they have a past. And before you start, I know that Shixen is an officer in Sable and that he's dangerous. We've had that conversation."

"Try not to get hurt while I'm gone, okay?" Kel asked. For a moment her eyes softened. "I like you being around, Rix."

"How about you try to avoid getting shot at while you're gone," Rix said. "I won't be aboard so I won't be there to fix things."

"I've managed this far in my career without a full-time mechanic aboard, I imagine I'll be okay."

"Talk to me about the legs of your trip."

"I'll be flying a Grelvox flag since that's technically *Calypso's* home port," Kel said. "That's why I took the delivery from Gestalt Station to Grelvox. I'm hoping you can contact shippers in Grelvox who need a load to come back this way. It doesn't have to be to Patience, but something within a few days travel."

"I'll do some research," Rix said. "How full is your hold from Gestalt Station to Grelvox and what are the things I need to be looking for?"

"We need an unbonded, self-insured load," Kel said. "Our little company doesn't have any bond, which means if the load is lost, the shipper needs to have it covered. That's not ideal and will knock us out of a lot of deals. Loads to any of the stations in the Surnac Belt are generally uninsurable, so make sure you add that to your criteria."

"Are you nervous for your first official job as a short-haul freighter captain?" Rix asked.

"I actually am," Kel said. She then picked up Rix's hand, pulled him in close and, without warning, gave him a warm, passionate kiss.

"What was that for?" Rix asked, confused and blushing. Kel had expressed some interest in him but mostly, they'd been too busy to consider anything personal beyond their partnership.

"Space is dangerous."

"That's not an explanation."

"Best you'll get. Now are you selling Collie's Reserve to anyone? All your bottles are empty.

Rix struggled to make sense of the moment and stumbled over his words. "Uh, no, well, sure, whoever wants the rum is good," he said. "Could you have Philo transfer from the twenty-liter containers into the bottles while you're sailing? Then, just see if you can get any bar owners to pick it up. I'd guess someone in Grelvox might be interested."

"I imagine we can handle it," Kel said.

7

BUZZBROOM

An unfamiliar sensation caused Rix's stomach to flop when a station alarm suddenly sounded. He reached for the atmospheric helmet that hung off the back of his collar and was prepared to pull it on when he realized his feet were no longer on the deck and he was starting to slowly rotate.

"What in the heck?" he grumbled to himself.

"Need a hand?" Kel asked. Instead of floating, Kel's magnetic boot locks were engaged, and she was firmly held to the deck.

"Does this happen often?"

"Oh, this is just the beginning," she said, reaching for his hand and pulling him back to the deck. "The good news is Philo just messaged me. He got the part you had manufactured and is on the way down. Are you sure you want to interface with Beverly? I wonder how Philo is going to feel about all that."

"It's Beverly's choice," Rix said. "I assume she's working it out with Philo."

"Can I ask you something personal?"

Rix leaned over and tapped a button which engaged the magnetic field in his boots, holding him to the deck. Satisfyingly, his boots clamped to the deck.

"Shoot."

"That's a weird idiom, by the way."

"What, shoot? I suppose. Is that what your question is about?"

"No."

"Are you going to ask it?"

"It's uncomfortable."

Rix chuckled. "I've seen you buck naked. I think we're way past uncomfortable."

"When? Have you been spying on me?"

Rix laughed again. "No, dumb butt. You walk through the crew space naked when you think I'm asleep. News flash, I'm not always asleep."

"Oh, that's so embarrassing. Why didn't you say something?"

"I figured it was just easier if I closed my eyes harder," Rix said. "I thought you knew."

"No, and it doesn't make this any easier."

"Seriously, Kel, ask what you want. Does this have anything to do with you trying to set me up with Amari?"

"A little."

"And your kiss?"

"Fine. Stop. I can't take much more of this conversation. Do you like me?"

"Yes."

"I heard a *but* in your answer."

"You do know that you can get to the point instead of going on a fishing expedition first," Rix said.

"Fine. Every time we kiss, I feel like I'm kissing my kid brother," she said.

"I didn't know you had a brother."

"I don't, and don't ask how I know what it feels like."

"Fine. I like you a lot," Rix said. "But, it's like you said. I don't think we're kissing friends. We're more like drinking friends and getting shot at by pirates, friends. Is that why you put Amari in my path?"

"She was interested."

"In me or in getting away from Shixen?"

"Does it have to be one thing or the other? If it's any consolation, I didn't think Shixen was still interested. Just be honest with her, okay? She's had it rough."

"I'm not letting Shixen run me off," Rix said. "Amari and I are working on a project together. I'm still interested in the project and if something develops between us, we'll work it out with him."

"How?"

"I'll talk to him," Rix said. "Besides, we only had lunch together."

"Well, I think she likes you."

"You see how you're all over the board on this, right?" Rix asked. "First, you're setting me up with Amari and then you're kissing me. You could see where that could be confusing, right?"

"It won't happen again," Kel said. "At least that's what I'm telling myself."

Rix gave half a grin. "Look, let's not get too focused on this. You're both pretty great. Any guy would be lucky to be with either of you."

The lazy station alarm that had been chirping the entire time they'd been having the conversation suddenly took on a more urgent frequency.

"Oh, frak," Kel said.

"What's going on, Kel?"

"Put on your helmet, Rix," Kel said, pulling her own on.

As Rix did as she suggested, the lights in his shop abruptly doused and the ever-present sound of air circulation fans stopped, leaving them in complete silence and darkness. A moment later, Kel's suit lamps snapped on, as did Rix's.

"What is it? Is the station compromised?" Rix asked. "Was there an asteroid strike?"

"Not a big one. Or we'd have felt it," Kel said. "No, I think this is just Patience Station being crabby."

"What do we do?"

"Well, back in the day, we'd wait for Geoff to figure out why the power's out."

"Great," Rix said as his helmet comms chirped. Picking up, he was unsurprised to find that Quixly had initiated. "This is Rix, go ahead, mayor."

"Where are you, Rix?" Quixly asked.

"In my shop."

"Do you have power?"

"No power, no gravity, no air circulation," Rix confirmed.

"Can you fix it?"

"Which?"

"Don't be a smart ass," Quixly said. "Patience Station is down. Can you fix her?"

"I have no Earthly idea what the problem is."

"Two month's rent forgiven if you can get us up and running in the next hour," Quixly bribed.

"Two month's rent forgiven when I get Patience back online," Rix said. "You can stuff that *next hour* business. I have no idea what I'm looking for."

"Fine. But hurry. People are going to panic."

"I might need access to Garba's warehouse. She has tools stashed that I might need."

"You can borrow whatever you need but it needs to be returned," Quixly said.

"How about I put useful tools back in the tool cabinets down in Environmental on Deck 3 so whoever does this in the future has them?" Rix said.

"Just get the power fixed."

"I'll do what I can," Rix said, closing comms.

"Let me guess, you're station maintenance, now," Kel said.

"I am today. How close is Philo? I need that cuff he's fetching so I can get help from Beverly," Rix said.

"He just pinged me, he's almost here," Kel said. "This emergency will make the conversation about Beverly moving easier."

"Just so we're not lying to Philo. He's a friend and deserves whatever the truth is," Rix said. "I hope that's Beverly's approach, too. Lies have a way of catching up with people and ruining friendships."

"Sounds like you have some experience with that," Kel said. "Are you going to be okay if I take off while Patience has no power? You can always send me a comm and I'll come back and pick you up if you can't get her back online."

"No, you guys go ahead and take off," Rix said. "I'm sure we can figure out whatever is going on. How hard can it be to power a space station?"

Kel inspected Rix's face for humor. "Are you serious right now?"

"No."

"I can never tell."

A sharp rapping on the station side hatch warned of someone requesting access.

"Philo?" Rix asked.

"Yes, it's him," Kel answered, turning the manual latch.

"Rixy, Rixy! Bevies ride with you today?" Philo asked, swinging into the space.

"Is that okay with you, Philo?" Rix asked.

"Bevies says you needs help," Philo said. "Bevies big helps."

"She certainly is," Rix agreed.

"Here Bevies' house," Philo said, handing what looked like a thin leather bracelet to Rix. "Be nice Bevies, okay?"

"I'll treat Beverly like she's my important friend, okay Philo?"

"Rixy good mans. Bevies be happy but still talks Philo. Put on. Bevies already in house."

When Rix touched the bracelet, Beverly suddenly appeared in front of him, still only ten centimeters tall and this time, she wore a slate gray jumpsuit with a green collar and cuffs.

"Tom Corbett, Space Cadet," Rix said, grinning. "Nice reference, Beverly."

"I've been saving that one," Beverly said. "Is Philo still okay?"

"Ask him yourself. He was excited that you were going to help me," Rix said.

"Has there been a power failure? I am unable to connect to Patience Station's computational network and there appears to be a failure of gravity and lighting," Beverly said.

"Good observation," Rix said. "Would you believe that Quixly wants us to fix it?"

"I assume he is unaware of my presence," Beverly said. "And yes, you have proven to be adept at resolving issues with the station."

Just then, the light flickered back on and a moment later, gravity returned, along with a small breeze as air handlers once again kicked on.

"Hmm, looks like it's fixed," Kel observed. "I guess you're off the hook, Rix."

"I guess so," Rix said as a chirp warned of an incoming comm. "Go ahead, this is Rix."

"Banner, did you fix the power?" Quixly asked.

"No. Do you still want me to look at it?" Rix asked.

"It's probably nothing. This happens occasionally. If it does it again, I'll have you get involved," Quixly said. "Since you didn't fulfill your end, I'm cancelling the emergency contract and your pay."

"I get it," Rix said, and found that he was talking to no one. "Boring conversation anyway," he muttered.

"Quixly?" Kel asked.

"Yeah. He cancelled the contract and hung up on me."

"He's not known for his tact. Want to help us load the rum into *Calypso*? I think that's our last cargo before we set sail."

"I'll send you a list of seeds I'm interested in for that project I'm working on with Amari," Rix said.

"Put what you're willing to pay on the list. I'm sure I can find seeds, it'll be a matter of how expensive they are," Kel said.

Rix nodded as he lifted a twenty-liter container of rum onto one of his grav pallets and then loaded the second. "I can do that. Beverly, would you be willing to make an initial list? I don't want to spend more than five hundred credits."

"Yes, and that should be sufficient to get you started on a small project. Diversity will be more interesting than volume as once your growing capacity is secure, you'll be able to reproduce the seeds," Beverly said.

"Are you really moving forward with your greenhouse project?" Kel asked. "What about Shixen?"

"Shixen shouldn't be threatened by a project that will pay Amari," Rix said.

"Because Shixen wants Amari to be financially independent?" Kel asked.

"Cold voice of reason," Rix said with irritation in his voice. "We'll just have to figure it out. Amari has expertise and interest. I'm not giving that up because of Shixen's ego."

"Good. Shixen shouldn't always get his way."

Rix pushed the grav pallet over to the man-sized door adjacent to the much larger hatch that allowed entry of smaller spaceships into the bay. Activating the airlock, he, Kel and Philo exited the bay onto a two-meter-wide catwalk that ran the length of the eighth level and over to a pier that jutted out into space and allowed for much larger ships to tie up. At present, there were three ships tied up, *Calypso* being the only vessel Rix knew to still be operational.

“Are you going to talk to Quixly about these runabouts?” Kel asked as they walked past the ships along the pier.

“I suppose I could ask about ownership,” Rix said. “I wouldn’t mind a junker project for when I’m not busy with other things.”

“Ownership isn’t hard. That one was Patience Station’s patrol vessel before it broke,” she said. “The other one is a freighter that was owned by a family that had to leave because it broke down and they couldn’t make money anymore. They were paying the docking fee for a while, but it might have lapsed. Talk to your buddy, Quixly. I bet he’d make you a good deal on the freighter, especially if you got his cruiser working.”

“Good eye on that,” Rix said, pushing the grav pallet over to the extended gang plank that sat between *Calypso* and the pier.

“Are you sure you don’t want to come along?” Kel asked. “You’re going to miss us while we’re gone. Also, just set the rum here in the crew space. Philo can load bottles on the way out to Gestalt Station.”

“I’m so far behind on getting my shop put together, it’d drive me nuts to be sailing around while I have so much work to do,” Rix said, helping Philo unload the rum containers beneath the galley table.

“Philo and I would love to have you along, but I understand. You have *special* projects planned with Amari.”

“You make it sound sordid.”

“Hopefully it is.”

Rix transferred a thousand credits to Kel and shook his head. He’d been making good money since he’d arrived but every turn he made seemed to nearly run him dry. “That’s for seeds and other arbitrage opportunities,” Rix said. “I’ll get you the list.”

“Gestalt Station is a good place to look for seeds,” Kel said. “I have a list of potential trade items for Petju, too. This could be a great trip.”

Rix smiled at Kel's excitement. "Godspeed, Kel," he said as she embraced him.

"I'm not sure what that means, but I'll take it," she said as Rix exchanged a complex handshake with Philo.

Exiting *Calypso*, Rix walked off the pier and leaned against the towering wall that made up the exterior of Patience Station. He didn't have to wait long for *Calypso's* systems to light up. Not long after that, mooring lines were automatically retracted and the ship gracefully slid away from the pier. Rix gave a respectful salute as his friends slipped away into the night.

"Do you miss them?" Beverly asked once Rix was back inside his mechanic's bay.

"They just left. I haven't had time."

"Will you miss them, then?"

"I've grown accustomed to being around them," Rix said. "I've also been by myself for much of my adult life, so I'm okay, if that's what you're asking. Nothing like getting to work to keep your mind off things. Can you open a channel to Quixly for me?"

"Yes, but now that I'm living so close to you, if you'd like, you can simply address the person you wish to speak to and I'll automatically route it," she said. "Before you do that, though, I'll need access to the earwig interface."

"You don't have that?"

"There's another level I'll need. Don't worry, it won't hurt," she said.

A prompt appeared on Rix's HUD asking for a new level of access. For a moment, Rix hesitated, wondering if giving more access to Beverly was potentially dangerous. He decided that he had no mechanism to weigh such questions, so he gave access, hoping his read of the tiny alien's moral compass was correct.

"This is Quixly. What do you need, Banner?" Quixly answered, his voice already testy.

"Those two ships moored to the pier," Rix said. "I'm interested in who owns them."

"Patience Station municipality owns them both. The freighter was left behind by the Carluf family. There's a through hole in the engine compartment. It's basically junk. We've had to run off salvagers. It's in bad shape. Why? Do you want to buy it?"

"What about the cruiser?"

"Not for sale."

"What's it worth to you to get it running again?"

"It's a bigger project than you think," Quixly said. "Why? Do you want to fix it for me? Are you that bored with your buddies gone already?"

"I was thinking you pay for parts, I'll do the work, in the end, you give me the freighter if I can get your cruiser working," Rix said.

"What is with you and all these trades?" Quixly asked. "Why not just make an offer on the freighter?"

"I have more time than money," Rix said. "Also, every project I do gets me more familiar with your technology. It's worth my investment, is what I'm saying."

"You're a strange person. It's like you never sleep, and when you do, you dream of fixing things."

"What, you don't?" Rix asked, grinning as he said it.

"Let me run your deal past the Town Council, first," Quixly said. "I'm inclined to say yes, but I need some coverage from the council since this isn't an emergency."

"Just let me know."

Comms terminated.

Rix chuckled at the prompt on his HUD. Quixly was, if anything, consistent.

"What now, Rix?" Beverly asked.

"Today, we're cleaning the bay," Rix said.

"How can I help?"

"Sorting the wheat from the chaff," Rix said. "I'd like to get all this crap out of the bay," Rix gestured, sweeping his hand over top of the piles of empty boxes, crates and litter.

"What kind of value are you considering wheat?"

"How about you notify me if something I'm piling into the trash has value beyond a credit or two," Rix said. "Or has a potential to be used in ship or station repair. I feel like I need a push broom to really get the job done."

"You have one, or at least it's analog," Beverly said. "There's an ion-broom to your right beneath that pile. It looks broken, but parts are certainly available."

With Beverly highlighting the broom's outline beneath the trash, Rix easily located it. As she'd said, the ion-broom was inoperable, and Rix brought it over to his workbench where he set about disassembling it.

"You are somewhat predictable, Rix Banner," Beverly said as she showed him the disassembly instructions for the relatively simple device. "These are called buzzbrooms by some. They ionize air currents to push dust and debris forward. They have a buildup of static energy that sometimes discharges, hence the nickname buzzbroom."

"I think I see the problem," Rix said. "This entire control wafer is corroded. Can you check the manufactory cost?"

"The closest part is the entire handle for fifteen credits."

"You're kidding. It's a simple swap out."

"As is the handle. Also, the wafer design is public domain."

"You're saying I could make a pattern and list it," Rix said. "Why wouldn't you just do that yourself? You could be making money just like I am."

"I have no need for wealth," Beverly said.

Rix wasn't sure what she meant but let the comment go. "Let's submit a new part, then," he said. "I'll record the repair process and attach the video to the part."

"I wonder if you'll find others who are equally interested?" Beverly wondered. "There are millions of these buzzbrooms in circulation, so perhaps. Who would know?"

"What's the manufactory cost now?"

"A single credit."

"I'll sell the IP for two credits," Rix said. "When can we have it?"

"For two credits, it'll be waiting for you to pick up if you leave now."

"Perfect."

Twenty minutes later, Rix had the buzzbroom's repair recorded and the new part placed out on the manufactory store, as well as a functioning buzzbroom to utilize. Switching gears, he laid out empty boxes against one wall and started filling them with obvious trash on the left side with progressively more potential value the further he got to the right. Three hours later, he'd filled and dumped into a nearby reclaimer a total of six cubic meters of garbage, earning him a scant six credits in return. He'd also found several common hand tools, some too broken to use, but several that were workable. Further, he had three crates of old spaceship parts that were in varying degrees of disassembly and disrepair.

"That's not a bad day's work," Rix said as he finished his first pass of sweeping the bay with his new favorite tool. The ion broom projected beams of blue light from the wide chromed head and the more slowly he moved, the more thoroughly it removed grit from the deck. He'd chosen a moderate speed due to a considerable buildup of grime, knowing that repeated scrubbing would bring the shop up to his high standards, eventually.

"The panels you ordered have been delivered to Bay 808. They were left in the hallway," Beverly said.

"All of them?" Rix asked with some surprise. As he'd been cleaning, he'd heard activity in the hallway, but since no one had knocked or tried to enter his bay, he'd ignored it.

"Yes."

Rix set the buzzbroom against the wall and opened the station side hatch. The normally open corridor was filled with thin panels leaning against the walls.

8

POKING THE BEAR

"I WONDERED if I'd ever hear from you again," Amari said, her eyes jumping between Rix and the panels. "I'm sorry I ran out of Petju's."

Rix held up his hand to stop her from continuing. "You don't have to apologize to me," he said. "Shixen is intimidating. I imagine you know that better than I do."

"I'm sorry I got you involved."

"Put it in the rearview," Rix said. "We have more interesting things to talk about."

"I don't understand. What is all of this?"

"Nano particulate polymeric strands in a planar configuration," Rix said. "At least that's what the pattern said. "I'd call them greenhouse panels."

"I don't think your greenhouse is going to work, Rix," she said. "Today was a perfect example. Losing power, sometimes atmosphere, gravity and even heat will kill plants. It happens often enough. We just don't have a stable environment."

"That's where this comes in," Rix said, holding up a box containing nine tubes of sealant. "Our greenhouse will be a self-contained microcosm with independent heat, atmosphere and lighting. I'm not sure if we should be equally concerned with gravity, but we can talk about that more as we put it together."

"We?"

"Last we talked, we agreed on a partnership. I've quite an investment in all of this. I figure it's time to start working toward a payout."

"I don't know if that's such a good idea. Shixen is focusing on me," Amari said.

"I could talk to him."

"No, that'd be a disaster. Don't you understand? He's dangerous. He's not going to be okay with us spending time together."

"It's your choice," Rix said. "If I must build this by myself, I will. I'd love your help and as far as I'm concerned, the Shixen thing will work itself out."

"I can at least help you put them in the bay," she said.

"That's the spirit. Grab the end of that."

The two worked in companionable silence for twenty minutes as they loaded the greenhouse panels, connectors and glue into Bay 807. Having not yet cleaned out the bay, they were forced to move some of the debris out of the way just to find room, but in the end, the hallway was cleared and the panels neatly stored.

"This doesn't look like anything," Amari said. "How did you afford all this material?"

"The polymeric strand material is cheap," Rix said. "It's my own design so there was no IP cost. The most expensive pieces were glue and delivery. Besides, I don't yet have the power and atmospheric units, although I think I might have a line on those."

"You talk funny."

"Sure, I'm from Earth, so ... you know, I'm an alien," he said.

Amari laughed politely. "Shixen doesn't have to know I'm working on this. It's not like he's down here."

"Are you saying you'll help get it set up? I have a whole lot of cleaning to do before I'm ready to put the panels together, but I haven't had much to eat all day, so I was going to take a break and grab some food."

"Hutari is expecting me back for dinner," Amari said. "I mean, I was thinking, maybe, if we ate in my apartment, you could join us."

"I don't want to cause trouble for you, Amari," Rix said.

"While we've been working, I've been thinking about how I want to live my life," she said. "I fear Shixen. I've been afraid of him since a couple of months after we started dating. I never had the courage to break it off and hoped he'd lose interest. It's like I'm his property. I make it more confusing because I let him pay for my apartment. It's not like we could live here if I didn't and we don't have anywhere else to go."

"Dinner sounds nice," Rix said, changing the subject. "How about you go home, and I'll join you in an hour or so after I do some cleaning up here."

"Okay," she said and walked toward the door to the hallway. "And Rix?"

"Yeah?"

"Thanks for being a decent person."

"Back at you."

Like he'd done in his shop, Rix started by locating empty boxes and lining them up against one wall. Unlike his shop, Bay 807 was filled with crates that were unopened, and his curiosity burned intensely about what might be inside. Instead of giving in, he dragged shelving against the same wall where the boxes were lined up and started stacking the crates on the shelves as he sorted debris into the same buckets as before. He was pulled from thought by a chirp requesting comms.

"It's Amari," Beverly said, appearing on one of the shelves with her legs hanging over the edge. "You know she's not wrong, right? Shixen isn't going to just give you a pass on being near her."

"Chips will fall where they may," Rix said, answering the comm. "This is Rix."

"Are you coming? It's been almost two hours," she said.

Rix checked the chrono on his HUD. "Son of a gun, Amari, I'm so sorry. Did I ruin dinner?" he asked.

"Hutari was hungry, so she ate, but I saved a plate for you. Can you break away?"

Rix looked around the bay. Two hours had him about halfway done with organizing the debris and he was feeling good about the fact that his shelving was full of heavy crates. Still having not opened the sealed crates, he'd found open ones with myriad parts he hadn't bothered to classify but had a feeling were made for repairing spaceships or space station subsystems.

While he wanted to keep working, he felt the pressure of having made a commitment. "Sure, I'll come right up. What's your address?" he asked, brushing at his jumpsuit ineffectively. "Say, do you have a suit cleaner? I'm pretty grubby."

"I do. You can even take a shower if you want," she said.

Rix couldn't help but look over his shoulder as he traversed the station on his way to Amari's apartment. He felt he'd made it in the clear and when he arrived, she ushered him to the shower with instructions to come out clean for dinner. He smiled as he luxuriated under the hot water of the shower and washed off the day's grime.

"Am I more presentable?" he asked, finding Amari at a small table in the kitchen.

"Yes, thank you for cleaning up."

"I appreciated the offer," he said. "Do you have your HUD still available?"

Amari tapped her ear. "I do now."

"While you serve, I'll project the greenhouse build onto the table. You can see how the panels go together and get an idea of what I'm talking about," he said.

"Is that something you want me to do?" Beverly asked, appearing in front of him on the kitchen table wearing denim coveralls, a hardhat and a hammer hanging from a leather toolbelt around her waist.

"Do you like greens?" Amari asked. "We don't grow many, but I have a few that are ready today."

"Please, show me," Rix said, looking at Beverly, hoping she caught the double meaning of his answer.

"Oh, it's just a little box garden I have over the sink. If you cut the greens at the right time, they grow right back," she said, her eyes turning to the table where greenhouse panels were carried by unseen hands and assembled one by one until a room six by eight meters came into existence. "Oh, Rix, that's a lot bigger than I thought it was going to be. Are you thinking hydroponics? Getting nutrient dense soil out this far is expensive."

"I'm not thinking anything, partner," Rix said. "My job is to build a weatherproof micro farm where you can get as creative as you'd like."

"I don't see any hydroponic tubes," she said. "We'll need those."

"How about we work on a design for your first phase while we eat?" Rix said.

"Do you have access to station water?"

"Yes."

Amari set a plate in front of Rix with modest portions of inexpensive station food. On the edge of the plate were several green leaves of a close relative to spinach. He took a few bites and, noticing Amari's watchful eye, he added a compliment. "This is delicious."

"Not by any standard," she said. "But I appreciate you lying."

Rix shrugged. "You prepare these proto foods better than I do."

"I've had a lot of experience. What if we run vertical tubes in rows with ports every twenty centimeters or so? We'll have a steady drizzle of nutrient water pumped through the entire system to keep the roots wet."

"That sounds about right," Rix said. "Honestly, I'm not overly familiar with it all. I was hoping you'd take the lead on that. Is there a source for the nutrient water or is it something we can manufacture?"

"A little bit of both," Amari said. "And, okay. You've got me. This is a dream project for me, and I won't let Shixen run me off. At least, not yet."

"This isn't anything more than two people working on a project for the benefit of Patience Station," Rix said, kicking back from the table. Watching Amari's face, he saw a micro expression of disappointment flash by, and he nodded in understanding.

"Where are you sleeping?" Amari asked.

"I was sleeping on *Calypso*. I have a cot I set up in the shop. I'll sleep there tonight and get a little more serious about all that soon."

"You could stay here."

"I'm not sure poking the bear is such a good idea. At least, not yet."

Amari sighed. "I know. And I probably would have changed my mind. It was just a silly idea that flitted through my head."

"You're a desirable woman, Amari," Rix said. "We'll get through this."

"Will we?"

"There's always a way," Rix said. "Thank you for the shower and dinner. I've got at least two more hours of cleaning to get done before tomorrow."

"What's tomorrow?"

"We're going to start building a greenhouse."

"This is so exciting!" Amari beamed. "I can't believe we're actually doing this."

The walk back to Level 8 was quiet, as it was getting late and most people were inside, preparing for sleep. Getting back to work, Rix continued sorting and dragging loads to the reclaimer for what seemed like forever. When he'd finally moved every scrap of material and done an initial sweep of the floors with his new favorite toy, the buzzbroom, he was exhausted.

"You have to be tired," Beverly said when Rix set the broom against the wall and scanned the bay with a satisfied exhalation.

"What time is it?"

"0130," Beverly answered.

"Can you set an alarm for me at 0800?" Rix asked. "I'd like to start opening those crates. I'm excited to see what was left behind."

"Some of the crates had part numbers on them. I did a little looking," Beverly said.

"Am I going to like what you found?"

"I'd estimate about six thousand credits worth of parts," Beverly said. "Although, out here, I'm not sure that is value you can realize."

"Oh, I'd never sell them," Rix said. "Every mechanic I've ever known hordes usable parts for a rainy day. You never know when something will come in handy. The biggest thing is knowing what you have. I'm hoping you'll help me with an inventory."

"In the morning, Rix," Beverly said. "Your vitals are showing that you're exhausted."

"You don't need to be a microscopic genius to know that," Rix said, crossing over to the shop. Settling almost immediately onto the cot, Rix pulled a thin blanket over his body and fell right to sleep.

The next morning, Rix was awakened by loud rapping on the door to the shop. He struggled from the cot and blearily made his way over to the door. "Beverly, what time is it and can you see who's out there?"

"It is 0730 and acting Mayor Quixly is your visitor," she said.

"Did he bring coffee?" Rix yawned, opening the door.

"He did not bring coffee," Quixly answered, stepping into the shop. "You've been busy," he added approvingly.

"I can't stand working in a messy shop," Rix said.

"Find anything interesting?"

Rix pointed to the small stack of crates he'd gathered from the shop's debris. "Look for yourself. I haven't inventoried anything just yet. It looks like anything of real value was taken, although there were some hand tools, so that's helpful."

Quixly nodded approvingly. "This bay had its share of renters in the past. Exterior bay doors are desirable, or at least they were when Patience Station was busier."

Rix padded over to the table where he'd set up his only kitchen gadget, which was a self-contained kettle. Pouring water from a jug, he started his water for coffee. “Join me for a cup?” he asked, gesturing to one of two chairs at the table.

“No, thank you,” Quixly said, sitting in the chair. “How serious were you about that derelict out there?”

“Serious enough to make the offer I did.”

“I have three more in similar condition.”

Rix poured coffee into a cup and gestured to a second cup. This time Quixly nodded his acceptance of the offer.

“That’s interesting.”

“Is it? I’m not sure there’s a working spacecraft amongst the four of them,” Quixly said. “I guess that’d be up to you to tell me.”

“What are your plans for them?”

“I have another cruiser, not the one you’ve seen,” he said. “I’ll trade you four derelicts for two working cruisers.”

“How long has it been since the cruisers were working?” Rix asked.

“The one outside of your shop has been a few years. The one I have in storage still moves, but barely. It’s nearly impossible to patrol local space without a cruiser.”

“You want to trade four derelict ships for parts and labor to fix two cruisers with unknown issues,” Rix said. “I can’t do that.”

“Why not? It’s a good deal,” Quixly said.

“You may need a part that is just too expensive to purchase. You don’t want me cutting corners, do you?” Rix said. “How about Patience Station pays for parts, I provide labor.”

“I had that deal when it was one derelict for a fixed cruiser.”

“True, okay,” Rix said. “I’ll put on credit however many hours I spend fixing your cruisers. If I take ten hours to get one working, I'll owe you ten hours for spaceship repairs."

"Time and a half and it can be for repairs to anything around here," Quixly said. "Patience pays for parts, but you have to get my approval for anything over a thousand credits."

"I need thirty meters on the big pier, closest to my shop."

"And time and a half?"

"And time and a half."

"You have yourself a deal, Mr. Banner," Quixly said. "I've provided temporary access to the municipal garage. And as a show of good faith, you don't have to move the derelicts until both cruisers are running."

"Looks like I'm going to be busy," Rix said.

"Your coffee is terrible, Rix Banner." Quixly shook Rix's offered hand. "Do you have a timeframe on when I'll have a working cruiser?"

"I'll keep you up to date. I have a couple of projects I'm finishing up and once I'm done with those, I'll get right to work. I imagine I'll get started the day after tomorrow."

"Fair enough."

"Aren't you quite the entrepreneur," Beverly said, appearing on the table while sitting behind a large walnut desk in a dark suit, complete with a fedora.

"*The Mob*," Rix said, identifying the movie Beverly modeled the scene on. "Let's get started on the greenhouse. I'm hoping we can get the floor laid out before Amari gets here."

Getting right to work, Rix had just finished sealing the final floor seam when Amari knocked and entered the bay. "When did you have time to get this all cleaned up? Is this the entire footprint of the greenhouse?" Amari asked excitedly.

Rix smiled at Amari's enthusiasm. "I worked late last night and Quixly woke me up this morning," Rix said. "I need your help with the side panels; can you hold this in place?"

"Sure," Amari said eagerly. "I brought some breakfast. It's not much, but that's not all that unusual around here."

"Well, maybe we can fix that," Rix said, snapping a corner piece into place. "Just push that panel over a little. It can't move too much. There's a track it's sitting in."

"Okay, got it."

Together, the pair worked doggedly, skipping lunch as panel after panel was installed and glued into place. It was 1730 when finally, Rix gave in. "I think that's as much energy as I want to give it today."

"I was hoping you'd get tired at some point," Amari said. "I'm exhausted."

"You should have said something," Rix said. "We could have stopped earlier."

"I didn't want to stop, we're just about fully enclosed."

"Why don't you take off, then. I'll grab some dinner and then finish up. I should be able to use the grav pallet to slide those last panels in place," he said.

Just then, the air turned off within the bay and a klaxon warned of imminent power failure. As there were several walls between the bay and space, Rix wasn't quite as worried about atmospheric pressure as he had been in the shop, so he didn't bother raising his hood. Instead, he flipped on a bank of portable lights just before the permanent lights flickered out.

"This is happening more and more frequently," Amari said.

"Elevators are out, we might as well finish the roof," Rix said.

"Nothing bothers you."

"Oh, that's a misread. Plenty of stuff bothers me. I just don't show it all the time. I figure we might as well take advantage of free moments. No sense in worrying about what we can't fix."

"If you say so. Personally, I like the idea of breathing."

The pair got back to work and with the artificial gravity no longer functioning, lifting the panels became considerably easier, allowing them to finish in twenty minutes what might have taken an hour otherwise.

Not unexpectedly, Rix received a comm request from Quixly twenty minutes later.

"I don't suppose I can get some of those time and a half hours in advance, can I?" Quixly asked.

"Sure," Rix said, clicking the last of the roof tiles in place. "I'll grab my tools and start making my way down." Just as he spoke, the lights and fans kicked back on. "It's like you're playing some sort of practical joke."

"It's no joke," Quixly said.

"Do you want me to go check things out, anyway?"

"Yes. Something's up."

"Good man," Rix said. "It's going to be a whole lot easier to figure out what's going on while the lights are still on and I can use the elevators."

Quixly chuckled. "I suppose you have a point there. Check in with me once you figure out what's going on."

"I'll let you know what I find," Rix said, terminating the call.

"Do you need to go?" Amari asked.

"Yes. But we were done for the night, anyway, weren't we?" Rix asked.

"We got more done than I'd expected," Amari said. "Are you going to seal the ceiling joints tonight? I could do it in the morning."

"Depends on what I find is going on with the power," Rix said. "If I can find anything."

"Okay, grab your tools. You can walk me to the elevators," Amari said.

"Sounds good."

Crossing over to his shop, Rix grabbed a tool bag that, due to his recent cleaning and organizing spree, was ready to go. It was a short walk to the elevators, and he waited for Amari's car to arrive before he called for one that would take him down.

"Okay, Beverly, talk to me about Patience Station's power generation, would you?"

"There's a lot, Rix, are you sure you want to get into this?"

"I don't see where I have much of a choice."

"What do you know about aneutronic fusion? Specifically, p-B11 or proton-boron fuel?" Beverly asked, appearing in a white lab coat in front of a black chalkboard, holding a pointer stick.

"Not a blessed thing."

"It's going to be a long night, my dear boy," she said. "You might have been wise to bring coffee."

"That tracks," Rix said with a resigned sigh.

9

RESTRAINT

"THERE SHOULD BE radiator fins outside the station," Beverly said, causing Rix to sit back on his haunches. The two of them had worked through the night, much of the time spent in a firehose of information about the extraordinarily complicated reactor complex that was Patience Station's power system.

"What do you mean, should be?" Rix asked.

"I can't find any references in the station's design about coolant ponds, but the actual information available when the station was built is dated."

"Dated, as in a different power system?" Rix asked.

"Got it in one," Beverly said. "The prior system used something called Fantastium, which is extremely efficient and is smaller by three orders of magnitude in its installation."

"A thousand times smaller," Rix said, whistling. "Why in the universe would you change from that?"

"Expense," Beverly said. "Fantastium is not only the single most energy-dense matter in the universe, but it is also the single most expensive material. So much so that it is often used as trading currency due to its extremely portable and stable resting form."

"How do we get some of that?" Rix asked.

"Ironically, go back home. Earth supposedly is lousy with the stuff," Beverly said.

"Lousy? What, now you're a mobster?"

Beverly's clothing shifted back to a black suit paired with a black fedora and a stubby cigar. "Do you want to make anything of that?" she asked with a gruff voice.

Rix laughed. "Does humanity know about Fantastium?"

"No. And I have some concerns that there might be those within the Galactic Empire who would take advantage of the untapped nature of Earth's Fantastium reserves," Beverly said. "Many emerging civilizations utilize the discovery of Fantastium to ascend to a new order of society, one that involves galactic travel via jump drives."

"But there are laws against pillaging such an emerging civilization, right?"

"There are. And laws are required because there are bad actors who have interest in taking advantage of the unwitting."

"Sounds like every piece of humanity's history I can recall," Rix said. "So, you're saying there needs to be coolant attached to all of this. Let's dig into diagnostics and grab some coffee before we start looking at spacewalks."

"That is prudent," Beverly agreed. "You should be at your peak physical capacity if you're to operate outside of the space station, especially in that there are few vehicles available for such a task."

"Surely there are some, though, right?"

"I do not know. That is a question for the acting mayor," Beverly said.

"Okay, we'll find him later," Rix said.

"You will not need to," Beverly replied.

"Why is that?"

"He has just arrived and is stalking toward us."

"Great."

"I hoped I'd find you down here," Quixly said without any other greeting. "What have you found?"

"I spent most of the night looking over the various subsystems and I was getting ready to do a deep dive on the logs," Rix said. "I suspect an issue with the cooling subsystem, but that'll require a trip outside. I was hoping you had some sort of maintenance vehicle I could utilize."

"You haven't found a smoking gun?"

"Not yet," Rix said. "I haven't been outside, nor have I dug as deeply as I'd like into the logs."

"How many hours do you have?"

"Six," Rix said.

"You look beat," Quixly said. "And if you haven't found anything after six hours, it's probably just one of those bugs we seem to have around here. How about you shut down your inspection and if it happens again, we'll send you outside."

"I haven't fixed anything," Rix said. "I think it's more than reasonable to expect this will happen again. If I could just look through the logs and go outside, I'd have a much better understanding of what could be going on."

"How long do you think that would take?"

"Another day or so," Rix said.

"Your time would be better spent getting the municipal cruisers working," Quixly argued. "Without them, we have nothing to say about the good people of Draven Knights dropping by any time they so desire."

"Did you know this system isn't the original?"

"I did not."

"There used to be a Fantastium reactor," Rix said. "Apparently, it was too expensive, so someone installed this proton-boron fusion reactor."

"That seems a good choice," Quixly said. "We haven't done much more than replace fuel every five years or so. It's expensive when it happens but not compared to the value of the power it generates."

"Does your contract for refueling include maintenance?" Rix asked.

"I don't know," Quixly said. "I can look."

"Feels like if it's available, it'd be worth the cost."

"Says everyone who doesn't have to pay the bills."

"Fair," Rix agreed. "To be clear, you want me to walk away, even though I haven't figured out what the issue is."

"Right. And don't worry about your reputation. It's a complex system. It was bound to happen that you'd run into something above your paygrade."

"It's not that," Rix said. "It just takes ..."

"Save your breath," Quixly interrupted. "I have a maintenance guy coming out from Grelvox. I'm sure he'll know right away what the problem is."

Rix gave Quixly a skeptical look. Having spent several hours digging into the subsystems and learning the technology, he wanted to continue working, but it wasn't his call. Having served in the Army where superiors often made baffling decisions, he had long ago learned how to let go of issues he didn't own.

"I'm sure he will too. You let me know if you change your mind," Rix said.

"You'll be the first to know," Quixly said. "Any estimate on when you'll have a cruiser up and running for me?"

"I haven't even been to the municipal garage yet," Rix said. "I've a mind for some coffee and breakfast from Petju. After that, I'm due a few hours of sleep and then I'll get to your cruisers."

"I'll walk with you," Quixly said. "I understand Petju has frosted breakfast rolls made from flour you and Kel brought back from Sout Atal. The way I understood it was you lost that load, though."

"We almost did," Rix said. "The cleanup was a pain."

The two men walked quietly to the elevator and rode up to Level 17 where most of the food services were available. "There's a rumor about you and Amari floating around."

"Didn't we already talk about this?"

"This is new. Something about the two of you building something."

"Nothing more than a business venture," Rix said.

"I'd keep it that way if I were you."

"Message received … again."

Quixly shrugged his shoulders and exited the elevator. Between the lack of sleep and the conversation topic, Rix decided to take his breakfast to go and, once he had what was best described as a cinnamon roll in hand, he excused himself and headed back down to his shop. Sitting in his chair, he promptly fell asleep, the roll falling from his hand to his lap and then onto the floor.

Five hours later, he was awakened by a chime at the shop's station side door. Looking down, he found a trail of frosting along his dirty coveralls and located his dried pastry on the floor. Hungry and a bachelor responsible to no one, he plucked the roll from the floor and carried it with him to the door, which he opened.

"You need to get a suit cleaner down here," Amari announced after giving him a once over.

"I have water hookups for a shower in the other suite," Rix said. "I just haven't gotten around to it yet. What's up?"

"I'm ready to get back to work," she said. "Have you had a chance to get the parts for the first towers? I have a few seeds from an extremely hardy leafy vegetable mix. It won't be a huge seller because a lot of us have little gardens on our counters, but they grow fast, so it's a good way to test our systems."

Rix scratched his head, barely having heard anything she'd said aside from wondering about the nutrient towers, which would require pumps, plumbing and water wells for recirculation.

"Sure, come in," he said, stepping out of her way.

"It's done?" she asked, her face lighting up.

"No. I haven't even started designing the space. I'm behind on the project."

"I have a virtual workspace I can share with you," she said. "I've been re-arranging the greenhouse all morning. Let me show you what I have. I think it's a good start."

Rix took a bite from the stale roll and realized he was thirsty. "Any interest in some lode bean coffee?"

"I'm good, thanks," Amari said, pinching the air in front of her and flipping her design to Rix.

As he worked on the coffee and scraped frosting from his coveralls back onto his roll, he started browsing Amari's design.

"That's a good start," he concluded as he wiped away the final bits of frosting.

"Use one of these," Amari said, producing a small wipe from her pocket.

"For what?"

"The frosting," she said.

Rix shrugged and did as she said. As he scrubbed, the stain was easily removed. "That wipe is fantastic. I should get some of those."

"Or wear less of your breakfast."

"Or that," he agreed. "I need you to add some room for a few pieces of equipment."

"Go ahead, you're an editor for the design," she said.

Rix nodded and dropped in the pieces of equipment he knew they would need. "We might be able to do better, but that's not a bad start. Take a look?"

"This looks expensive," she said after a few minutes of review.

"We can manufacture your sixteen towers going for four hundred credits," Rix said. "I have that now. What about nutrient solution? Do you have all the mixing stuff you need?"

"If you're okay with me using some space next to the greenhouse, I won't have to lose space inside," she said.

"Why don't you start gathering what you need for that and I'll send the tower parts over to the manufactory," Rix said. "We can get this all set up tomorrow morning."

"What are you doing this afternoon?" Amari asked.

"Well, I can't get the parts created until later tonight," Rix said.

"Oh, I know," she said, disappointment on her face. "Do you need me to go?"

"It's not that," Rix said. "I was under the impression that spending time with me caused issues with Shixen. I was trying to be sensitive to that."

"Oh. That," she said

Rix nodded. "There are a lot of people worried about how Shixen will respond to us spending time together. I got it again from Quixly this morning."

"I'm so done with all of this. He has no right," Amari said. "I don't understand why he thinks he can own me."

"That's not right," Rix agreed. "He's a powerful man, though."

"I'm sorry I've dragged you into this."

Rix shrugged. "We'll keep it simple, just two business partners working toward a common goal."

"I told him that was our relationship. He didn't respond well."

A pang of concern shot through Rix's being. "Talk to me about not responding well."

"You have to promise me you won't react," she said. "I won't be able to trust you in the future if you do."

"That's not exactly fair," Rix said.

"Like that's our standard," she said sarcastically.

"Okay, I won't react."

Amari pulled another wipe from her pocket and swiped at the side of her face. A large, deep blue and dark purple bruise in the shape of a hand appeared just beneath her eye. He'd thought her eye was bloodshot from lack of sleep, but with the bruise, the mystery was resolved.

"My God," Rix said, aghast. "Have you had someone look at this for damage?"

"Get closer, Rix," Beverly said. "I need to see it better."

"No," Amari said. "Shixen is always very careful to make sure he doesn't cause permanent damage."

"I want to react," Rix said, leaning in to get a better look.

"You can't, his Sable brothers would respond, and you'd be dead," she said. "I think that's what he wants."

"He needs to be stepped back," Rix said angrily. "Did he hurt you anywhere else?"

"Yes, but I'm okay, Rix. Really. I'm going to handle this on my own," she said.

"Don't do anything brave or stupid," Rix said. "If he's willing to do this to you now, he's capable of worse."

"I know what Shixen is capable of. I've seen some very bad things, Rix. Trust me."

"I'm sorry you've been exposed to this," Rix said. "I'm sorry he's hurting you."

"Why? It's not your fault."

"I'm sorry that you have to feel pain and be afraid," Rix said. "I can't control Shixen. Do you want to step away from this project? That might be the smart play here."

"No."

"Are you sure it's worth it?"

"Me building a future for Hutari and myself?" Amari asked. "You're asking if that's worth it?"

"You know what I mean."

"I do," she said. "I'm afraid you won't like me once I deal with this."

"Amari, please don't do anything that will get you hurt."

"Like talk to another man? Because that's what got me hurt this time."

"I have money. You could go away," Rix said.

"Would you be willing to let this drop for a while?" she asked. "Working with you is safe and good for my spirit. I don't want to think about Shixen right now."

Rix sighed. "Okay. We can do that."

"So, what are you doing this afternoon and can I help?"

"Repairing municipal cruisers for Quixly," Rix said.

"Perfect, what's our first task?" Amari asked.

"Finding the municipal garage."

"I know where that's at—Level 7."

"Lead the way," Rix said.

"Do you have access?"

"We're about to find out. Oh, first, I need to blow the shop's atmosphere so we can pull them in when we get back. Hood up?"

"I'll wait in the hallway," Amari said.

"Suit yourself."

"Funny."

Rix gave her a sidelong glance. Given their conversation, humor was the last thing on his mind. It was only when he raised his suit's helmet that he saw the possibility of a pun he'd inadvertently used.

With the atmosphere purged from his shop, he slipped through the temporary airlock and into the station's hallway. Joining Amari, the pair walked quietly toward the elevators. And when Amari's hand sought out his own, he didn't push it away, but wrapped his fingers around hers.

"Level 7," Amari spoke to the elevator. "The garage entrance is just across from the elevator. It hasn't had staff for quite a long time."

"Were you around when people worked here?" Rix asked as they exited the elevator.

"No. Well, yes. If you count the harbor master function, that's staffed sixteen hours a day," Amari said.

"Hutari works down here?"

"Yes."

"Should we stop in?"

"She's expecting us. We can get to where she's sitting if we go through the garage."

"Let's see if I have access," Rix said, placing the palm of his hand on the security panel. The panel recognized his handprint, and a magnetic click informed them the door was open. "I'll admit I was expecting to have to call Quixly to get access."

Amari smiled and followed Rix into a foyer of sorts where a reception counter sat empty behind another closed door locked by a security panel. Again, the door unlocked when Rix scanned his way in. Behind the second level of the door, there were several empty offices and hallways leading in two directions.

"She's down here," Amari said, gesturing to the right. "Straight ahead is where the vehicles are kept."

The pair walked through a doorway and saw a lighted hallway from within which they heard a woman's voice.

"Hello," Amari called, announcing their presence.

A moment later, Hutari stepped into the hallway with a big grin on her face. "Hey guys, what brings you down here?"

"We were off on adventure, and I told Rix I'd show him your office," Amari said.

"Fun! Thanks for coming by. It gets super quiet down here most days," Hutari said.

"How many ships do you have come through here in a day?" Rix asked.

"At any given time, there are two or three smaller, short hauls running deliveries. If it was just them, I probably wouldn't need to be here," she said. "Once or twice a week, we'll get a freighter in. Seems like that's less often nowadays. How did you get in?"

"I have access to the garage. I'm helping Quixly with his cruisers. Apparently, there's also an old freighter that was seized a few years ago that's still impounded," Rix said.

"You're fixing them all up for the constable?"

"Hutari, that's Rix's business."

"I don't mind, Amari," Rix said. "No, the trade is, I fix his cruiser and I get the impounded freighter and the three derelicts that are up on the pier on Level 8."

"Oh, that wasn't a good trade. Well, I don't know about the impounded freighter, but for sure those derelicts have been picked over by just about everyone," she said. "Why would you trade for them?"

"Hutari, be kind," Amari warned.

Rix laughed. "It's just labor on my part, so nothing much spent. As a shop owner, I need parts ships. In some cases, I might just need hull panels. I doubt the engines were fully removed and people probably haven't taken things like coolant reservoirs or hoists or actuators. You'd be surprised what people leave behind."

"Sounds like you're the right guy for the job," Hutari said. "I still think you're going to regret taking ownership of those ships down on the pier."

"Maybe," Rix said. "Worst case, I'll cut them up for reclaimer credits. I think the steel on them is worth something."

"If you don't mind getting really dirty."

"Well, we've proven that, now, haven't we," Amari interjected.

"Mom! Things I don't want to hear, already," Hutari said, feigning horror.

Rix chuckled as the two women argued for a moment.

"How about you guys figure this all out while I go check out that impounded freighter? I admit, it has my curiosity," Rix said.

"Don't let her run you off," Amari said. "She knows everything between us is perfectly innocent."

Rix smiled but didn't answer.

"I actually need to get back to work," Hutari said. "Thanks for stopping by!"

Rix's smile widened as the energetic young woman pulled him in for a hug and then jogged back into the office that she'd come from.

"Nice kid," Rix said.

"Pain in the ass you mean," Amari said, a little more loudly than necessary.

"I heard that!"

Walking back the way they came, Rix had to authorize one more entry to get into the garage portion of the municipal complex. Much larger than he'd expected, the garage had bays for ten vessels, each with photonic generators sitting next to tall, closed doors. Only two of the bays were occupied, the first with what was best described as a local space-only vessel that was roughly the size of a school bus, painted with gold and blue stripes over a white background. A Patience Station logo was in good shape on the starboard side. A small turret sat beneath the cockpit with a pair of guns pointing forward.

Sitting in the next bay over sat the half again bigger impounded freighter Rix had traded his time and energy for. "Well, that's interesting," he said, taking it all in. "Do you suppose I can get either of these started up?"

"I hope so," Amari said. "You're the spaceship mechanic."

"It'd be just my luck that I can't get it to work when I bring a pretty girl along. I bet Quixly would love to hear about that."

"Which, the pretty girl part or you can't fix his broken cruiser?"

"Either."

"I was afraid you'd say that."

10

BLOOD ON HER HANDS

"YOU SHOULD CONSIDER WEARING your helmet when you go in there," Amari warned as Rix slipped around the constable's cruiser to look at the larger impounded freighter.

"Why's that?" Rix asked, turning with a big smile on his face.

"You love this, don't you?" Amari said.

"What's not to love? With a bit of work and some extra parts, we can make something that's completely useless have value," Rix said. "What's this about helmets, though?"

"I've spent a lot of time around unsavory types and seen more than a few ships seized," Amari said. "You can count on the idea that nobody went inside and cleaned up trash or unsealed foodstuffs. Your freighter was left in an atmosphere-controlled space, which means bacteria, molds, fungus and worse have had a fertile breeding ground for however long it's been sitting here."

"Well now you're just taking the fun out of it," Rix said, pulling on his helmet and approaching the freighter. Like the municipal garage, the security panel next to the freighter's hatch lit up, sensing their presence. Unlike the garage, however, Rix's palm was not accepted. "Bah, Quixly has me locked out, still."

"Have you paid him?"

"It's a trade, but your point is valid, I haven't fulfilled my end of things. I just wanted a look is all," Rix complained.

Amari shrugged, not having an easy explanation for him. "Check the cruiser?" she offered.

Turning around, the pair approached the cruiser. When they were within a few meters, the cockpit lights turned on in addition to several external lights along the dorsal line on its side. Rix pushed up on his tiptoes but was unable to see over the lip of the glass bubble that made up the forward cockpit.

"Door is back here," Amari said, gesturing to a man-sized hatch flanked by the cowls of what looked like oversized engines for the smaller, bus-sized vessel.

"You seem awfully knowledgeable of police cruisers," Rix said.

"Oh, you have no idea," she said. "Hang out with a man like Shixen for very long and you'll end up being dragged into more than one of these."

"Did that really happen?"

"Multiple times. Multiple locations," she said. "That's one reason I've settled on Patience Station. I still have a few active warrants."

"We should bookmark that conversation," Rix said. "I didn't know I was travelling with a fugitive from justice."

Amari raised an eyebrow. "Do you think less of me?"

"I barely know you," Rix said. "And Kel has set me straight about being overly trusting of local law enforcement."

"Well, I've lived a rough life," she said. "If you know what's good for you, you'll run away at your first opportunity."

"Maybe after we steal this police cruiser, huh?" Rix asked jokingly, pressing his gloved hand onto the security panel. The aft hatch popped inward in response and when he pushed on the door, it swung open.

"You make recovering a broken ship sound so exciting."

"It can be. I used to help my town sheriff recover stolen vehicles. People can be testy when they think you're stealing their already stolen vehicles."

"Why wouldn't your sheriff arrest the people who did the stealing?"

"Sometimes, he was moonlighting for bank recoveries. Once, we tried to find a guy named Old Earl, but he was hiding. That all changed when I opened the door to his truck. He probably wouldn't have shot at us if he hadn't been drinking. We got out of there right quick."

"You have funny stories. Mine aren't nearly so lighthearted," Amari said. "When pirates take things, people get hurt. I've seen some awful things. I used to try to run away, but Shixen would find me. He made sure I knew he wasn't happy."

"I'm surprised how easily you talk about it," Rix said. "Most battered women back home really struggle to ask for help. We need to do a better job of protecting them. It's not okay that Shixen uses you as a punching bag."

"I still don't want you trying to fix anything."

Rix found the cruiser's interior lighting and turned it to full. The ship was both bigger than he'd thought by looking at it from the outside and smaller than he expected, given his experience aboard *Calypso.* On the port side was a holding cell, separated from the rest of the cruiser by a thick transparent ceramic panel. On the starboard side there were cabinets, which Rix discovered contained components for the various subsystems. A locked cabinet was labeled armory.

"What are you looking for?" Amari asked.

Rix moved forward and scanned the ship. Unobvious to the external view, there was seating for six behind the bulkhead that separated the cockpit from the rest of the vessel. The door which segregated the seating from the cockpit stood open, and a pair of old, worn synthetic leather chairs completed the cockpit's lived-in vibe.

"Mostly just getting a lay of the land," Rix said. "I have a bunch of reading to do to get caught up on how this vessel's subsystems are organized. Having a picture in my mind before I start reading is always helpful. We'll have to figure out how to open the bay doors. I wonder how many of those photonic barriers are still working."

"Two years ago, at least one of them was," Amari said. "Not exactly the best memory, though."

"Should I ask?"

"You, for sure, should not ask."

Rix nodded and slid into the portside pilot's chair. As soon as he did, Beverly appeared on the dashboard in front of him, wearing a red spacesuit with a glass bowl top, her legs dangling in front of the cracked display that had been left behind.

"You got that outfit from my *Galaxy* magazine. Now help me. I need to figure out how to get this thing started," Rix said, addressing Beverly but not caring that Amari heard him. So far, Beverly had chosen not to reveal herself to Amari and Rix wanted to honor that.

"Clever," Beverly said. "You'll need to warm up the injectors, kind of like glow plugs. Here's the sequence."

"I don't know how to start it," Amari said. "This is older technology than I'm used to."

"I found a decent description," Rix said, allowing his eyes to focus on his current reading of a manual related to the cruiser. His actions were part ruse and part genuine. "Looks like it'll take a minute since it's been sitting in storage for a while."

"We should figure out if any of these photonic barrier generators are working. It'd be a shame to have to purge all the atmosphere in this big old space."

Rix pushed up out of his chair, but Amari was quicker and more nimble. She giggled as he followed behind her and he took that as an invitation to get closer, which only served to spur her on more quickly.

"There's a control station over there," Rix pointed to a workstation with a few dark video screens arranged on the wall in front of a narrow desk. Walking briskly, he crossed over to the desk and sat, tapping at a built-in keyboard that caused the panels on the wall to light up.

"Bay door controls are on the top, left," Beverly said, reclining on the desk against the bottom panel. "Tell me, Rix, do you like her?"

"Too early to tell."

"What's that?" Amari asked, stopping behind him, her hands coming to rest on his shoulders as she watched him work.

"I'm wondering about those photonic barriers," Rix said, flipping virtual switches as he tried powering them up. Of the ten bays, only one of the barriers came online. "Looks like we have one. Big surprise. It's where the cruiser is sitting."

"That suggests the other barriers have been broken for a while," Amari said.

"Smells like opportunity."

"Explain?"

"Helmet up and magnetics on," Rix said. "I'm opening the bay door."

"You like to play it safe."

"One of ten of those barriers are working. Are you willing to risk that the last one is solid?" Rix waited for Amari to tap on her boots and raise her helmet before he opened the exterior bay door.

"You make a good point."

"I've already fixed one of these barrier controls. Maybe I could make a deal with Patience to fix the broken ones in trade for one for the shop."

"You think differently about things. You look for where you can add value and then how you can negotiate for something you want," she said.

"Isn't that what most people do?"

"Not at all. Most people think about what they want and the minimum they can give to get it. Your approach is more two-sided."

"Holistic and repeatable. If everyone feels like they got a good deal, it's easier," Rix said, pushing away from the desk and casting a wary eye toward the barrier, which flickered as if in recognition of his concern.

"Maybe we hurry," Amari said, also glancing at the unstable barrier. Without waiting for his response, she took off at a run.

"You're fast!" Rix said racing after her.

"Try to catch me," she said, laughing. When they reached the ship, she necessarily slowed in the cruiser's narrow corridor and Rix tapped her shoulder. With nowhere else to go she grabbed the back of one of the passenger seats and used it to help her spin around. Rix thought she would avoid him by jumping into a seat, but instead she stepped forward, causing him to run into her.

"Oh, I'm so sorry," Rix said, trying not to let his momentum drag them both to the floor. He was too late, though and their legs intertwined. With Amari's grip on the chair, she slowed their fall but ended up on her butt with Rix right atop her. The moment slowed and she became quiet as she investigated his face earnestly.

"Hello," she said softly.

"Hey there," he answered. In their fall, he'd put a hand behind her back, looking to ease her impact with the deck. Trapped, his arm held them close together. He discovered that was okay with him.

Amari made the first move and pushed her head forward slowly until their lips met. It was a chaste kiss, but one that promised more than the moment held.

"It'd probably be best if we got going," Amari said.

"I'm sorry, Amari," Rix said.

"Don't," Amari said, placing a finger on Rix's lips. "It was a nice kiss."

Rix helped Amari to her feet. The status of the cruiser's engines had changed to ready, although Rix noticed several complaints from the vessel's status indicator. Tapping in, he briefly read the messages and discovered there were substantial problems with many of the subsystems.

"I'm not sure how this will fly," Rix said. "The engines are toast. It has some attitude jets available, but I'm not sure how that helps."

"You haven't spent much time behind the stick, have you?" Amari asked.

"Just what Kel let me do on *Calypso*," Rix replied. "You have an idea?"

"Your bay is two thousand meters away. This isn't that hard," she said. "Do you mind?" Amari's focus was on the flight stick in front of her.

"By all means."

"Call it in. Let Hutari know we're entering local space."

Rix nodded. "Patience Station, this is Rix Banner in the municipal garage. We're taking out a cruiser for a spin and will be headed to Bay 807. Over."

"Rix, you're cleared for transit. What's the status of your cruiser? Over," Hutari responded almost immediately.

"Hutari, we're navigating with attitude jets only," Amari answered. "It's probably best if folks stay clear for a while."

"I'll close the corridor for the next thirty minutes. Let me know if you need more," Hutari answered. "Patience Station out."

"Let's close that aft hatch and we'll get going," Amari said. "Otherwise, it's going to get breezy in here."

"Good call," Rix said.

It was not without some trial and error that Amari navigated the constable's cruiser from its parked position through the barrier and into Patience Station's local space. As soon as they passed through, the lack of artificial gravity eased Amari's workload, and she easily turned the vessel and gently nudged it around and back toward the station.

"Five meters per second is slow, but I doubt we're in that much of a hurry," Amari said. "Close your suit, we'll evacuate the atmosphere so you can EVA and open the shop doors."

"See why I want a photonic barrier, now?

"Certainly do, but we'll get along just fine."

She was right on with her assessment. Twenty minutes later, Rix had exited the vessel, opened his shop's bay door and ushered Amari through with a wave of his hand.

"You made that look easy," Rix said when Amari settled the cruiser onto the deck and he'd closed the bay doors behind them. Refilling the shop's atmosphere took a moment and the pair stood quietly with their helmets in place as they waited.

"What now?" Amari asked.

"I need to go back to the garage and lock up," Rix said. "I don't think Quixly will thank me if I leave his house open."

"No, I don't suppose he would," she said. "And it's getting late. Hutari's shift is nearly done and we have a show we were going to watch together."

"Thanks for the company," Rix said. "And the expert sailing. I would have struggled to accomplish the same.

"What do you have left for tonight?"

"After I lock up, I'll eat something. Working on the power generator last night messed up my days and nights," Rix said.

"Come watch a show with us," Amari said. "We have a couch you could sleep on."

"I'm not sure Shixen is ready for us to have sleepovers," Rix said, trying to keep it light.

"And yet, I have to figure out how to move forward with my life."

"Maybe let's not ruffle any more feathers tonight," Rix said.

"I respect that. Tomorrow we install nutrient towers?"

"I just checked the manufactory order. We'll have supplies by 0400."

"Do you want to get started then?"

"Please, no. Let's shoot for 0800. Is that okay?"

"I'll bring pastries."

Rix accompanied Amari to the elevator where they split, with her heading up to her apartment and him heading down to the municipal garage. When he returned, he considered getting to work on the cruiser, but exhaustion prevailed and when he sat in his chair, he fell asleep.

With a full night's rest, Rix was wide awake at 0600 and decided to make a trip down to the manufactory to pick up the hydroponic equipment he'd produced. The tubes were unwieldy, but with help from a manufactory worker and a substantial tip, he had the equipment loaded into Bay 808, resting next to the greenhouse.

"Rix, I'm hearing some chatter on Patience Station's municipal bands. Something's going on," Beverly said as Rix walked back to his shop, fully intent on making a fresh pot of coffee.

"What do you mean? Are we under attack?"

"No, I picked it up on the medical emergency channel," Beverly said.

"Who's hurt?" Rix asked, turning quickly from the door and jogging toward the elevator.

"I heard Amari's name, but they're trying to speak in code so I'm not getting everything. "Atrium, behind the fountain, Level 17." Beverly directed.

"Shoot, shoot, shoot," Rix said. "Level 17, emergency."

"Five credits charged for emergency conveyance," the elevator answered.

A thrill in Rix's stomach warned of the elevator's faster than usual travel and before he might have expected, the doors opened to Level 17.

Right off the elevator, he could feel a difference in the atmosphere of the normally relaxed environment. The sound of feet running and shouts of excitement were coupled with anxious voices. Rix didn't hesitate, sprinting toward the fountain where he found a growing crowd. Pushing through the gathered, he found Amari with blood all over her hands, kneeling on the ground next to a body. His anxiety spiked as he tried to identify the person on the ground.

"Amari!" Rix called out, not even aware he was doing so. Her head turned to him, a look of dread filling her face. He started forward, but his path was cut off by a large figure. He struggled to get around the man in front of him, but it was to no avail. Rix struggled to figure out who was blocking him.

"Turn around, Banner." The voice belonged to Quixly, his large hand grasping Rix by the shoulders. "You can't be here right now."

"She's hurt."

"No. Lords of Gavenar, get out of here, Banner," Quixly said angrily. "Your life is in danger."

Rix shook his head, the words Quixly said making no sense. "Amari is hurt," he insisted again.

"I'll get her help, but you can't be here," Quixly hissed. "You need to leave, now!"

Rix jostled with Quixly for a moment, only to get a look over the big man's shoulders. He finally was able to identify the figure on the ground. It was Shixen, and he had blood seeping from a chest wound. Emergency personnel worked to stabilize him and started to help Amari. Briefly, their eyes met, and in her expression, he could only see confusion and pain.

"I'm here for you," Rix said.

"Stop. You'll make it worse," Quixly said, pushing Rix away.

"You need to keep me in the loop."

"I will. Go."

Rix walked away, his mind busy trying to parse what he'd seen. That Amari was hurt was foremost on his mind and he wondered just what had happened between her and Shixen. Had there been a third party? Was there some sort of struggle? Given Quixly's disinterest in cameras in public spaces, Rix wondered if there was a recording of the event. His mind was filled with questions.

"Rix, you're being followed," Beverly said when he was only ten meters from the scene. She appeared in front of him wearing a black long-sleeved turtleneck sweater, slacks and leather gloves.

"How many?" he asked quietly.

"Two. One of them is Greasle," she said.

"That's not good."

Rix patted his pocket, hoping to find a knife. He had a multitool, which wasn't much. Instead of turning toward the elevator, Rix shifted away and headed toward Petju's Pub.

"They're still following."

An idea formed in Rix's head. Taking a quick turn, he ducked around one corner and then the next. Level 17 wasn't much of a labyrinth and Greasle would find him soon enough, but all he needed was a few moments.

"Am I clear?"

"For now."

Multitool in hand, Rix opened a panel labeled *pipe chase*. Without hesitation, he climbed into the chase and pulled the panel closed behind him while bracing against the vertical pipes. Taking no chances, he slid down, his feet periodically running into supports which held the pipes in place.

"What's on Level 16, do you know?"

"It is called the suburbs," Beverly said. "There are a few eateries, but it's mostly apartments. Level 15 is where most of the municipal offices are located. If Amari is to be arrested, she will likely be brought there."

"Why would she be arrested?"

"You are not thinking clearly, Rix," Beverly said.

"Are you suggesting she stabbed Shixen?"

"The visual evidence would suggest exactly that, Rix."

"How so?"

"Stop moving for a moment, I'll show you the scene and you can make your own judgments."

Rix slowed his descent and held himself in place. "Go ahead."

Overlaying his own view, Beverly projected the scene where Amari sat next to Shixen's body. Her hands were covered in blood. Protruding from Shixen's chest was a long, narrow knife. Amari's face had fresh cuts atop the old bruises, and her right eye was puffy and starting to discolor.

"There was a struggle, that much is clear," Beverly said.

11

FUGITIVE GIRLFRIEND

RIX STRUGGLED to even look at the cruiser sitting in his shop. The scene of Shixen's death played time and time again through his head, interrupting anything that resembled forward progress.

"Is there any word from Quixly?" he asked Beverly again.

"No, Rix," she said patiently.

"I'm going up there."

"Quixly was clear about that. It would be dangerous for you. You don't want Sable associating you with Shixen's death," she said.

"I can't help what they'll associate," Rix fumed, although he knew that wasn't true. Pirate gangs were notorious for guilt by association and, while he wasn't specifically worried about tying himself to Amari, he knew he'd be helpful to no one if he died while they were taking revenge.

"Let's focus on the cruiser for the moment," Beverly said. "You need to give Quixly time to work this out."

"He's shown himself to be a patsy," Rix argued.

"Or was he being practical?"

"Kel wouldn't mince words like that."

"No. She wouldn't. You're not Kel."

"Capture the main engine logs," Rix said, sighing. He'd plugged his diagnostic scope to the log port and opened the bay to space so the small amount of exhaust created by the normally efficient engines wouldn't build up. Ideally, he'd have an exhaust capture system, but that would cost quite a bit more than he could afford.

"Capturing," Beverly acknowledged.

"If an Olds pulled into my shop sounding like that, I'd be tempted to take it over to the salvage yard," Rix said. "What's the primary issue?"

"There are numerous. I am not certain I can reduce to one."

"Okay," Rix said distractedly as he started scrolling through messages. The engine logs were stuffed with messages of events both expected and unexpected, making the search more difficult to parse. "There, tell me about those messages." Rix highlighted a section of errors.

"How do you do that?"

"Do what?"

"Home in on an issue so quickly. I saw those messages but didn't think they were more or less important than the others," Beverly said.

"Well, I don't know that's the issue. I just think it's interesting. We have power to the engines, and the matter coils are spinning just fine. The output from there is where we light up the patrix chain. There's nothing flowing from the patrix chain and that's why we're not moving with main engines, but the thrusters work."

"That is sound reasoning, although you've skipped a number of other blatant issues."

"Such as?"

"Carbonized volume is four hundred percent normal."

"Because it's not joining with the patrix chain."

"I see no evidence of that," Beverly argued.

"No, but what produces that message?" Rix asked.

"How are you so familiar with this engine?"

"There are only a dozen engine designs for small vessels that are widely used," Rix said. "Eight of those designs use Fantastium, which the people I know can't afford. That leaves four architectures for me to study. Which I did. Everyone thinks all this is extraordinary and some of it is, but most of these systems just aren't that complex, once you strip away all the bells and whistles."

"How do you know it's not a problem with the smaller subsystems? The bells and whistles, as you call them," she said.

"It might be, but I also know for sure there's a problem between the main power and the end of the patrix chain. So, I'm going to dig in and see what I can find there. It's going to be a long night because, of course, that's behind seven hundred kilograms of machinery."

Rix got straight to work on disassembling the compact engines of the constable's cruiser. Minutes gave way to hours. Finally, exhaustion won out after he'd removed the final part and had the patrix chain assembly laid out on his workbench.

"There is an announcement on the municipal board," Beverly said as Rix settled into his chair.

"Tell me it's good news–that Amari didn't kill him."

"It's a report about a mugging in the Atrium. Apparently, Shixen came to Amari's defense but was injured in the process. The report says that Amari attempted to perform lifesaving first aid but was unsuccessful. Further, there were no cameras in the location of the incident and Amari was released from custody and cleared of wrongdoing."

"See if you can raise her on comms."

"I'm trying. She's not answering."

"Send this message: Amari, contact me when you can. I'm concerned," Rix said.

"It is sent," Beverly said. "But, Rix, I don't believe the scene supports Amari helping Shixen at all."

"I know," Rix said and settled back into his chair for sleep.

Several hours later, Rix awoke to the beeping on his HUD for a queued message of moderate importance. He tapped on the message and was surprised that it was Kel and not Amari.

Rix, we'll arrive at Gestalt Station tomorrow and have made good contacts for sale of your Collie's Reserve. I expect to move fifteen liters, if not more. Also, I read that Amari was involved in a mugging where Shixen was killed. She's going to need your help. Sable will be suspicious and may cause her trouble, regardless of innocence. I hope you're finding things to keep you busy. Calypso *is sailing great, and it looks like we're going to meet our deadline on Gestalt. Also, you could send a comm once in a while, you know. Sincerely, Kel Warp.*

Rix moved slowly from his chair and filled his coffee pot, always the first task of the morning. After that, he poured a serving of proto protein with a nutritional supplement designed for human consumption. The taste of the manufactured food was reasonable, but the texture left a lot to be desired. Finishing a little more than half, he set the bowl into a cleaning station and cleaned his hands, just as lode bean coffee spilled over the top of the carafe because he hadn't thought to check that it was empty.

"Darn it," he cursed to himself as coffee splashed onto his work pants.

He checked his comms and found that neither Amari nor Quixly had called, so he composed a message back to Kel.

Dear Kel and Philo, Times are difficult as I'm unable to contact Amari, and I worry that Sable is threatening her. Nonetheless, I'll continue to look for ways to help her. We've made significant progress on the hydroponics farm. Today, I expect to install the towers and possibly pumps, heater and filter. Our design will eventually have full isolation from station life support and will include backup atmospherics, vacuum control and even power for things like heat and circulation. Our first phase, however, will last twenty hours without support from the station, with some assumptions. Please send a message when you've landed and then again when you take off from Gestalt. I'll let you know when I find out more regarding Amari. Sincerely, your friend, Rix Banner.

A signal from his newly installed door alert indicated someone was approaching the station side door. Inspecting the video, he found a woman with short-cut black hair and piercing blue eyes. By every standard he was familiar with, she was attractive, and she even smiled as she pressed the buzzer to get his attention.

Opening the door, there was an audible pop as the bay's atmosphere equalized with the hallway. "Good morning. How can I help you?" Rix asked, suddenly self-conscious of the coffee stain on his jumpsuit.

"That's a nice greeting," the woman said, stepping around him and into the bay.

"I'm sorry but did we have an appointment?" he asked, catching up with her as she made her way over to the workbench where Rix had left the patrix chain soaking in solvent. A dark film formed ovals in the liquid and small black specks had fallen off the device, sinking to the bottom.

The woman looked over her shoulder to see that the door had indeed closed. Immediately, the smile on her face dissolved. "Oh, Rix, I'm in so much trouble," she said, stepping in to him and resting her head on his chest as if they were old lovers. Rix could think of nothing else to do but wrap his arms around her.

"I don't know what's going on right now," he said, but as he looked down at the woman, he realized it was Amari's face that was looking back at him.

"Amari?"

"I thought Kel told you of my heritage," she said. "I'm Tjelari, like Kel."

"Wait, no, she did," Rix said. "Amari?"

"Yes," she said, her face slowly returning to the foreign version. "I go by Nerali in this form."

"That's going to take some getting used to," he said.

"It's critical that you do, Rix," she said. "Sable will kill me if they figure out who I am."

"Can you maintain this shape for that long? I thought it was difficult," Rix said.

Amari's smile was gentle. "There are some differences between Kel and me," she said. "It is also a form I've used occasionally around Patience Station, so I am familiar to some."

"Are you okay, Amari?"

"Please, use my correct name, Nerali," she said. "I don't know how to answer your question. It has all been so horrible."

"Sit," Rix said, leading her over to a chair. Once she was seated, he brought her a coffee, which she set on the table next to her. "Do you want to talk about it?"

"You're not asking me if I did it," she said.

"It's your story to tell."

"He was so angry, Rix."

"About us? That's absurd."

"No, about the farm," she said. "He didn't care about you. He did, but he didn't. He thought you were too much of a ghespi ... wimp, I think is the closest translation. That you were running from him."

"I don't love the characterization, but I wasn't thrilled to stand up to him, either," Rix said. "I guess that doesn't make me particularly brave."

"Doesn't it? Foolhardy is the correct description for challenging a pirate boss on his home station, Rix. Shixen would have had you killed or done it himself if he'd thought you were any competition," she said. "No, he was angry that I was pursuing the farm, and I might have enough money to support myself. We argued and it turned physical. He was hitting me so hard. I almost blacked out, and do you know what was worse? People heard it, and they walked away. They let him beat me, right there in public."

"That's horrible," Rix said. "I'm sorry he did that and that no one came to help."

"I'm so glad you weren't there," she said, setting her face into her hands as she started to sob.

"I would have stopped him," Rix said. "You wouldn't have been hurt."

"And you would be dead. I wanted you to be there so badly and I nearly broke because I knew you couldn't be," she said. "I didn't even know I was doing it."

"You don't have to tell me," Rix said.

"I don't know if it was me, Rix. It could have been. Maybe. But he hit me hard and I blacked out for a time," she said between sobs.

Rix nodded. "I'm so sorry."

"Do you think it was me?"

"What is Quixly saying?"

"There is a trace of my DNA on the blade. He's saying it's because I was trying to help Shixen," she said. "Quixly won't admit it, but he thinks I'm the killer."

"More like the victim that fought back. Why do you care what Quixly knows? He made a cover story. It sounds right," Rix said.

"I've not had good luck when men have power over me," she said.

"I hate to point this out, but you're telling me things you shouldn't. Don't I have power over you now?" Rix asked.

"Would you use that against me?"

"No. But how can you believe me?" Rix asked.

"I'd argue because I just know, but I don't think my history with that is good. I need to trust someone, Rix. I'll go insane if I don't," she said.

"The last thing I want to do is betray you, Amari," Rix said.

"Nerali."

"Sure," Rix agreed. "What's next for you, then?"

"I rebuild my life," Amari said. "I can't go back to my apartment. Shixen was paying for it, and no doubt Sable will be watching it. Waiting for me."

"What about Hutari?"

"She works for Quixly. I hope Sable isn't dumb enough to go against her while she's employed by the station."

"Sable is afraid of Quixly?"

"'Afraid' isn't quite right. There is peace between Patience Station and Sable. Attacking Hutari would change that. Quixly has controls for all levels of Patience Station. That is a tremendous amount of power."

"I guess I hadn't thought of it that way."

"Imagine what would happen while we're just standing here if he opened the bay doors. He can do that and more, like cut off atmosphere to an entire level while they're asleep," she said.

"That's dark."

"Right?"

"I'm sorry this happened to you," Rix said.

"Would you mind if we didn't talk about this for a while? I didn't get any rest last night. I kept thinking they were coming for me."

"Where did you sleep?"

"In jail. Quixly let me out this morning."

"You can sleep right there, if you want," Rix said. "I can keep the noise down."

"I'm not going to sleep now. Maybe I could help you work on the cruiser?"

"Or we could go work on the hydroponics farm. I have all the equipment. We just need to set it up."

"Do you believe me?" she asked.

"About what?"

"That I don't know if I killed him. Because, otherwise, I'm just a murderer."

"I believe you, Amari," Rix said. "But I'm not the one you're going to need to convince."

"Oh?"

"Right, that's you," Rix said. "You're questioning yourself and how you might have reacted."

"It sounds like you have some experience with this."

"I was in a war. It's easy to blame things on war. That is, until it isn't," Rix said. "At the end of the day, you have to work this out for yourself. Then and only then will you have enough energy to begin to worry about what others think."

"What's that thing on your workbench? It looks dirty."

"It is," Rix said. "It's part of the cruiser's engine. Part of it is broken, but some of it is just dirty."

"And that's why it's not working? The engine, I mean?"

"It's at least one reason. I was just about to order parts. I need someone to scrub what I have sitting in the solvent."

"Scrub? With what?"

"A toothbrush," Rix said. "If I had more credits, I'd have a parts agitator. I don't, so we need to go old school on it, and that means scrubbing with a toothbrush."

"Sign me up," Amari said. "I'm not afraid of a little work."

"I have a few more pieces that need the same treatment. I'll get you started and order my part. After that, we can run over to the farm and start assembling the hydroponics. I don't suppose you brought the seeds with you? Or did you leave those at home?"

"They're in that box I brought yesterday," she said. "I left it in the greenhouse."

"Perfect."

Rix showed Amari how to clean the part and left her to her thoughts. Back in the cruiser, he pulled several other parts that were equally dirty, if not broken, and stacked them in a container, which he brought out with him.

"When you're done, let's give these a solid scrubbing, too," he said.

"How do I know when I'm done?"

"No more dirt comes off. Generally, just scrub each surface, nook and cranny. The solvent makes it easy," he said.

"I like the smell."

"Everybody does."

It was lunchtime when Amari finished washing parts. The manufactory would take another two hours to create the replacement part for the patrix chain, which sent the two over to what they were affectionately referring to as 'the farm.'

"I can't believe we're actually doing this," Amari said as they set the vertical tubes with regularly spaced plant openings onto the floor and snapped them into the matrix Rix had manufactured. It took a bit more finagling to attach the tops of the vertical tubes into the custom-designed holders, which also routed nutrient water for a steady drip.

"You had a good idea. All I did was send your ideas over to the manufactory," Rix said. "Help me move this nutrient tub into the corner, would you?"

"Of course."

The tub would hold a week's worth of nutrients to be recycled through each tube and dripped across the seedlings' roots.

"So now, we just drop the motor into this tub, fill it with water and we can see if we have leaks and how well water makes it through the system. I assume you have an idea of how we'll get your seeds to sprout," Rix said. "I've been looking. I think we can just place them in a sponge to get them started. Is that right?"

"It's close," Amari said. "I'll show you how we do it. We'll start them outside of the hydroponic tubes. I have a pattern for you to print. We can just set them on the ground in here or build a bench for this kind of work. It doesn't matter much."

"We'll be doing this fairly often," Rix said. "How about we make shelves so we can have stacks of seedlings at different ages? We can slide light panels between them."

"Show me," Amari said.

"It'll take me a minute to draw it up ...," He paused. "How about this? You finish up here and I'll run down to the manufactory and grab the part for the cruiser. We'll have some dinner and draw up the seedling production line."

"What should I do while you're gone?"

"How about you sit down for a minute," Rix said, leading her back to the shop.

"I could sit. I'm tired."

Rix nodded and gestured for her to take the recliner he often used as a bed. She started to protest but wasn't committed to the objection. Rix dimmed the shop lights, pulled a blanket over Amari and set a glass of water and a pistol on the table next to her.

"Do you think I'll need that?" she asked with concern in her face.

"No. I'll lock up behind me, and I won't be gone much more than fifteen minutes," he said. "Catch a quick nap and when I get back, we can talk seedlings."

"That sounds like a plan."

As promised, Rix returned twenty minutes later, carrying the parts he'd replicated for the cruiser. Amari's sound sleeping was something he wasn't about to interrupt, so he quietly made his way back into the aft of the cruiser, where he started reassembling the ship's power plant. Hours ticked by as he worked and slowly but surely the engine came back together.

"You've been busy," Amari said, shuffling into the cruiser with the blanket Rix had laid on her still wrapped around her shoulders. "I thought we were going to talk seedlings."

"I figured you needed the sleep."

"You were right. How's it looking in here?"

"Your timing is perfect. I was just about to fire it up. We'll have to suit up. I need to open the bay due to the fumes," he said.

Making a quick run through the shop, Rix and Amari stowed everything that might be disturbed by the change in pressure. Because it wouldn't be an immediate evacuation, they didn't need to worry about losing items–just those that might freeze, boil or explode due to the change in pressure and exposure to space.

"There has to be a better way to do this, right?" Amari asked.

"These engines are designed to connect to a low-pressure exhaust tube. I just don't have one yet because the one I want is two thousand credits. I'm saving up," Rix said.

"It doesn't help that your fugitive girlfriend is spending all your money on hydroponics," she replied.

"Hmm, is that how you see yourself?"

"I'm for sure a fugitive."

"I meant girlfriend."

12

SMOKE SCREENS

"THAT'S NOT BETTER, RIX," Amari said as Rix fired up the main. "I thought you fixed it."

"Hang on," he said. "We did fix the patrix chain. There could be something else."

"You don't know?"

Rix chuckled. "I'm not all-seeing. Let's check what the diagnostic logs are reporting." He plugged the diagnostic scope in and, with Beverly's quiet help, started filtering. Jabbing a finger at the screen, he grinned. "That's a great sign."

"What?" Amari asked.

"Whatever's causing trouble is way past the patrix chain. We're getting clean power up to that point," he said. "Looks like there's something in the combiner manifold."

"I don't see those words."

"I'm a simpleton, those are my words. Look here," Rix pointed at the diagnostic terminal, where he'd limited the messages to a repeating sequence of errors.

"Do you need to tear it all apart again?" she asked with exasperation in her voice.

"Sometimes that's how it goes," Rix said. "Not this time, though. Those errors are further back. Time to get wrenching again."

"Isn't this frustrating for you?"

"Fixing broken things?"

"Yes. You just keep taking things apart and putting them back together."

"That's the price for fixing things," Rix said. "When I take things apart, I learn about them and get a chance to check their general level of wear and tear. You can't let it get to you. Breaking things down, cleaning, repairing and reassembling, that's the life of a mechanic."

"You missed learning how they operate," Amari said. "There's no way you already knew how this engine works."

"I see your point," he said. "Yes and no. Each engine has its own specific implementation, but the big ideas are always the same. Debugging and diagnosing are more art than science. Most of the time, when you find a broken piece and replace or fix it, the entire assembly starts working again. In this case, there are multiple subsystem failures. That's how it goes, so we fix the next thing."

"Patience is your superpower."

"Hah, I'm not sure about that, but I appreciate the sentiment."

As they'd been talking, Rix had started working to remove the large panels that surrounded the failing subsystem, which, if anything, had gotten worse with the current repairs. "So, in this case, it's likely the patrix chain was damaged by whatever is broken back here."

"How?"

"Think of it like a big assembly line. If the end stops working, everything behind it starts backing up."

"Look at all this black stuff," Amari said as she took a panel from Rix and set it aside.

"Good detective work," he said. "We're on the hunt, now."

"You really do get a kick out of this."

"Don't you? We're about to get this cruiser working again. It's sat for how long now?"

"A couple of years, I'd guess."

"And here's the problem," Rix said, pointing at a blackened part. Unplugging the diagnostic scope from the main, he moved it directly to the small subsystem. The subsystem provided virtually no feedback, aside from general errors. "Looks like we have another smoking gun."

"That looks bad."

Rix started removing the part and watched out of the corner of his eye as Beverly researched replacement potential. "I wonder if it's possible to clean the part enough to get it running," he said, his intended target being Beverly, but understanding that Amari would think he was asking her.

"I don't mind trying to clean it," she said. "That solvent bath works really well."

"Eight hundred credits and you'll have it in the morning if you give approval," Beverly said.

"Give it a try," Rix said. "I'm going to get a new part manufactured, though. If you can get that one working, we'll save it for future repairs."

"Do you want to give Quixly a warning? This is close to his threshold of one thousand credits," Beverly said.

"If it works, why would you buy a new one?" Amari asked.

"That part is worn, and municipal vehicles are in service nearly nonstop. Replacing is the right answer. I don't like to throw away anything that's potentially useful, though," he said.

"You're the boss," Amari answered cheerfully.

"Change of subject?"

"What's on your mind?"

"Won't it be suspicious if you simply disappear and no one is curious?"

"Suspicious to whom?"

"Anyone who's paying attention."

"What are you thinking?"

"I have reason to talk to Quixly about these repairs. I think I should ask him what happened to you," Rix said. "To push him to find you."

"What good would that do?"

"I think the presumption is that someone in Sable took you out, right? Isn't that why you changed appearances?"

"Well, yes, but Sable will know it wasn't them."

"Is that right?" Rix asked. "Would they advertise who took revenge on you?"

"That's a good question. I'm not opposed to you asking Quixly about me," she said.

Rix nodded. "Let's get this replacement part installed. I'll spend the extra fifty credits to have it expedited. Your seedling planting media should be available by then, too. Meanwhile, I'll look for other issues that need fixing on the cruiser so we can wrap up this project."

"Do you think we're close to finishing?"

"We're getting down to cosmetics, which feels pretty good."

Recharging the atmosphere in the bay, Rix sent Amari out to start cleaning the part while he began reviewing all of the ship's major systems, one by one. There were small issues that would require minor repairs in four other locations, so he added to the list of replacement parts he'd need and shipped the bill to Quixly, as it added to twenty-four hundred credits. He then moved to the outside of the vessel and inspected the hull, looking for additional issues. The cruiser had its fair share of bumps, nicks and scrapes, which if he were back on Earth, he'd have recommended be sent to a body shop. As he had tools for filling and patching, and it would only require labor to repair, he set to work.

"I have your parts bill," Quixly said on comms a few minutes later. "You've racked up twenty-four hundred credits. Are you sure you're done?"

"As sure as I can be without those parts," Rix said. "Trust me, when I'm done, your cruiser will be in better shape than it's been in years."

"I don't easily trust."

"Okay. Where does that leave us?"

"I'll approve the parts, but no more," the constable said. "I don't want this to be an endless rabbit hole."

"This cruiser, new, costs ninety thousand credits. How much maintenance has it seen in the last ten years? I'd bet, given the shape of things, not much," Rix said.

"You'd be surprised."

"I imagine I would," Rix said. "Hey, quick question, have you seen Amari? I know she's probably laying low after what happened with Shixen, but she's not responding to my comms."

"Give her some time," Quixly said. "There's a lot going on and she's most likely scared."

"Are you going to protect her?"

"Best I can. Look, I can't play bodyguard, and Sable has twenty times as many people here as I have officers," he said.

"You can't protect her."

"Not like she needs. I told her as much and I think she'll probably leave the station. It's best for her and the station."

"I'm going to stop by her place and see if she's around," Rix said.

"No."

"No?"

"If anyone from Sable sees you sniffing around, you'll be drawing a bullseye on your chest. Like it or not, you need to stay away from her. You can't possibly protect her, and you'll end up getting yourself killed. If she stays in her apartment and is careful, this thing might blow over long enough that we can get her out of here."

"Will you check on her?"

"Yes."

"Thank you," Rix said, ending comms.

"Was that Quixly?" Amari asked, looking up from where she was working at his bench.

"Yes."

"You've a more devious mind than I expected."

"Problem solving is kind of my thing. I don't feel devious," Rix said. "Are you getting hungry?"

"I'm starving."

"That's a good sign. I was looking at the chandlery's stock. They have a case of instant meals. Have you ever tried those?"

"Nutritionally, they're fine," she said.

"But they taste like engine sludge?" he asked.

"More like reconstituted dust. Like someone dumped too much spice onto bean curd," she said. "But given I need to keep a low profile, they're probably a good call."

"I was going to have them delivered. I can get them for ten credits a meal."

"They last forever and you have storage. That's not a poor choice."

Rix filled out the order with additional coffee and a selection of desserts. The bill came to six hundred credits, but it would keep them in food for the foreseeable future and no matter what, the meals had to be a step up from the proto nutrition he'd been eating.

Two hours later, a delivery was brought to the door, which was just about the time Rix finished repairing most of the small dents and tears in the cruiser's hull. He had no way to paint the repairs, and the dissonance of the patches was just too much. Back on the manufactory marketplace, he searched for a paint gun, which he discovered was more reasonable than he'd expected at twelve hundred credits.

"I'm feeling poor again," Rix said. "Every time I get two nickels to rub together, I blow it on tools."

"What'd you get now?" Amari asked.

"Paint. Twelve hundred credits, and it'll match existing colors as long as I keep the tints filled," he said. "*Calypso* could sure benefit from it, too. We have your growing media and some parts available at the manufactory. Would you consider making a couple of these meals and I'll run down and grab them?"

"Sure."

When Rix returned, the smell of cooked food permeated the shop.

"This is better than you gave credit," he said, enjoying the first several bites.

"They're not bad," she said. "Give it a few meals, though, you'll see what I'm talking about."

"I might not be the pickiest customer."

"Thank you, Rix," Amari said, looking up from her meal.

"For what?"

"All of this. You've kept my mind off Shixen. Given me a place to hide out. And you haven't bugged me about what happened. I know you've got to be curious, but you're giving me space to work it out."

"Maybe I'm just that self-involved."

"Why do you do that?"

"Do what?"

"Insult yourself when you get a compliment."

"I didn't know I did that."

"You're consistent. It's okay to have people appreciate you," she frowned.

"I'll work on it," Rix said. "How about you get started putting together the first seedling rack, and I'll see about installing these parts. If we get your seeds planted and Quixly's cruiser returned, it'll be a banner day!"

"It's a race."

After cleaning up their lunch, the two set themselves to their individual tasks. It was only two hours later when Amari brushed off her hands and approached Rix, who was using a vacuum cleaner to pull ages-old dirt and crumbs from the cruiser's cockpit.

"What are you doing?" she asked.

"Finishing touches," Rix said. "My uncle was a repairman, and his motto was to always leave things cleaner than how he found them. How's your seedling project coming along?"

"I'm done. I planted the first rack, and we need to get the lights connected to a power source. Every four days we'll plant another rack. We'll have sprouts by twelve days, and we can move them into the hydroponic towers. Two weeks after that, we'll have our first crops and a whole assembly line of seedlings behind that."

"Will we need to expand your hydroponics farm?"

"In a few weeks, I'll want to add another bank of towers," she said. "But I have another project I want to start designing, first."

"What's that?"

"It's a mat of greens that turn every six days. I didn't think we could grow them, but I think if we reinvest from our initial sales, we can bootstrap the costs," Amari said. "None of this makes a huge amount of money at one time, but it should be recurring."

"We can work on projections at some point," Rix said. "I'd say that as long as we're not losing too much money to begin with, we just plow forward. There's no doubt fresh food has a lot of value out here."

"That's what I'm counting on."

"Let's move your seedlings over to the farm so we can vent the bay again. I'd like to take the cruiser out for a quick spin," Rix said.

"You think it's ready?"

"Only one way to find out."

Twenty minutes later, they were sitting inside the cruiser looking at the cockpit's instrument cluster. Rix ran through the startup sequence and watched for error codes, of which there were several. Capturing the codes, he nudged the cruiser backwards and out of the bay until he was several hundred meters from the space station.

"I miss this view," Amari said, looking back at the station nostalgically.

"It's quite a sight," Rix said. "Hold on to something. I don't have a ton of experience with this." And without further warning, he engaged the primary power plant to the main engine and watched his diagnostic scope, looking for issues.

"Are those errors on your screen?" Amari asked.

"Maybe. I'm hoping those are calibration errors."

"Why?"

"In my mind, they're easier to fix."

Rix pushed the craft up to speed and raced out toward the Aegis asteroid. Unlike *Calypso*, the cruiser accelerated quickly and turned easily, although given its size and purpose, that lined up with Rix's thinking.

"It feels like grumpy old Quixly is going to have a shiny new cruiser to run around in," Amari said.

"Let's hope it lives up to expectations. I've logged enough time fixing this, he's going to own my butt for a while, fixing things around Patience."

"The deal you made, where he gets to use the same amount of hours for station repair as you spend fixing his cruiser, is counterintuitive. You're incented to not spend many hours getting the cruiser to work," she said.

"That might be the incentive, but doing a fantastic job is my actual objective. Always let your work speak for you."

"Another of your uncle's sayings?"

"Good guess," Rix said, turning back for the asteroid. "Have you thought of how you going missing is going to affect Hutari?"

"Neither Hutari nor I are safe if she doesn't play the distraught daughter once I turn up missing," Amari said.

"That'll be rough."

"I feel so guilty about it, but I can't think of anything else to do. I might need you to talk to her, so she feels like someone's on her side."

"But not tell her what's really happened."

"Right."

Rix nodded as he guided the cruiser back to Bay 807 and slid the ship into place. "Well, I have a few more things to work on, but I should have this project wrapped up tonight."

"There are crates in the hallway," Amari said.

"Oh, good," Rix said, repressurizing the bay. "It's the paint rig I ordered, and there's a bunch of basecoat and dye packs. I kind of went all out."

"Was painting part of your deal?"

"Nope, but ..."

"Under promise, over deliver," Amari filled in, impatiently. "I know. I know."

"See, you're learning," Rix said cheerfully as he retrieved the packages. "Any chance you'd like to make some dinner? Not your job, I know, but it'll give me time to adjust for the calibration errors and get the hull painted."

"When will you give it back to Quixly?"

"Tonight," Rix said. "Do you have anywhere you could go? He might want to see what we're doing in Bay 808."

"I'll make myself scarce," she said. "Do you mind if I sleep here tonight?"

"No, make yourself at home," Rix said.

The pair fell into a comfortable rhythm of work. Three hours later, they were seated in Rix's hand-me-down chairs, eating meals he'd ordered from the chandlery.

"Chocolate mousse dessert?" Amari asked. "We could split one if you're not too hungry."

"Sure," Rix said. Amari smiled and slid an already prepared package over to him. Rix grinned as he tried the smooth dessert. "Not bad."

"I can see you thinking about something," Amari said. "Just tell me."

"Are you okay if I give Quixly a call? I'd like to have him come get his cruiser."

"Of course, I've inconvenienced you enough."

"It's not like that. You've had a rough couple of days," Rix said.

"And you've been a good friend. I'm sorry for pushing myself on you so much," she said.

"Look, you need a friend," Rix said.

"I think that's about all I can handle, right now."

Rix replayed in his mind how she'd referred to herself as his girlfriend. When she'd said it, he'd thought she was forcing things, but he hadn't been about to argue with her while she was processing her trauma with Shixen. "We're good, Amari," he said.

"Thank you, Rix."

"Open comms with Quixly," Rix said.

"What do you want, Banner?" Quixly asked.

"Feeling grumpy, Mayor?"

Quixly sighed into the comms. "No, it's just been a long day. Have you heard from Amari at all?"

"I have not. Is she missing? I tried to reach out to her earlier."

"I went over to her apartment. Not only is it empty, but it's also trashed. Someone was looking for something," he said. "Or maybe they were just upset about Shixen and wanted to leave a message. I don't know."

Rix was surprised to hear Quixly expressing his concerns so openly. "Maybe my news will lighten your day."

"Oh?"

"That cruiser from your garage is fixed up and ready to go. I owe you eight hours of fix-it time, even subtracting the time I spent looking into the power system," Rix said.

"Oh? How is it running?"

"I'd like your opinion on that. Do you have a minute to run down here?"

"Now?"

"I'm just sitting around, doing nothing," Rix said.

"Since when has that been a thing? Aren't you always jumping on the next project?"

"Guilty. But I do want to get this to you so I can pick up that freighter sitting in the municipal garage," Rix said.

"The deal was you fix two cruisers, and I hand over four derelict freighters," Quixly said. "Let's not get out of sequence."

"I read you," Rix said. "We'll play it your way."

"I do have time, though," Quixly said. "I could use a cruiser instead of having to hire freight runners every time I want to look at something outside."

"I'll be here all night."

"Give me twenty minutes." Quixly closed comms.

Amari left shortly after that, and Rix had the first quiet he'd experienced for a few days. He sat back in his chair and closed his eyes, not expecting to fall asleep. Almost as soon as he relaxed, Beverly was talking in his ear, telling him to wake up, that Quixly was at the door. A few loud knocks in addition to an electronic chime jolted Rix from his chair.

"Sorry, Constable," Rix said, answering the door. "I must have fallen asleep."

"You look like crap, Banner."

Rix ignored the comment and gestured excitedly. "Come on over and take a look."

"That's ... what did you do?" Quixly asked.

"I've attached an invoice, similar to what you'd receive if I was billing Patience," Rix said. "You'll notice it shows paid in full."

"We didn't talk about paint. Why would you do that?"

"There was quite a bit of cosmetic hull damage, so I took care of that," Rix said. "Something big hit one of the structural members, so I cut it out and added reinforcement." Rix pointed to the section where he'd repaired the vessel's structure and as he did, a short video of the damage was sent to Quixly's HUD. "Other than that, there were mechanical issues and several subsystems that needed calibration. But that should all be cleaned up, now."

"This is more than I was expecting, Banner," he said. "You did this knowing you were adding hours to what you owe me?"

"I can't be sloppy and expect repeat business," Rix said. "Do you want to take it out for a run?"

"Yes. Are you going to do the same for my other cruiser?" he asked.

"Every repair is a whole new adventure," Rix said. "I hope we can get it back to something like this. It depends on if you have the budget. Paint and hole filling are just labor. That's easy. Broken subsystems are where we'll spend money."

"I'll run it out for a shakedown cruise, but I'm bringing it back if it's still broken," he said.

"I'd expect nothing less," Rix said. "Also, be careful when you take it back to the garage. The only working photonic barrier generator you have is unstable. You might dump the bay's atmosphere if you're not careful."

"It's been like that for a while."

"Doesn't that feel dangerous? You do know that I already fixed a pair of those generators for Sable, right?"

"I do," he said. "Are you offering to fix the ones in the municipal garage?"

"You have ten bays," Rix said. "I'll get five of those bays working in trade for a pair of generators. You pay for parts."

"Patience can't afford it."

"I won't spend over a thousand per barrier," Rix said.

"That's a real offer?" Quixly asked.

"It is."

"I don't know how you make any money. Every deal you do is barter," Quixly said.

"I need equipment more than credits right now, although I'm getting tired of proto protein," Rix said.

"Order meal bars, they're good in a pinch," Quixly said. "Try the berry."

13

ASS CLOWN

Rix set his lode bean coffee on his workbench and rubbed his hands together. Income from the manufactory marketplace was averaging four hundred credits daily but was only slightly ahead of ongoing expenditures. In five days, he had a fifteen hundred credit bill due on the lease for the farm. His account was sitting at twelve hundred fifty, so he felt good about finances. Add to that a pile of fourteen nonworking photonic barrier generators and a broken-down municipal cruiser sitting in his shop, Rix was in a good mood and ready to get moving.

A chime at the door brought out a sigh, as he wasn't excited about having his morning redirected. When he saw Amari's face in her alternate form, he smiled, knowing that his day certainly would be redirected.

"Good morning," Rix said, opening the door.

"That might be overstating it, some," she answered. As Rix took her in, he became aware of her disheveled state and stains on the tight-fitting jumpsuit she wore.

"I thought you were coming back last night," he said.

"That's not a good idea, Rix," she said somberly.

"Has something changed?"

"No. Not really," she said. "I came this morning to let you know that whatever this is between us, is over."

Rix knit his eyebrows together, searching his memory for something beyond the trauma of the last few days that would lead her to that decision. "What's going on?" he asked simply. He'd come to enjoy Amari's company and didn't love her decision.

"There are things you don't know. Things I haven't told you," she said. "I'm not who you think I am."

"That sounds ominous," he said. "For the record, I don't know that much about your past, aside from what you've told me."

"Right. Which is roughly nothing."

Rix couldn't decide if she wanted him to be inquisitive or let her keep her secrets. He chose a middle ground. "I'm a good listener, Amari. And our relationship doesn't need to be anything more than a couple of friends building a business."

"That's the part you don't understand," she said darkly. "Did you know that up until thirty years ago, this entire region of space was at war? I've heard you talk about your war back home and how it was a big deal. This war was a big deal too, only in this case, the bad guys won."

"Dravari?"

"That's right. Most of the pirate gangs around here are old Dravari soldiers who got mad about Dravari making nice with the Galactic Empire," she said. "The reason Dravari leave the pirate gangs alone is because of old alliances and financial arrangements."

"Sable and Draven Knights pay Dravari protection money so they can have free reign in the Surnac Belt?" Rix asked

"Just so. Do you understand what I'm telling you?"

"What's this have to do with you? You'd have to be over fifty years old to have been part of that war," Rix said.

"I'm a shape changer, Rix," she said. "My body doesn't age like yours. I'm older than you think."

"I see."

"Do you, Rix Banner? Because I don't think you do. Let me spell it out for you. I was an extraordinary Dravari agent. My specialty was infiltration, and I was good at it. Men like Shixen, Greasle and even Jacknie from Draven Knights are all ex-military. You've stepped into a viper's nest, Rix, and you're going to get killed, and I don't want to be the reason that happens."

"How would that be your fault?" Rix asked.

"Do you want to know what Shixen and I were talking about the day I killed him?" Rix could hear regret and self-loathing in the way she said *I killed him*.

"I don't know, do I?"

"Jacknie put fifty thousand on your head, Rix," she said. "Shixen wanted me to kill you. And I know you're going to miss this part because of what I said, but you need to hear me. *Shixen wanted ME to kill you*. This was reasonable to him because it's something I used to do. It's a part of me."

"You kill for money," Rix said.

"No!" Amari spat. "Aren't you listening? I was a Dravari agent. I infiltrated enemy strongholds and dismantled them. Sometimes, I had to kill people."

"You were an assassin," Rix said.

"No, but does it really matter?" she asked. "I didn't take assignments that were kill orders. I *did* take assignments that put me at extreme risk, and I did what I had to to survive. Good people died because I showed up."

"Why did you fight for Dravari?" Rix asked.

"Because that's the side I was on. Tell me something. Did you choose which side of the war you fought on? Or was that decided for you by where you were born?"

"Born," Rix said. "I've killed people too. I guess I got lucky to be born to the winning side and that side held the moral high ground. I get your point. I don't see how you staying is any more dangerous to me than you going. If I have a price on my head, that doesn't say anything about you."

"I gave up sneaking around and killing people, Rix. I don't want that to be part of my life," Amari said. "When I figured out Dravari were the bad guys and that I was part of that, I walked away. I let Shixen control me because I didn't think I had a choice. When he told me to kill you, I told him no, and he got mad."

"And he hit you, like he's done before," Rix added.

"Yes. Remember, I'm not built like you. I feel pain, but I can also make it go away," she said. "It's more insulting than it is painful. He knew this, so he was trying to hurt me after I refused."

"Like really hurt you," Rix said.

"That's right."

"It sounds like you made a decision to survive."

"I don't know what happened. Trust me, if I could remember killing him, I'd tell you. It's not like you don't already believe it. Shixen told me to leave you alone, but I didn't. I should have walked away when I saw this coming," Amari said.

"Instead, you stuck around, and I think you saved my life," Rix said.

"Why aren't you more revolted by me?" she asked. "I just told you I'm a killer, that I was part of the evil that plagues the Forantic Quadrant. If you'd been here during that time, I'd have been your enemy. I probably *did* kill Shixen."

"In our war, there were people who'd come to our country and settled, which wasn't that unusual. Our country was founded by immigrants, so just about everyone came from somewhere."

"Like Patience."

"That's a good analogy."

"Japan was on the other side during the war. So, we decided to take these people, strictly based on their family history, and put them in internment camps, because we were worried about their loyalties," Rix said. "Were Japanese Americans our enemy? Just so we're clear, they'd already given up their homes to come live in our country. If they'd gone back to Japan, a place where they had no home left, would they have been welcomed back or looked at as enemies?"

"I don't get your point, here."

"My point is, governments make big decisions that put people on sides they haven't chosen," Rix said. "Japanese Americans were placed in an impossible position."

"You're saying I'm like them," she said. "But that doesn't hold water, Rix. I was part of the war. I killed people. I was good at my job."

"I guess I just see things differently. I don't know the specifics of your missions, and I don't need to. What I do know is that when the war was over, you stopped."

"I was a pirate after the war, Rix."

"And you kept killing people?"

"Yes ... no, not really. But people around me did," she said. "I tried to walk away. I only managed to get so far, though."

"Don't leave," Rix said. "Do something important for Patience Station. Build a farm with me."

"You'd really just look past everything I just told you?"

"If you'll accept that I might have some things in my past I'd like to leave buried," Rix said. Amari didn't say anything, but Rix saw the change in her face. "So, yesterday, I picked up the pump, a heater and some material we can use to build a bench," he prompted. "I figured we could put that together."

"It looks like you have your hands full here," she said. "If you give me the plans, maybe I could work on that by myself, if you're okay with that."

"Nothing wrong with wanting some alone time," Rix said. "When will you move plants into the towers?"

"Soon," Amari said. "I have a generation growing in the nursery stack. When we move those to the towers, I'll start the next generation. We'll have to use the first generation to harvest seeds, so it'll take a little longer. I have a timeline I've built. I was going to leave it with you."

"But since you're staying, you can work on it," Rix said.

"Something like that."

"I was going to spend some money today on a private head for 808," Rix said.

"Are you tired of using the public restrooms?"

"I found a shower I could use on seventeen, but that's getting old," Rix said. "Otherwise, I need to get Quixly's second cruiser out of my shop before I spend too much on that."

"You should have let me go, Rix," Amari said. "I'll be nothing but trouble for you."

"According to you, I'm the one with a price on his head," Rix said. "I'm the actual trouble, if we're keeping score."

"Well, we'll just have to see about that," Amari said. Gone was the self-doubt in her voice and in its place, Rix heard resolve.

"Hold on there," Rix said. "Don't you go getting yourself into trouble for me."

"Trouble finds me no matter where I go, Rix," Amari shrugged. "If it finds me because I'm helping one of the few decent men I've met, that's probably something worth my attention. Also, if Skef comes looking for me, send him over to 808."

"Why would he do that?"

"I sent him a message asking him to meet me," she said. "I've known Skef for years."

"And he recognizes you as Nerali?"

"Skef won't have questions. He's a survivor, just like I am."

"I won't ask anymore."

"That's probably for the best."

For a moment, Rix and Amari looked at each other. Only minutes before, Amari had been set on running, but now she had flipped from remorseful veteran to something seemingly much more dangerous. Rix realized in that moment that if they were to have a relationship beyond friendship, they would need to take it slowly.

"I don't suppose this cruiser is going to fix itself," Rix finally said, breaking eye contact.

"Put a pistol on your belt, please," Amari said, opening the tool cabinet where he stored the weapons he'd taken from various visitors who'd had ill intent. Wordlessly, Rix accepted the gun she handed him.

Back to work, Rix repeated the diagnostic process he'd utilized on the first cruiser. Significantly more battered than the first, the vessel's issues were much more about visibly damaged parts than complex subsystem failures. With Beverly's help, he first collected an inventory of the damages. Like the first cruiser, the main engines weren't working, but unlike the first, these engines wouldn't even come online. Again, though, it was physical damage that prevented their operation.

"Will Quixly baulk at this repair bill?" Beverly asked. She was wearing her Rosie the Riveter outfit, which had long been her go-to for working repairs. As Rix uncovered failures, she'd created a document containing myriad pieces and parts that needed replacing. In the end, the parts bill alone was fourteen thousand credits.

Rix shrugged. "That's his call. We're looking at fourteen hours of work, so I won't be sad if he says no."

"You should include the labor hours. That might convince him. He'll never get a better deal."

"Do that and send it over to him," Rix said. "In the meanwhile, let's get started on these photonic barrier generators."

Time slipped away as Rix organized the devices in a long line and started methodically running diagnostics. He learned that he had two different manufacturers, and different models within those manufacturers' lines. By mid-afternoon, he'd finished diagnostics and identified the parts required to bring them all back into specification. The bad news was, he'd committed to keeping the cost down to a thousand per unit. With twelve units, he was sitting at nineteen thousand, or a sixty percent increase. He was just considering how to approach Quixly when he received his call.

"That's good timing, Mayor," Rix said.

"Oh? I was calling about the bill you put together for the other cruiser," Quixly said. "That's more than I was expecting."

Having run his own business for years, Rix was used to the *price* conversation. "It looks like that cruiser was in a war," Rix said, addressing the problem straight on.

"That's not wrong," Quixly said. "My predecessor, Bari Goalstead, was killed in that cruiser while on active duty."

"I'm sorry to hear that," Rix said.

"It's been a few years."

"Fourteen thousand is a bargain for the damage on this vessel. I'll have fifteen hours labor if everything goes to plan. Are you still interested?"

"I'll find the money," Quixly said. "Go ahead. Can you manufacture everything locally?"

"Yes," Rix said. "I'll send it to the manufactory and put a requirement for your signature."

"That works. I'll sign it right away. Thanks for the call."

"Don't hang up."

"Oh?"

"I was off on the photonic barriers. Do you have any flexibility on repairs? I need another five thousand," Rix said.

"I thought you were committed when you made that deal," Quixly said.

"It is what it is. I can return the units if that's too much. Like the cruiser, though, I'm not sure where you're going to get free labor."

"It's not free, you're keeping two of those units," Quixly pointed out.

"Don't hear that I'm not grateful, but I just don't have the funds to make up the difference."

"No, I understand," Quixly said. "Put the order in with my signature requirement. It'll be tomorrow morning, most likely. I want to put this to the council."

"Should I hold off on disassembly? Is there a chance you won't get approval?"

"It's your call," Quixly said neutrally. "But I'd say there's a better than good chance I'll get them to agree to the repairs. Without patrol vessels, we can't very well see to law enforcement around here, and that's a touchy subject, what with reports of Draven Knights running around and now Shixen."

"Tomorrow morning, then," Rix said.

"Rix, you have an incoming comm from Kel," Beverly said after terminating comms with Quixly. "Will you spend ten credits for an upgraded communication link?"

"What's that?" Rix asked.

"She's on Gestalt Station and they have quantum communication connection with Patience if you're willing to pay for the upgrade. The conversation isn't necessarily private, though, so be careful."

"Yes," Rix answered. "Heya Kels, how's it going?"

"You're feeling mighty chipper," Kel said. "Are you and Amari hitting it off, or what?"

"I'm not sure we have the credits to finish that conversation," Rix said. "No, big things happening around here. I just learned Jacknie has fifty large on my head. Not loving that. Otherwise, I fixed up one of Quixly's cruisers, working on a second, and I made a deal for another photonic barrier pair. Labor on my part gets me a working set."

"What's fifty large?" Kel asked.

"Jacknie wants me dead, Kel," Rix said.

"What a clown," Kel said. "Gah, we need to get you off station."

"Not happening," Rix said. "This is my place. I'm just getting it set up. I'm not getting run off."

"Make some body armor, at least? Nobody on station would expect that from a mechanic. There's some nice, light stuff available. It's pricey, though."

"What kind of pricey?"

"Fifteen thousand, give or take."

"I don't have that kind of money."

"Well, a couple thousand would at least put some armor on your chest. That's probably the right play," she said.

"I have rent due in five," Rix said. "And I have other things to spend money on."

"How is Amari doing? Word is she's a ghost," Kel said.

"That's the right word," Rix said, not sure who might be able to intercept the transmission. "I feel bad about that."

"Yeah, you sound all broken up about it. What in the heck, Rix? I thought you guys were getting along."

"I met someone while you were gone," Rix said. "We're just talking right now."

"Who? How'd you meet?" Kel asked.

"Gal named Nerali," Rix said. "You probably don't know her too well, she's new to the station and was interested in helping me start a farm."

"You said Nerali?" Kel asked suspiciously.

"I did."

"A real looker, this Nerali? Youngish, maybe thirties, long, jet black hair. Kinda, you know, womanish looking?"

"No *kind of* to it," Rix said. "She's in Bay 808 setting up the rest of the greenhouse. Say, if you can barter for seeds, do it. We have basic greens right now, but it'd be nice to get that dwarf wheat or even micro-oats."

"How much do you want? I think there's a decent supply on Gestalt. There's also hops and barley, given they have a fermentation plant here."

"No kidding? They sell beer, then?"

"Gestalt is big, they sell just about everything if you have the credits."

"Grab a good selection. I'll put up another four hundred in the company account," Rix said.

"I will. I have a couple of hours to kill before we take off for Grelvox. Philo isn't back yet," she said. "So, you met Nerali, huh? That's darn interesting. I guess I'm not overly surprised you two hit it off."

"After Grelvox, what's your plan?" Rix asked.

"We'll get paid for this load once we get to Grelvox; I was going to try to turn that cash into a supply run for several of the Patience vendors. Are you good with that? And keep your credits. We have enough in the corporate account to cover seeds."

"You're picking up Brian Kurth in Grelvox and bringing him back, right?" Rix asked.

"That's right. Why? Are you getting tired of playing station maintenance?"

"There's something off with the power generator," Rix said. "I spent five hours looking it over and just about the time I was going to take a walk outside, the heat overload reset and Quixly called me off."

"That's been happening on and off for a couple of years. It's nothing new," Kel said.

"This frequently?"

"How many times has it happened since I left?"

"Twice," Rix said. "The first one lasted five hours, like I said."

"Yeah, that's a bigger one than usual," she said. "That's why plants don't do so well. You're fixing two of Quixly's cruisers. What are you getting for all that?"

"Three derelict freighters and one that he has locked up in the municipal garage," Rix said. "I didn't get to go into any of them and they're all looking rough, but they're worth more than a few days of my labor, so it'll be worth it in the long run."

"What, now you're a junk collector, too? What need do you have for old freighters? You already have part ownership in *Calypso* and she's not a junker."

"No, she's certainly not," Rix said. "But these old ships will have usable parts, at a minimum. If we're lucky, I'll be able to strip out power generators, gravity generators, and hull plating. Also, I ended up getting a paint gun. I have a date with *Calypso* when you get home. Any trouble with Dravari so far?"

"A little chase, but nothing I couldn't handle," she said. "They gave up when we ducked back into Surnac. And before you ask, I could have outrun them if we were in open space."

"Why won't they just grab you at Grelvox?"

"Near a major city there are too many eyes on what they're doing. It's out here in the deep dark where they get to unleash their inner ass clowns."

"Did you just say ass clown?"

"Fitting, right?"

"I guess I can't argue with that. Okay, Kel, safe sailing. I want to see you guys back in one piece. You read me?"

"Loud and clear, Rixy," Kel said.

14

AVENGING ANGEL

NOT HAVING HEARD from Amari for most of the day, Rix crossed the hallway and entered the farming space. The greenhouse took up only a small fraction of the warehouse he'd rented, and as he walked over to it he attempted to locate Amari. With windows running around the entire building, he was relatively certain she wasn't inside when he entered.

"Amari?" he called but received no response.

"I don't think she's here," Beverly said, appearing on a shelf that sat within the tall rack where seedlings had been planted to germinate.

Rix took quick stock of the greenhouse and saw that sometime during the day, she'd completed all the work possible, aside from connecting the pumps and heaters to power. No more had he thought it but did the lights in the room flicker and shut down.

"That's not getting old," Rix said sarcastically, exiting the greenhouse and making sure the door was closed behind him. "I hope her seeds don't get too cold."

"They would survive freezing temperatures at this stage of their growth, Rix," Beverly answered.

Shining a small flashlight he'd taken to carrying, Rix used the manual release on the bay doors, moving from the farm back to his shop. "Do you suppose we'll get the call this time, or is he going to wait it out?"

In preparation for Quixly's call, Rix assembled a toolbox and pulled on a spacesuit. He'd inspected all the interior components of the power plant and believed the problem to be one of overheating due to excessive demand and an insufficient mechanism for shedding the extra warmth. Even before he'd successfully pulled on his suit, his comms buzzed.

"This is Rix."

"Can you run down to the power station and see if there's anything you can do?" Quixly asked.

"You have plenty of hours on credit," Rix said. "I'm headed down. Did you update my security credentials?"

"I'm not sure that will matter with the power off," Quixly said. "But yes, you have been given full access to maintenance hatches and corridors."

"Thank you," Rix said, closing comms. "Are you ready, Beverly? We're off on adventure!"

"You certainly know how to show a girl a good time. It's no wonder you have so many women flocking to you," she said, grinning from where she hovered close to him.

Rix exited the shop and turned left in the hallway instead of right, as he'd need to take the maintenance stairwell to get to the power station. Walking in the dark, Rix was keenly aware of the sounds around him as he thought about the fact that Jacknie had put a large bounty on his head. For fifty thousand credits, many would be coming for him, and while he wasn't exactly prone to worry, he wasn't thrilled about being in the open. Several flights of stairs later and the echo of his own boots the only noise to keep him company, Rix was grateful to arrive at Level 2, the lowest level available by stairs.

Stopping at the primary consoles, he plugged in his diagnostics scope and started capturing data. Having already built a profile for the events he was most interested in, Rix was able to drill in quickly to the problem which was, as he predicted, the system had overheated.

"Do we have any historical data on consumption?" Rix asked. "Or can we find any?"

Beverly appeared on the console next to where he'd been typing. "Yes, I'm sending it to your scope for analysis."

"Perfect," Rix said, scrolling and pinching as he worked to filter the data into a usable view.

"What are you looking for?"

"Load comparisons. I want to know if something special is happening to cause these outages or if there's an arbitrary failure. As far as I can see, the power generation system is operating within specifications, but it can't get rid of heat fast enough to satisfy the demand."

"Do you want to call Quixly?"

"No. Now that I have maintenance access, can you help make something to warn me when we're getting close to a shutdown? Back home, when we had similar problems, we'd brown out parts of the city."

"Brown out?"

"They'd get less supply until the crisis was over."

"You don't think this is broken."

"No, I think there's something broken, but I think there's also a mystery," Rix said. "Let's go outside and confirm a suspicion I have."

"I go where you go," Beverly said, now donning a winter parka.

Rix pulled his suit closed and worked his way over to a maintenance hatch that sat next to thick shielded piping, which he knew to carry superheated fluids out to a radiant field.

"I suppose you know this, but space isn't exactly cold," Rix said. "It's a common misnomer."

"I do know this. Space is mostly devoid of anything."

"So that means it's not great at radiant exchange," Rix said. "You'd think it'd be fantastic. It's not."

"Is there a point?

"The design of the radiant field should have it connected to a mass of some sort that pulls the heat off and lets it shed that heat over time due to exposure to vacuum," Rix said.

"You're saying this to me for a reason," Beverly said.

"That's all obvious stuff, huh?" Rix asked.

"Obvious, maybe not. In the specifications which, due to your interest in the subject, I've thoroughly read and committed to memory, yes," she said.

Rix chuckled as he ducked through the small airlock and outside to Patience Station's large asteroid. After his first step, he realized that while the station and asteroid were quite massive when compared to himself, they were not enough to generate meaningful gravity, and he caught hold of the roof's overhang before he tumbled out into space.

"This is a clip-in moment, isn't it?" he said, pulling himself along handholds back to the ground.

"Yes," Beverly said. "I'll warn you next time. It didn't occur to me, either."

Rix opened his tool bag, extracting a retractable line that clasped to his spacesuit on one end and a carabiner on the other. Back outside, he connected to a long cable that mostly went where he wanted. It became an odd dance as he tried to figure out how to move along the line and remain vertical. Finally, he gave up and simply pulled himself along.

"This doesn't look right at all," he said, arriving at the wide fins that looked like the fan of a peacock's tail, all lying flat and slightly elevated from the asteroid's barren rock. The fins were cherry red in color, which Rix imagined meant they were quite hot. They were, however, interrupted about a third of the way from their base by a color shift from red to black.

"What were you expecting, Rix?" Beverly asked.

"Hang on," he said, carefully sifting through the tool bag he'd decided to bring along. Inside, he found the laser thermometer he was looking for and started taking readings. As anticipated, the red fins were bordering on white and running at nine hundred degrees Celsius. Moving forward, the black fins ranged from a few hundred degrees where they were closest to the cherry red to negative one hundred degrees furthest at the tip. "Are you catching that?" Rix asked.

"I assume there is a break in the fins," Beverly said.

"Agreed. First, the cherry red is way hotter than specifications. Second, remember the radiation conversation? Those fins aren't supposed to be suspended above the ground, they need to be in contact with a mass. Ideally, they'd be buried under a whole bunch of ice. It's handy they're not though, given the break."

Rix shifted along the line and found himself precariously positioned above the fins, like a common housefly sailing over top of an electric stove coil.

“Be careful, Rix. Vacuum might not allow for radiative transfer, but any part of you that touches certainly will,” Beverly said.

“You’re not wrong,” Rix said, reeling in the retractable tether so a misstep on his part wouldn’t send him into danger. “I need to see why these aren’t conducting. Would you do your video recording thing so I can look at this in detail after we’re back?”

“Yes,” Beverly answered.

“Are you seeing this?” Rix asked, pausing above the break on the rightmost radiative fan. “It’s not even connected. I can’t tell from here if it’s broken or just not installed correctly.”

“I have the capacity to project a magnified view if you would like.”

“Yes. Do that.” On Rix’s HUD it quickly became clear that the top of the radiative fan had no connection to the bottom and it was missing bridge components. “I’m not seeing any obvious signs of sabotage. Is it possible they decided not to complete the installation for some reason? Do they keep notes on things like this?”

“There are notes. I’m scanning for details,” Beverly said. “It appears this is by design. When the station was first built, it was considerably smaller. The fins were added for future expansion, but I don’t see a project in the station’s history to make the connection. There are also notes about a project to move two thousand cubic meters of ice onto the field once the expansion project was completed.”

“And you don’t find that in the project? How have they been getting along for so long with crappy power like this?” Rix asked. “Low demand is my best guess. I suppose I need to look at historical logs to figure out if something has changed or what.”

“There isn’t a significant change in demand,” Beverly said.

"Can you get measurements for the connective braces? Connecting the entire field would probably help a lot. Also, it looks like we could expand the field further," Rix said.

"That's correct, and I have measurements. There is a pattern on file for this project, and I've verified the dimensions. There has been some shifting of the asteroid, so we'll need to adjust slightly, but the pattern is flexible," Beverly said.

Rix's attention was drawn to a flash of light from above his position several hundred meters. "What in the heck is that?" he asked, staring intently, trying to make out what he was looking at. Without warning, a panel popped up on his HUD with a zoomed view. Perched on a narrow ledge, a pair in spacesuits held long weapons and he suddenly realized the display he'd seen were muzzle flashes. "Shoot. We're being shot at." With a quick yank on the cable, Rix pulled himself back toward the station.

"It appears someone has figured out your location and has interest in Jacknie's bounty," Beverly said.

"I'm glad they're lousy shots," Rix said, settling in beneath the overhang. "And what is it with station maintenance that people figure they should shoot at me?"

"Fifty thousand credits is a fortune to most folks out here," Beverly said.

"I should never have gone to Sout Atal. I was so naïve, and Kel tried to tell me, but I wouldn't listen."

"She has local knowledge."

"You don't have to tell her about this conversation," Rix said.

"Loose lips sink ships," Beverly said agreeably. "I have Quixly on comm. I assume you want to report this."

"This is Quixly. Go ahead, Banner. Did you fix it yet? Power is still out," Quixly said.

"We're going to be down for another two hours," Rix said. "It overheated again."

"I thought you fixed it last time."

"No. I figured out that it was overheating. I have a plan now, but that's not why I called."

"Oh?"

"Someone is taking shots at me from Level 9," Rix said. "I've got a location if you want it. I imagine they're not hanging out, though."

"What is it with you that so inflames folks that they want to shoot you?" Quixly asked. "Oh, never mind, asked and answered."

"Very funny, Quixly. Maybe you could take your new constable scooter out and see if you can sneak up on them. I've sent you coordinates," Rix said.

"I will. Also, I was in a meeting with the council. They've approved both the fix to the second cruiser as well as the photonic barriers, although a couple of them were irritated that I made a trade with you for station equipment that's quite expensive."

"Expensive boat anchors are still boat anchors," Rix said.

"If I understand your analogy correctly, I'm inclined to agree. I'll take a run out and see if your new friends are still in position. I wouldn't get excited. Will you be able to repair the power while it's still out?"

"No. I need parts. Also, once I'm done with this, we're going to need to get someone to move a bunch of ice."

"How much?"

"Two thousand cubic meters," Rix said. "The power plant was never finished."

"That's not possible. Patience Station had over twenty thousand inhabitants at one point. We're not using more power than back then. Check your data, Banner. You're off on this one."

"Maybe so," Rix said. "I haven't had time to sit down with it. I'll send you a report, but trust me, once I have a repair in place, you'll need to get someone to move ice and not that crappy stuff with all the rocks you were using for the atmospheric concentrators."

"There's an ice field on the back of the asteroid. I'll need you to work with Fentral Boggs. He's the only one I know who can move that kind of material," Quixly said.

"Okay. I'll talk to him once I get this all drawn up and estimated," Rix said.

"Two hours before power is restored?"

"About that."

"I'll be in touch. Quixly out."

"Rix, do not be alarmed," Beverly said.

"What's going on?"

"There is a figure moving along the side of the station where it meets the asteroid surface. To your right, up forty meters if you consider the gravity of the station to be down," Beverly said.

Rix thought about what she was telling him and he looked in the direction she'd indicated. A blue outline surrounded an otherwise invisible figure that was moving quickly, using the joint where station met rock as a handhold.

"He's moving fast," Rix said. "Was he shooting at us? That doesn't seem like the right angle."

"I do not know. I recommend getting indoors, though."

"That sounds like a solid plan," Rix agreed, captivated by the figure's speed as it moved out of view, blocked by the overhang. “I don’t think I’ve done enough to warrant the kind of anger Jacknie seems to have.”

“You stood against him and caused embarrassment when you defeated his soldiers,” Beverly said. “It is a matter of pride and reputation, I suspect.”

“He’s not going to give up easily, is he?”

“It does not seem likely.”

Rix leaned out from beneath the overhang so he could check out the climbing figure. Without slowing, it was halfway to where the shooters had set up, and Rix’s curiosity got the better of him. He poked out from beneath the overhang just enough to have line of sight to the shooter’s perch on Level 9. A muzzle flash warned him that his presence was noted and he popped back in as blaster fire chipped away at the steel apron where he stood.

“Oh, man, they’re waiting on me. That’s probably not a bad thing if Quixly is going to check them out,” Rix said. “I’m glad they’re not military snipers. Without gravity to mess up trajectory, that can’t be that hard of a shot.”

“An inexperienced shooter, perhaps?” Beverly offered.

“No idea,” Rix said. “Kel suggested I get some armor. I think she’s probably on to something. When I checked, it looks like a chest plate is in the two thousand range. I just don’t have the funds for something like that.”

“It seems a reasonable priority.”

“I hear you. Let’s get back to the shop. We can finish plans for the radiator repair and then tonight, I’ll start dismantling the cruiser and get a parts request for power off to the manufactory. For all the work I throw their way, I should get a discount, don’t you think?”

“Perhaps.”

Returning to the shop was uneventful, and Rix took a moment to make coffee and open a couple of meal bars. He'd taken Quixly's recommendation for berry to heart and ordered an entire case. He found that the mayor was right on, and the meal bars were a considerable upgrade from the protein and carbohydrate paste that were so much cheaper.

"What do you think of the plans I've put together for the radiator repairs?" Rix asked, pushing the electronic file over to Beverly's virtual form.

"I have a few improvements to suggest. Would you review them?"

"I don't understand how you do that so quickly."

"I've been watching you work," Beverly said. "I had my proposed changes complete when you sent your work to me."

"That's fair," Rix agreed, jumping through each proposed change. He accepted twelve of fifteen changes and was grateful for her feedback. With that complete, he submitted the parts requests and plan to Quixly for review. "I'm glad to have that off my plate."

"What will you do now?"

"No rest for the weary," Rix said. "We'll start disassembling the cruiser. I think we'll have parts for that and the barrier generators first thing in the morning. It might take a little longer to get the power station parts. I suppose it depends on how urgent Quixly perceives it."

Two hours later, Rix was on his back pulling parts and setting them neatly in a row when he was alerted to a visitor at the shop's door.

"It's Quixly," Beverly announced.

"Were we expecting him?" Rix asked.

"We were not."

Brushing off his hands, Rix slid out and sat up. It took him a moment to get to his feet and before he'd succeeded, Quixly was banging on the door again. "Open up, Banner. I know you're in there."

"No need to get pushy," Rix called as he approached. "I'm coming."

Rix opened the shop door and looked expectantly at Quixly, who was flush in the face. "I know it was you, Banner. Just tell me what happened."

"You're going to need to be a bit more specific," Rix said. "Tell you what about what, now?"

"You reported shooters. When I went to the location you identified, I found a couple of corpses floating next to a balcony," he said.

"I don't mean to be obtuse, but fresh corpses or old ones?" Rix asked carefully.

"Are you fooling with me?"

"No."

"Dead corpses. Recently made that way. By the coroner's report, dead about the time you called me," he said.

"Gunshot?"

"Don't play coy."

"I'm not playing anything," Rix said. "Although, I did see something else while I was there. Someone was climbing up the station wall. Like they were headed up to where those guys were shooting from."

"This is bad, Banner. Those men were Sable. You're going to start a war," he said.

"I don't know where you've been, but I'm already in one. I was informed earlier that there's a bounty on my head, courtesy of Jacknie from Draven Knights."

"Let me search your shop, Banner."

"Why?"

"These men were killed by knife," he said. "I'm looking for a murder weapon."

"Search all you want. I didn't do it."

"I almost believe you."

15

MOUTHS TO FEED

Waking early due to a buzz at the station side door, Rix groggily looked through the camera's view of the hallway. Lined up on both sides were packages from the manufactory. With the pending death threats, Rix had taken to requesting deliveries from the manufactory instead of picking parts up by himself. Cautiously, he moved parts for both the cruiser and the photonic barrier generators into his shop. He smiled to himself. There was something hopeful about new parts that always put him in a good mood. Rix turned his attention to making coffee and grabbing a light breakfast, which consisted of a single meal bar. He'd no more than filled his cup and sat down in his chair when the buzzer alerted him to a visitor.

Rix sighed as he found Quixly standing impatiently in the hallway. "Good morning, mayor," he said.

"Why don't I think you mean that?" Quixly asked with a raised eyebrow.

"Think of it as a sincere wish on my part," Rix said. "Cup of lode bean?"

"If you have enough."

"Always," Rix said, moving so Quixly could enter. Filling a cup, he turned back to Quixly and handed it to him. "How can I help?"

"Your proposal for refitting the power generator is put on hold," he said. "The counsel wants this new fella, Brian Kurth, to take a look at it when he arrives in a week."

"And if the power drops between now and then?"

"We'll be down for a couple of hours, just like yesterday."

Rix nodded. "I'm fine with that."

"This will be the first order of business I take up with Mr. Kurth once he arrives next week," Quixly said.

"I assume that's not what you came to tell me," Rix said.

"Good guess. When was the last time you saw Amari?"

"Right after you released her from jail. I was going to ask you the same thing."

"Why?"

"Because we were working on a project together," Rix said. "Amari is a friend. I'm concerned. Have you seen her?"

"No. I have video of her walking out onto the concourse shortly before a small freighter pushed off. She hasn't been seen since."

Rix nodded. "You could have asked me that over comms. Why'd you come, really?"

"I found evidence that the two men found dead were in possession of long rifles and there is a witness that saw them shooting in the general direction of the field where you were working," Quixly said. "I need to know if you killed them, Banner."

"With a knife? You're asking if I scaled the side of the space station and surprised two men with long rifles who were shooting at me and killed them with a knife," Rix scoffed. "I'm telling you that not only is the idea ludicrous, but also that my only involvement was hiding once I figured out I was being shot at. No, I did not kill those men. You're not telling me something."

"I'm not telling you a lot of things. That is part of my job as constable," Quixly said. "But, since this involves you, I will tell you that the men were killed in a way that is often associated with sending a message. The details are part of an ongoing investigation, so I can't share, but I would say that whoever killed those men has an interest in protecting you."

"I don't understand. What was the message?"

"That you are off limits and further attempts to collect Jacknie's bounty relating to your death will be responded to with malice."

"That's a lot to read from a knife wound."

"And a reason why I don't believe you sent it."

"I guess it's good to be a simple guy," Rix chuckled.

"If Amari contacts you, tell her I need to talk with her," Quixly said, setting down his coffee.

"Okay."

With his routine interrupted, Rix set his own cup on the workbench and started reassembling the photonic generators after replacing the parts he'd manufactured. In that the devices had already been cleaned and sufficiently disassembled, the work went quickly, and by mid-afternoon he'd tested the entire lot of them and was satisfied with the results. With only a small break for lunch, Rix then moved over to the cruiser and continued disassembling and cleaning in preparation for installation of the parts. It was 2200 when he finally rolled out of the stripped-down cruiser and stretched out sore muscles and joints.

"I wondered if you would be in that thing all evening," a man's voice caught him by surprise.

Startled, Rix spun around, his heart hammering as he found Greasle sitting in his favorite chair, a bottle of Collie's Reserve open on the floor, with a glass of rum in one hand and a blaster pistol in the other. "Oh, shit," was all Rix could manage.

"I have to admit, that's damn satisfying," Greasle said. Rix wasn't sure if he was referring to the rum or the fact that he had fully alarmed Rix.

"What are you doing here, Greasle?" Rix asked, allowing his hand to fall to his side and mentally face-palming as he realized the pistol, which Amari had been so adamant about him carrying, had been left on the workbench. When he glanced over, he noticed the pistol was missing.

"I have your pistol, Mr. Banner," Greasle said. "Come. Join me for a drink. We need to talk."

Rix scanned the room but as he did, Greasle sat forward and gestured with his own pistol. Reluctantly, Rix crossed over and sat in the chair near him. A second glass of rum was already sitting on the small table between them, and with some urging from Greasle, Rix took a small sip.

"Do you plan to kill me for the bounty?" Rix asked.

"You're a bit of a ground around here," Greasle replied.

"I don't know what you mean."

"I suppose that's a spacer saying. A ground attracts electricity, just like you attract trouble. I've been sitting here trying to decide if you know what you're doing or if it's just all this activity you're generating that puts you at the center of trouble."

"Maybe it's something else," Rix said. "I've been in my shop just minding my own business, fixing things."

"Oh, I completely understand. I've had eyes on you even before Shixen got taken out. You're about the most boring person I can imagine. You literally spend all day taking things apart and cleaning them," Greasle said. "Where's the fun in that?"

"When they work once I put them back together," Rix said. "I'm creating value. Instead of buying something new, I fix it for a fraction of the cost of replacement. It's a win—win."

"Please, stop talking. I'm already bored," Greasle rolled his eyes. "I need to talk to you because, intentional or not, you're causing me trouble."

"I don't know how."

"You're involved in Shixen's death. That part, I'm just guessing, and honestly, thank you. About the only way for me to be promoted was for Shixen to die. However, two of my soldiers are dead. They were killed by someone who is very good at what they do," Greasle said. "That someone left a message to leave you alone. I can only assume that someone was you, and that you employ or hired a heavyweight to get us off your back. Message received. No Sable soldier will be taking shots at you. You leave us alone. We'll leave you alone. We don't have to be friends."

"Does that include my associates? Kel, Philo and my new business partner Nerali?" Rix asked.

"We'll leave yours alone as long as you leave mine alone," he said.

"I just want to live a simple life," Rix said. "I don't have a quarrel with you or Sable."

"I'm glad to hear that," Greasle said, pushing his blaster into the holster at his waist. "Now that we've had that discussion, are you open to taking work outside of normal channels?"

"What are you thinking?" Rix asked.

"We have vessels that need repair," he said. "Atom, a local I hired to run the shop that Shixen took over from you, doesn't seem to know what he's doing. I'm not asking for special service. I just need someone who can fix them."

"How many?" Rix asked.

"Three, but one is of importance. I'm willing to pay above market rate for priority service."

"Have someone tie it up to slip 807A by tomorrow afternoon and I'll take a look."

"Good, now I can fire Atom. What a waste of time and money," Greasle lamented. "Also, you should get some decent food in your refer. There's no reason to live on that paste."

"It's not like there's a grocery around here," Rix said. "I'm not sure what my options are if I don't want to have Petju making it."

"Maybe I can throw in some decent food if I like your service," Greasle said, slicking back his hair as he stood. "I'm glad we could come to an understanding. There's no reason for us to be enemies on such a small station."

Rix nodded. He didn't love taking work from Greasle, but he also didn't need to make an enemy, as long as the work he was doing was fully above board. The ability to walk in public on the station, however, had plenty of value. "I was just about to head out. Is there anything else?"

"Put this bottle on my bill, would you?" Greasle asked.

"Let's call it a peace offering," Rix said.

"See, now, that's a solid gesture," Greasle said. "I knew I was going to end up liking you."

Rix winced internally as Greasle slapped him on the back. Worse, he couldn't seem to shake the grungy pirate, who decided to accompany him out to the elevator bank. Fortunately, Greasle selected a different floor when they entered the car, and by the time Rix was to the Atrium on Level 17, he was by himself.

"I haven't seen you around for a few days. Where have you been hiding?" Petju asked as Rix entered Petju's Pub. Much had changed in the small restaurant and bar, with upgraded seating and even a server walking between tables.

"Busy, busy," Rix said. "Sorry I'm covered with dirt. I'm just looking to grab some dinner. I don't mind taking it to go. What's going on here? You've been updating. It looks nice."

"We just had a freighter make it in from Caldrin-3," she said. "Haven't seen Felitini for fourteen months or better. I bought him out of food stock, so I figured I'd better let people know I'm serious about business. What are you interested in? The board up there shows what we're making tonight."

"Chef's choice," Rix said.

"Good and hungry, then?" Petju asked, gesturing for Rix to sit.

"And then some."

Rix sat back in the booth and relaxed. He hadn't realized how much stress he'd been carrying with the knowledge that Sable had such easy access to him with the bounty in place. The ability to be seen in public was quite a relief.

After several minutes, the server, an older woman with a kind smile and oversized ears brought out a plate piled high with steaming green vegetables, mashed something he hoped was like potatoes and brown meat. It was the closest to a meal he was used to from home that he'd seen since arriving on Patience, and he dug in with zeal.

"Are you Rix Banner?" a high-pitched voice asked, interrupting him after he'd barely gotten started. He tamped down his irritation and forced a smile onto his face. At first, he missed the small alien who stood next to his table, looking over the top of the speaker. With shoulders roughly the height of the table, the thin, green-skinned alien, with a slightly enlarged head, pointy, oddly moving ears and yellow eyes was something of a surprise.

"Oh, hello there," he said. "Yes, I'm Rix. How can I help you?"

"Greasle fired Atom," he said. "I'm Atom."

"You were his mechanic?"

"Yes. He said I no fix things right."

"I'm afraid you'll need to take that up with Greasle," Rix said. "I have no idea of the quality of your work. I only understand that he needed you to accomplish some things and you struggled. Is that an unfair assessment?"

"You use big words, Rix Banner," Atom said. "Atom good with hands. No read good. Atom hungry."

"Atom, what are you doing?" Petju asked with irritation evident in her voice. "You can't come in here begging for food."

"Hold on, Petju. I've got this. I'd forgotten that Atom and I were to have dinner tonight," Rix said. "Atom, grab a seat, tell Petju what you'd like for dinner tonight. My treat."

"Are you sure this is what you want, Rix?" Petju asked. "Atom can be pesky."

"Probably a good warning, but I think I've got this. Go ahead, Atom, sit with me, we'll talk and have dinner together," Rix said. "Petju, get him what you got me, would you?"

"You're making a mistake," Petju said, but walked away.

"Rix Banner is saying true? Atom eat here?"

"Take a seat, Atom. Otherwise Petju won't know where to put the food," Rix said, pushing his plate to the side. "So tell me why you couldn't fix Greasle's ship?"

"Cleaned injection points. Cleaned exhaust recirculatory. Bad wires. Greasle no want spend. Needs works on meat tricks, but too hard open," he said.

"I think he means matrix," Beverly said, showing up on the table between them. "Atom is a Grintok, Rix. He likely understands more than he can communicate. Grintok speech centers are underdeveloped. He is likely truthful about being good with his hands. Grintok are known for having extraordinary dexterity. They're also often blamed for being thieves. There's a not so flattering saying -- *If you want something cheap, fast, and probably illegal—ask a Grintok.*"

Rix nodded to Beverly and turned his attention to Atom who was staring greedily at Rix's plate. "How did you clean the injector and exhausts?" Rix asked.

"Hard work. Brush with orange, good smelly. Atom get much dirty," Atom said.

"Solvent."

"Good smelly."

"Is Atom good at cleaning?"

"No people pay clean. Atom no clean. No get pay."

"That wasn't what I asked," Rix said. "Are you good at cleaning?"

"Atom good fixing."

"Atom, I won't ask again. Are you good at cleaning?"

"Yes. Atom no like clean. Atom good clean."

"You don't like to do it but you can do a good job. Is that right?"

"Yes. Lots of words."

"Does Atom want work for tomorrow? One day only," Rix said.

"Atom fired. No work tomorrow."

"How about you come work for me tomorrow," Rix said. "I'll pay twenty credits for half a day. If you do a good job, I might have more work."

"Twenty credits, yes!"

Rix was saved by Petju sliding a smaller plate onto the table in front of Atom. "There you go. Just be careful, Rix. Grintok have trouble with sticky fingers if you get my meaning."

"Thank you, Petju," Rix said, noticing that Atom hadn't started on his food. "Go ahead, Atom. The food on that plate is yours."

Atom didn't need further prompting and started shoveling the food into his mouth using his hands. The food slipped from his mouth from time to time, spilling onto his front, which didn't seem to bother him in the least.

The two ate in relative silence, aside from the smacking of Atom's lips as he seemed to thoroughly enjoy the meal. When he'd finished, Atom belched loudly three times and then lay over on the seat and closed his eyes, falling asleep.

"Strange little fella," Rix said when Petju came over to the table and noticed the sleeping alien.

"Annoying, more like. Most restaurants won't let them in. I would have stopped him if I'd seen him enter," Petju said. "It was a nice thing to feed him. I'm afraid you might have trouble getting him to leave you alone now, though."

"I can imagine," Rix said. "Could I get a bag for my leftovers?"

"Certainly. And you can leave him on the bench. I'll get him to leave."

"Atom, wake up," Rix said, and when he didn't get a response, he poked the small alien's shoulder and repeated himself. It took several tries, but finally, Atom awoke and sat up.

"Why Rix Banner bother Atom?"

“I’m leaving and I’m sure Petju will want you to leave, too,” Rix said.

“Atom leave,” the small alien said dejectedly. “Twenty credits tomorrow?”

“Twenty credits,” Rix agreed. “Come 0800 tomorrow morning.”

“Atom come morning.”

With a full stomach and feeling good about having a bit of social interaction, Rix was in a pleasant mood as he returned to his shop. In the hallway, only twenty meters from the entrance to his shop, he heard the scrape of a shoe behind him, and spun around, only to not find anyone. He quickened his step, not sure what might be behind him.

“Going somewhere?” a woman’s voice asked, right after a pair of feet landed heavily on the deck still several meters back. Rix spun around, fully expecting to find nothing, but instead finding Amari, in her Nerali guise, holding Atom by the collar.

“What’s going on?” Rix asked, jogging back to their position.

“This one was following you,” Amari said. “Kind of an unlikely assassin, though.”

“That’s Atom. We had dinner together and I thought he was coming tomorrow to help me work on the cruiser,” Rix said.

“I not trouble! I not trouble,” Atom screeched. “No hurt! No hurt!”

“You can put him down, Nerali,” Rix said, unwilling to use her real name.

“Settle down and I’ll let you go,” Amari said, struggling not to drop Atom on his butt due to his frantic struggling.

“Where did you come from?” Rix asked, looking at Amari. “I didn’t see you.”

"A girl can't give away all of her secrets," she said. "What are you going to do with this one?"

Atom looked about as uncomfortable as he could as Amari continued to hold onto the sleeve of his poorly fitted jumpsuit.

"Let him go. He'll be okay. I don't think he was following me to cause trouble," Rix said.

"Why then?" Amari asked.

"Atom, would you care to explain?" Rix asked.

"Atom sleep by Rix door. Early work," Atom said.

"What is he talking about, Rix?" Amari said. "Did you hire Atom? Are you serious?"

"He lost his job because Greasle wants me to do some work on his cutter," Rix said. "Apparently, he was Greasle's mechanic."

"You can't be serious."

16

CRITICAL DAMAGE

"Atom, where do you normally sleep?" Rix asked, opening the door and ushering both Amari and Atom into the shop.

"Atom sleep hallway, no people," Atom answered.

Rix nodded and then noticed Amari eyeing the leftover food he'd brought from Petju's Pub. "Would you eat this?" Rix asked, offering the box to Amari.

She started to turn him down but then thought better and took the food from him. Without hesitation, she found a seat and started eating. While Rix was curious about what was going on with Amari, he figured to deal with Atom first.

"Atom, you don't have a regular place to sleep. Is that what I'm hearing?"

"Move much. Constable mean."

"It looks like you found yourself a little friend, Rix," Amari said between bites. "It's like you're making a fun clubhouse for misfits."

"Atom go. Sleep hallway. Work tomorrow," Atom said plainly.

"Do you want to sleep in the shop?" Rix asked. "Constable Quixly won't bother you in here."

"Can okay?"

Rix thought about the poorly worded response and figured Atom was asking permission. "Well, it won't be free," Rix said.

"Atom work work."

"Good," Rix said. "Two small tasks. First, you will crate up the photonic barrier projectors. Be careful, though. They are expensive. I'm keeping two of them and I'll be installing them before I sleep tonight. After you crate them up, you'll sweep the shop with the ion broom. I'll work on making a bed for you."

"Atom sleep floor."

"No," Rix said. "Now get to crating those projectors and take it easy. We don't need to damage them. The ion broom is leaning against the wall next to the tool cabinet."

"You're nuts," Amari said, watching with some amusement as Atom got to work.

"Where crates?" Atom asked almost immediately.

"Stacked right there," Rix pointed.

"Big heavy," Atom said, struggling to climb the stack of crates so he could take the top one down.

Rix was about to intervene when Amari stopped him. "Don't, Rix, let him work it out. Grintok are stronger than they look."

Sure enough, Atom grabbed a crate from the top and awkwardly held it with one hand while he climbed down the stack. Rix looked on as Atom packed the first projector. It wasn't the most efficient way to hold the projector and wouldn't allow for three per crate like he'd wanted, but Rix decided to let the small alien work.

"Want to help me, Nerali?" Rix asked.

"Sure, what are we doing?"

Rix grabbed one of the two projectors he'd set aside and started carrying it back to the exterior bay doors. "Grab the other one. They're a little heavy, maybe use a grav cart."

Having installed a photonic barrier in his previous shop, Rix set the first in place, returning to the workbench for a boltgun and tools for pulling station power. Back in the flow of things, he worked efficiently and quietly, stripping wires, building out small power boxes and connecting the devices. All in all, the process took less than an hour, and by that time, Atom had started sweeping, although his efficiency at the task was very poor.

"You're not going to say anything to him?" Amari asked. "He's not really sweeping. You know that, right?"

"First day, I let new workers do things their way. If it works out, they get to keep going. If not, I step in. It helps if I know what I'm working with," Rix said. "It's getting late, are you staying here tonight?"

"No, I was just checking in on you when I found Atom following you. I was worried it was someone who intended you ill," Amari said. "It's not like there are a lot of places to sleep here."

"How are you doing for credits?" Rix asked.

"I'm okay, for now," she said. "I need to check in on the seedlings. Will you be around tomorrow?"

"Yes. I'm delivering the photonic barrier projectors first thing in the morning. After that, I'll put the cruiser back together. I need to give a bid for fixing the hull plating. That's extra work that's not part of our original deal."

"You did it for the first cruiser."

"I'm not feeling as generous today. The first time was to show Quixly what it could look like," Rix said.

"Clever."

"Thanks for coming by tonight," Rix said. "I appreciate the help."

"Do you want me to stop by after I check in on the seedlings?" Amari asked. "We could have a nightcap or something."

"That'd be swell," Rix said, seeing Amari to the door.

Once she was gone, Rix set to the task of creating a temporary bed for Atom. Given the alien's size, it was an easier job than it could have been. Breaking down crates and reconfiguring with boltgun in hand, he soon had the makings of a reasonable bed. Seeing that Atom was still at work, Rix decided to add a canopy, which would give Atom some privacy, given his bed was open to the shop.

"For Atom?" Atom asked, pushing a pile of dirt in Rix's direction.

"Yes. Atom's bed," Rix said.

"Use now?"

"Are you tired?"

"Yes yes. Atom sleep."

"Go ahead, little guy," Rix said.

Without preamble, Atom released the ion broom's handle and raced over to the bed, pulling back the cloth as the handle clattered on the floor. Looking out once, he pulled the curtains closed, leaving Rix wondering what he'd just seen.

Shrugging his shoulder at the odd behavior, Rix cleaned off his workbench and poured a couple of fingers of rum into two glasses, adding ice to his own. He'd been on Patience Station for almost a month and as he reflected, he slipped off to sleep in his favorite chair.

"Rix sleep." Atom's high-pitched voice somehow made it through Rix's subconscious, waking him.

"I'm awake," Rix said, looking around to find Atom standing uncomfortably close. "What's going on?"

"Morning. Work work time," Atom said.

"Did I miss Nerali?" Rix asked.

"No Nerali. Morning."

"Okay," Rix said, struggling to get out of the chair where he'd spent the night. Looking at the table, he found his half empty glass of rum right where he'd left it. "If you're sticking around, there are things you need to know."

"Atom stay?"

"At least today," Rix said.

"Learn what?"

"Coffee," Rix said. "Make coffee first thing in the morning. I'm going to show you how, but you need to remember what I show you so you can make it."

"Atom try."

"That's all I ask."

While it took longer than usual to make the coffee, Atom seemed to understand the concepts, although Rix knew only time would tell. After loading four crates onto grav pallets, Rix and Atom set off for the freight elevator and one level down to the municipal garage. Installing four bays worth of photonic barriers took only thirty minutes each as the fittings were already in place. Rix found that while Atom wasn't particularly proactive, once he understood a task, he worked diligently to complete it.

"That was good work, Atom," Rix said as they brought the grav pallets back to the shop.

"Bring others, too?" Atom asked.

"Do you think you could install the last ones without me?" Rix asked.

"Atom know how."

"Let me know before you turn them on. I'll come down and double check, just to be sure. Okay?" Rix asked.

"Okay."

If Atom was offended that Rix wanted to double check his work, he didn't show it. It was with some satisfaction that Rix watched Atom leave with the remaining projectors, knowing it would give him more time to complete work on the broken cruiser.

Picking up where he'd left off the day before, Rix finished the final cleaning tasks and started dragging parts back into the cruiser and bolting them into place. Three hours passed and he was well over halfway done when he realized Atom hadn't returned.

"Beverly, do we have any way to track Atom?"

"No. It didn't look like he was carrying comms. I didn't find him in the station registry, either."

Rix sighed and retraced his steps down to the municipal garage, fully expecting to find that Atom had either not arrived or had walked off, chasing something more interesting. Instead, he found Atom struggling with one of the projector units. Somewhere between crying and cursing, Atom wasn't aware of Rix's approach and startled when he realized he wasn't alone.

"I'm sorry. Atom stupid. No get part fit," he said, throwing a tool onto the deck with a loud clangor.

"No reason to get upset. You should have come and got me," Rix said. "Show me what the problem is. We can work it out together."

"Atom not fired?"

"No. Show me what isn't working," Rix said.

Atom did just that, demonstrating that the projector wouldn't fit into the left-behind fittings. He then turned the projector around both left and right and then upside down. "It no fit."

"There are two models of these projectors," Rix said patiently. "This is not for the model you're holding. Try this other one, here." Rix pointed to a device on the pallet and watched Atom to see how he'd react. Understanding hit the small alien like a hammer and his eyes widened at the same time he jumped back.

"Atom very stupid."

"Go ahead, then. Install the other one." Atom got right to business and this time had no trouble seating the device into place and connecting it to the various fittings and wiring harnesses. "Atom is not stupid. That is a fine piece of work you just did there. I believe this last one goes over there," Rix said, pointing to an opening.

"Oh no. Big boss office there," Atom said.

"Quixly?"

"Yes."

"I don't think he's coming down," Rix said. "Let's get this finished up, we'll grab some lunch and then you can help me finish the cruiser for Mayor Quixly."

"Eat again?" Atom asked.

"Three times a day until I start getting a gut," Rix said, testing the other devices Atom had installed. With one exception, they were correctly done, and he didn't feel badly about what Atom had missed. Although Rix showed him the error, he made little of it otherwise.

Back at the shop, Rix shared a meal bar with Atom and then the two got back to the cruiser. This time, with twice as many hands, the job moved along more quickly. It was well past dinner time when the final part clicked into place, not even requiring so much as a set screw.

"Done?" Atom asked.

"Except for diagnostics," Rix said. "Let's get it started and we'll work front to back through the subsystem logs."

"Much work. Much reading."

"How about I give you twenty credits, and you buy dinner at Petju's?" Rix asked. "I'll run diagnostics."

"Yes. Food good!"

With Atom gone, Beverly appeared on the dashboard just in front of the cockpit seats. "He's not incompetent," she said. "I don't think he was well suited to a lead mechanic position, though. What are you thinking about? Can you afford an employee?"

"Eighty credits a day is probably what I have for him. I could use a helper, though," Rix said. "Otherwise, I end up doing all the running and jobs will get backed up. I need to make sure I charge accordingly, though."

"You don't charge anything, right now," Beverly said. "You only do trades."

"We're still solvent, though."

"And you owe Patience Station fifteen hundred credits tomorrow for rent. If you hadn't made the deal you had, that number would be thirty-five hundred credits," she said.

"That's a good reminder, I'll send that rent off now while I'm thinking of it," Rix said. "It's easy to see a lack of credits and think that we're running out of money. I have two bays, part ownership in a freighter business, four old freighters that I haven't had a chance to look at, and part ownership in a fledgling farm. Oh, and photonic barrier generators just got added to my shop. That's quite a lot of progress."

"I can't exactly argue with that. You also have a bounty on your head and the space station you live in keeps losing power," she said.

"You're grasping at straws. How do those diagnostics look?"

"You do good work, Rix," she said. "There are a couple of calibrations you need to work through, but otherwise, systems are all working. Have you heard back from Quixly regarding the hull repairs?"

"I didn't even send the request," Rix said. "Other than a test drive, I think we're done here. After dinner, help me with an estimate?"

"Six hours labor, four hundred credits in supplies," she said. "I assume you're looking to work off the hours you credited for the cruiser repair deal?"

"What's my balance on that?"

"Sixteen hours if you remove the time spent fixing the first cruiser's hull and painting it," she said.

"Do you want to send that to Quixly, then?"

"It's sent."

"Okay, activate the doors. We'll take this out for a quick run," Rix said. "That is, if I can figure out how to sail it."

"Amari has arrived. If you'll permit, I could let her in," Beverly said.

A screen showed on Rix's HUD providing him options to give Beverly: *single-use, time-limited,* or *unrestricted* access to the secure entry to each of the doors for bays 807 and 808. Rix selected *unrestricted* access for all of it and then opened the forward bubble of the cruiser, which hinged up and allowed a direct exit from the front of the vessel.

"You've really cleaned up in here," Amari said, looking around. "Where's the little green monster?"

"I'm not sure Atom would love that characterization but he's up grabbing dinner. We'll have plenty if you'd like some," Rix said. "It looks clean in here because Atom and I have been knocking off projects, left and right. I just have hull repairs to complete, and that's only if Quixly is willing to pay."

"You've accomplished a lot in the last couple of weeks," Amari said.

"We still have a few minutes. Do you have any interest in taking the cruiser out and putting it through its paces?"

"You'd let me do that?"

"I have virtually no experience with small craft like this. I'm not the right guy to sit behind the wheel," Rix said.

"Wheel?"

"Sorry, Earth term," Rix grinned. "So, are you interested?"

"Sure."

Rix walked back to the exterior bay doors and turned the photonic barrier projectors on. Once they were humming along and a light blue film seemed to cover the entire opening, he tapped the button that would open the exterior doors. For a moment, he felt anxiety, wondering if the barrier would hold, but his worry was for nothing as the vastness of space came into view.

"What a treat to have this kind of view," Amari said. Rix turned and smiled, relishing Amari's attention. Without further conversation, the pair walked back to the cruiser, where the forward stairs had popped out, and took seats in the cockpit. "How hard do you want me to take it?"

"Is this a trick question?" Rix asked.

Amari's cheeks pinked and she shook her head. "I'm not being crass," she said.

It was Rix's turn to blush as he realized what his question must have sounded like. "No, no, I didn't mean that. Just take it slow, then try things that are more rigorous to the ship's systems," he said, fumbling his words to get them out quickly.

Amari grinned. "You're cute when you're embarrassed," she said. "Be a dear and call Patience and let them know we're headed out, would you?"

Rix glanced quickly at Amari, trying to figure out if she was still giving him a hard time. Before he could put his mouth fully around his foot, he established comms with Patience Station.

"Patience, this is Rix Banner. Requesting permission to take a small vessel out from Bay 807 on a test run," Rix said.

"Thanks for the heads up," Hutari answered shortly thereafter. "And way to go, getting the municipal garage running again! Quixly's taken his shiny new cruiser out and back like half a dozen times since this morning. He'll never tell you, but he sure appreciates the work!"

Rix glanced at Amari questioningly but kept comments to himself. "Over and out, Hutari. Hope you have a good night."

"Thirty minutes left on my shift," Hutari answered. "Best thing to happen today. Patience Station out."

"What was that look for?" Amari asked.

"Hutari is awful chipper for someone who's supposedly just lost her mother," Rix said. "You've been talking to her. Isn't that dangerous?"

"I wasn't going to disappear and not tell Hutari. She'd never forgive me."

While they'd been talking, Amari had gently lifted the cruiser from the deck and was slowly backing it out into the vacuum of space. Rix watched as they passed through the barrier and continued to be astounded by how a curtain of light somehow held back pressurized atmosphere. It was something he planned to research further, but not at that moment, because the cruiser's display was filled with diagnostic messages.

"What is all of that?" Amari asked as she punched the bow thrusters at the same time she applied thrust from the main engine. The messages flew even faster across the display, making it nearly impossible to understand what was happening.

"Verbose event data," Rix said. "Hold on, I'm dialing it back since I don't need most of what's being shown." As he worked, the scrolling messages slowed. "That's better. And wow, that's looking fantastic."

"I can punch it up, now?"

"Go," Rix said. With little experience relating to engine capacities and ship masses, Rix hadn't put together the considerable difference between a law enforcement cruiser's potential acceleration and a freighter's. "Oh ... my ... gosh!!"

"Whee! This thing is amazing!" Amari cheered as she pushed the small craft hard at a nearby asteroid and banked around it. "I want to be a constable now!"

"Or a race car driver in Le Mans," Rix said. "You'd for sure like to do that."

"Earth cars?"

"Really fast ones."

"That does sound like my speed. What more do you want me to test?" Amari said, the thrill of the moment evident in her voice.

"How about a ten-minute burn out and back," Rix said. "Shake it up a little. You figure a constable is likely to be mixing it up with the criminal element. Best if we find a problem now."

"Can do," Amari said, banking hard and allowing the cruiser's inertia to carry them uncomfortably close to an asteroid before their new acceleration pulled them out of harm's way.

Rix focused his energy on reviewing the subsystems. As Amari sailed, he worked through all of the calibrations by asking for small tweaks in her navigation. And, by the time they'd returned to Patience Station, Rix was certain that the cruiser was ready for business, as long as Quixly didn't mind that it was missing significant portions of hull plating.

"Looks like Atom is back with dinner," Rix said.

"I'm not sure what to think of him," Amari said.

"What's there to think about?" Rix said. "He works hard and does a decent job of listening."

"Doesn't he mess up a lot?"

"Atom? Sort of. It's hard to blame him for things he's never had a chance to learn," Rix said. "He follows instructions decently and he has a good attitude."

"You know what? I like this part of you, Rix Banner."

"Which part?"

"Where you're defending the guy who is generally considered a joke by most of the people on the station. Where they see limited intelligence, you see someone who just needs a little more training."

"Doesn't feel fair, otherwise, does it?"

Amari set the cruiser back down in Rix's shop, surprising Atom so much that the small green alien ended up dropping dinner onto the deck. Shock and horror showed on his face as he looked up at Rix through the cockpit's glass.

"You were saying?" Amari asked, trying not to laugh.

"We might need a warning system," Rix said, popping the canopy. Tears welled up in Atom's eyes and he cowered, clearly worried at Rix's response. Crossing the deck, Rix knelt in front of the small alien, trying to avoid dipping his knee in whatever gravy had covered the meal. Rix gently grabbed Atom's arms. "Hey, you don't need to be afraid. Accidents happen. How about you go get three meals this time, Nerali is going to join us."

"No yells?"

"None at all."

"Rix Banner, this is Patience Station, are you available?" The emergency comms had cut through the conversation he'd been having.

"Go ahead, Patience," Rix said, once again recognizing Hutari's voice.

"We've received an emergency distress call from *Calypso*. The signal was weak, but we have a lock on the origination."

"Can you put the message through?"

Patience Station, this is Calypso. *We've sustained critical damage to major systems due to an unprovoked attack by unmarked hostile ships, which I suspect to be from the Draven Knights pirate organization. I've attached data streams of the entire incident to be shared with Galactic Empire Trading Authority if we're unrecoverable. Please contact my partner, Rix Banner. Time is limited.*

"Oh, crap," Rix said.

17

GRAVITATIONAL PULL

"WHAT IS IT?" Amari asked. "I see stress on your face."

"It's Kel," Rix said. "*Calypso* was attacked and is disabled. I have a data stream."

"Play it," Amari said without hesitation.

"I'll use your projector to put it on the wall," Beverly said, appearing in her Rosie the Riveter coveralls and polka dotted scarf.

The video data stream showed all of *Calypso's* combat and navigational displays in addition to a comprehensive video of the local spaces around the ship. On the ship-to-ship comms, Kel was heard negotiating with a trio of ships that had her cornered near a moon Rix didn't recognize.

"This is Kel Warp, captain of Calypso*, a Galactic Empire registered freighter. I'm transmitting my license. Please stand down,"* she said.

"Negative. You are to heave-to so that we might take you and your crew into custody and seize your vessel."

"We're fully licensed and have a civilian aboard. You have no authority to corner us like this."

"Our scanners indicate your power plant is cycling up. Cease this action immediately or be fired upon."

"Wait, what? My engines are cold. We're coasting, waiting for you jack wagons to figure out that you're breaking Galactic Empire law! I'm recording and will send it to the trade commission!"

"All frequencies are jammed. You will cease hostilities."

"We're not moving. We're not firing weapons. What hostilities!?" Kel's voice was thick with concern.

"Kels. Bad ship, firing!" Philo panicked.

"*Evasive action. Kurth, strap in. This is going to get dicey!"*

Suddenly, the trio of ships closed on *Calypso*, firing both energy weapons and a single missile, which caused rolling flames and smoke to fill the cockpit and then blink out.

"What in the hell?" Rix asked. "They didn't stand a chance."

"Do we have a location?" Amari asked. "We've got to go get them."

"With what?" Rix asked. "Quixly's police cruiser?"

"No, Rix, you have a freighter up in the municipal garage, right?"

"We don't even know if it works," Rix said.

"It was impounded and has sat there for several years. We might be able to make a deal with one of the local haulers, but if that's out by Gestalt, their ships aren't sized right," Amari said.

"Hell," Rix said. "Okay. Take Quixly's cruiser around to the municipal garage, I'll run through and open a bay."

"Aren't you worried about whoever has a price on your head?" she asked.

"Quixly said someone put a message out that I wasn't to be touched. I don't know what that means, exactly, but he seemed to think I'd be relatively safe on Patience," Rix said.

"Did he now?"

"Yes."

"Okay, go, I'll bring this one around," Amari said, running over to the cruiser and jumping in.

"Beverly, raise Quixly, would you?"

"This is Quixly," came the reply a moment later as Rix dashed down the hallway toward the elevators.

"Quixly, I have a problem."

"Oh? Let me guess, you need my help."

"Not exactly," Rix said. "I'm delivering your cruiser and I need you to free up that freighter in the municipal garage."

"Does this have anything to do with the message you got from Kel?" he asked.

"Did you watch that?"

"It was encrypted, so no."

"Does it matter, then? I'm delivering the second of two cruisers. That freighter is my payment," Rix said.

"And you plan to do what with it?"

"Does it sail?" Rix asked.

"I have no idea. It did a few years ago."

"Are you going to release it or not?"

"I'm coming down," he said. "If the cruiser is in good shape, I'll honor the deal."

"Thank you. And, not to be a pain, could you come fast? Kel is in trouble," Rix said. "... Quixly?"

"Comms were terminated, Rix," Beverly said.

"Okay, connect with Atom, would you?"

"I can't. He does not have an earwig that he uses."

"Seriously?"

"He has lived in poverty for most of his life, if his description is to be believed," Beverly said. "That earwig has been outside of his financial means."

"How is it that I can talk to him while I'm in the ship and he's in the shop?"

"I've been routing through the public address."

"Your intelligence is underestimated."

"I suppose that puts me in good company."

Rix pushed at the hatch to the municipal garage and found that it was locked. When he tried the security panel, his credentials were denied. "Beverly, tell Amari to hold on, Quixly has me locked out for the moment."

"We've discussed it before, but if you simply address the person first, I'll correctly route your conversation to include opening a comm channel," she said.

"I'll hold," Amari responded a moment later.

"What in blazes are you in such a hurry about?" Quixly asked.

"I'll send you the video. I hope that legal action is possible. They attacked her, unprovoked."

"Who attacked whom?"

"Unmarked ships attacked *Calypso*."

"Kel skirts Dravari law. If that's Dravari, they're unlikely to give her much latitude."

"I don't think Dravari. I'll send it to you," Rix said. "This isn't a lack of latitude. It's a hit job. Maybe as mayor, you can send it to someone who will recognize the injustice."

"I believe you overestimate my influence." As they'd been arguing, Quixly had opened the municipal garage and was walking toward a bay door, where he flipped on the photonic barrier and then opened the metal exterior doors. "Tell your pilot to bring it in."

"Nerali, go ahead," Rix said.

"I thought you were going to fill the hull voids and paint it like you did the last one," Quixly complained.

"Not part of my work order," Rix said. "I sent an offer for what I'd need to complete that work. Once I get back, I'll be happy to do that for you. Just sign the invoice."

"You certify this cruiser is in good mechanical working order?" Quixly asked.

"I'll warrant my work for thirty days," Rix said. "As long as you don't get into a dust-up, I'll fix whatever issues come up, labor free."

"What, not parts?"

"Sorry, it's an older craft. I have no idea what might be ready to break next," Rix said.

"I can see you're in a pinch," Quixly said. "I hereby authorize transfer ownership of freighter, *Gravitational Pull*, to Rix Banner and revoke all other ownership claims of same vessel."

"*Gravitational Pull*," Rix mused with half a smile. "That's clever."

Amari settled the cruiser onto the deck and popped the cockpit so she could walk out the front. Looking square at Quixly, she nodded professionally and then gave a quizzical look to Rix, clearly questioning what their next move was.

"You look almost familiar," Quixly said.

"Nerali Sa'Vel," Amari said without batting an eye. "I come from Nerath-Vel but arrived a few months ago."

"Ah, right, I've seen you around. What are you doing with Rix Banner?"

"He offered me employment. We're working on a farm project together," she said.

"Are you curious or interrogating?" Rix asked. "Nerali, I have ownership of *Gravitational Pull*, we need to see if we can get her going. I'm sorry, Quixly, we're short on time. We need to go."

"Of course, Banner. It's always some kind of emergency with you," Quixly said.

"Give me a break," Rix said. "My emergencies come from Patience Station's outdated subsystems, most of the time."

"No need to be sensitive. You have your ship, already."

Rix shook his head and turned toward *Gravitational Pull.* Blocky and half again bigger than *Calypso*, *Gravitational Pull* had the aerodynamic profile of a brick mortared to the front of a cinder block.

"Can you sail this thing?" Rix asked, looking at Amari.

"If you can get it running, I can," Amari said.

"Open the bay doors. I'll get it started," Rix said with determination, forgetting about Quixly's presence and jogging over to the homely craft. As he approached, he realized his mental description of block and brick wasn't that far off. "Are there two sections to this thing?"

To the outside observer, his question likely sounded like he was talking to himself. Beverly, however, knew better.

"*Gravitational Pull* is much like the tractor trailers of your home world, Rix," she said. "The large boxes that trail the forward passenger compartment are stackable, removable and standardized."

On Rix's HUD, outlines of a pair of stacked, cubical containers lifted from a long, narrow frame that was connected to the forward passenger compartment. Along the frame were outriggers upon which hung hefty engines made for pushing heavy loads.

"Not overly sophisticated," Rix observed, stepping onto a tall platform that gave him access to the starboard hatch of the freighter's cab.

"There's little power in the reserve batteries," Beverly said, highlighting a slowly throbbing indicator on the dash.

"Holy cow, this thing isn't much for luxury accommodations," Rix said. "I can't imagine taking this on a long haul."

"You're right, Rix. *Gravitational Pull* is an intrasellar hauler, designed for two pilots and trips that can be accomplished in days, not weeks. There have been multiple lawsuits against the manufacturer due to physical injury incurred by long haul freighter pilots. These vessels have been phased out due to the lack of crew quarters."

"Do we have enough power to run diagnostics?" Rix asked.

"We might have enough power to start one of the engines. I will capture the diagnostics log regardless of success," Beverly said. "I'm projecting the startup sequence onto your HUD."

"Thanks," Rix said as he started working through it. "Good Lord, this thing sounds like one of those old diesel Caterpillars trying to start in the winter." And he was right. As the heavy freighter engine internal mechanism started to slowly spin, it made a deep, slow chugging sound that very much resembled the large bore diesel of an earth moving machine.

"My gosh, what is this thing burning?" Amari called over comms.

Rix looked up and through the wide, flat glass that stretched from one side of the cockpit to the other. Black soot poured from the starboard engine, which was struggling to start. The soot had almost entirely filled the municipal garage.

"Beverly?" Rix asked. "Is this a problem?"

"I don't know. Generally not. This engine has a purge facility that expels impurities in the fuel. That subsystem can fail and you end up getting what you're seeing here."

"What does it take to fix?" Rix asked. "Is it harming the engine?"

"We'd need time to look through the engine, Rix. It could be a number of things, including a bad batch of fuel," she said. "According to what I can find, this isn't particularly harmful to the engine, although the efficiency of the fuel usage is quite poor under these circumstances."

"How poor? Fifty percent worse or a thousand times?" Rix asked. "Do we have enough fuel to get to Kel and back?"

"It is a seventy-five percent increase in fuel consumption," Beverly said. "The recommendation is to purge the existing fuel and refuel. Repairs are called for if that does not resolve the issue. I cannot find much data on the impact of sailing long distances with this kind of ongoing failure."

"There's no part we can have manufactured expeditiously and put on before we leave?"

"No."

Amari climbed into the cab and shook her head. "Just so we're clear, I've never sailed something like this before. I'm not going to be good at it."

"At least you have an idea," Rix said. "Run us over to the fuel depot if you can."

"She's hemorrhaging greasy black smoke, Rix. We don't need fuel. We need a mechanic. Know one?" Amari asked pointedly.

"Turns out, this isn't a life-or-death mechanical failure," Rix said. "We just need extra fuel."

"That's crazy," Amari said, holding Rix's gaze for a moment.

"If you have another option, I'm all ears," Rix said.

"Okay, fuel it is. Then what?"

"Back to Bay 807. Are you going out to rescue Kel with me?"

"Of course, I am," she said, slowly nudging the unwieldy freighter out of the bay and into space. "You've admitted it yourself. You have no idea how to sail this thing. At least I'm just intimidated by its size."

"At least we're holding atmosphere," Rix said.

With the first engine started, a generator started filling the nearly depleted batteries and provided more than enough power to the cab to get everything going. A string of colorful lights hung from small hooks over the cab's forward glass shield. On the dash, centered between the two seats was a doll that resembled a middle-aged woman. As the ship trudged along the doll did a sort of belly dance.

"She's not exactly sleek," Amari said, raising her voice over the increased noise in the cab. Rix realized the noise must have been from the engines because just as soon as the cab passed into vacuum, the noise abated instantly.

"I don't think we'll be talking about how roomy she is, either," Rix said. "I think this must have been built for a solo or two-person team. And I think I have a broken spring in this chair digging into my back."

"What did you expect in exchange for a couple of days' work?"

"Fair point, but it's not like this thing had value to Quixly," Rix said, climbing from his chair into a small space behind. On one side, directly behind where Amari sat, was a countertop and several closed cabinets. There was a water tap, which unsurprisingly didn't work, a small food re-heater and a half-sized refrigerator. Opening the cabinets, he found several bottles of water and a stack of old meal bars. When he opened the refrigerator, a foul smell accosted his nose and he failed to recognize what might have previously been stored within it.

"What is that smell, Rix?" Amari asked.

"Refrigerator needs cleaning."

"Do you know how many days it'll take to travel to Kel?"

"Not yet, we'll need to plot it. Maybe punch it into this navigation computer, although it is beyond old."

"Five days if at full acceleration," Beverly answered.

Rix did a little math. "Working water would be a good idea. We're going to be in here for a while."

"It could just be out. Is there anything in the reservoir?" Amari asked. "Did you figure out how long it'll take?"

"Five days," Rix said.

"Patience Station, this is *Gravitational Pull* entering local space, destination fuel depot and then Bay 807," Amari called.

"You are cleared, *Gravitational Pull,*" Hutari answered. "*Gravitational Pull,* are you aware of off-gassing coming from your aft engine on starboard?"

"Thank you, Patience," Amari answered. "We're working through maintenance issues."

"Good luck, *Gravitational Pull*. Patience Station out."

"If I didn't know better, I'd say Hutari isn't impressed," Rix said, turning around in the space behind the chairs. Opposite the micro-sized galley was what was once a compact exercise machine that doubled as extra seating. Lines, handles and a treadmill belt were a jumble of junk that had been ignored long before the ship had been given up to Quixly.

"She's probably seen worse, but not much worse," Amari said.

"I'm not sure where we're supposed to sleep."

"Look up," Amari said.

Even before she'd said it, Rix's eyes had been drawn to a hatch in the deck below his feet and an open hatch above. A slim ladder was built into the aft wall, something Rix had mistaken for shelving. Climbing up, he stuck his head into a space that was as large as the galley and cockpit area combined, although not tall enough for someone to stand within. Grimy old mattresses lay on the upper room floor, and two more seats were built into the floor right above the cockpit with a strip of glass on the forward bulkhead, giving a great view of space. Rix was certain he wasn't about to sleep on the mattresses and wondered if he wanted to know what the source of the black stains he discovered might be.

"There's a sleeping bunk above," he informed Amari when he climbed down. "It's kind of disgusting, but I can see the value of it."

"That sounds like a common enough configuration," Amari said.

Rix opened the hatch in the deck and climbed down. He could almost stand in the narrow confines of the lower deck, which was packed with the craft's micro-sized subsystems, including grey/black water handling, atmospheric filters, navigation, flight, gravity and inertial systems.

"Is there a console?" he asked, only to have Beverly use his HUD to highlight a flip-down shelf that exposed a keyboard and screen. "Let's get some diagnostics going. I need to figure out if this will get us out to Kel and Philo or not."

"Copy that. Give me maintenance access, would you?" Beverly asked.

A prompt on the console asked for exactly that access and Rix agreed. With that done, he started working through the subsystems, checking for critical issues that could end their flight. There were many and his heart sank. In essence, *Gravitational Pull* was operating on a hope and a prayer, not solid mechanical underpinnings.

"We need to shift gears on this," Rix said. "Can you help me identify every filter and fluid that I'll have access to while underway. We'll do a bunch of cleaning, refitting filters, greasing bearings, you know, basic maintenance."

"I don't believe there are bearings to be greased," Beverly said. "That is, unless that's a euphemism for sex."

"Stop," Rix said dryly.

"Three hundred for fuel, water and a change-out of atmosphere and emergency atmo," Amari said.

"Are we registered under my name? I authorize the expenditure," Rix said.

"That worked," Amari answered and then muttered. "Not exactly sure how, though."

"Take us back to the shop. I need to load up tools for the road. I think we're looking at an hour before we roll. I have items at the manufactory."

Rix looked around for something to scoop the contents of the refrigerator into. There was a bucket in the engineering deck, complete with a rag. Bringing both back to the galley, he set to scooping out the glop into the bucket as best he could. Opening one of the water bottles, he washed most of the residual out, but it wasn't clean enough to hold food. He tried the sink tap and discovered it still didn't work.

Having not found a bathroom, Rix once again went below so he could trace the greywater lines, which he did easily. Back up to the galley area, he found a hidden door that opened to a tiny all-in-one head where the toilet folded down from the wall, giving just enough room for a shower when uncompacted. He tried the hose that functioned as both showerhead and sink tap and discovered he had water. Cleaning the rag he'd found, Rix was then able to make more progress on the refrigerator, and while it would do for an emergency, he promised himself he'd scrub it more.

"We'll need to release the containers from *Gravitational Pull* if we're putting her into the shop," Amari warned. "Are you up for doing that?"

"One minute," Rix said. "Beverly, I need some quick training on how to do what she's saying."

"Who are you talking to?" Amari asked.

"Hold on," Rix said, watching the release sequence for the storage containers *Gravitational Pull* had locked onto her cargo rails. Like most things, the sequence wasn't particularly complex, but Rix imagined there'd be complications due to the amount of time that'd passed since *Gravitational Pull* had been in operation. "Go ahead and pull up to our slip. I think I know how to get these containers off."

"Really?"

"I'm pretty good at this sort of thing," Rix said, donning the helmet of his space suit. Opening the cabinet in the mechanical's room, he found a retractable tether in reasonable working shape. Next to that tether was the main tool used to detach the storage containers, and it didn't take much imagination as to why the two items were found together.

Twenty minutes later, *Gravitational Pull* was sitting on the shop floor, with a very surprised Atom looking on. Rix smiled, grateful that the excitable alien hadn't once again dropped their food.

"Machine smells, bad," Atom said as Rix and Amari climbed down from the cab.

"There's been a change of plans, Atom," Rix said. "Nerali and I are going on a trip."

18

ROAD TRIP

"Atom come?" Atom asked.

"We're going in that," Rix said, pointing at *Gravitational Pull*, which beneath the bright shop lights looked even more dilapidated than it had in the municipal garage.

A flash of confusion crossed Atom's simple face. "No good trip. Bad ship."

"My point is, it's too small, Atom," Rix said. "I have a parts order at the manufactory, though. I need you to go fetch it, would you?"

"Eats?"

"Sorry, we're going to have to eat later," Rix said, grabbing a grav pallet atop which he began stacking tool bags. "You can stay in the shop, though. I'll leave some money for food while we're gone."

"Get manufactory," Atom said with an irritated look.

"I think I pissed him off," Rix said after Atom exited the room.

"You two are awfully familiar for only having met yesterday," Amari observed. "You can't treat a Grintok like you do. He's never going to leave the safety you're offering."

"I've hardly done that," Rix said.

"Making him a bed and buying him dinner? Those are probably the two nicest things anyone has ever done for him. If you don't plan to keep him around, you better make a clean break, right now, or it won't be fair to him," she said.

"I'll deal with it when we get back," Rix said. "I can't add something in the middle of an emergency."

Amari nodded but it was clear she wasn't in complete agreement. "I'll pack the meal bars. Are we trying to get fresh foods for the trip? Trust me, I'm fine without."

"I'm out of cash," Rix admitted. "I think we're surviving on meal bars and protein paste for now."

"Welcome to much of my life," Amari said with a sideways grin. "I'll pack enough food for two weeks."

Rix nodded and shifted to something that had been bothering him. "I don't understand why you're coming," he said. "Have I obligated you somehow?"

"You can be dense. Did you know that?" Amari asked.

"I don't even know what that means," Rix said. "My point is, if you want to step away from this, you can."

"Do you have any idea how to sail something like *Gravitational Pull*?"

"No."

"Then there's your simple answer. I'm coming because Kel and Philo have a better chance at surviving if I do."

"That's noble," Rix said, pushing a pallet over to *Gravitational Pull* where he started unloading tool bags and carrying them up into the vehicle's cab.

"Not exactly the word I'd use," Amari said with some exasperation. Instead of continuing the conversation, though, she set to the task of counting out food for the trip. "Hey, tell me about the water situation," she called over comms.

"Oh, shoot," Rix said. "I need to manufacture an earwig for Atom."

"You're doing it again, Rix. Giving him a gift is cementing your relationship."

"And he's at a huge disadvantage in society without it," Rix argued.

"Forty-five credits for an expedited run, Rix," Beverly cut in.

"Done."

As much as Rix wanted to leave immediately, he also knew that once they were in space, there would be no coming back to the shop for forgotten items. "Beverly, would you inventory the items I've packed and make recommendations?"

"You have a comprehensive set of tools. You lack necessary cleaning supplies and from our prior interactions, I believe this will likely cause considerable problems. Also, it is unlikely you will sleep on the mattresses in the sleeping bunk. I suggest ejecting them and taking them to the large item reclaimer station. I detected a dormant infestation of space mites."

"Oh yikes, seriously? Okay, make a list of cleaning items, but we need to get going," Rix said, climbing up into the overhead bunk. "How does this come out?" Rix scanned the walls for a hatch to push the mattresses out of but didn't find anything.

"You will compress the mattresses with load straps. Also, first wrap them with a tarp or you will spread mites to other surfaces."

"This is disgusting," Rix said, climbing out so he could grab both load straps and a tarp. It took half an hour for Rix to remove the mattresses and another fifteen minutes to stuff them into a nearby reclaimer slot. The reclaimer credits were negated by the poor condition of the mattresses, but Rix felt good about removing the mess, regardless.

"Heavy load. Clear way," Atom called, pushing a cart filled with filters of various sizes and bottles of different kinds of fluids. It was enough that Rix wondered what he might have gotten into. Walking ahead, he opened the door to the shop for Atom.

"Is there any of this that I need to install before we get underway?" Rix asked.

"I don't know," Amari said, not realizing Rix was asking Beverly.

"Yes, see the maintenance bulletin," Beverly said, starting a short video that showed how to drain two hydraulic reservoirs lashed to the backside of *Gravitational Pull's* cab. The bottles were enough to completely replace the contents of the reservoir.

"That's a forty-minute job," Rix complained.

"And it controls the main engine positioning," Beverly retorted. "Amari was unable to make adjustments which suggests the lines are likely shot or at least they have air within them."

"Did you make new lines?"

"Yes."

"That's probably faster. Atom, here's an earwig," Rix said, picking up the small package containing an unregistered earwig. "Put that in so we can talk without being next to each other."

"For me?" Atom asked, his face blank and untrusting.

"Yes, for you, put them in," Rix said, struggling to hide his frustration at the delays. "And then bring the black hoses in package number four over to me."

Rix grabbed a plastic barrel and dragged it up and behind *Gravitational Pull's* cab, where he proceeded to disconnect long braided lines that ran within a channel in the cargo rail, leading back to the batwing braces, which allowed the main engines to swing up and down in an arc. Leaving one end of each of four lines in the barrel, he moved aft where he was able to disconnect the lines and allow fluid to seep out. Instead of waiting for the discarded lines to finish draining, he just stuffed them into the barrel and then drained the reservoirs before attaching new lines.

"What more do you need me to do, Rix?" Amari asked. "I used your buzzbroom to clean the bunk deck. It was filthy and still needs a more thorough cleaning. I put in as much bedding as I could find, but you're seriously lacking in that department."

"It'll take twenty more minutes to get these lines bled," Rix said. "I think we're good for takeoff after that. Remind me to send Petju some money to feed Atom once we're off, okay? Atom, load the rest of the supplies into the galley area behind the main seats. I'll organize things once we get on the road. Beverly, what am I missing?"

A sharp turn of Amari's head told Rix that she'd heard the last. "That's the third time. Who is Beverly?" Amari asked. "Are you working with someone on the station? Rix, I need to know if there are other people involved."

"We'll talk about it once we're moving," Rix said, putting the cap back on the reservoir he'd just topped off. "And I'm done with that. Atom, how are you coming with those supplies?"

"He's almost done," Amari said. "I'm bringing a couple of the larger filters right behind him."

"Okay, Atom, now here's the deal," Rix said. "We're going to be gone for ten to twelve days. My partners, Kel and Philo, are in a spot. They might need our help. Geez, I hope they still need our help."

"Don't talk like that," Amari said. "We'll get there in time."

Rix pursed his lips, suppressing emotion he hadn't realized he was carrying. "I know," he finally managed. "I'm going to give Petju money for food for you while we're gone."

"Atom not stay. Philo friend."

"Atom, you're not coming. *Gravitational Pull* is already too small. There's no room."

When Atom didn't respond, Rix hoped it was the end of the conversation. As a last consideration, Rix grabbed his lode bean coffee stores, a couple of bottles of Collie's Reserve rum and the makings of the Fisherman's Folly drink that he and Philo both enjoyed.

Like all good road trips, there were packages, crates and bags stuffed everywhere, as neither Rix nor Amari had spent any time considering how best to organize *Gravitational Pull's* extremely limited space.

"Have you seen Atom?" Rix asked, not seeing him in the main part of the cab, nor when he looked up into the bunk.

"Last I saw, he was headed back for those boxes you're standing next to," Amari said. Rix opened the hatch to the lower deck and peered around, making sure the little alien wasn't hiding. "He was upset with you telling him he couldn't come."

"Atom, we're about to take off. Please get clear of the ship," Rix said. He waited for a few minutes. "I guess he's not responding. We need to go."

"Without the containers, you should have an easier time backing this thing out," Amari said. "No time like the present to learn."

"That's a good idea," Rix agreed, running through *Gravitational Pull's* startup sequence. As before, a greasy black cloud of exhaust filled the shop just as the exceptionally loud, throated rumble of the poorly insulated engines coughed to life. “Boy, that does not sound good.”

“You better get it out before you set off air quality alarms on Patience,” she said.

“This thing is irascible,” Rix complained as *Gravitational Pull* slipped sideways, even though he’d applied no pressure to the flight stick.

“Feather it the other direction, the trim adjustments are worn,” Amari said. “Keep a light touch, though or you’ll—“

Metal against metal screamed as Rix’s adjustment sent *Gravitational Pull* careening off the wall, leaving a deep jagged scratch. Generally difficult to flap, Rix nudged the stick away, uninterested in repeating the damage on the opposite side, which he very nearly did.

“Like ice skating without skates,” he grumbled, recalling long winters back home in Wisconsin.

“Ohh, you’re close,” Amari said, tensing up, fully expecting to hit the station again. Fortunately, Rix managed to just miss sideswiping a second time and cleared the threshold of Bay 807’s opening. “Good job.”

“I’m not sure *good* is the word you’re looking for,” Rix said, nudging the stick so the craft turned away from the station. “Patience Station, this is *Gravitational Pull*, we’re departing for a time, over,” Rix said.

“*Gravitational Pull*, you are cleared for local space and beyond. Safe travels and hurry back. Patience Station, out,” Hutari answered.

“Hutari’s working late,” Rix observed.

“She knew you’d be making a run to retrieve *Calypso*,” Amari said.

“And Kel and Philo,” Rix said sullenly.

“Oh, I’m so sorry. Of course, them too,” Amari said. “Would you like me to take the controls while we’re negotiating the asteroid belt?”

"That's a good idea," Rix said. "I'll see about organizing."

Rix moved back into the galley area and just sat for a moment. It had already been a long day before the news of *Calypso's* trouble. The pressure of launching a vessel with an unknown, likely suspect maintenance history had been a lot of added stress, and he took a moment to just sit and reflect.

"Are you doing okay back there?" Amari asked after an undetermined time, as Rix's eyes had closed and he found himself waking to her voice.

"I'm apparently tired," Rix said. "I fell asleep."

"I saw that," she said.

"How long was I out?"

"Two hours."

"Oh, shoot. I'm sorry. Do you need me to take a shift?"

"We're on a long straightaway," Amari said. "The autopilot is mostly working, so I think we're okay for the time."

"What does mostly working mean?"

"No matter what we do, there's drift in our course," she said. "It's like the ship doesn't know what straight is."

"It probably doesn't," Rix said. "There are calibrations to keep that working right."

"Well, it's not a big issue," Amari said. "We'll lose maybe twenty minutes on the journey out."

Rix nodded, blinking away the sleep that pulled at him. "Um, right, okay. Let me do some unpacking and then we can see about shifts for the overnight."

"Take your time, although if you can get the coffee set up, I'd be up for a cup," she said.

"I'll focus on stowing the food and getting that set up."

Knowing he hadn't done a great job of cleaning the cupboards over the actual galley, Rix set to that task, first removing every object and then using the cleansers they'd brought along to remove decades of sticky grime from every surface. Aware they had more time than anything else, Rix scrubbed hard and had to dump out dirty water several times into the drain within the head.

With cabinets clean, Rix first packed away the meal bars and protein pastes. He then moved on to the liquor and then finally the coffee beans. Setting up the coffee maker had him extending straps from the wall behind the counter to hold it in place, and after forty minutes of work, the smell of fresh lode bean coffee filled the cab.

"That smells amazing," Amari said when Rix brought a pair of cups forward and sat down next to her.

"You're a good sport for coming along," Rix said.

"Kel's been a good friend," Amari said. "I'm glad you're okay with me coming along."

And then, unexpectedly, Amari reached over and picked up Rix's hand. Turning, Rix looked at her, trying to read her face, but found she was leaning back against the padded chair and staring out into space.

"Is this okay?" she asked after a few minutes, lifting Rix's hand.

"It feels nice, Amari."

"It doesn't need to mean anything more than what it is," Amari said.

Rix looked at her with raised eyebrows. With every part of the last few weeks being busy beyond belief, and then the death of Shixen, he hadn't considered Amari a romantic potential. They'd danced around the topic a few times, but with all the stress, it just hadn't seemed honorable to Rix to pursue her.

"I like being with you, Amari," Rix said, seeing if there was room to open the door. It had been a long time since he'd been in a relationship and, while their timing wasn't great, he was interested enough not to let things drop.

"Thank you, Rix. Same. I don't think you know how much I appreciate you peeking into my life and not running away screaming," she said.

"I'm the one on the hit list," Rix said, chuckling. "You should be the one running away, screaming. Apparently, in space, I'm a danger magnet. Back home, I was just a simple guy, fixing cars."

"Do you miss home?"

"Sort of?" Rix said, as more of a question than an answer.

"You don't sound convinced."

"Life around here is more exciting. The people are more alive," Rix said. "It's hard to come back from war and then turn everything off. Don't get me wrong. I love mechanical work. But now, with all this technology, everything is so thrilling."

"You're holding hands with an alien," she said. "That's probably something none of your friends back home did, right?"

"A gorgeous, shapeshifting alien," Rix corrected. "I hope that isn't offensive."

"Not at all," Amari said. "I worked hard to make this form as pleasing to the eye as I possibly could."

"So, it's not as much of a compliment, though, since it's not really you," Rix said. "I guess I'm not sure how you think about it."

"A compliment is a compliment," she said, shrugging and releasing Rix's hand.

"You're a little offended?"

"Oh, because I let go of your hand?" she asked. "No, that's not it. This chair is made for a different person than me. It's digging into my butt, so I have to adjust."

"Are you feeling good about *Gravitational Pull's* performance, so far?"

"It's doing what we talked about. I'm a little nervous about its condition, but these old cargo haulers are built tough, and we have a brilliant mechanic aboard," she grinned at Rix.

"Is it offensive to ask about your natural form?" Rix asked. "It's just a curiosity and I don't mean anything by it."

"Tejlari only share their natural form with people they have built strong, trusting relationships with. This Nerali form can be replaced with some effort. My true form cannot be replaced, so it's a bit of a secret."

"I understand," Rix said.

"I'll show you if you want," she said.

"Why? It's a secret."

"Sometimes, a person wants to be known," Amari said.

"I have a question, first."

"Sure."

"Is Amari your real name? You don't have to tell me what it is. I'm just wondering if I should be calling you something else," Rix said.

"You're asking because my Amari form is who you were introduced to," she said.

"Right."

"Yes, it's Amari," she said. "It's close to my natural form. Not easily confused for the same, though."

"That's mysterious," Rix said.

"You'll understand. Are you sure you want to see this? It might change your opinion about me."

"Is that what you're afraid of?" Rix asked. "We're starting to get a little close and you're worried I won't like the real you?"

"Something like that." Amari said. "How about this? I'm going to go up into the bunk room. It'll take a couple of minutes for me to shift. Come up in five, okay?"

"Will all this be okay?" Rix asked, gesturing at the vessel's controls.

"We're clear for one hundred thousand kilometers in every direction," she said. "I'll set a proximity alarm."

"Okay."

Rix watched as Amari climbed from the seat and escaped through the galley and up into the bunk. She was an attractive woman in her shifted shape. He worried about what she wanted to show him. Would he find her so unattractive that it changed his opinion? It was plain to him that she wanted to see if her alienness would run him off.

"I'm ready, Rix," she called after a while.

"I feel like I'm thirteen and at a party playing seven minutes in heaven," Rix said.

"I don't know what that is," Amari said. "Are you nervous? I promise, I won't hurt you. Just close your eyes on the way up."

"Well, heck, now I'm nervous. I wasn't thinking you'd hurt me."

Amari sighed but didn't say anything more. Rix climbed the ladder into the bunk room and padded his hands around until he found the elevated ledge at the aft where he could sit.

"Now, open your eyes slowly," she said.

The suspense was killing him, and he wasn't certain why if the shift was something like Amari form to Nerali form, it would require moving to the bunk. Opening his eyes, he was careful to locate her head so he could make sure he wasn't looking at her in a way she'd misinterpret. Her face came into focus, and she was right, she closely resembled the Amari form, except her features were edgier, her cheekbones more pronounced and her jaw a little sharper. Amari's natural form was almost painfully beautiful.

"You're beautiful, Amari," Rix breathed, suddenly needing a bit more air.

"Honorable to keep your eyes up, but you need to see all of me," Amari said. With peripheral vision, he could tell that Amari wasn't wearing much, if any clothing and while the idea was alluring, he wanted to be respectful. "You have my permission to look, Rix Banner."

Rix allowed his eyes to jump to something that'd been bothering him but he'd forced himself to ignore. There was something behind her that undulated, waving. Suddenly, all worries about catching a glance at her naked chest were lost as he found that the thing he'd missed were gossamer wings with dark veins running through them. "Wings," he managed through the dryness of his mouth.

"Yes, wings, Rix," she said calmly. "Look more. You need to see everything."

Rix couldn't keep his eyes from her chest and to his great relief, he found that she had what he would describe as a very natural human form with a bit more pigmentation in critical areas. Not wanting to stop there, he continued to look at her, his brain picking out incongruities and drawing his eyes to her arms and then hands. Beneath pale skin, dark blood ran through her veins, making them more prominent than usual. Her hands were slightly more elongated than that of a human woman, perhaps thirty percent longer, and her fingers were tipped with long, blood red nails that ended in sharp points. His eyes then flicked to her feet, which, not unexpectedly, were similar.

"Are you afraid now, Rix Banner?" she said in a sultry voice. "Do you find me terrifying to behold?"

"Do they work?" Rix ignored her question, looking from her wings back into her face, which was framed by jet black hair.

While she'd been trying for seductive or menacing, Rix's question caught her off guard. "My people have been called angels of death to those who know of our true form," she said. "It is a name that has been earned through the generations."

"I don't know about what you've earned or not," Rix said. "I wasn't expecting some of what you've got going on, but if your question is am I scared, I don't fully understand. Are you grumpier in this form? Because mostly, I wasn't thinking your personality changed."

"You are serious. Are you not overcome by lust for me? Do you not wish to control me?"

"Well, I don't want to be closing any doors here," Rix said. "You're, for certain, drop-dead gorgeous. Going naked, however, is probably why you get that lust thing, if that's your opening move. Guys love ... well, all of what you've got going there. So you have long fingernails. I'm still getting stuck on if they work ... the wings."

"I was told there are men like you, Rix Banner. I did not think I would meet one," she said.

"Is that good or bad?"

"In my true form, I can sense things such as attraction, fear, excitement, and yes, lust," she said. "There are many who are attracted to Tejlari in a way that is controlling. You have no difficulty controlling this urge."

"I'll admit, you're quite attractive. Enough to make my heart speed up, I'm sure of that," he said. "But you're wrong about one thing."

"What is that?"

"I have *no* urge to control you," he said. "And are you purposefully ignoring my question about the wings? Because that'd be incredibly cool, aside from my thinking that they're not big enough to really lift a woman of your size."

"And now I'm fat?"

Rix laughed. "And this is why I fail."

19

SPACE FLEAS

"Aaah, crap!" Rix cursed as the wrench he was twisting slipped off the nut and his knuckles skimmed across the rusted edge seam of the fuel transfer junction case. He hopped up and down for a moment as he shook his hand, wondering just how much skin he'd removed and what kind of bleeding he was in for. He'd been working for a couple of hours on what should have been simple filter replacements but had turned into a frustrating exercise in frozen bolts.

"Are you okay?" Amari called back, her voice filtering down to the lower deck. "What are you doing down there?"

"Is it that much to think anyone in an advanced society would *actually* service the highly advanced, technically superior equipment," Rix called back, irritation evident in his voice.

"Look Bub, don't get testy with me," Amari answered. "You bought this piece of poop, not me. I'm just doing my best to keep it moving forward."

"Ah, sorry, that wasn't meant for you," Rix said, grabbing a laser drill to vaporize the bolt. Unlike drilling bolts back in his garage in Wisconsin, the laser drill's ability to control temperature was so fine that the bolts could be slagged and sucked out without damaging the housing, made from alloy with a higher melting point. "It's just this equipment would be in much better shape if people *actually* used filters, you know, where they're designed to fit. Also, power off for ten minutes, okay?"

"Go ahead," Amari answered.

Rix didn't even try to free the final bolts, but instead blasted them away, losing patience that would potentially save him from running out of spare bolts, something he hadn't previously worried about but which was starting to become a concern.

"Figures," Rix said, wedging a screwdriver into the seam between filter housing and the junction case. Not unexpectedly, it took more power than he'd hoped, and when it suddenly released, he was unable to catch the housing before it crashed onto the deck.

"Sounds like my favorite mechanic is having one of those days." Amari's voice was much closer than it had been and Rix looked up, finding her leaning over the edge of the main deck so that she was looking at him upside down. "Can I make you a drink? I noticed you brought that Collie's Reserve."

"No thanks. Do you see this?" Rix asked, swiping two fingers along the inside of the junction case. When he removed his fingers, he brought along a thick black sludge and the remnants of something unrecognizable.

"Is that the old filter?"

"Yes. This power plant has forty-seven thousand hours on it," Rix said. "Believe it or not, it only needs to be serviced every two thousand hours. Care to guess how many hours ago this filter was replaced?"

"Like ten thousand?" Amari asked innocently.

"Never. In forty-seven thousand hours of operation, not one engineer, mechanic, pilot, owner, or head cook thought to open this housing up and swap out a filter. It would have been better if they'd simply taken the filter out after a few thousand hours, because all this gunk is equal parts the stuff we wanted to filter, plus the decay of the actual filter."

"You're passionate about this. I can tell," Amari said, working hard not to sound patronizing. "It'll be all fixed up after you clean that out and put in a new filter, right?"

A smile tugged at Rix's face but was quickly erased when a large goober of black goo splattered on his coveralls, catching his chin as it did. "Yeah," he sighed. "This and twelve more like it. Thing is, if I have to burn out all the bolts, I don't have enough replacements."

"What are you thinking about for dinner?" Amari asked, unperturbed. "I'm thinking a nice pairing of rum and crunchy meal bar. You can get cleaned up and we can watch something from the media library you got from Earth. You know, you never did tell me how you managed to get that library. The story I recall hearing was you and Kels were running for your lives when you took off from Earth. Doesn't seem like you had the technology to grab all that."

"Tell her most of the library is from broadcast signals and it was Kel that put it together for you," Beverly said, appearing in clean coveralls, sitting on the junction case.

"We don't have things with storage like you have," Rix said. "Well, we do, but we call them tapes and they're not the sort of thing you can easily access. The programs are constantly being transmitted and Kel picked a bunch of it up for me. I'd be in to watch something before going to bed. I'm a little frazzled by just how bad of shape this thing is in."

Judiciously, Rix spread solvent into the housing and magically, all the gunk pulled away. The process was mesmerizing enough that Amari enjoyed watching the transition from sludge to spotless with a few expert strokes.

"That cleans up nicely," Amari commented.

"I can't complain about this solvent," Rix said. "I have good stuff back home, but this is incredible." With the housing clean, Rix put a new filter in place and set the cover back. With a tap, he cleaned the threads of the housing and spun bolts into place with just the right amount of torque.

"Why aren't you using a boltgun for that? You should have plenty of bolts available there, right?" Amari asked.

"That's a reasonable question," Rix said. "The boltgun is more for semi-permanent or permanent fixtures."

"Oh, so because you need to do this every couple thousand hours, you want them to be easier to remove."

"You're not just a pretty face."

"Aww, you think I'm pretty?"

"Funny," Rix said as he started cleaning the mess he'd made.

"Why is that funny? You think I'm funny looking?"

"Well ... yeah," Rix said, deadpanning. "You're an alien. Of course you're funny looking."

"What in the heck, Rix?" Amari asked. Her face turned dark as she pulled back from the hatch she was hanging over.

"Good looking for an alien?" Rix called after her and when he didn't hear anything he continued. "I mean, no tentacles or antennae is a pretty low bar, but I like it."

"Oh, you're for sure going to pay for that!" she said, suddenly showing up in the hatch with a piece of fruit that was well beyond its expiration, holding it menacingly.

"You wouldn't," Rix said, raising an eyebrow.

"Wouldn't I?" Amari challenged, whipping her arm around and releasing the fruit. Rix was caught off guard when he discovered that Amari's skill with fruit chucking was quite good, and his right shoulder was tagged with a gooey mess.

"Oh, it's on, now, missy," he said, rushing forward, which caused Amari to yelp with anticipation. Reaching the ladder, he scrabbled up toward her as she reeled back, then hurtled into the ladder space leading up to the sleeping loft.

"Don't come up here, you'll make everything a mess!" she called, her voice a full octave higher than it normally was.

"Oh, no, there's nowhere to run and you're throwing rocks from your glass house," he said, chasing her into the loft.

"Don't ... don't," she said, pointing a finger at him. "I'm all clean. I just took a shower, and I don't have that much clothing aboard." As she spoke, she lunged to the side, trying to avoid his advance, but it was a hopeless move, as he had her trapped and she knew it. "You're going to get our bed dirty. Stop, Rix, really."

"This would be a good time to make a bargain," Rix said. "I'm already dirty, thanks to you. I don't have much to lose."

"Wait, wait, wait," she said, holding up her hands defensively.

"For?" Rix asked, moving vertically with her as she looked for an escape.

"A kiss," she said.

"Hold on, now. You splat me with spoiled fruit and think you can get out of it with a little kiss?" Rix asked. "What must you think of me?"

"No, no, no, not just a little kiss," she said, talking quickly. "You go get cleaned up. Put your suit into the cleaner and I'll make you dinner, a nice drink, and I'll show you a kiss, the likes of which you've never experienced."

"Oh? That good?"

"Shape shifting, exotic alien girl, good. A full twenty seconds of kissing that will change the way you measure every other kiss in your life, good," Amari answered provocatively.

"A minute," Rix bartered.

"Forty seconds," Amari countered.

"I'll get cleaned up," Rix agreed, dropping his arms and turning back to the stairs, which he climbed onto.

"Wait a minute," Amari said.

"What's up?"

"Am I not pretty, you know, compared to Earth girls?" she asked, sounding vulnerable.

"Let's see how that kiss goes."

"You're impossible!" she said, her face flashing with humored frustration as she threw a boot at him. This time, he was ready for her and ducked out of the way, slipping down the ladder.

It took another hour for Rix to finish cleaning up the job he'd started, get himself clean and set his coveralls into the suit cleaner. The two had reached a sort of detente, as *Gravitational Pull* was too small for them to avoid each other while they went about their duties in preparation for the promised, simple dinner.

"You smell a lot better," Amari said.

While Rix had been working on *Gravitational Pull*, Amari had organized the galley and even discovered a small table that folded down from one wall. On the table, she'd set a thin towel that resembled a tablecloth. With two coffee cups filled with a fruit and rum drink she'd invented on the fly and packaged meal bars as the place settings, she'd invited him to sit with her.

"There's something about an alien girl who knows how to put on the Ritz for her special fella," Rix said.

"You're this special Ritz fella, are you?" she asked, turning her head demurely.

"Well, maybe I could be," Rix said. "You know ...,"

"Still wondering about that kiss, are you?" she asked. Rix shrugged, playing innocent. "Stay there. Don't move."

Rix nodded and watched as Amari slid a leg out from beneath the small table and stood with a grace he hadn't expected. Locking eyes, her half smile kept his attention as she slunk around the table and placed a well-manicured hand beneath his chin, holding him transfixed as she lowered her head until their lips were scant millimeters apart.

"Do I have your attention now?" she asked quietly, her warm breath blowing against his face.

"You don't have to do this, Amari," Rix said quietly. "I was just playing."

"Do you want me to keep going?" she whispered, brushing her hand so just the tips of her fingers rested under his chin.

"Yes."

"You're sure?"

As Rix opened his mouth to answer, Amari made her move and pressed her lips into his own. The sensation of her soft lips ran all thoughts from Rix's mind and he responded, careful to keep his excitement in check. For ninety seconds, they kissed, a give and take of emotion and pent-up desire. When they finally parted, they were both left gasping quietly.

"And?" Amari asked, creating distance between them, her hand releasing his chin.

"I don't know. What?" Rix asked, his analytical brain struggling to catch up with the moment.

"Do you find me pretty, Rix? Or am I offensive to the eyes of an Earth man?" she asked with a self-satisfied grin on her face, clearly knowing his answer.

"Well, I can say, without question, that kiss was top five," Rix said.

"Top five?" Amari asked, skeptically.

"At least second place," Rix said. "But it's not a fair comparison."

"Oh?"

"Junior High, Jill Parker, seven minutes in heaven," Rix said.

"This Jill, she was a looker?"

"You have no idea. I was an eighth grader, she was a ninth grader, cheerleader, the works," Rix said. "I had such a crush."

"Good kisser, this Jill Parker?"

"Well, if I'm honest, not really," Rix said. "But man, I was in love."

"You dated after this? I've never heard you talk about yourself, tell me about you and this Jill Parker."

Rix laughed. "Not even close. The next year, she was in high school and I was still in junior high. She was embarrassed about the whole thing."

"That must have felt bad to you."

"At first, a little," Rix said. "But the whole school knew. I was hot stuff after that."

"It is hard to compete with an adolescent crush," Amari said, smiling gently, all pretense of competition gone from her voice.

"You do know I'm kidding, right?" Rix asked.

"Do I?"

"Amari, no Earth girl could compare to you," Rix said. "Physically, every facet of you is perfection."

"Because I've constructed this look."

"Sure, that's reasonable, but your Amari persona is pretty great, too," Rix said. "There's no competition, even with Jill Parker."

"Aside from your crush."

"A man my age is capable of crushes," Rix said. "Play your cards right."

"I love your swagger, Rix Banner," she said. "Perhaps Jill Parker was very good for you, after all. Why did you not pursue her once age was not so important?"

"Jill? Nah, she got married to Barry Hawkins. They have six kids. Nice family," Rix said. "I've never wanted to settle down like that."

"Well done, in that case. You're currently sailing through space in a vessel most wouldn't consider space-worthy, toward unknown danger, to save a friend you don't even know is still alive," Amari said. "You have officially not settled down."

"What do you want out of life, Amari?" Rix asked, leaning back as he picked up the glass of rum punch she'd prepared. "And this isn't bad. The rum is a little rough, but your juice covers well."

"I want to be in charge of my own life," Amari said.

"That's fair. Feels like you're mostly there in this moment. What else?"

"I'm not, though. I've done things that will attract the wrong kind of attention."

"You blew your cover, somehow. Shixen had something on you and when he died, he put you in danger."

"I did something to help a friend. People are looking for me now."

"This isn't about Shixen, is it?"

"Let's leave this alone for now," Amari said, taking a long drink of rum.

"Okay," Rix said. "You were right, though. It was a good kiss; one I'll not likely soon forget."

"And I'm quite the cook," she said, snapping off a chunk of her meal bar.

"Very high rating on your domestic skills," Rix said, grinning.

"I wondered when you'd pick up on that," she said, scrunching her nose and smiling. "Are you tired yet?"

"Getting there," Rix said. "Being in space kind of messes with me, though. My body can't figure out what time it is."

"Oh, I'm glad you said something about that," she said. "That could be a real problem if we don't address it."

"I don't follow."

"Your brain is used to the patterns of a daylight schedule," she said. "On Patience Station, the lighting is controlled so that there is directionality and varying brightness based on time of day. It simulates an optimal twenty-six-hour day in a single star solar system."

"I wondered about that!" Rix said. "I hadn't investigated it yet, but I thought it was strange that it felt like evening was darker than midday. I guess I hadn't picked up on the direction thing."

"The movement of the star overhead is subtle," she said. "The brightness is quite a bit different. Some people have mental struggles without a sense of day and night. We have limited lighting aboard *Gravitational Pull*, but we can do a lot by turning down the lights after 1900 and back up at 0700."

"What time is it now?" Rix asked, checking his HUD as he spoke. "Holy cow, it's 2300, I didn't realize it was so late."

"That's why I was asking if you're tired. I had planned to pull the covers off the bedding and get them cleaned while I scrubbed out the loft. It's just late for that."

"What if we worked together at it? We could do a thirty-minute scrub down while the covers are cleaned. I know I'd feel better about sleeping in clean bedding."

"You've got a deal!"

Cleaning up dinner took little effort, and they agreed that Rix would push the bedding down from the loft to the main deck, where Amari would pull it apart and get it started in the wash while Rix started scrubbing.

"You're seeing these little bugs, right?" Rix asked after ten minutes of scrubbing. The first pass he'd taken had been with his ion broom, but it had quickly become clear that hand-and-knees scrubbing was required.

"Yes," Amari said with obvious disappointment in her voice. "And it's not a good thing. We'll have to set off an aerosol treatment when we get to a space station and after every shower, I have a lotion you need to spread on the back of your neck, or you'll get little bug bites."

"We have space fleas?" Rix asked.

Amari barked out a surprised laugh. "That's a perfect description. They can go dormant for years. I should have anticipated we'd have problems."

"But you brought the lotion."

"I did, and it'll work. I just don't like sharing space with your so-called space fleas. The thought of them crawling over all our stuff is icky."

"Back in the war, we had trouble with lice," Rix said. "Well, more the disease they carried than the actual bugs, but loads of people died from those diseases."

"This would be a similar problem."

"But you were thoughtful enough to bring space flea soap along," Rix said, finishing her thought.

"You're funny," she said, "Let's give this another twenty minutes and then could you bring back the beds, and I'll get the covers out of the cleaner? We'll have made enough progress that we can probably sleep."

"You're not worried about keeping watch?" Rix asked.

"I have a proximity alarm set up," she said. "We'll have at least an hour warning if anything gets close now that we're outside of the Surnac belt."

"So, do pirates have trouble with space fleas?" Rix asked.

"People who don't clean and treat their ships have trouble with space fleas. It really depends on the pirates," she said. "Some pirates are lazy thugs who've found that stealing is easier than finding productive work. Others take more of a business approach."

"Feels like disease really isn't much of a problem, so I'd imagine there isn't the same level of concern for dealing with the fleas," Rix said.

"Red welts that don't show up for a few days is about the extent of it. There's a whole legend about the ghost of a girl killed by pirates and how the welts are left by her kiss and are given to the most heinous pirates."

"So they make it a badge of honor," Rix said, chuckling as they worked together to stuff the bedding into the cover.

"Do you want first shower?" Amari asked. "This talk of fleas is making me rather itchy."

"No, go ahead," Rix said.

"But you'll take one?"

"Of course."

"And you'll sleep in the bed with me?" Amari asked, and when he gave her a questioning look, she hurriedly added, "It's just for companionship. Sometimes I like to be next to someone. It helps me sleep."

"Oh, good. I was afraid *all this* was giving you ideas," Rix said as he struck a ridiculous pose while flexing his muscles.

"You're so weird," Amari said and disappeared down the ladder.

20

SALVAGE RECOVERY

"I wish Kel would respond," Rix said nervously, tapping closed the communications equipment.

Amari and Rix had been under sail for five of the six days it would take to reach *Calypso's* last known coordinates, and there had been no response to any attempted communications.

"I've sent a back-channel message to Hutari. We'll see if *Calypso* has sent anything more to Patience Station," Amari said.

"All this has to be hard on her," Rix said.

"It is and it isn't. She had a rough time growing up with my involvement with Shixen. It wasn't all bad, but as much as I hate to say it, me disappearing for a couple of weeks isn't a new idea to her."

"I'm sorry to pry."

"It's okay. There are some things I don't love talking about. Shixen wasn't a good man, but he sometimes wanted to be. It could be confusing. He wanted to use my covert skills and mostly didn't care how I felt about it."

"I'll try to stop asking," Rix said.

"No, it's not that. I'm not offended by the questions," Amari said. "There's just some stuff I'm not ready to talk about. You're a good man, Rix Banner. I'm trying not to screw this up."

Rix nodded. He and Amari had been dancing around each other, flirting and then backing off. His own experience with relationships hadn't been stellar, and hearing that Amari valued their friendship mirrored his own feelings. "I feel the same, Amari. I don't want to jump into something and lose a friend because it wasn't right."

"I should have warning labels all over me," she said. "And you should run."

"We're in a ship that has twenty square meters of living space. I'm not sure I can run anywhere," Rix said.

"You know what I mean, though," Amari said quietly. "How much more maintenance work do you have? That fuel pre-pass you did yesterday brought up our efficiency by eight percent, that's a twenty-four percent gain since we started."

"One more and it's a big one. I'm going to need to shut down the power plant for upwards of an hour. Is that going to work for you?" Rix asked. "Also, I see what you did there, changing subjects."

"Thank you for not pressing," Amari said. "You're going to need to be patient with me if you decide I'm someone you want around."

"You'll find I'm a patient man, Amari," Rix said.

"I need to make some changes to our acceleration plan to get us an hour of down time," she said. "Ideally, go work on it now and I can make those calculations while you're working. Do you need any help?"

"No. It's tight down there."

"Have you communicated with Atom lately? How's he doing?"

"Honestly, I don't know," Rix said. "He's not a very good communicator. I sent more money to Petju for food for him. Petju says he seems to be okay."

"You're not worried he's going to trash your shop or sell all your tools?" Amari asked. "You're very trusting and Grintok don't have the best reputations."

"I guess I hadn't thought about it that much," Rix said. "I've always had employees and sometimes they cause trouble, but mostly it works out."

"That's an endearing trait, Rix," Amari said. "I hope it doesn't come back to bite you."

"Did you know that Grintok, when on their home planet, live in large, cooperative family dwellings?" Rix asked.

"I did not," Amari said, tilting her head. "You've done research. You're not as naïve as I was thinking."

"Communal living and shared ownership don't necessarily mix well with how most people view property," Rix said. "I think it's more likely that he's using my shop to make money of his own and I'm perfectly fine with that. He's also making a mess. Again, no problem. I'll work with him to fix that when I get back, but my choice was either leave him behind or bring him along and we don't know what we're getting into, so that could be a lot of stress."

"And this gives us a nice trip to learn about each other," Amari said.

"Okay, I'll be back in an hour or so," Rix said. "Maybe I'll even get lucky and every bolt in the housing won't be frozen."

"I wouldn't count on it," Amari said.

The work now familiar, Rix found it easier to navigate the tight space of the lower deck and was grateful to find unseized bolts that were easily removed. His anticipation of a need to replace the fluid was confirmed when he drained off several liters of thick material that in no way resembled what he put back in. That the machines managed to operate under such outrageous conditions was a real testament to the quality of their design and materials used in manufacture.

"You're filthy, go take a shower already," Amari said when he joined her in the galley an hour later.

"You didn't ask how it went," Rix said.

"If you're not complaining, I already know," she said. "Did you know that this time tomorrow, we'll arrive at the coordinates Kel sent?"

"Hopefully she'll be okay," Rix said.

"I'm nervous, Rix," Amari said. "Six days on a ship that's not moving is trouble. If they lost power, they'll have had trouble keeping warm and scrubbing the atmosphere."

"I've been running scenarios that would put them in a space where they can't communicate," Rix said. "Not much of it looks good. When will our scanners pick them up?"

"They're in a small cluster of asteroids which are blocking our scanners," Amari said.

"Kel loves a big entrance."

"She probably used the asteroids to make it so the ships attacking them couldn't get a good line on *Calypso*," Amari said. "Kel is a brilliant pilot. She's very instinctual."

"And she's flying through space where she has more enemies than friends," Rix said.

"You do know that these coordinates are next to a jump point, right?" Amari asked.

"I don't know that," Rix said. "What are you suggesting?"

"That she wasn't just sailing locally. The trouble she ran into might have come from out of this system," Amari said. "We're assuming Dravari or local pirates."

Rix sighed. "Can we tell if she was coming back or leaving the system?"

"No. Why does that matter? She hasn't been gone all that long, so I'd at least guess she was trying to leave."

"This doesn't add up," Rix said. "Her route was all local. What's she doing headed out to a jump point?"

"Not just headed out, she was there," Amari said. "Kel knows her stuff, so rethink your question and assume her location makes sense."

Rix sighed. "Hopefully we'll know more tomorrow when we talk to her."

"That's the spirit. Now, what are you going to work on next? I know you're not done with this old girl, yet."

"I've never put her under much of a scope," Rix said. "So now I'm going to start running diagnostics on all her subsystems so I can get a comprehensive understanding of what's really going on with her. I feel lucky to have made this trade. She's a real find."

"You've got to be kidding me. *Gravitational Pull* is going to cost you more in the long run to keep sailing than if you bought something newer," Amari said.

"I'm not kidding at all," Rix said. "Structurally, this old girl has some big old bones to her and there's some corrosion, but nothing in the super-structure."

"Some? The entire loft is pocked with holes just ready to be punched through," she said.

"I saw it," Rix said. "Makes me wonder what they had going on up here, but when I looked, it was all on decking and bulkhead panels.

Look underneath and you find that the structure is in really good shape."

"Are you trying to convince me or you?" Amari asked.

Rix chuckled. "Probably a little of both."

And with that, Rix and Amari got back to the tasks they'd given themselves. Without the ability to remove surface rust, lay down paint or manufacture new parts, there was only so much that could be done. Even so, in the five days since they'd set sail, *Gravitational Pull* was considerably more usable than when they'd first adopted the ship.

"*CALYPSO* SHOULD BE on scope in thirty seconds," Amari announced as she navigated *Gravitational Pull* around the large asteroid that had blocked their ability to get line-of-sight on *Calypso's* last known coordinates.

"There she is," Rix said as a positive indicator lit on his tactical display. "I'm getting a read on her passive transponder panel."

"Nothing on the automatic response?"

"No, and we're not even getting a power reading," Rix said and then gasped. "Holy crap, something big hit her. Are you seeing this?" Rix zoomed the visual tactical display in, taking it over with a live view of *Calypso*, which rested within a depression on the surface of an asteroid twenty times *Calypso's* mass.

"Those scorch marks are telltale of a direct missile strike. Someone wanted her badly," Amari said. "I'm trying a high power comm signal which should permeate her hull, regardless of if her antennae are knocked out."

"Nothing?" Rix asked. "Dang, that missile holed her good, I can see into the passenger compartment just forward of the engine bay."

"That can't be good. Are you seeing foam?"

"For what?"

"When you get holed like that, you can deploy foam to erect a temporary barrier so you can hold atmosphere. This isn't looking good, Rix. You need to prepare yourself for the worst case."

Rix nodded gravely, sealed his vac suit and strapped on the toolbelt he'd set aside for the purpose of boarding a disabled ship. "How close can you get me?"

"Five meters. *Gravitational Pull* might not be the most comfortable long-distance cruiser in existence, but she more than makes up for it in maneuverability," Amari said.

"I'm sealing off the lower deck in preparation for EVA," Rix said, sliding down the ladder rails into the lower compartment. While *Gravitational Pull* didn't have a traditional airlock, the cockpit/galley deck could be closed off, allowing the lower maintenance deck to have atmosphere evacuated for the exact purpose of moving to and from local space without dumping the entire living quarters.

"One minute to arrival," Amari said.

Rix spun the manual hatch wheel from below and started the evacuation process. Unlike more sophisticated vessels, atmosphere from *Gravitational Pull* evacuated straight to space, leaving a long white plume.

"I'm clipping in and opening up," Rix said. "How is your pressure in the main cabin?"

"We're losing some, but I have my helmet up," Amari said. "We'll need to look into that when you get back."

"Good copy," Rix said, swinging the hatch open and flipping on the flood lights, which brightly illuminated *Calypso's* port side. "Dang, that's a lot of damage." Rix stepped away from *Gravitational Pull* with enough force to carry him over to the gaping hole in *Calypso's* side.

His heart hammered in his chest as he considered just how unlikely Kel and Philo's survival were and how he might find them.

"Can you see anything?" Amari asked.

Rix understood she was asking about bodies and his eyes were locked in on the frozen torso of a suited individual who no longer had legs attached. "I've got a partial body. I can't tell who it is, but they're dead, for sure."

"I'm sorry, Rix," Amari said.

Rix grasped the jagged steel of *Calypso's* hull plating and guided himself within, landing softly next to the corpse. A spray of blood and mist had frozen to the inside of the helmet making identification impossible. That the suit clearly belonged to *Calypso* had Rix's blood pressure sky high as he reached for the mask's release. He mentally braced as he opened the suit. For a moment, he struggled against the crystalized moisture which held the helmet in place.

"It's not Kel nor Philo," he relayed, blowing out a breath and momentarily fogging the interior of his own helmet. "I don't know who this is, but it's someone I don't recognize."

"Female?"

"No. Older male, not sure of species, but there are features on his temples that are for sure neither of our people," Rix said and then to himself he breathed, "Thank you, God."

"Check his wrist, should have an ident," Amari said.

Rix waited for his view to clear and then pulled the man's wrist. The name suddenly rang a bell. "Brian Kurth," Rix said. "The new maintenance guy for Patience Station. Quixly isn't going to love this. I'm sorry, Brian."

"Look around, I can only see what you're pointing at," Amari said.

"Copy," Rix answered, turning slowly to take in the ship's interior. "Aside from this big hole, I'm not seeing a huge amount of damage. I'm going to move forward. Kel was probably in the cockpit."

"Okay. Take it slow, Rix," Amari said.

Locking magnetic boots to the deck, Rix moved forward through the ship he was once so familiar with but now felt entirely foreign to him. Focused on the cockpit entrance, he batted away floating objects that occupied the space between him and his destination. "Geesh," he said quietly.

"Are you okay, Rix?" Amari asked.

"I'm okay," he said, listening to the sound of his own breathing as he advanced.

"Hold on, I see something," Amari interrupted.

"What?" Rix asked, his eyes scanning every surface in front of him, fully expecting to discover body parts of his friends. The emotional trigger back to his time in The War weighed heavily on him as he recalled a particularly bloody scene he'd visited after an air raid had struck the hangar where he'd been stationed.

"Starboard bunks. I thought I saw a pulsing light," Amari said.

"Philo's bunk," Rix said, hope rising in his chest as he recalled how the small, gregarious alien liked to sleep through long space flights. "I see it. There's power."

"Okay, go slow," Amari said. "If there's someone in there, you can't afford to open it up. They might not be suited."

"Good call," Rix said. "Beverly, I need that foam, do we have any on *Calypso*?"

"Amari, and I don't know," Amari answered with a questioning tone to her voice.

Beverly appeared in front of Rix wearing a nurse uniform from WWII. Rix didn't feel like playing games but appreciated that her appearance felt appropriate for the moment. "Look in cabinet 12-A on the portside. I believe there was a foam capsule there. Be careful when deploying, we don't want to interfere with the primary hatch operation."

"Smart," Rix said.

"What?" Amari asked. "I think I'm missing something. You're not making sense. Rix, check your O2 levels. You might be experiencing hypoxia."

"Negative, Amari," Rix said. "Sorry, I've got a lot going on. I'll explain later."

"I'm worried about you, Rix. Hypoxic victims don't often know they've got a problem."

"Beverly, send her my bios," Rix said, opening the cabinet and discovering the foam container. "I hope this thing is still loaded."

"Your bios are good," Amari said. "We're still going to need to talk about whoever this Beverly is."

Rix ignored the comment as he paced aft.

"I have you on local comms with me only, Rix," Beverly said.

"Thank you. Show me how this foam thingy works, would you?"

A video appeared on Rix's HUD, showing how to twist and release the foam disc in a way that would correctly fill a void. Positioning the bottle, Rix initiated the sequence, which started with a spinning beam of light that showed how the foam would deploy. Ten seconds later, foam rapidly disgorged itself and filled the space.

Without lights from *Gravitational Pull*, the passenger space within *Calypso* darkened significantly, which had the effect of highlighting the pulsing light of Philo's sleeping quarters. "Do we have enough atmo to fill this?"

"You should have hull patch ready, just in case there are additional holes," Beverly instructed.

"Good call."

Having utilized quite a lot of hull patch from *Calypso's* stores, Rix easily located an applicator and opened the manual release for atmosphere. Slowly, *Calypso* pressurized.

"Rix, there are many leaks, but there is also enough atmosphere remaining in *Calypso's* stores to maintain pressure for several minutes," Beverly said.

"Gotcha," Rix said, moving to the sleeping bunk and tapping it open. Within, he found Kel and Philo, unmoving. "We're too late," he moaned fatalistically.

"No, use the hypos she's laid out," Beverly said, highlighting a pair of syringes resting between Kel and Philo. "She's induced a deep sleep that utilizes significantly less oxygen."

Rix struggled to keep his hands steady as he injected first Kel and then Philo with the twin syringes. At first there was no reaction, but then both drew deep breaths. Kel apparently drew too deeply and coughed, causing her to sit up violently.

"Rix?" she asked, when she turned and looked at him. "What is happening? Why are the lights out? Why am I sleeping with Philo?" A sudden thought must have crossed her mind because she patted down her clothing but said nothing more. "Were we drinking?"

"*Calypso* was attacked and holed," Rix said. "You hid in Philo's bunk. We just got here."

"Rixy! Rixy!" Philo said excitedly. "Tolds Kels Rixy come. Good mans. Bring good drinks?"

"How did you get here?" Kel asked.

"Save the questions. Do you have suits?" Rix asked.

"Uh, oh, yes, right here," she said.

"Put them on," Rix said. "We need to EVA over to *Gravitational Pull*."

"I don't know what you're saying."

"The newest add to our fleet. I have a container hauler. She's not in the best shape, but she made it out here," Rix said.

"You sailed out here all by yourself?"

"Amari came," Rix said. "Don the suits, already? I don't know if whoever did this to you is still around, but I'd appreciate getting out of here while the getting's good."

"Oh, crap, it's starting to come back. What about the maintenance guy … Keith? I think he took a bad one."

"Kurth. He didn't make it."

"Shoot," Kel said, pulling the suit over thin sleeping clothes. "Is *Calypso* done for? We took a big hit. That foam is covering real trouble."

"Well, I was thinking we'd tow her back to Patience," Rix said. "This container hauler is plenty big and if Beverly will help me figure out the right tie downs, I have plenty of cable."

"Seriously?"

"Wouldn't be the first time I've hauled her with one of my trucks," Rix said. "I'd think you'd be used to that, by now."

"Very funny," Kel said.

"Philo, are you up for helping me get *Calypso* settled onto the back of *Gravitational Pull*?" Rix asked.

"Ready now, Rixy. Promise drink?"

"Promise."

"Good, good."

"Beverly, give me comms back with Amari," Rix said. "Amari, they're alive."

"Both of them?" she asked.

"That's right. I'm sending Kel over on that line I extended. I'll need you to cycle the atmo for her and then reposition so we can get *Calypso* loaded up."

"And Beverly, is she coming too?"

"She'll come with me," Rix said. "I promise there are no shenanigans. You'll understand once I explain."

"Okay."

"Are you ready, Kels?" Rix asked.

"Did I miss something? Amari sounds pretty interested in Beverly. Is there something going on between you two? I mean, I for sure tried, but I didn't think you and Amari were good," Kel said.

"You can harass me all you want once we're aboard, okay? For now, let me and Philo get this ship lashed down."

"Count on it."

21

MULTI-TOOL

"ARE you sure this old rust bucket can bring *Calypso* home?" Kel asked once Philo and Rix had returned to *Gravitational Pull*. As there were only two sunken chairs in the cockpit, she sat behind, on the deck, her legs hanging over the back of Rix's seat.

"Hey now," Rix objected, patting the forward bulkhead sympathetically. "If you talk about her like that, she might not feel like taking us home."

"Sure. That's likely," Kel answered. "Where did you even come up with this old relic?"

"I made a deal with Quixly: I fix a couple of his cruisers in trade for a few of the derelicts hanging around Patience," Rix said. "I got lucky with *Gravitational Pull*. She's in great shape compared to the others."

"Why would you trade for any of them?" Kel asked.

"Parts and materials," Rix said. "Eighty percent of the vessels I've worked on use similar components. How do you think we're going to fix *Calypso*? We need hull plating and who knows what else."

"*Calypso* is dead, Rix. I don't know if you saw it, but there's a hole where one of the power plants used to be," Kel said.

"I wouldn't be so quick to judge that," Rix said. "Let's get her back to the shop and we'll do an inventory on what needs to happen to get her squared away."

"You're crazy," Kel said, reaching over to tussle his hair, which Rix managed to avoid. "But you're my kind of crazy."

"I assume we're headed back to Patience," Amari said, still tapping on the navigational computer. "It looks like it's going to be a long slog. Twelve days, optimistically."

"Yikes," Rix said. "Anything I can do to help?"

"No, *Calypso* has a lot of mass for a container hauler of this size and with engine power at forty percent, this is what we're left with," Amari said. "Also, things aren't adding up with this whole thing. Are we going to talk about it?"

"What do you mean, not adding up? We were attacked by pirates, and they left us for dead," Kel said.

"You're not that naïve," Amari said. "What kind of pirate leaves *Calypso's* hold un-popped?"

"They didn't take the hold? Are you sure?" Kel asked, sitting forward.

On the primary navigation display, which happened to be the only operational display, *Calypso's* hold suddenly appeared. Stacks of neatly tied down crates remained undisturbed, fastened to the deck.

"We need to get out of here," Kel said nervously. "Cut *Calypso* loose, now!"

"What's going on, Kel?" Rix asked.

"She's right. I'm cutting engines," Amari said. "Rix, how quickly can you untie *Calypso*? We can set her adrift and record her heading. If we get out of this, we can come back and recover her."

Hearing the concern in both women's voices, Rix gave up on questioning what was happening and set to moving. "Philo, I need you, Buddy. We're going to cut *Calypso* loose. I need your help."

"No good, Rixy. Just got Caly strapped in."

"Philo, please. Go now," Kel said. "Emergency."

"Philo go," Philo answered quickly.

Donning his helmet, Rix stuffed tools into the various pockets of his suit and slid into *Gravitational Pull's* lower deck with Philo right behind him. "We need to be careful to keep tethered, Buddy," Rix said, pulling a line from his waist and reaching up to the small alien who was closing the hatch to connect a safety line.

"Closed good," Philo said.

Rix punched the depressurization release and spun the manual lock mechanism for the outer hatch. Before stepping out, he clipped a second line to *Gravitational Pull.*

"Beverly, give us a disconnect sequence, please," Rix said, handing a multi-tool to Philo.

On both of their HUDs, connection points were highlighted with pictures of either Philo or Rix next to them, making the work easy to understand.

"Rix, you need to hurry, we have ships inbound," Amari said, her voice strangely calm.

"Copy," Rix grunted, following Beverly's plan.

Fortunately, disconnecting *Calypso* was considerably easier than connecting, as the ship itself didn't need to be maneuvered.

"Thirty seconds," Rix said, tugging on Philo's line to draw him back.

"Wheee!" Philo giggled, his arms flailing comically.

Rix shook his head at the small alien's antics in the face of danger.

"We're aboard," Rix said, pushing Philo into the hold and swinging in behind.

Amari, waiting for the *go* signal, accelerated hard, causing Rix to stumble back toward the open hatch, through which he might have careened out, if not for Philo's quick reflexes. The alien's strong arms pulled him to the side and the pair worked together to pull the hatch closed and lock it down.

"Thanks, Buddy," Rix said. "I've missed you."

"Rixy is my people," Philo said, hugging Rix awkwardly. "I worried. Rixy came."

"Just like you'd do for me, Philo," Rix said, returning the hug.

"Hold onto something, Rix," Kel said over comms. "We have trouble up here."

No more had Kel said this but did *Gravitational Pull* lurch hard to the side, its inertial dampeners not keeping up with the sudden movement. Philo and Rix were tossed around for a moment until they managed to find handholds.

"What's going on, Kel? We're getting banged around down here."

"Don't blame me," Kel said. "That's your girlfriend at the helm."

"She's not– ," Rix stopped midsentence. He was about to say she wasn't his girlfriend, but that didn't seem quite true. "Talk to me, Kels."

"We've got a three on one sort of thing going on," she said. "And this old tub just doesn't have the maneuverability. They're hailing us. What do you want to do?"

"Beverly, put them through," Rix said. "Unidentified vessels, this is *Gravitational Pull*, please identify yourselves and break off attack."

"*Gravitational Pull* you will heave-to and prepare to be boarded. You have twenty seconds to comply or you will be destroyed."

"Kel, is that your read?" Rix asked, hoping Beverly would mute the outgoing transmission and route his message to Kel.

"Oh, yeah, this is the same group that holed *Calypso,*" Kel said. "Amari's flying is only going to keep us alive for so long. We better do what they say."

"Unidentified vessels, please hold your fire, we're complying," Rix answered. "Amari, cut the engines. They've got us."

As soon as *Gravitational Pull* settled its flight path, Rix recharged the lower deck's atmosphere and spun open the hatch leading to the main deck.

"I'm sorry, Rix, Amari," Kel said. "I didn't put together what was happening."

"Do you want to tell me what's happening?" Rix asked. "Besides the obvious?"

"Get ready, Rix," Kel said. "They're going to come in hard. Best to get on your knees. Hands behind your head. Clench stomach muscles, it's a good bet you'll get a foot to your gut. It's a dominance thing."

Atmosphere vented from the main deck as a trio of armed men in light armor moved into the already crowded space. A flash of light against a rifle butt was the only warning Rix got as his head was struck, and he was momentarily stunned. Doing his best to comply with the rough treatment, he and his friends were pushed out onto a line connected to a larger vessel and into a waiting hold, where new but similar rough treatment was provided until all four were kneeling on the deck and atmosphere was pressurized.

"Aww, see, that wasn't so hard."

Still a bit groggy from being struck in the head, Rix struggled to take in the group who'd captured them. Looking at the trio of heavily pierced and tattooed captors, there wasn't a uniform between them.

The speaker's voice belonged to none other than Jacknie from Draven Knights of Sout Atal.

"What are you doing, Jacknie?" Kel asked. "Why the elaborate trap?"

"I thought you, of all people, would understand, dear," Jacknie said. "Can you not imagine why we wanted to take the entire, festering hive of you all at once?"

"You're nothing more than a lieutenant," Amari said. "This isn't your idea. You don't have the prestige required for a mission like this."

"You can show your real face, Amari. There are no secrets here," Jacknie said. "Just to show there are no hard feelings, I'll even clue you in that it was Vigno who asked me to bring back his lost sheep."

"What does Vigno want with her?" Rix asked angrily.

"*Them*, my boy. They're sisters. I bet you didn't know that did you?" Jacknie said. "And do mind your tone. Vigno said nothing about you or the monkey making it back alive, so do make sure you're not more trouble than you're worth."

"Where are you taking us, Jacknie?" Kel asked.

"Won't you just be surprised when we get there. Search them and then close them in," Jacknie said, turning to one of the guards. "You others, don't take your eyes off them. They can come back wounded if we need. Don't kill the women unless there's no other choice."

The search for weapons was quick. As none of them had been visibly armed to begin with, only knives were found on both Amari and Kel. Fifteen minutes later, the four were left in the hold with a single guard to watch over them.

"I don't suppose you want to tell me what's going on here, do you?" Rix asked.

"No talking," the guard said without conviction.

"Vigno is trouble," Amari said, ignoring the pirate. "All of the local clans pay Vigno tribute. Think of him as a kind of overseer."

"What would he want with us?" Rix asked.

"He must have figured out who we are," Kel said. "And by we, I mean Amari and me."

"But Jacknie knows, doesn't he? And Shixen?"

"Something changed. Neither of those two would have given up that information," Kel said.

"Why?"

"Like it or not, Jacknie thought he had some control over me," Kel said. "Likewise with Shixen and Amari."

"He sets a trap in deep space, just hoping Amari would come with me on a rescue?" Rix asked. "That feels improbable."

"It's my fault, Rix," Amari said. "I put out a warning to let people know you were off limits."

"Off limits?"

"Jacknie put a price on your head. I sent a message when I took out those two who were stalking you while you were looking at Patience Station's power system, outside of the station. They were shooting at me."

"That makes so much more sense."

"And Vigno figured out who I was because of my proximity to you," Kel said. "It's a leap, but Jacknie knew the truth. He probably spilled the information."

"I don't get it," Rix said. "The truth about what?"

"Amari and I are special, Rix," Kel said.

"I'm aware."

"Are you? Have you thought about how what you know fits into a covert operation? What if you were a pirate boss who wanted to keep the gangs in check? Or you wanted to infiltrate a Dravari station? Can you imagine how we could help, given what you know about us?"

"I find it hard to imagine your technology doesn't circumvent that," Rix said. "So, what, we're going to go meet with Vigno and he's going to make us a deal we can't turn down?"

"Not us," Kel said, gesturing to include the four of them. "Us." This time she pointed to only Amari and herself. "He'll use you and Philo as leverage."

"What are we going to do?" Rix asked.

"I feel like we need to have a conversation with Vigno," Amari said.

"That sounds like a terrible idea," Rix said.

"You have another plan?"

"I might if I had some privacy," Rix said.

"There are twelve people, give or take two on this vessel," Kel said. "Think this through a minute. We can get you some privacy, but there are a lot of variables."

"I need ten minutes."

"Hey, enough already," the pirate guard said from where he sat on a crate several yards away. "Sit down and shut up."

"Okay," Kel said, nodding at Rix and then to Amari.

Kel stood, her features softening as she slowly transformed. "You know, Jacknie never said you couldn't have fun with us. I'd be down for some fun."

A momentary mask of lust crossed the pirate's face but was just as quickly replaced by one of anger. "Sit down. I'm no fool. You get me distracted while your friends take me out." The pirate advanced on the group, his rifle raised and pointing directly at Kel's waist. "Sit, I said!"

"What are you doing, Kedgie!?" Amari demanded, her voice changing to a lower register as she stepped to the side. One moment, Amari was in her Nerali form, the next, her body shape had transformed away from her curvy figure, and her face had taken on Jacknie's appearance.

"Sir, I'm trying to quiet the prisoners," the pirate guard said, clearly surprised to see his boss suddenly showing up in the hold. Looking over to the hatch, the guard's expression was that of confusion as he tried to figure out where his boss had come from. "Why are you wearing ...?"

Amari's fist lashed out and struck the guard in the face. So violent was the blow that the guard fell back over the crate he'd just stood up from. On the way down, Amari grabbed the rifle and turned it on the man. "Don't move a muscle, or I'll end you," she growled, stepping forward so the muzzle of the rifle stuck in the man's chest.

A crackle of a speaker filled the hold. "Bravo, bravo!" Jacknie's voice said over the speakers. "I needed proof. You provided even more quickly than I thought you might. Nighty, night."

The hiss of gas sounded as a mist floated down from the ceiling.

"Cover your face," Rix said, doing exactly that. His warning was for naught, as whatever was in the gas took over and he slumped helplessly to the ground.

An indefinite amount of time passed as Rix slipped in and out of a drugged consciousness until finally, he started to awaken.

"Kel? Amari?" he asked quietly.

"Rix, you are awake," Beverly said. "You have been separated from the others and we have moved vessels. I have heard talk. You are on one of Vigno's vessels, and I believe you are in grave danger."

"What kind of grave danger?" Rix asked.

"The kind where I believe there was discussing how to dispose of your body."

Rix's eyes searched the makeshift cell he was stuck within. "That sounds important. How much time do I have?"

"You have been unconscious for four days. It is quite early in the morning. I believe they will act before the end of the day. Perhaps first thing. There is a guard stationed outside of this room."

"Closet," Rix corrected. "What kind of ship? Do you have a floor plan?"

"Why would that matter?" Beverly asked.

"Let's not argue. Do you?"

"I believe so," Beverly said as Rix's HUD showed the layout of a vessel at least three times *Calypso's* size. The identified closet Rix had been put in was two thirds aft and on the starboard side.

"I hate to complain, but are you serious?" Rix asked, digging into the side of his boot, where he pulled out a small multitool.

"I do not understand," Beverly answered. Rix pushed aside some of the detritus on the deck and started to work on a series of screws. "You're escaping? Where will you go?"

"Bear with me," Rix chuckled quietly. "Their complete lack of understanding of how ships are put together is embarrassing."

A few minutes later, Rix had removed the bolts he'd targeted and wedged up a deck panel, which he then slipped beneath, slithering uncomfortably through a morass of pipes and wires that were nearly too small to allow passage. When his head finally dropped beneath the deck, he pulled the floor panel back in place and wiggled through, dropping to the 'tween deck's floor.

"How did you know you would fit?" Beverly asked. "I looked at that possibility and there was no room on the drawing."

"There's always wiggle room," Rix said. "How do you think I get into small spaces to fix things? Mechanics are pros at getting into tight spots."

"What will you do? Will you try to send an emergency distress?"

"No. Who would even come for us?" Rix asked.

"That is my concern."

"Were you aware that Kentil atmosphere is only two percent oxygen?" Rix asked.

"I am."

Rix worked around the dimly lit space until he stood next to the atmospheric processors for the small vessel. "I'm thinking you can reprogram the ship to support Kentil. We need to suppress the oxygen alerts, but I feel like if they can gas us, we can gas them."

"Won't that impact our people as well?"

"It will," Rix said. "We only need to knock them out. With hands-on access, we can give you control of the atmosphere. We'll find the girls and get their helmets on. Look, it's the best idea I can come up with on short notice."

"It is a good idea, Rix," Beverly said. "If I have control, I can make sure only those with helmets on are able to move. We should locate Amari, Kel and Philo before we proceed."

"Can you do that?" Rix asked.

"It is unusual for me to consider this type of covert planning," Beverly said. "It is taking some adjustments to the way I think. And yes, we may gain access to environmental sensors. It will not be difficult to locate the biosignature of Philo. If we are lucky, he is still with Kel and Amari."

"Show me where," Rix said.

A small subsystem attached to a support member suddenly throbbed with a medium blue outline. Rix approached and started disassembling the front panel as indicated by Beverly. A few minutes later, Beverly announced her access. "It is surprising how ineffective security is if direct access to the subsystems is gained."

"Have you found them?"

"Yes."

"Is it possible to get to them before we start all of this?"

"I do not believe so. Let us make changes to the atmospheric processing system and then position ourselves to reach them quickly," Beverly said.

Once again, Rix located the subsystem Beverly identified and fifteen minutes later, the atmospheric mix on the vessel was changed. It took another ten minutes for the air to be cycled through.

"If this has worked, it is critical that we locate our people," Beverly said. "I do not wish to endanger them with hypoxia. I am providing low levels of oxygen to reduce the danger."

Rix started to work on the deck panel that would give him access to the hallway in front of the room where his friends were being held. With easy access from below, he was through the floor in minutes.

"Looks like the plan worked," Rix said, noticing a guard slumped over in a chair outside of the door where he was certain his friends were.

"Use his hand to open the door," Beverly suggested.

Doing as instructed, Rix opened the door and quickly moved between his friends, donning their masks.

"They don't look comfortable," Rix said.

"Hypoxia, while dangerous, is not painful," Beverly said. "The resultant headache, however, will elicit many complaints."

"Can you check the environmental sensors to determine if there are others up and moving?" Rix asked.

"I am able to account for eleven crew, including those of the bridge," Beverly said. "None are moving. Also, I am bringing oxygen levels up. It is not my wish to kill or injure our captors."

"Ugnh," Kel complained, her hand coming up to her head.

"Hey, sleepy," Rix said, crouching in front of her.

"Rix?" Amari asked. "What's happening? How are you free?"

Rix held up his multi-tool. "More dangerous than a gun in the right hands."

22

SETTING THE TRAP

"You shut down this entire ship with a multi-tool?" Kel asked disbelievingly.

"They stuffed me in a coat closet. It wasn't that hard to get access to the 'tween deck where all the systems are," Rix said. "With Beverly's help."

"Okay, stop," Amari said. "Who in the hell is Beverly? I've been patient for long enough on this."

"I have a nano-sized symbiote living in my shirtsleeve," Rix said.

"I've moved," Beverly said. "I'm living under your eyelid–and don't scratch your eye. I'm too small to cause you to itch."

"What kind of symbiote?"

"Are you okay with me sharing this, Beverly?" Rix asked.

"There are only a few possibilities," Amari said.

"Go ahead, Rix," Beverly said.

"Beltigersk," Rix answered Amari.

"There's a whole lot more conversation that's needed, but this isn't the time or place. What's the plan, here, Rix?"

"It's evolving as we go," Rix said. "I figured I'd get you guys freed up and then we could figure out what to do with our circumstances. At a minimum, we can cuff everyone and put them in the hold."

"Or we can lock one of them up and see what's at the end of this snake hole," Kel said.

"Can you mimic him?" Amari asked.

"Might be better if you do," Kel answered.

"What are we talking about?" Rix asked.

"We need to capture Jacknie," Kel said. "If it's Vigno that's causing trouble, it's time to deal with him."

"How?"

"I just need a change of clothing." While Amari spoke, her face started to change to that of Jacknie's.

"I hate to say it, but you have boobs, Amari," Rix said.

"So glad you've noticed," Amari said. "And while I can't fully change, I can reduce, and with the right equipment, I'll fit his clothing just fine.

"Right equipment?" Rix asked. "And you're quite a bit shorter than Jacknie."

"She's talking about a big bandage to flatten her chest," Kel said. "Unless standing next to someone, people do not notice height differences. We're good at not allowing those kinds of comparisons."

"My assumption is that Jacknie is forward, on the bridge," Beverly said, looping Amari, Philo and Kel into the communication channel. "Otherwise, he is in the owner's cabin. I've sent the ship's layout to each of you. If you accept the permissions request I sent, I'll be able to project relevant details onto your HUD."

"We need to find Jacknie," Amari said. As she moved, her figure continued to change; hips narrowing and chest flattening, only her clothing would give her away.

"Bridge is forward ten meters," Beverly said. "Environmental systems show there are no moving crew members and the door stands open."

"You're getting all that data from environmental subsystems?" Kel asked.

"Yes. Environmental systems adjust flow rates based on position and activity levels of the crew," Beverly said.

"Let's go," Rix urged, snagging a pistol from the guard who had been watching the room-turned-cell where Amari, Philo and Kel had been stowed.

As they moved forward, they passed several crew who had collapsed and were suffering from varying degrees of hypoxia, which, if not dealt with soon, could result in the deaths of many.

"Leave them," Kel said. "If our gambit is to work, they'll need to believe they haven't lost control of the ship."

The ship's bridge wasn't large, just big enough to seat six. Rix immediately recognized Jacknie's slumped figure seated in a central chair that was positioned to give him a good view of each crews' display.

"What are we doing with him once we have his stuff?" Rix asked, moving Jacknie around as he started removing the pirate's clothing. "He's going to make noise, and we can't afford crew talking to him. They'd discover our ploy."

"I believe your Earth idiom fits this – it's not my first rodeo, sheep boy," Kel said as she helped Amari into Jacknie's clothing.

"Cowboy," Rix corrected.

"You boys put him in my vac suit," Amari said. "We'll lock him in that closet you were in. We can gag him so no one understands what he's saying."

"Would you entertain an alternative?" Beverly asked, appearing on the forward bulkhead above the pilots' flight controls. She wore a black outfit that closely resembled Jacknie's clothing.

"Cute," Amari said, acknowledging the outfit. "What's your proposal?"

"With a little help from Rix, I could keep a modified level of oxygen flowing into a cabin. Jacknie and whoever else you put into that cabin will remain unconscious until we choose otherwise," Beverly said.

"Are you sure you have time to do that?" Kel asked.

"It is well within his capacity," Beverly said. "I believe the only cabin with a dedicated air supply is the owner's."

"I'm game," Rix said as Kel started removing clothing from the only female crew, a pilot, on the bridge. It wasn't a surprise that Kel was shifting her own look to match that of the crew member's.

"Philo, help Rix move Jacknie and Bella to the owner's cabin," Amari said. She turned to Rix. "And while you're at it, find someone to switch clothing with that's roughly your size. I bet these pirates don't know each other so well that a new face is unlikely. With Jacknie to back you up, you should be fine, and you'll have better access to the ship."

"Can do," Rix said.

Thirty minutes later, all except Philo, who would spend his time below on the 'tween deck, were dressed in pirate clothes and in position.

"Oxygen levels are returning to normal," Beverly warned.

Hamming it up, Kel and Amari slumped in their chairs while Rix lay prone on the floor, as if he'd fallen asleep while standing guard at the entrance to the bridge.

At first, not much happened. Rix wondered if Beverly's O2 mixture had been too lean for the crew. It took several minutes, but soon there was a small groan here and a surprised complaint there.

"Snap out of it you! Give me that navigation plot, now!" Amari as Jacknie ordered.

The crew member seated directly next to Kel struggled to sit up and gave her a confused look. Kel responded quietly. "You fell asleep. It must have been some sort of flare. Jacknie didn't, and he's mad. Hurry."

"Aye, aye, Captain," the crew answered. "I'm sending to your primary display. Oh, wait, your credentials aren't reading. Can you reauthorize?"

"I don't know what game you're playing here. I am authenticated. You've put the wrong credentials. Authorize me now, dammit!"

"Right, sir! It looks like something got scrambled. You're not authorized for anything."

"Fix it, now!" Amari said forcefully.

"Debsil, reauthorize the captain," the crew said, clearly desperate to hand the work to someone else.

"Very strange," Debsil said.

"Is there a problem?" Amari as Jacknie asked.

"No sir. I do not know why authentication failed. I've run a full replace. You should be up and running again," Debsil said.

"Debsil, you are relieved," Amari said. "Banner, take his place."

"Captain, I ... that wasn't me. Something happened to your credentials. I'll dig in and figure out what it was," Debsil said.

"No. Give Banner full control over systems and then put yourself on limited duty. Be happy I'm not investigating your incompetence right now. I have more important tasks ahead," Amari as Jacknie said imperiously. "And if I find you've been poking around systems while on limited duty, I'll be seeding the stars with your worthless body. Do you read me?"

"Loud and clear, Captain!" Debsil said.

"Beverly, do you see our access now?" Rix asked quietly.

"It's looking good. I've removed all administrative rights to everyone except you, Kel and Amari," Beverly said.

"Where are we going?" he asked her. The screen in front of Rix showed a simplified navigation plan. "Twelve hours to our rendezvous," Rix announced to the bridge.

"Fine," Amari said. "I feel like a walk. Banner, you have the bridge. Call me if our status changes."

"Aye, aye."

With that, Amari as Jacknie skulked over to where Kel sat working at her station. "So Blumeo," Amari said suggestively. "How about we take a little break together."

"Captain?"

"Come with me. We'll get some rest. Sitting on the bridge is so boring." Amari as Jacknie turned. "Someone tell me, did we recover any rum from that trade ship, *Calypso*?"

"We did not have time. There was a Dravari patrol closing in on sensor range," a crew member said, not daring to look at Jacknie, who should have known that information.

"Ah, right you are. I have a good stash in my cabin. Come, dear. We have much to discuss."

Kel stood and did her best to look nervous as Amari pulled her from the bridge.

"Oh, man, I thought we were all in trouble," the remaining pilot confessed. "I've never fallen asleep while in the chair. What happened?"

"The ship registered a gravitational anomaly," Rix said. "We had trouble with several systems. Some crew were affected like you. And not to be repeated, Jacknie was knocked out too. That's why he gave you all a break. You'd be smart to stop talking about it. Jacknie is irritated."

"He's happy because his trap worked and we're bringing the prisoners to Vigno."

"You seem to know a lot of things, Chemp," Rix said, reading the man's name from his HUD overlay. "What's a freighter pilot and her friends to Vigno? We've spent all this time hiding out. What's your take?"

Chemp looked at Rix skeptically. "Sir, I don't know you very well. I don't want to be caught speaking out of turn. I respectfully decline to speculate."

"That is a tough stance to take, Chemp," Rix said. "Are you sure that's your best answer?"

"I ... what do you want from me?"

"What's the crew saying about why we're out here doing this? I know what I think. I'm just passing time here. You can keep your secrets," Rix said, trying to sound disappointed but no longer irritated.

"Word is," Chemp started surreptitiously. "Vigno set this trap because he thinks one of the people we grabbed is an old intelligence agent from the war. Maybe both, I don't know. But the rumors say they're assassins and Vigno wants them to work for him."

"Why wouldn't he just reach out and make an offer?" Rix asked.

"Are you for real? Why would anyone work for Vigno if they didn't have to? No, he's going to hold their friends hostage until they do what he wants. Then he'll probably kill them all."

"That sounds like Vigno," Rix said, nodding in agreement.

"Apparently, they've been in hiding for a couple of decades. It's a big deal for Jacknie."

"I imagine that's right," Rix said. "Hopefully some of that flows downhill to us little guys."

"Guaranteed bonus if we deliver. Aren't you in on that?"

"I won't believe it until it's on a chit in my pocket," Rix said.

"Smart."

"What do we have to do to get some food up here?" Rix asked.

"We ate two hours ago. If you order, though, we can get just about anything."

"Well, whatever that anomaly was, it really took it out of me. Have them send up a few lunches."

"Aye, aye."

"Captain, we have *Bonehook* on long range," Rix called over comms to Amari. "We have a comms request."

"Hold on, I'm coming," Amari answered.

Arriving together, Amari and Kel took their places, Kel in the second pilot's seat, Amari in the captain's chair, which moved Rix to first officer position. "Clear the bridge," Amari as Jacknie ordered. "Banner, Blumeo, you stay put."

Having put in at least a twelve-hour shift, the bridge crew was glad to clear out. Chemp gave Rix an apologetic look for leaving him behind, as the two had just spent their shift together chatting. Rix nodded and gave a smile. He also found it ironic that, if not for the circumstances, he might have found Chemp to be a decent enough person to get to know.

"Close the bridge, Banner," Amari ordered imperiously.

"Aye, aye," Rix answered smartly, closing and locking the bridge.

"Let's see what Vigno has to say," Amari said. "Go ahead, *Bonehook*."

A deeply wrinkled, gray-skinned, hairless alien showed on the forward screen. "Did you get her?" Vigno asked, not bothering with pleasantries.

"Her?" Amari as Jacknie asked. "*Her*? How about *them*."

"Silken and Smoke? You said you were going to try. Are you certain? How?"

"They got careless. One of them decided to protect that pain-in-the-ass Earthling on Patience Station and they killed Shixen."

"You think Smoke killed Shixen, or Silken?"

"Could have been either," Amari as Jacknie said. "I knew Smoke quite well, and I only saw her just recently. I am not surprised they found each other after all this time."

"Or maybe that's how they've been living."

"Maybe," Jacknie said.

"How did you keep them? I want to see them," Vigno said.

"I can show you Smoke. Silken is locked down. She's too dangerous to let out."

"I feel we've grabbed the tail of a boxen beast," Vigno said, chuckling. "We will no doubt find ourselves scarred if we do not tread carefully. Are you certain the companions are enough to motivate them to our needs?"

"Yes. They are both quite fond of their little semi-sentient pets," Amari as Jacknie said.

"Bring me Smoke so that I might see her. It has been some years."

"Banner, you and Blumeo go get the one called Smoke. She is locked in the starboard officer's mess."

"Aye, aye," Rix said as he and Kel exited the bridge.

"Not a word," Kel said. Stepping into the mess, she pulled off her shirt, exposing the spacesuit beneath. "This should be enough change."

"You still look like Blumeo," Rix said.

Kel smiled wanly and as she did, her face shifted to a visage that Rix didn't recognize. "This is Smoke."

"I should be more afraid of you guys, shouldn't I?" Rix asked.

"You keep being this sweet, honest, slightly naïve human, you'll have nothing to worry about. Has Amari talked about any of this yet?"

"Not yet," Rix said. "Truthfully, we're moving pretty slowly."

"But you like her, don't you," Kel said.

"Maybe this is a conversation for later?" Rix asked.

"Fine."

"I'm binding your wrists, okay?"

"Got you worried, don't I?"

"Not really."

"We'll have to work on that," Kel said as Rix lightly tied her wrists behind her back.

As they entered the bridge, Kel suddenly swung around, bringing a knee up, just barely missing Rix, who dodged out of the way. Not missing a beat, Rix roughly pushed Kel against the chair where Amari sat.

"How delightful!" Vigno said. "Welcome my little warrior hiding as a freighter pilot. We have so much to catch up on."

"Why are you doing this, Vigno?" Kel asked angrily. "I paid off *Calypso* and then you come and shoot it down? What's the logic in that?"

"It is a shame. She was a nice little ship," Vigno mused. "You ignored my invitation. I could not have that."

"Invitation?"

"Don't play dumb. It does not suit you. Jacknie gave you a chance to rejoin our ranks. He told you there would be consequences. Today is just that. Maybe after you sit quietly in a cell for a few months, you'll remember just how to properly appreciate your betters."

"I'd rather die."

"We'll entertain all options, my dear," Vigno said. "I have a few small jobs for you and Silken. I'm certain I can make you both very comfortable."

"Drop dead."

"Take her back, Banner," Amari as Jacknie said and watched as Rix and Kel jostled together, making a show of removing her from the bridge. Just as they were almost through the door, Kel swung her head in such a way as to impact the door frame, splitting the skin and causing blood to flow. Amari as Jacknie turned back to the screen where Vigno was looking on with amusement. "You have your work cut out for you, boss."

"Smoke is quite the feisty one. I cannot wait to bring her and Silken back into line. To discover they've been sitting right under my nose this entire time. You took a great deal of risk hiding this from me. Only bringing these two back has saved you the punishment you are due."

"It is as I have said," Amari said, guessing how Jacknie would respond. "I have been faithful."

"We will see," Vigno said. "You have attracted Dravari attention. We must make this transfer quickly. I cannot afford to be caught in open space."

Amari tapped on the console as Rix and Kel as Blumeo returned, pulling up long range sensor data. A contact at two hundred thousand kilometers was all that she could see, aside from *Bonehook*. Drawing lines between the ships with her finger, she discovered there would be only an hour between their rendezvous and the arrival of the fast, oncoming vessel.

"I cannot resolve the vessel that is at the edge of our sensors. *Bonehook's* sensor suite must be better than ours. Please transmit updates," Amari said.

"You would be wise to invest in the best equipment. A blind pirate is a dead pirate," Vigno said with disdain.

"I imagined you would be more pleased," Amari as Jacknie said. "You are not the leader I once thought you were. I do all the hard work and you receive the benefit and then complain of my methods."

"Watch your tongue, Jacknie, or I will cut it from your mouth."

Kel and Rix exchanged questioning looks as Amari seemed to be jumping completely off script.

"I have captured your reluctant, hidden assassins and even as I bring them to you, you pay me no respect," Amari said. "I stand for you, even when the others talk of your demise. Ask yourself, Vigno. Where would you be without me?"

Vigno's nostrils flared with contempt, his eyes growing wide. "You freely admit to plotting against me? Why have you not told me before this?"

Amari sighed. "I have not plotted against you. As I have said, I support you, Vigno. The others have spoken of organizing to remove you. I told them that was unwise. It is nothing more than you would expect."

"We will talk more of this when you arrive," Vigno said. "Fix your attitude, Jacknie. I am in no mood for your whining." And with that, Vigno closed comms.

"What were you doing?" Rix asked after closing the bridge door.

"Testing their relationship," Amari said. "We need to know how close they are."

"Doesn't sound like they like each other, but Vigno did back off a little on the hostility."

"Vigno wants us," Amari said. "It's my fault. I had to stop the assassins who were sent to Patience Station to remove you, Rix. I did so in a way that exposed my presence."

"Why did Jacknie hide Kel for so long?"

"We were close at one point," Kel said. "Jacknie can be charming. He is also a narcissist and was certain he could get me back. Together, we could have easily toppled Vigno."

"Why didn't you?" Rix asked.

"Because we weren't at war anymore," Kel said. "The only people who suffer when Jacknie and Vigno fight for control are innocents like the people of Patience. It's hard enough to make a go on a space station.

Pirates don't want work. They want to take from people who do. I have no interest in being associated with that."

"What I'm hearing is that Jacknie is patient enough to wait around for you. He had to have suspected you weren't coming back, though.

"I think he realized I wasn't coming back when we destroyed his little fighter craft. He put a price on your head as a warning to me. He wasn't expecting to find Amari in the process."

"That hasn't worked out for him," Rix said. "What's our play with Vigno?"

"I wasn't entirely sure until I heard how afraid he is of Dravari catching up with him," Amari said. "Now, I know exactly what we need to do, and I'll need both of your help. It's going to be risky, but if we're successful, we could get rid of Jacknie and Vigno in the same moment. That would be good news for everyone. Imagine how Patience Station would fare if trade ships didn't have to pay protection fees to the pirates."

"I'm in," Rix said. "And, if you're looking to give that Dravari ship a minute to catch up, I have some ideas."

"Oh, do tell," Kel said, rubbing her hands together excitedly.

23

DOPPELGANGER

"*Bonehook,* this is *Draven Primary*, requesting docking permission," Kel called over comms. "Our forward hatch cowling is fouled, requesting portside aft umbilicus."

"Wait one."

"Affirmative," Kel answered and then muted. "They won't like it. We'll be coming in at the back of their ship."

"Our plans are harder, otherwise," Rix said, fidgeting. "And I don't love that we're splitting up. Things always go wrong when we split up."

"You need to trust us, Rix," Kel said. "Amari and I have spent a lifetime doing this sort of thing. Trust me when I say Vigno is in more danger than you are."

"I'm not worried about me."

Amari laughed out loud and then looked at Rix with compassion. "Oh, Rix, you are so cute. During your war, you were a mechanic, which don't get me wrong, was a perfectly patriotic and valuable commission. What is it you think Kel and I were doing during our war?"

"Well, I guess I don't know for sure."

"Don't you? Think about our skillsets and how they might be utilized in war," Amari said.

"I'll be honest, the first thing that comes to mind is something I'd rather not talk about."

"Sex," Amari said. "I understand. And, yes, that is something most men consider. Do you not see how easily fooled Vigno is in this moment? I'm twenty kilograms lighter than Jacknie. His clothing hangs on me. Yet, Vigno has not questioned my identity even once. Our brains fill in discontinuities for what we see."

"Give it to him straight, Amari," Kel said. "He doesn't understand the other part. He won't be okay with this."

"Are you sure?"

"What's going on, girls?" Rix said. "What other part?"

"Rix, I haven't told anyone this before and I'm trusting you with an extraordinary secret," Amari said. "I need your word that you won't tell anyone."

"You've shown me your true form, Amari," Rix said.

"Really?" Kel asked, suddenly interested.

"Yes Kel, and no, that's not what we're going to talk about right now," Amari said.

"Hold on. I'd like to know the circumstances of how that went down."

"Stop it already, Kel," Amari said.

"Now you're blushing," Kel said. "You guys got freaky, didn't you?"

"Oh, for the love of the Lords of Gavenar," Amari said. "No. We didn't get freaky. We did not have sex. Can we move on, now?"

"*Draven Primary*, this is *Bonehook*, you are directed to line up with our aft coupling," a voice filtered in through the conversation.

"Hold on a sec," Kel said and then unmuted. "Good copy, *Bonehook*, we'll be around in a jiffy."

"*Draven Primary*, you are admonished to keep communications professional. *Bonehook* out."

"Well, that was awful snippy, don't you think?" Kel asked.

"Shall I continue, or do you have more?" Amari asked.

"Oh, you go ahead. I need to fly this ship. I don't know why you're dawdling. We have work to do."

"Good," Amari said.

"Wait! Did he touch your wings?" Kel asked and then looked at Rix conspiratorially. "That's a hint for the future. I'm just saying."

"This is why we can't take you anywhere," Amari said. "Rix, before Kel starts up again, you only need to know that because of our heritage, we are both difficult to capture, injure or hold."

"Injure?" Rix asked.

"That's right. What would kill another person of a different species is not nearly enough for a Tejlari. And even when we are injured, we heal quickly. There is more, but you should be confident that we can handle ourselves aboard Vigno's vessel. I am much more concerned for your and Philo's wellbeing than our own. To us, you are both quite fragile."

"Is that how you see us, Kel?"

"Well, I see Philo as a scruffy, chubby, sexy little fella who gets along great with the girls," Kel said. "But she's not wrong. You're like walking eggs for as much damage as you can take."

"That's the worst analogy I've ever heard," Rix said.

"*Bonehook*, we're all snuggled up tight," Kel said. "Roll out the red carpet whenever you're ready."

"Do you have to provoke them, Kel?" Amari said.

Kel nodded her head with a chagrined look on her face. "I think the actual answer to that is yes," she said. "I mean, everyone is so serious. Why do comms have to be so serious all the time?"

"Clarity of communication?" Rix suggested.

"Was there anything unclear about what I said?"

"Don't get into it with her, Rix," Amari said. "I'm sorry I even brought it up." Shifting her face back to that of Amari, Amari approached Rix, but before she could continue, they had to put up with a taunting *oooh* from Kel. Rix smiled, knowing that Kel was just having a little fun.

"You're going to be safe, right?" Rix asked, holding Amari by the shoulders.

"Yes. And if anything goes in the wrong direction for you, you know what to do, right?"

"Call you right away. I think I have this, though," Rix said. "As long as the crew acts like you said."

"They're gonna kiss, boys and girls," Kel said in her announcer voice, as if there were more than three people on the bridge.

"There are days when I do not like that woman," Amari said, leaning in with her head tipped to the side.

"She kind of grows on you, though, right?" Rix asked, moving in so their lips met. And for a moment, Kel left them alone.

When they separated, Amari blinked a couple of times. "We don't do that nearly enough," she said. "Promise me that after this, we'll spend more time doing that."

"I promise," Rix said as Amari's face shifted back to that of Jacknie's. "I'll go back and get Jacknie, now."

"Wait, I need my cuffs," Kel said, holding out her hands as she shifted. "And maybe you could promise we'll do more of this when you get back," she added with a sultry voice.

"You're so naughty," Rix said.

"If only you had any idea how true that is," Amari said ruefully.

"True," Kel agreed.

Rix shook his head and stepped off the bridge, carrying a rifle in one hand and a spacesuit hood and cuffs in the other. He didn't love the idea of binding and blinding Jacknie in the way they'd agreed, but it was part of the plan, and he'd work with it.

"I won't wake him until you have him bound," Beverly said, floating next to Rix as they walked the short distance to the owner's cabin.

Once inside the cabin, Rix quickly bound Jacknie's wrists and attached the hood to his spacesuit. He then overrode the controls that allowed Jacknie to turn off the one-way blackout filter that would keep people from seeing his face.

"Wake him, please," Rix said.

Jacknie struggled for only a moment before he realized his hands were bound. From his actions, Rix imagined Jacknie was talking, and he waited for the pirate to stop speaking before he responded.

"Jacknie, your hood is not transmitting externally on purpose. We don't mean to harm you, but if you put us to the test, I can't guarantee your safety," Rix said. "For now, you can hear and see everything.

That might change, depending on the situation. I need you to stand and I'll escort you from the ship over to *Bonehook*."

Jacknie appeared to have a response and Rix patiently waited for it to subside.

"If you're done, we'll get going," Rix said. "Go ahead and stand when you're ready."

Jacknie's shoulders sagged after a minute and he then stood.

"Good. It should be a short walk," Rix said, leading him to the hatch they would exit from. As they walked, several of the Draven Knights stepped out, curious at the events they'd had no warning about. Apparently, however, leading a prisoner through the hallways at gunpoint was well within the norms, as there were no challenges, nor even any questions.

At the hatch, they were met by Amari, who once again wore Jacknie's face, and Kel, who had reverted to her normal form. Leaning against the wall, Philo watched with some interest, as if the events were as normal as the pirate crew seemed to think they were.

"After you, Rix," Amari said, grasping the cuffs at Kel's back and holding a pistol to her side.

"Philo, grab the hatch, please?"

"Got it, Rixy!"

Entering the umbilicus that joined the two ships, Rix gaped in wonder at the starscape that unfolded in front of him. On the ship, behind a thick glass screen, surrounded by steel bulkheads was one thing. It was another thing entirely to have only a thin sheet of transparent material between himself and the heavens.

"Your jaw is hanging, sailor," Amari said with her best Jacknie impression. "Let's look professional." Just then, the hooded Jacknie bucked angrily, trying to draw attention to himself. His move was poorly timed and resulted in a quick correction from Amari.

Rix's blood pressure rose as he crossed over to *Bonehook* and rapped on the hatch. The protocol he'd been given was to close access to *Draven Primary* before *Bonehook* was opened to limit pressure adjustments. The greeting party on *Bonehook* was composed of no less than four well-armed pirates.

"I'd chastise you for overkill, bringing four scary pirates to bring to heel two bound little girls, but I do understand how legends have so pervaded our culture," Amari as Jacknie said. "I promise to protect you from these little gals, best I can."

"Cut the crap, Jacknie," one of the armed pirates said. "Your goon stays behind and Vigno doesn't want the monkey."

"What am I supposed to do with it?" Amari as Jacknie asked.

"Toss it into space for all I care. There's a hatch right there."

"Be a doll and do just that, would you?" Amari as Jacknie asked.

"No!" Kel cried out. "Leave him alone!"

"No, please!" Philo added.

The pirate grabbed Philo, who started to struggle. and a second joined in the tussle. In all, it took three of them to push and then hold Philo in the hatch until it was closed. At the same time, quicker than lightning, Kel, whose wrists weren't properly bound, and Amari lashed out at the remaining pirate, stripping him of his weapon and placing Kel's blacked out helmet over his head.

"Turn away," Amari whispered harshly as Kel struggled to adjust her facial features to match that of the pirate they'd hooded. As a final move, they swapped Kel's overcoat with the pirate's.

"Why did you hood her?" one of the pirates who'd fought with Philo asked.

"You just spaced her best friend. We had to cut off her visual," Amari as Jacknie said.

The captured pirate struggled against the freshly applied restraints and Rix drove the butt of his weapon into his side. "Knock it off. Nobody cares."

"Let's go," the lead pirate said. "Your boy isn't welcome. We've got the security from here."

"I'll stay here," Rix agreed.

"Pelco, you stay behind," the lead pirate said.

"I've got this," Kel said.

"Let's move. Vigno's waiting."

"Does it always work like this?" Rix asked after Amari and the hooded Jacknie had disappeared with the other pirates. "They didn't even question it."

"The brain sees what it wants," Kel said. "Now, where do we need to go?"

"Beverly?" Rix asked.

"I believe I have the layout of this vessel in my stores," Beverly said. "Head across and then aft. There should be access to the power plant on the starboard side. It might be locked. If it is, I'll deal with it."

"How?"

"This will go a lot faster if you're not always asking questions," Kel said.

"That's fair."

When they reached the door that Beverly had identified, Kel gestured to it and Rix attempted to open it. As expected, it was locked. As they'd been walking, Kel's face had changed from Pelco to that of the pirate who'd led the armed party that had taken Amari as Jacknie.

"You, open this door," Kel demanded of an unsuspecting crewman who happened into the hallway.

"That's a secured space," the crew answered and then took in Kel, who was glowering back. "Oh, I've got it, Rast. I'm sorry, I didn't recognize you with that new cover."

"Just open it," Kel growled.

"Is there something wrong?" the crew asked. "I didn't get any reports of something going wrong."

"Leave us," she snapped. "We're working on something."

"Yes. Okay, Rast."

Inside the small engine room, Rix inspected the subsystems. He was unfamiliar with the make of the engine, but the general principles of space flight and power plants were all relatively similar. He hadn't spent a lot of time working with interstellar jump drives, but the reading he had done told him of a crystal component that, when met with a particular frequency of wave, helped the ship move into jump space. The crystals were common and easily manufactured, if worth a few thousand credits on the open market. Opening an enclosure, he removed a total of four crystals, two from the jump drive's subsystem and two from an alcove where backup crystals could be stored.

"Is that it?" Kel asked.

"You know, this goes faster if you don't ask questions," Rix said with a snarky grin on his face.

"Good one," Kel said, grinning back. "Is it?"

"That's jump space. If we're just trying to slow *Bonehook,* we need to interrupt the flow of power in a way that's not quickly repaired."

"And you're comfortable you can do that," Kel said.

"I need my tools."

"Lead on," Kel said.

"Beverly, this is on you," Rix said.

"I doubt there are many crew back here at this time of day," Beverly said. "We'll head around the aft corridor."

"Hey, you can't be here," a crewman said. Next to the larger crewman who was the first crewman Kel had intimidated as Rast. "What are you doing? I'm calling this in."

Once again, Kel moved with speed Rix hadn't anticipated. One moment, she was next to him, the next, she was standing in front of where the crewman who'd challenged her was now slumping to the deck.

"We don't like tattletales," Kel said, punching the one who'd turned them in and had been hiding behind the now fallen larger crewman. "Grab the big one."

Together they pulled the unconscious pair of crewmen back into an engineering space where they propped them against a bulkhead.

"If someone finds them, it's only a few minutes before they find us," Rix said.

"We only need a few minutes," Kel said. "Right, fixit man?"

"I hope so."

"That's the spirit."

Hurrying through the aft mechanical spaces, Rix found himself in front of an airlock hatch. He spun the wheel to open the hatch and was presented with a tool bag, held by Philo.

"Kels right. No lock hatches. Pirates lazy."

"You could have just gone back to *Draven Primary*," Kel said.

"And I'd be without tools," Rix said. "Open that panel, would you little buddy?"

"Open, yes," Philo said.

And for a few minutes, the pair worked together.

"I hear someone coming," Kel said. "Close it up."

Rix returned the panel to its spot as he and Philo spun bolts back into place. "We need to move," Rix said.

"Well, technically, we're not supposed to be here," Kel said. "Let's head home."

"What about Amari? Us leaving wasn't the plan."

"Well, it really was," Kel said. "Amari and I talked. We knew you wouldn't be okay leaving her behind, but that's just what we're doing."

"They'll catch her."

"You'd think that, but you'd be wrong," Kel said. "It might take her a couple of weeks to get out of this mess, but I'm telling you, she'll figure it out."

"We can't leave our people behind."

"That's how she gets hurt, Rix. She'll make mistakes if she's trying to keep you safe. Let her do her thing. Trust her."

"I can't believe I'm doing this," Rix said as Kel led them over to the hatch where they'd brought Philo aboard. Once outside, Philo grabbed the small bag that had contained the equipment they'd pushed across from *Draven Primary* prior to boarding. Going hand over hand, they pulled themselves back to *Draven Primary* and re-boarded.

"Vigno is going to know something is up when we just take off," Rix said.

"Oh, he'll know before that when I put a few holes in his escort," Kel said.

"You're doing what?"

"Welcome back, Jacknie," one of the bridge crew said as Rix and Kel returned. Rix winced as Kel's change to Jacknie was one of the worst he'd seen so far. About the only thing she had right were the facial tattoos. Even so, the crew that had taken over the bridge after they'd left seemed completely unsuspicious. "How'd prisoner transfer go?"

"Vigno is a jackass," Kel said angrily. "I have half a mind to leave him a piece of my mind."

"That's a dangerous game, Boss," the crewman answered.

"Well, I'm a dangerous man," Kel snapped. "How are we fixed for missiles?"

"We have a full complement of four."

"Toss one at his escort," Kel said. "Then let's make tracks. I don't really want to tangle with *Bonehook* today."

"Are you sure, Boss?"

"Do I sound unsure?" Kel asked. "You know what? Clear the damn bridge except for Banner."

"I'm sorry, Boss. Missile away on your command."

"Set in navigational path for Sout Atal," Kel said. "Fire up those engines. As soon as we're moving, throw that missile."

"Target any part of the ship? We're at four hundred meters. We're not going to miss at this range."

"Target engines, there's no need to create a blood feud."

"Navigation is online," a second crew answered smartly.

"Launch missile. Full power to engines. Go!" Kel shouted. "Go! Go! Go!"

"Missile has hit," the first crewman said. "There's too much noise to get a reliable reading on damage. It was a clean strike on the portside engine, though."

Kel sat back in the captain's chair. "Well, that's probably gonna get a little sticky."

"*Bonehook* is turning and they're firing up engines," reported the first crewman. "Boss, I'm not sure what's happening, but *Bonehook's* struggling."

"Is that so?" Kel asked, unimpressed by the information.

"It's like their engines are offline. They're trying to establish comms."

"How close are we to their weapon's range?"

"They don't have much of a shot. Are you sure that was a good idea? Vigno will send people."

"We're pirates, man," Kel said. "We don't answer to anyone except ourselves. It's time we started living like that again. Tell me you're not tired of getting bossed around by Vigno. Everyone has a boss, and all, but that man is too much, don't you think?"

"He has two hundred men. If he comes for us, we'll have to scatter."

"Give me a position on that Dravari frigate. Do we have anything on that?"

"Yes, they're about six hours out and still headed directly at *Bonehook*."

"I sure hope Vigno gets those engines working. It'd be a shame if he got caught out here," Kel said.

"*Bonehook* is sitting atop the jump point to Garenod, you know that as well as I do," the crewman said. "He'll just jump. It's not like Dravari can follow *Bonehook* through. They don't have those crystals."

"Well hells, I'd forgotten about that," Kel said. "I guess we'll just have to see how that all works out."

"You need to be careful, boss. The crew isn't going to like what you did there," the crewman said. "You've put Draven Knights on the outs. We're going to have to run now."

"We'll be just fine. And I need you all to clear the bridge. Banner, you stick around," Kel said.

"Aye, aye, Boss," Rix said. "Beverly, I think we're going to need to run that sleeping protocol again."

"That does sound prudent."

"Jump crystals to Garenod," Kel said. "I'd heard rumors about crystals that work on a different harmonic for private jumps. What do you suppose they've got hidden on the other side of that jump? I bet with the right people, those crystals would fetch quite a tidy sum?"

"You're tempting fate, Kel," Rix said.

"I'd forgotten how much fun this can be."

24

JOURNEY HOME

"*Bonehook* is trading punches with that frigate. This should be interesting," Kel said.

"Amari is on *Bonehook,* Kel," Rix said. "She could be killed. I can't believe you're so casual about this."

"You're assuming it wasn't Amari who started that fight," Kel said. "Besides, *Bonehook* has armor thick enough for at least five minutes of scrapping with that frigate. Trust me, once they're through that armor, *Bonehook* will change their tune."

"Assuming you're right, why would she do that?" Rix asked.

"I can only make an educated guess," Kel said.

"And that is?"

"Somehow Amari got control of *Bonehook* and mouthed off to whoever is sailing that frigate. Maybe she calls their mother some names, or makes lewd suggestions about Dravari breeding habits, who knows, but she gets Dravari all fired up. She does this all while looking like Vigno. She then starts a fight and makes her escape. It's straight out of the playbook."

“That’s a dangerous game,” Rix said.

“Is it, though?” Kel asked. “Every time you get into a spaceship, there’s a chance you’ll run into that magic piece of space junk that holes the ship and you. Dravari are way more interested in taking Vigno alive, so they’ll target engines and navigational systems.”

“How in the world does Amari escape that?”

“I’m telling you, it’s not that hard,” Kel said. “Why don’t you wait a couple of weeks and ask her yourself when she’s back on Patience?”

“If she can do this, why is she living on Patience Station in relative poverty?” Rix asked.

“This sort of thing can draw attention. Neither of us want to get collected by a government and used like we were last time. Either we go cold turkey and only use our skills when it’s critical or we use them all the time and risk getting found,” Kel said. “This was one of those moments where the risk was entirely worth it. With Shixen gone, now Jacknie and Vigno gone, too, places like Sout Atal and Patience Station will have a chance to wiggle out from beneath pirate control.”

“Sable is still on Patience Station. Greasle is running things now,” Rix said. “We’re not out from under anything.”

“Without Vigno backing up Sable, Quixly can enforce our laws. He just needs to get a start,” Kel said. “Trust me, he’ll know what to do when he hears about Jacknie and Vigno.”

“With all of your skills, why would you settle for being a freighter pilot? Or Amari, looking to be a farmer. How does this make any sense?” Rix asked.

“You were in a war, Rix. What did you do after it was over? Did you go look for a place where you could get shot at while fixing whatever lame tech humanity has?”

"Look, a P-51 Mustang is hardly lame," Rix said. "And the technology would blow away any engineer around here for its craftsmanship and innovativeness."

"Okay, sorry, I didn't mean to insult you. Do you get my point, though? Your mechanic's shop and diner, was that you settling for a lesser life?"

"No."

"Then why are you struggling to see that sailing a freighter is what I want to do? I don't have a boss, and I get to be free. Using my skills would mean I lose all of that," Kel said. "Same with Amari. She might be the best spy in the history of the Narlux-4 system. She might be in the bottom ten percent of farmers in the same. What is it that she wants?"

"Peace," Rix said, recalling a conversation he'd had with her.

"Now you're catching on," Kel said. "Also, look at the data stream. It's over and *Bonehook* is just venting some gasses. It's still mostly intact."

"I can't believe it's over, just like that," Rix said. "What are we doing with this ship, by the way?"

"What do you want to do? We could go somewhere," Kel said. "We could probably find a buyer for this ship, although we wouldn't get much for a hot pirate ship that's probably, right now, on the tactical screen of every Dravari Patrol ship in the solar system."

"I'd like to go back and grab *Gravitational Pull*, then pick up *Calypso* and head back to Patience Station," Rix said. "If Dravari are tracking us, though, that might be tough going."

"They'd be communicating with us if they had us on their long range," Kel said. "They had to make a choice to chase us or take *Bonehook*. I'm not sure how we'd find *Gravitational Pull* or *Calypso*. We don't have any systems that tracked their last known coordinates and vectors."

"Do you mind if I weigh in?" Beverly asked, appearing on the forward bulkhead, wearing a jumpsuit.

"Of course not, you're part of this," Rix said.

"I can get you to *Gravitational Pull* and *Calypso,* both," she said. "We'll put this ship adrift and set off a distress signal. I agree that if you try to keep this ship, you'll bring more trouble your way than it's worth."

"I'm all about leaving trouble behind," Kel said. "Can you give me a rendezvous point?"

Beverly mimed pinching something in front of her face and flicked it at Kel, who pushed the data into *Draven Primary's* navigational computer.

"Two days if we take a leisurely pace," Kel said. "One if we push."

"Let's go fast," Rix said. "I have contracts to get back to, and I just got a message from Quixly that the power is down again on Patience Station. He's wondering where his new, genius maintenance man is and when we'll be bringing him back."

"Oh, that's not going to be a good conversation," Kel said. "I was just beginning to like Brian, too."

"I say we push it. I'd hate to be aboard any longer than is absolutely required."

"Done," Kel said. "You know, just because we're not taking the ship doesn't mean we can't look through Jacknie's stuff."

"I'm not doing that," Rix said. "That seems like something that would come back and bite me. Besides, I'm no thief."

"Nothing that's on this ship is ever making it back to Jacknie. How about you stay here? I'm going to go have a look through his quarters."

"See if you can find some food while you're at it," Rix said, settling into the pilot's chair.

~

"SHE'S NOT ALL that pretty, but she looks like home to me," Rix said.

Thirty-six hours had passed since they'd left *Bonehook* behind and, as unlikely as it had seemed, Beverly's intercept coordinates had put them within ten kilometers of *Gravitational Pull*, which was close enough for Rix to contact the vessel's autopilot.

"Are you sure we can't keep this ship?" Kel asked.

"I imagine it depends on how badly you want whatever's left of Draven Knights chasing you," Rix said.

"Right. I forgot about that," Kel said. "Your ... whatever it is, is ugly. Anybody tell you that?"

"It's a wrecker," Rix said. "Like that truck I pulled *Calypso* out of the cornfield with. It's not supposed to be pretty. It's supposed to have a strong superstructure and big engines made to pull the extra weight of a second ship. It's also the only ship in our little fleet that currently is space worthy, if you've forgotten."

"It smells," Kel said as they and Philo made their way down to the airlock.

"Did you set the autopilot to take this ship back toward the Dravari patrol routes?"

"It's set," Kel said. "I'm still pissed that I didn't find anything of real value in Jacknie's cabin."

"Does he normally live aboard?" Rix asked.

"Only once in a while," Kel said.

"Then why would he store his stuff on the ship?"

"A girl can hope, okay?"

Rix chuckled. "That's fair. I can tell you, I won't miss all this cloak and dagger, flying a ghost ship full of semi-conscious pirates around, thing."

"Where's your sense of adventure?"

Rix clipped his safety line to the side of the pirate ship and pushed off, spooling out a thin cable behind him. Landing gently against *Gravitational Pull*, he grasped a handhold and rearranged the safety line so that the two vessels were connected before he entered the lower deck through the hatch.

"Come on across, guys," Rix called, peeking back out of the hatch.

First Philo and then Kel used the line to guide their space flight, with Kel unclipping the line so that it was no longer connected to the pirate ship. Once inside, Rix set *Gravitational Pull* to repressurize after closing the hatch.

"You don't smell that?" Kel asked after they'd doffed their pressurized helmets. "It's kind of a burned metallic smell."

"I do," Rix said. "She has some mechanical issues we need to work out. I didn't have time before we came out to rescue you."

"It's all about priorities, Rix."

"Have I mentioned how you can be annoying sometimes?" Rix asked.

"No, you've been good about keeping that to yourself. I feel like I made up for it by introducing you to Amari. How are we fixed for food? I'm dying. I've had nothing but paste and meal bars for weeks."

"I hope that means you like that," Rix said. "Because that's all we have, too."

"You've got to be kidding," Kel said.

"Nope," Rix said, clambering up to the main deck so he could fire up the primary power plant. "Beverly, would you mind sharing coordinates for *Calypso*?"

"I've loaded them into the navigational subsystem already," Beverly answered.

"Look out to starboard, *Draven Primary* is making her way out of here," Kel said. "That's going to suck for them. Can you imagine falling asleep and waking up a couple of weeks later with a giant headache in a Dravari prison?"

"Not something I'd be interested in," Rix said, steering *Gravitational Pull* around so that they were in line with their new heading.

It took all of five hours for them to catch up with the unmanned, unpowered *Calypso* and another hour to cinch her down to the extendable rails that made up the bulk of *Gravitational Pull's* length.

"Can you read me, Rix?" Kel called just as he and Philo had finished tying the larger ship down.

"Go ahead, Kel," Rix answered.

"Are you up for checking out our galley?" Kel asked. "We picked up a couple days' worth of food on our last stop. It'd be better than this paste and meal bar slop we have going."

"Can do," Rix answered.

The scene within *Calypso* was grim, with the contents of the ship having been tossed about, frozen, thawed and refrozen. Rix tried to avoid looking at the remains of the maintenance man who'd been killed in the attack but knew it would likely fall to him to clean up the mess once they'd returned to Patience Station. Focusing on the task at hand, he was gratified to find that the case of food Kel was referring to was still intact, and he wrestled it from the ship and pulled it behind him as he worked back to *Gravitational Pull.*

"Six days, twelve hours," Kel announced as Rix struggled to carry the food crate up to the main level.

"To Patience?" Rix asked.

"That's right."

"I'll admit, I'm a little impressed with how this old girl pulls," Kel said. "*Calypso* is a big load and we're only down thirty percent on acceleration. We're using fuel like a champ. We'll need to offload fuel from *Calypso* if we want to keep burning at this rate. Did you know we're leaving quite a particle cloud behind us?"

"I've seen it," Rix said.

"What's causing it?"

"No idea," Rix said. "I haven't had time to do any kind of diagnostics yet."

"You could now," she said.

"Not like what I'd want. We need to be back at the shop," Rix said.

"Has my mighty little Earthling mechanic finally met his match with this old rust bucket?"

"You're feeling saucy today. What gives?"

"I feel bad for that guy, Kurth, getting killed on *Calypso*. I also feel badly about the damage we took. Are you going to be able to get her sailing again?" Kel asked.

"I could do some preliminary work out here in space, but without access to the subsystems, I have no idea how bad things are," Rix said. "Whatever hit you knocked out a good three-meter swath of expensive gear. I was just looking at the original drawings and I'm pretty sure we lost the entirety of the navigational system, and if I'm right, the power plant is going to be junked."

Tears formed in Kel's eyes; she tried to blink them away. "Dammit," she whispered, wiping angrily at her cheeks.

"I know it's a hard blow," Rix said, resting his hand on her arm.

"She's the only thing I've ever owned, Rix. She's my home."

"And because of your smart thinking, you and Philo survived long enough for us to come get you," Rix said. "We'll get her sailing again. I promise you that."

"You can't make that promise. You haven't even looked at her."

Rix laughed. "Spaceships are just a collection of subsystems, framing and plating. We have a total of five ships, not all in as good shape as *Gravitational Pull*, but, well, it's progress. We'll beg, borrow and make our own parts. You'll see."

"I know you're just saying that to be nice, but thank you," Kel said. "I needed to hear that in this moment."

"Kels, Rixy, Philo make foods?" Philo asked, swinging down from where he'd been resting in the bunk overhead.

"What are you doing up?" Kel asked.

"Philo hungry. Make foods?"

"Sure Buddy, go ahead," Rix said. "I left a crate next to the galley. Do your best."

"Yay!"

"Do you really think you can fix *Calypso*?"

"I know I can fix her. The real questions are 'how long will it take' and 'what expensive pieces of equipment are we missing?' The old derelicts I talked Quixly out of might have some parts, who knows?"

"You're going to put equipment into *Calypso* from other ships? How will you get those systems to work with what's already aboard?" Kel asked.

"How is it you think the ship's designers do it?" Rix replied.

"It's part of the original plans?" Kel guessed.

"Well, true, but those subsystems aren't unique for just one design, they all can be reprogrammed to work with different ships. It's just a matter of finding a programmer and plugging in all of the details."

"A programmer, what's that?"

"Another piece of equipment that allows reconfiguration. There are maybe a dozen different protocols for ship subsystem configuration remapping," Rix said. "If we're lucky, we won't need a different programmer for every different piece of equipment."

"That sounds horribly complex."

"It is," Rix agreed. "And, if you spend time learning how to use those programmers, you don't have to buy original equipment, and you can get away using parts from other ships that don't need them anymore. What we really need is access to an old junkyard that has a lot of old ships."

"I know where there's one," Kel said.

"Really?"

"Xandarj, I think it's called Pocile Aerie. I don't know all of the details, but I believe you pay a fee to visit and then price-per-kilogram varies depending on what type of thing you take."

"And it has a lot of old ships?"

"It's one of the approved locations where old ships can be dumped without recycling. Xandarj has taken a bunch of crap from the Galactic Empire for not requiring recycling, but they basically have told everybody to shove it."

"That sounds very interesting," Rix said. "Back home, we had junkyards just about everywhere. I used to spend my weekends scouring the local junkyards, pulling parts I knew had value and offering discounts to my customers who didn't have the money for new."

"Like me," Kel said.

"Like us," Rix amended. "Philo, what are you making? That smells fantastic."

"Rice pasta with tomato puree that's only a few months old," Kel said. "We have a few kilograms of animal protein that he sometimes adds. Hold onto your socks, this is probably going to be pretty good."

Rix kicked back and directed his data searching to Xandarj and the Pocile Aerie junkyard. Right out of the box, he was shocked at the size and scope of the yard. At its base, the junkyard was an ancient, generational cruise liner designed to host a family of avian-descended people who lived on massive ships for lifetimes, handing down and caring for them from one generation to the next. Pocile Aerie had a legend around it related to its failure in Xandarj space, where it had come to rest. Year after year, decade after decade, when ships would fail or need to be retired, instead of paying to have their materials reclaimed, ship owners would pay a small fee to abandon them next to the ancient cruise liner, thus, over time, creating a trove of old vessels.

"Here you go," Philo said, handing over a plate of pasta with red sauce.

"That looks great," Rix said. "So, Philo, have you been to this Pocile Aerie?"

"No, no, no," Philo said. "Ghosts and bad peoples. No good to visit."

"Really?" Rix asked, forking a pile of pasta into his mouth.

"There have always been rumors," Kel said. "It's hard to know what's real and what's not. Xandarj people have a different take on personal safety. Generally, you're on your own. So people tend to make up stories to keep people away."

"No. Bad peoples. Mads says," Philo said, referring to a close friend from Xandarj.

"The smart money would be to hire a guide," Kel said. "Get a local guide to accompany you so you're not stepping into trouble."

Rix nodded. "Ghosts or otherwise, that sounds like a good idea."

"Rixy drink Philo's Folly?" Philo asked, offering a short glass of offensive smelling liquor.

"Philo, are you sure?" Rix asked, sniffing the drink. "This doesn't smell right."

"Yes. Yes. Better than Rixy's," Philo said.

"You've created a monster, Rix," Kel said.

"We'll see," Rix said, giving the drink a try. "Where'd you get the fish sauce and pickle juice?"

"Gestalt Station," Kel answered for Philo. "He was beside himself." Kel seemed anything but impressed as she spoke.

"It's a little different," Rix said as Philo watched him carefully for a reaction. "But I think you might have improved on it. I can't quite taste the sake, but if we are having rice pasta, you must have found a rice spirit that's similar."

"Matcha, was hard to find," Kel said. "He's been dying to share this with you."

"Great job, Buddy!" Rix said, relaxing as the potent drink filtered through his system.

"Are you interested in more sailing lessons, Rix?" Kel asked. "We have six days of nothing but open space ahead of us. Might as well learn something as we go."

"I'm in."

25

OPPORTUNITY COSTS

"The Guardians," Kel said. "I never feel like I'm home until I see them."

Rix had been sleeping and woke at Kel's quiet pronouncement. The trip home had been slow and uneventful, aside from daily, urgent pleas from Quixly to return quickly due to recurring power failures at Patience.

"Can you tell if there's power on Patience?" Rix asked, moving his head to attempt visual on the station around Aegis, the largest of the five guardian asteroids.

"Hutari says they've been down for over twelve hours, and emergency backup is down to pushing atmosphere and heat to only the interior levels," Kel said. "People are scared. Are you sure you can fix this?"

"I'm never sure, but last time I looked at the problem, it was caused by overheating due to poor installation," Rix said. "He was also depending on Kurth to come fix things, so he asked me to stand down."

"He's an odd one," Kel said. "What are you going to do?"

"I've already started," Rix said. "We're rerouting some of the emergency power to the manufactory to build the remainder of the heat sinks that weren't installed when Patience Station was first built. Then we'll move a whole lot of ice from the back of the Patience Station asteroid over that entire heat sink field. That should get rid of the overheating that's shutting down the system."

"Seems like you already know what needs to be done, then," Kel said.

"I'm bothered by this being as simple as excess heat," Rix said. "It feels like there's no good reason the system is so fragile."

"Right, and do you know what's happening in three days?"

"No idea. I hope I'll have power restored by then," Rix said.

"Let's put a pin in that and talk about my thing," Kel said. "In three days, Patience Station is electing a new mayor. You need to put your name out for consideration."

"I've been here for months," Rix said. "I'm hardly a good candidate."

"Quixly is compromised," Kel said. "He shouldn't be elected."

"And I should? Kel, I want to build my shop and fix spaceships," Rix said. "Do you know what happens every time I get done fixing something for Patience Station?"

"What happens, Rix?"

"I get pulled into something new and I don't get to work on my shop. My floors are rusty. My lifts are only temporarily installed. I have about a third of the tools I need. I have three derelict ships, one barely operating tow truck and our money maker, the freight hauler, *Calypso*, has a hole the size of Texas where her power plant used to be. When would I have time to be mayor, much less make any sort of decent campaign for election? Nobody even knows who I am."

"Patience Station, this is *Gravitational Pull*, we're twenty minutes out and on approach to Bay 807," Kel called over comms.

"Welcome home, *Gravitational Pull.* There are a lot of anxious, cold citizens awaiting your arrival," Hutari answered.

Kel looked at Rix with self-satisfaction. "Do I need to say more? And I can help."

"How? You're always gone, running freight."

"Technically, I've never had a successful freight run," Kel said. "And you told me *Calypso* was going to be down for a while. What else do I have to do other than get your campaign running."

"I don't know what's involved. It sounds like a full-time job. I don't want a full-time job."

"Hire assistants," Kel said. "You can get help at your shop and also in the mayor's office. As far as I know, every mayor in history had a second job. I don't think the pay is that good."

"You're not exactly selling this idea," Rix said.

"And you know you need to do it," Kel said. "I can see it in your face."

"You're so full of crap."

"I am, but that has more to do with how much I despise the plumbing on this ship," Kel said.

It took Rix a moment to catch up and he shook his head. "Funny."

"You're just going to let Quixly do this, then?"

"It's a waste of time. I don't know how to run a space station."

"And Quixly does? He was the constable, something he wasn't very good at," Kel said. "Then because there was nobody else, he was put in as the acting mayor. Tell me, Rix Banner, how's he doing?"

"You're exhausting," Rix said. "I'll think about it."

"Good," Kel smiled. "That's all I can ask."

"You'll stop pushing me, then?"

"No, silly, but I'll give you a few hours to fix the power," Kel said. "You should check if your parts are finished at the manufactory."

"I don't need your help in organizing myself."

"Feels like you do. You wouldn't even know you needed to be mayor if it wasn't for me."

"Atom, are you available?" Rix called over comms.

"Boss?" came a very confused answer thirty seconds later.

"Hey, Buddy, time to wake up. We're pulling into the station and I need you to open the exterior doors. Make sure we have power and the photonic generators are running, first."

"Boss, it's cold here. No powers. Atom no feel good."

"Can you put on your suit and get those doors open for me?" Rix asked.

"Atom open doors."

"I'll get you some help when we get there."

There was some grunting followed by a wet, splashing sound. Rix grimaced. Atom was sick and needed help.

"Did you hear that?" Kel asked. "He threw up, and who is Atom?"

"A new helper I hired. A young Grintok."

"You hired Atom the Grintok," Kel said, deadpanning.

"I did. He just kind of moved in."

Kel shook her head. "They do that. Getting rid of a Grintok is like getting rid of an STD. You think it's gone and then it comes back."

"Sounds like there's a story behind that," Rix said. "Atom is a decent mechanic with a little oversight."

"Right ... oversight. Rix you've made some bad decisions before, but this one is a top five kind of mistake."

"Why?"

"He'll never leave. He's got the IQ of a cockroach, and they're messy."

"Atom knows the rules. We clean before we work. We clean after we work. He's not as dumb as you think and he's honest and hard working."

The doors to Rix's shop started swinging open and with them, a flurry of junk swirled out on the winds of residual atmosphere.

Kel chuckled. "You needed to consult me before hiring a Grintok."

"What is all that stuff?"

"Trash," Kel said. "You weren't home to tell him not to make a mess. Grintok hovels are notoriously dirty."

"I'll deal with it."

"Let him go as soon as we set down," Kel said. "Don't draw it out."

"I'm not letting him go," Rix said as Kel slowly spun *Gravitational Pull* around and backed *Calypso* into the shop. As she did, a cloud of black smoke billowed out from the old cargo hauler, filling the space.

"Did you know you were smoking like that?" Kel asked, having momentarily forgotten about Atom.

"It's unprocessed fuel getting carbonized. I know about the problem, but I can't find the cause without being home," Rix said. "Atom, close the doors and repressurize."

"Yes, Big Boss."

"You like him calling you boss," Kel said, grinning as the two extracted themselves from the pilot's chairs.

"You're in a mood," he answered, shaking his head. "I'll have *Calypso* off in twenty minutes. Can I get you to run *Gravitational Pull* down to the manufactory to pick up the parts for the power station? I need them delivered to the heat sink field behind the station. I bet Philo could help strap things down if you took him."

"I don't even know what you're talking about. What's a heat sink field?"

"Beverly, could you send coordinates to Kel?"

"Of course," Beverly said, appearing in her blue jumpsuit and polka dotted scarf. "It's nice to be home, isn't it?"

"It is," Rix agreed, climbing down the narrow stairs and into the shop. "Oh, Lord, what happened in here?" he asked as he took in the general disrepair of his once clean shop. Tall, empty cans of bulk rum were tipped over, and puddles of things better left unknown dotted the living area closest to the entry back into the station.

"Atom worried, no Big Boss come home," Atom said, looking up at Rix with concern.

"I'm sorry we had to leave in such a hurry," Rix said. "What's all this mess, Atom?"

"Atom drink much, feel sick."

"That rum was something I was going to sell, Atom," Rix said. "That was worth good money."

Tears formed in Atom's eyes as he heard the disappointment in Rix's voice. "Sorry, Big Boss," he said, shuddering. "No think Big Boss come back. Atom lonely."

"And sick," Kel said. "A lot."

"Big bottles. Hard drink all," Atom said.

Rix closed his eyes and shook his head. "Okay, we have some things we need to talk about next time," Rix said. "For now, get this place cleaned up. Get the buzzbroom and clean up all those piles. After that, pick up all of the remaining trash. Let me know when you get that done."

"Atom feel bad."

"I bet," Rix said. "Go to the infirmary and get some of those hangover pills."

"Atom no money."

Rix pinched ten credits on his HUD and flicked it to Atom. "Now you do. Go, now, then come back."

"You're going pretty light on him," Kel said. "He downed five hundred credits in rum. How's he going to pay for that?"

"He's not," Rix said. "Look, I know he's a mess, but I feel responsible for him."

"You have too soft of a heart," Kel said.

"Philo, help me get *Calypso* off the back, here?" Rix asked.

"Sure, Rixy!" Philo said excitedly. "Atom part of team now, Rixy?"

"Yes. Is that okay with you?"

"Atom is okay," Philo said. "Smells bad, though."

Rix didn't respond other than to start working on the lashings that held *Calypso* in place. Without her gravitational systems operational, *Calypso* was difficult to maneuver. Rix added a gantry crane to his always growing list of missing tools, which would allow him to lift heavy loads. Fortunately, with no power to the station, there was no gravity within the bay, and it was just a matter of tying *Calypso* to the station's super structure and driving *Gravitational Pull* out from beneath it.

"You're free, Kel," Rix called over comms.

"Do you want to ride along, Rix?" Kel called back.

"No, it's not that much of a walk and I have tools I need to collect."

"Copy that. See you over there," Kel answered. "Philo, are you coming?"

"Yes. Yes!"

Pulling over a gravity pallet, Rix started stacking tools. The actual work of installing the heat conducting fins was a simple process that was only made more difficult by the size of the fins and their fasteners, which turned out to be bolts as big around as a woman's wrist. While he didn't have the perfect tools for the job, he could make do.

"Quixly, did you get word that we're on station?" Rix called over comms.

"People are cold, Banner," Quixly answered with obvious irritation. "Why hasn't the power turned back on? It's been hours."

"I don't know. We're loading up the new parts and heading over to the field. I hope you left me on the access list. If I'm locked out, that's going to make things harder."

"I'll meet you over there," Quixly said, not admitting he'd removed Rix from having access.

"Sorry about Kurth," Rix said. "I know you were hoping this would be his job."

"I'm going to need an explanation of your and Kel's involvement in his death," Quixly said.

"Do you think?" Rix asked. "Don't see how that's any business of Patience Station's given where it happened. Go ahead and take it up with Kel, though. My report is that by the time I got there, Kurth wasn't alive."

"We're not done with this," Quixly grumbled. "And we haven't talked about your rate on this repair."

"Bay 808 for a year," Rix said.

"That's robbery. That's almost twenty thousand credits."

"Twenty-two thousand credits," Rix corrected. "And it doesn't cost Patience Station anything. You know as well as I do that both of these bays would sit empty for the next year, regardless of all the work I'm doing."

"Patience Station needs that income, Banner."

"Okay, let me pick through those tools left behind by Geoff and Garba," Rix said. "I take anything I want that's related to repairing a station or ships."

"I have no idea what the value of those things are," Quixly said.

"And if I'm going to keep fixing everything around here, I'm going to need tools," Rix countered. "I'm trying to do this in a way that doesn't cost you credits, but you keep acting like I'm doing you dirty."

"I'll get approval from the council," Quixly said. "Just get the power back on."

Rix closed comms and rolled his eyes. Quixly's attitude was irritating and his reticence to fix critical systems bordered on criminal. Quietly, he stewed on these problems as he made his way down to environmental systems.

"There's a rumor Jacknie from the Draven Knights and Vigno got scooped up by Dravari," Quixly said, catching up to Rix as he sat in front of a locked door with his pallet of tools. "According to what I heard, it happened not too far from where *Calypso* ran into trouble."

"Is that right?" Rix asked, not interested in linking his or Kel's name to the troubles of pirates.

"Don't be coy, Banner," Quixly said. "If you know about a power play for control of Sable or Draven Knights, I need to know for the safety of Patience Station. With Shixen, Jacknie and Vigno out of play, there's going to be trouble as those organizations try to figure out who's in power."

Rix stopped moving forward and turned back to Quixly. "Is that your question, Quixly? You want to know who's going to be in power when you hear about the top dogs in two pirate organizations getting captured. What about Patience Station being in power? What about the good people who've struggled to live and pay their taxes have someone who cares about keeping pirates off this station instead of giving them a free ride?"

"You're an idiot if you think Patience Station is anything more than a place for the next angry pirate chief to make his mark," Quixly said.

"Can I quote you on that?"

"Don't be an ass," Quixly said. "Everyone knows that we can't stand up to the pirates. Vigno's organization is all ex-military. They were the rebels who fought Dravari and got chased out to the Surnac Belt and lost."

"Were you part of that war, Quixly?"

"I was, and if you're suggesting I've got anything to do with Sable, you're dead wrong," he said.

"The only one who's made that suggestion is you," Rix said. "I've tried to keep my head down and play by whatever dumb rules you come up with. In return, you ignore everything I suggest, and look at where we're at now. We have no power, which is slightly less scary than having no atmo. You can hide behind fearing Sable, but people here deserve more than that, especially if like you say, Vigno, Shixen and Jacknie are all out of the picture now."

"Greasle and his crew aren't going anywhere," Quixly growled, opening the final lock for Rix.

"Sounds like you have some decisions to make, then," Rix said.

"Stick to fixing things, Banner. You have no idea what you're getting into."

"At least we agree on that," Rix said, glancing up to find *Gravitational Pull* slowly descending to his position. "Beverly, mute him and let's get some heat readings."

"You're pushing Quixly's buttons, Rix. Are you sure that's how you want to work with him?" Beverly asked. "And the fins are cool again. There must be a new problem."

"We'll get this work done before we figure that out," Rix said. "We can't install the remaining heat sinks without the current ones being cool enough to work with. Show me how to shut the entire system down, would you?"

"It's not hard. There's a few, large paddle style switches you need to drop," Beverly said, showing a video of the devices and their correct *off* position.

"Got it," he said, moving back through the airlocked doors and into the generator room. He easily located and turned the switches off and moved back outside where Kel and Philo had already started moving the fins into place, setting them into the cradles that had been waiting empty for decades.

"Great job, guys," Rix said, setting out the bolts next to each joint. In addition to reattaching the disconnected fins, he'd taken the liberty of completing the heat dissipation field with a final row of fins. If Patience Station were to ever flourish, infrastructure short-cuts couldn't be allowed.

"Crank bolts?" Philo asked, reaching for one that he had set down.

"Not yet," Rix said. "We'll connect them all loosely. Once we have them all in place, I'd sure appreciate help getting them tightened up."

"Will this get power up and going again?" Kel asked.

"There's something else going on," Rix said. "But this can't be done with a hot system, so it's a perfect time to install these fins."

"What do you think the problem is?"

“No idea,” Rix said.

And with that, they set to the task at hand. An hour into the job, Quixly was on the comms demanding an update. “Talk to me, Banner. What’s your progress?”

“We’re working, Quixly,” Rix said. “I’ll get you an update as soon as I know something. Did you get a contractor to move the ice field like I specified?”

“I have someone,” Quixly said. “I don’t know why we need this if you’re expanding the current system.”

“Look, the current system isn’t working, and you may have burned out more subsystems by waiting,” Rix said. “I’ll know more fairly soon, but I need to get back to work.”

“The council is displeased with the speed of your repairs, Banner,” Quixly said. “I was asked to share that message.”

“Sounds like you’re not playing fair, Quixly,” Rix said. “I just got back ninety minutes ago. I’d have had this fixed two weeks ago if you’d let me work on it. Does the council know that?”

“Just get it fixed, Banner. Quixly out.”

26

SLAGGED

RIX STARED at a vertical run of wires, thick as his forearm, unshielded and ten meters tall. Each wire attached neatly to the heat distribution panel with long, wide u-shaped cradles. It took him several minutes to understand what he was looking at. His approach for finding the newest problem plaguing Patience Station's power was to start at one end of the system and visually inspect it going forward. He knew something was wrong, but wasn't certain what.

"What are you looking at?" Kel asked when she couldn't take the silence any longer.

"I've never seen this thick of conductor material before, and I'm thinking it's also what's preventing the power generator from coming online," Rix said.

"I don't see a problem. You have big old wires. I'd expect that," Kel said.

"Look closer."

"At what?"

"Watch this," Rix said, taking a forearm-length wrench and smacking the closest of the wires. When the wrench hit the wire, instead of bouncing off, the thick wire cracked, with a shower of debris.

"Should it do that?"

"No. Beverly, grab specs on this, would you?" Rix asked.

"I do not need to," Beverly said. "Look above where it enters the sheathing. This is not the correct material. This wire is tied directly to the heat exchange and requires an alloy that can survive the constant extreme heating and cooling cycles."

"Let me guess, they're expensive to produce," Rix said.

"Fourteen strands at twelve thousand credits each. That is 168,000 credits," Beverly said. "The closest manufactory capable of producing these lines is on Grelvox."

"That's a long round trip. Ten days, minimum," Kel said. "How did this happen? Who installed these wires?"

"Beverly, can you get any sense of time when these might have been installed?"

"I need to be closer to the sheathing," Beverly said.

Rix considered the problem. The sheathing was barely visible, disappearing into the deck above and below. Making up his mind, he set to removing a panel in front of the closest wire. It took a few minutes before he got the decking panel removed and had access.

"This wire was manufactured a month ago here on Patience Station," Beverly said. "There is a manufacturer's stamp on the casing."

"What is the cost of producing these?" Rix asked.

"Twenty-eight thousand credits," Beverly said.

"A month ago? Who installed them? That was after Geoff," Kel said.

"Can we track down who made them? You have to go to Quixly with this."

"Do I?" Rix asked. "We need to take this to the council. There are two possibilities. One, Quixly is aware of what's happening or two, he isn't aware and is inept at securing critical infrastructure."

"That's a dangerous path, Rix," Kel said. "Quixly might be a grump, but he's kind of been on your side."

"I thought that too, until the council started complaining about my work and he didn't own that he prevented me from repairing the heat exchange field," Rix said.

"Would that have solved this problem?" Kel asked.

"No. But he couldn't possibly have known that unless he somehow knew the heat exchange wasn't the actual problem," Rix said as the pieces of the puzzle started falling into place.

"Aren't the fins we just installed the actual fix, though? Everything is too hot, right?" Kel asked. "That problem goes away with the new radiant field and ice dump."

"The inferior parts are less efficient at transmitting the heat," Beverly said. "Rix's solution would have extended how long these parts were effective."

"Beverly, would you help me make a report of this problem into a video," Rix said. "We'll stick to the facts and send it directly to Quixly. We'll give him a chance to present it to the Town Council. Also, we need an emergency request to produce these crappy wires and then a second request for delivery of a full set of proper alloy wires."

"I have it," Beverly said after a few moments. "Would you like to review it?"

Rix, Kel and Beverly spent twenty minutes reviewing and revising the video until it was ready to be sent.

"You're not sending this to the council. I don't understand," Beverly said.

"Because he's either a genius or incredibly lucky," Kel said. "Sending it to Quixly's mayoral account ensures it becomes part of municipal archives. The odds of that account being monitored by someone other than Quixly are extremely high. Rix stays above reproach."

"Rix, you have incoming comms from Quixly."

"Put it through," Rix said. "This is Rix."

"Banner, what are you thinking, sending that through the municipal message queues? What if I hadn't been looking for it? We're in an emergency here! We don't have time for you to be messing around!"

"I hope you watched it and you're calling to approve both temporary exchange wires and production of the alloy on Grelvox," Rix said.

"I've sent approval for the local manufacturing request. We'll reroute emergency power to the manufactory to get these produced," Quixly said. "The other is going to require council approval and I don't think they'll go for it."

"The temporary exchange lines are only going to last maybe six to eight weeks," Rix said. "I told you that in the summary I sent."

"Patience Station doesn't have two hundred thousand credits to spend on wires, Banner," Quixly said. "Why else do you think I'm making ridiculous deals with you that don't have me paying you in credits?"

"My dealings with Patience Station have been more than fair," Rix said.

"No. You've been taking advantage of crisis after crisis to line your own pockets, Banner."

"So that's how you're playing this?" Rix asked.

"I'm launching an investigation into what happened to Kurth," he said. "Your partner was responsible for his well-being. I don't find it coincidental that she and her mutt partner both survived and my new maintenance man did not."

"We killed a man so I could barter for shop tools?" Rix asked incredulously. "Are you listening to yourself?"

"Desperate people do desperate things, Banner," Quixly said.

Rix terminated the call. "Boy, he's hot," Rix said, pinching a recording of the conversation from his HUD and flicking it to Kel. "Let's run Gravitational Pull around and wait for the temporary heat exchange lines."

"You're so calm," Kel said. "I'd be pissed. I *am* pissed! He's calling us murderers."

"No reason to get upset. His accusations are ridiculous. Murdering a man and wrecking our ship doesn't add up to the value of a few shop tools."

"I'll work on a full accounting of our deals with Patience Station for the consumption of the town hall. I believe an investigation is likely. Maybe we can head it off," Beverly said.

"Please do."

With nothing else to produce, the heavy, inferior lines were already stacking up in the large warehouse adjacent to the manufactory. And with everyone focused on the return of power to the station, no less than twenty workers had shown up to help load the materials. Each of the workers volunteered to join Rix and crew back at the power generator room to help manage the heavy pieces.

"It's not a big space," Rix explained. "But four volunteers would certainly speed up the process of moving these lines to and from the ship."

"You've got it," Thudd Gaveshod said. "I've helped move these in the past. They're a pain."

"Is that right?" Rix asked. "I might have some questions about that install if you don't mind."

"Happy to help," Thudd said. "I'm surprised Quixly isn't down here helping. He and Greasle were running this last time."

"I think he has other things on his mind," Rix said, not immediately jumping on the information.

"People are rightfully upset. Power is a big deal to a station like Patience," Thudd stated the obvious.

"We'll meet you guys down there," Rix said, climbing into Gravitational Pull with all fourteen lines securely lashed down. Trailing a cloud of black smoke, Kel pushed the container hauler to its limits as she scooted around the station and lined up on the bay that was closest to where they would work.

Thudd and friends showed up minutes later and cheerfully got to work, easily maneuvering the long, heavy wires through the dark, gravity-deprived hallways and into the power distribution room, where Rix and Kel worked to remove the existing lines.

"These should go to the reclaimer, then?" Thudd asked, eyeing the growing pile of discarded, brittle wires.

"All but a couple," Rix said. "I'd like to run some testing on these before we destroy them."

"Sounds good."

Another hour passed before all lines had been replaced. A small crowd gathered behind Rix as he made his way over to the heavy power switches.

"We'll prime the generator with the smaller magnetic motor," Rix explained. "Without it, it's impossible to start the main generator."

Rix depressed buttons in sequence and watched with interest as gauges reacted to his actions. "Kel, lock that heat transfer cage. Anyone touches anything in there and they'll pop like a cherry bomb in an apple."

"A what in a what?" Kel asked, chuckling. She followed his instructions and closed the cage, locking it.

"Here goes nothing," Rix said, pushing the large paddle switches to their *on* position, one after another.

Suddenly, gravity returned with the patter of smaller items falling to the deck and boots finding purchase. Lights and a flow of warm air followed. Rix tapped on the diagnostics panel, moving from deck to deck, searching for problems.

A small cheer erupted from behind him as Thudd and his helpers contacted personnel around the station and received word about systems and spaces powering up.

"Dang, we're already heating up fast," Rix said.

"Is there a problem?" Thudd asked.

"I'm not sure," Rix said. "Those wires we installed aren't the right material, and we know that starting up a system like this is a big pull on resources."

"Why not make the right lines?"

"The alloy we need isn't available on Patience," Rix said. "We need a run to Grelvox and a big bag of credits."

"Are we going to be okay?"

"I think so," Rix said. "We also need to get a bunch of ice moved onto the radiant field where those fins we had you manufacture got installed. Quixly has someone doing that, but with all this heat, that's a priority, now."

"Hmm, haven't heard of that getting done," Thudd said. "There are maybe three guys on station that can do that work. I'll make some calls and find out what the holdup is."

"Would you?" Rix asked. "I'd really like to know when that's happening."

"Certainly would. Who knew a mechanic would be the hero of the day, but that's becoming a repeating theme around here. I bet I can get that work started this afternoon, yet."

"Quixly has the specifications. I can send them along if someone needs it," Rix said.

"I'll be honest with you. I don't think that work has been scheduled yet. I'm pretty sure I'd know about it," Thudd said. "I'll make some waves. Quixly can be cheap, and that's not a good thing if it means we're not getting power. Send me the specs. I'll make sure it gets done, one way or another."

"Careful, Rix. You already have enough trouble with Quixly," Kel warned.

"I don't understand the trouble, Warp," Thudd said. "If the work needs doing, we need to get it done. We're all in this together. We have no time for politics and egos."

Rix knew in that instant that he and Thudd were destined to be friends. He pinched and flicked the specifications for the ice field that had been designed but never implemented. "That'd be a big help, Thudd."

"Consider it done."

"Where to now, Big Boss?" Kel asked with a dumb grin on her face.

"Not you, too," Rix said.

"Now that you have power, I bet you're itching to get that shop cleaned up. Am I right? I know I want to get access to Calypso's hold and see if we have anything left. That hole in the ship probably opened a piece of the hold. I'm not sure. Do you think Atom is coming back?"

"Why wouldn't he?"

"You told him to get sober and come clean up his stuff," Kel said. "I don't think most Grintok see that as a good time."

"I think he likes having a place to lay down at night," Rix said. "I give him that, food and pay him to work. It's a better gig than what he had before we met. You should give him a chance."

"All that vomit in the shop isn't doing much for magnanimous feelings," Kel said. "I don't want to be cleaning up after him."

"Same," Rix said, climbing up into *Gravitational Pull*. "Everyone has to pull their own weight around here."

"Are you taking us back?" Kel asked with a hint of humor in her eyes. It was one thing to navigate the unwieldy container hauler through space, and another thing entirely to maneuver close to a space station.

"Maybe next time," Rix said. "My focus isn't that great just now."

"I've got it," Kel said, easily lifting off and avoiding the various obstacles that were in their way. "Park it on the slip?"

"Yeah, we have thirty meters of slip. We'll have to park at the end until we move those derelicts around," Rix said.

"I don't get why you traded for those," Kel said. "They're junk. Every two-bit salvager has already been through them looking for things to sell."

"They both have their engines," Rix said. "Also, Quixly has one more that we made a deal for. Would you and Philo be willing to grab that in the next couple of days?"

"I'm sure we can make time, especially considering we don't have a ship to fly."

"I'll probably get started on that tomorrow," Rix said. "I have a bunch of things I need to work on today."

Kel gave him a surprised look. "Like what?"

"Don't you think I have my own life?"

"In a word ... no," Kel said, snugging *Gravitational Pull* up next to the slip. "Philo, lock us down, please."

"Yes, yes, Kels!"

Working through the airlock and into his shop, Rix found Atom walking toward a pile of trash, carrying a fresh load.

"Good job, Atom," Rix commended as he scanned the room. Atom had only just begun but that he was working on it without prompting was all Rix cared about for the moment.

"Big Boss make powers," Atom said. "Smarts."

"Oh, boy, I'd have lost that bet," Kel said. "I can't believe he's cleaning."

"He does a good job," Rix said, making sure Atom could overhear them. "Let's go check on Amari's farm."

"Farm?"

"Oh, yeah, we made good progress before we came out to grab you guys," Rix said, leading her across the hall to the farm space.

"How is this still green?" Kel asked. "They've been losing power left and right."

Rix checked the readouts on the monitoring systems. "They're struggling," he said. "But closed in like they are, they keep a lot of their heat. They don't consume oxygen, so that was okay. They need more light than they've been getting, though. I'm glad they're not all dead."

"Some over here are," Kel said, finding a tray of sickly yellow shoots.

"Those are the youngest plants," Rix said. "We can get another generation planted and going. We're not that far behind. The plant computer says we'll have harvest on some of whatever this is in a week."

"You don't know anything about this, do you?" Kel asked.

"Mechanically, yes, biologically, not at all," he admitted. "I bet Skef would help out, though."

"Do you think? He's been surly."

"Nerali made friends with Skef," Rix said, using Amari's pseudonym. "He was pretty interested in what we were doing down here."

"Skef's not a bad guy, he's just had to live through setback after setback between losing atmosphere and losing power all the time," Kel said. "I can talk to him if you want. It would free you up to work on your shop."

"Don't you mean work on *Calypso*?" Rix asked.

"If you need to hear it that way, sure," Kel agreed and then looked around. "You have a lot of space in here. What are you planning to do with the rest of it?"

"I'm not sure. We were putting in a decent head," Rix said. "That's all those parts over there. I'm getting a little tired of sleeping in a chair, so I was thinking about making a bunk room or something like that."

"Amari isn't going to want to live in a bunk room, Rix," Kel said. "You need to do better than that."

"Every credit I earn goes to fixing *Calypso* and buying tools," Rix said as they walked back to the shop. "This is all temporary down here."

"Have you given any more thought toward running for mayor?" Kel asked.

"Not even a minute," Rix said and looked to change the subject. "How about we grab showers and then go up and get some grub at Petju's?"

"Are you buying? I'm broke right now. Every credit I own is in *Calypso's* hold ... or not."

"Let's open her up and see what we're looking at," Rix said. "At least you can eat dinner knowing which direction the wind is blowing."

"I'm not going to be able to hold my end up on fixing *Calypso*," Kel said, her face falling. "You've been paying for everything. I feel bad about this."

"This is a long-term investment," Rix said. "Let's see what it's going to take to get her space-worthy again. We'll make decisions after that. But for now, let's check out the hold. We'll go from the back. I think there's some mess where I put the foam in that you're not going to want to see."

"You mean where Kurth got mushed?"

"Yes," Rix said, inspecting Kel's face to see how upset she was. In The War, Rix had seen plenty of death and, while he didn't like it, it didn't have quite the impact on him as he expected it would for someone who hadn't been exposed.

"It'll be fine," Kel said, to Rix's slight surprise. "I'll help you clean all that up after we've had something to eat, how about?"

Moving to *Calypso's* hold door, Rix attempted to spin the manual lock. Unsurprisingly, the frame of the door was tweaked and the lock was unmovable. "Did you have anything that couldn't deal with vacuum? I think we lost the seal."

"Nothing much," Kel said. "How are you going to open it?"

"I'll use a cutting torch."

"Won't that ruin it?"

"No more than it already is," Rix said. "Atom, grab the cutter and bring it over, would you?"

"Yes, Boss," Atom answered.

A few moments later, Rix started cutting into the door frame. At first, he'd hoped it wouldn't require much cutting. In the end, it was a total loss.

"That's not ideal," Kel said as Rix pulled the door free, allowing it to fall to the deck noisily.

Climbing on a ladder and peering in, Rix was gratified to see stacks of cargo still strapped to the deck. "I think you might have some good news here, Kel."

"Temper your expectations," Kel said. "I think we had maybe a max of six thousand credits of cargo. I arbitraged the earnings from the Gestalt Station deal into trade goods to bring home."

"That was good thinking. Let's get it unloaded, and you can work on selling it," Rix said. "Grab some dinner first?"

"Yes, but there's a stack of crates for Petju. We might as well bring them along," Kel said.

Rix nodded and, in the end, they found it easier to simply unload the entire small hold into the shop. With a little organization, Kel identified the crates for Petju, which they put onto a grav pallet.

"Keep cleaning, Atom," Rix said. "We'll bring you dinner, unless you're slacking off."

"Atom work hard, Big Boss," Atom answered cheerily.

"I know you will."

And with that, they set off for Petju's Pub and their first warm meal in weeks.

27

DREAMING BIG

THE MOOD of the folks they ran into as they made their way up to The Atrium was overwhelmingly positive, with people whispering, pointing and some even clapping Rix and Kel on their backs when they passed.

“Wow, people are happy,” Rix said.

“What did you expect?” Kel asked. “They’ve been without power for almost a day and the rumor was the station was dead. We come back and a couple hours later it’s back on. You’re a hero, Rix. I guess my question is, what are you going to do about it?”

Rix didn’t get a chance to answer, as they’d arrived on Level 17, which was crowded with station inhabitants and a raucous celebration that was already well underway. Music blared out from hidden speakers and sounds of loud talking and clinking glasses and the sights of people dancing with no abandon enveloped them as they stepped from the elevator warily. When the party goers closest to the elevator noticed their arrival, the pair were pulled along until they were in the center of it all.

"This is crazy," Rix shouted to Kel, attempting to be heard over the excitement. Just as he spoke, a tall mug of beer was shoved into his hand and Hutari cut into his personal space, pulling him around to dance with her.

"Go with it!" Kel called back, raising both arms and gyrating happily to the music.

"You're the best, Rix!" Hutari shouted exuberantly, dancing lithely next to him.

Rix shook his head. He didn't feel like any kind of hero. Maintenance was an important job, but in his estimation, just about anyone with any mechanical bone in their body could have done exactly what he'd done. That said, he didn't feel it was his place to get in the way of a good party, as there was no doubt in his mind the citizens of Patience Station certainly needed one.

"I need to talk to you," he said when Hutari's dancing brought her closer to him once again.

"No work now! It's party time!" Hutari said as she started moving away.

"It's about your mother," Rix said.

This stopped Hutari cold, her dancing transforming to standing still as she took him in. "What?" she asked, suspiciously.

"Not here," he said.

Hutari nodded and pulled him along behind her. The move caught the attention of several partygoers who cheered them on, making assumptions about their intent.

"What do you mean, *about my mother?*" Hutari asked, after pulling Rix into a nearby, abandoned office. "What do you even know about her?"

"I know plenty," Rix said. "She was with us when we were brought aboard Vigno's ship, *Bonehook*. She got left behind, by her own wishes and probably got scooped up by Dravari."

"I need more words. What do you mean, she got scooped up by Dravari? What were you doing on *Bonehook*?"

"What do you know about your mother and the war?" Rix asked.

"I know I'm not supposed to talk about it."

Rix nodded. "That makes sense. I'll approach differently. Your mother has special skills. Jacknie had Kel and Philo trapped. He was trying to capture your mother and Kel to take to Vigno because he knows how special they are."

Hutari's eyebrows shot up into her hairline. "Do *you* know how special they are?"

"Let's just say neither were acting like themselves when we got picked up," Rix said. "Your mother asked us to get off the ship. She said she could handle it."

"Why didn't Vigno just leave?"

"We disabled the ship because Dravari were coming."

"She's been wanting to do that for a long time," Hutari said. "And Jacknie? Was he caught, too?"

"The headline here is that your mother is in trouble."

Hutari's face relaxed. "Oh, that's funny. Mom handled the three most heinous pirates in this sector of the Galactic Empire in the last two weeks, and you think she's in trouble? Do you understand how special she really is?"

"Probably not, because I appear to be the only one who's worried," Rix said. "I'm sorry. I just don't think she's in a good place. She needs help."

"She might. Highly unlikely, though," Hutari said.

"You're not worried," Rix said.

"You have it bad for her, don't you?" Hutari asked. "She told me there was someone. Funny, the signs were all there, but I didn't figure it was you."

"Not her type?"

"Not really."

"I wondered," Rix said glumly.

"Men are dumb," Hutari said. "No. You're dumb."

"Nice."

"You are. Don't worry. I was dumb, too. Mom clearly has a thing for you. I'm guessing by your reaction, you have similar feelings, otherwise, you wouldn't be so concerned about how I feel about all this."

"I think I probably would," Rix said.

Hutari inspected Rix's face for a few beats and a small grin tugged at her lips. "Man, you're good. I, for sure, want to believe you. Mom has a history with bad boys."

"Be that as it may, I've told you what I needed to. I'm sorry I couldn't do more," Rix said.

"I hear you, Rix Banner," Hutari said. "And now you're officially missing your party."

"You're really not concerned?"

"Not even a little."

And with that, she pulled him back out to the party, which if anything, had intensified in the short time they'd been talking. Once on the main floor, Hutari became distracted by friends who drew her off. Not quite knowing what to do with himself, Rix moved through the crowd, fully intending to find food inside of Petju's Pub, but before he could get there, he was stopped by the man from the manufactory who'd organized help to move the heavy conductor wires.

"I wondered if you could actually pull off the save of the century," Thudd said. "You're the man of the hour! Why don't you have a drink in hand?"

Rix thought back to where he'd left the tall beer someone had handed him and realized he'd abandoned it in the office where he and Hutari had been talking. "I set it down," Rix said.

"I know this is your moment, but there are some of us who'd like to talk to you," Thudd said.

"*Us*?" Rix asked, suddenly concerned that Thudd and his men were the remnants of Sable.

"Council," Thudd said. "There's a rumor you're interested in running for mayor."

"That's Kel's doing," Rix said. "I've no interest. I'm a mechanic, not a politician."

Thudd nodded thoughtfully. "Your popularity would probably earn you the position. No politicking required."

Rix shook his head. "I don't mind helping to keep things running. I don't want to be mayor."

"That is a shame. Would you still be willing to talk with the council? We'd like to get a first-hand understanding of how Patience Station got into such poor repair."

"I can tell you what I know," Rix said. "There's a lot of history I haven't been around for."

"Tomorrow morning, would you be available for a few hours?"

"Will there be food?" Rix asked, his stomach growling loudly.

"I'll make sure of it," Thudd said, smiling and then moving off.

Rix was at the entrance to Petju's Pub when Kel caught up with him. "What were you talking to Thudd about?" she asked.

"Meeting with the council tomorrow morning," Rix said.

"Did you talk to him about running for mayor?"

"I told him I wasn't interested."

A look of disapproval crossed Kel's face but was just as quickly dismissed. "I didn't think you were serious. Most people are drawn to that kind of power."

"Yeah, not me," Rix said. "Besides, who would fix *Calypso* if I became mayor?"

"There's that," Kel said, brightening and then pushing past him into the pub. "Are you buying lunch? Because I'm starving."

Petju's Pub was crowded and the two struggled to make it up to the bar. When they did, Petju saw them. "I'll be there in a minute," she said, handing a platter to a server Rix had seen before. It took closer to ten minutes before Petju was able to free up enough to get to them. "Can we talk business tomorrow? I'm slammed here." Her question was directed at Kel.

"We're just looking for dinner," Kel answered. "We need four of your specials."

"You should have led with that," Petju said. "I heard *Calypso* got hit. Did any of your supply run make it?"

"I thought you were too busy to talk business," Kel said.

"With all this today, I'm going to be back to selling comera in paper cups by tomorrow," Petju said.

"I've got a load," Kel said. "I'll get you inventory and prices."

"Excellent news!" Petju said and turned to Rix. "Mayor?"

"No way," Rix answered.

"Wise man. Four specials coming up," Petju said, nodding with understanding. "Did Thudd already find you?"

"Yes."

"You'll still come tomorrow morning?"

"Of course. I don't mind talking about what I know," Rix said.

"Appreciate that," Petju said. "Okay, I need to get to work here."

Rix nodded and caught Kel looking at him.

"What?" Rix asked, accepting a fresh beer from Petju.

"I can't figure you out," she said.

"I'm not that complex," Rix said.

"Every time I think that, you do something that makes me question it," Kel said. Rix tipped his beer glass into Kel's and took a long drink. When he was done, he struggled not to frown. "What?" Kel asked.

"We need to talk to Petju about cleaning the lines to her taps. This beer is horrible," Rix said.

Kel shook her head. "And then you say stuff like that."

"What?" Rix asked. "I'm serious. Mold grows in the lines and then it tastes bad. Those lines need to be cleaned every couple of weeks."

"I'll let you talk to Petju about that."

"Maybe I'll get a test kit and show her the bacterial growth," Rix said.

"You do that," Kel said, rolling her eyes.

"Here you go! Four specials, on the house," Petju said, handing a bag over the counter.

"Thank you," Rix said, figuring it wasn't the right time to argue about payment.

"I think I'll stay and enjoy the party for a bit longer," Kel said.

"Sure," Rix said. "I'm exhausted, this beer is about to put me down."

"You're an old man, Rix Banner."

"I keep trying to tell you that."

Kel rolled her eyes and then let go with a whoop as she danced out of Petju's and into the courtyard. Rix smiled and followed behind her, moving through the crowd with his head down, trying to be inconspicuous. He was only partially successful, and it took him the better part of an hour to worm his way out of introductions and conversations until he was on the elevator. The elevator stopped on Level 11, which by itself wasn't a huge surprise. That Greasle and two rough looking men joined him, was.

"Greasle," Rix said by way of greeting, nodding his head.

"Word is, you're quite the celebrity," Greasle said. "Why aren't you up enjoying the festivities with all the other sheep?"

"I'm not looking for trouble, Greasle," Rix said. "I'm tired and just looking to get back to my shop so I can eat some dinner."

"I'd hate to keep you from your dinner," Greasle said, his tone sarcastic. "There's a rumor you had something to do with Vigno getting grabbed."

"Hardly," Rix said. "I went out and grabbed Kel's ship, *Calypso*. Bandits put a hole in her the size of this elevator car. Can't imagine what that's got to do with Vigno."

"He's right, boss," one of the men said. "He was sailing a crappy old cargo hauler. Had *Calypso* strapped onto the back. She's in bad shape, that one. My guess, they'll need another loan to get her good and fixed up again."

"Is that what you think?" Greasle asked angrily. "Was I asking you?"

"No, Greasle."

"Then shut up when your betters are talking."

"Yes, Greasle." The man looked at the floor of the elevator, which had stopped on Level 8, where Rix wanted to get off.

"What about it, Banner? Did you have something to do with Vigno getting nabbed?"

"No," Rix said. "I'm a mechanic. I pretty well stick to my lane in things. I have no quarrel with Vigno."

"That's smart," Greasle said. "What about this rumor about you looking to be mayor?"

"Only a rumor," Rix said. "No interest in that, either. It'd just get in the way of my work."

"You know what? I think I like you, Banner," Greasle said. "I like a man who knows his place. When are you getting started on my ships, then, given you're the mechanic?"

"Bring the first one by tomorrow afternoon," Rix said. "I'll get started on diagnostics and get you a price by the end of the day."

"With a friends and family discount."

"I'll give you my best price," Rix said.

"You do that," Greasle said, stepping out of Rix's way so he could exit. "Won't go well for you if I find out you had something to do with Vigno."

"Understood," Rix answered.

Returning to his shop, Rix flipped the lock and sighed. "Heya, Big Boss," Atom said. "Floor good. No?"

Rix set the bag of food onto the workbench and withdrew a box of food and handed it to Atom. "Eat something. Have you seen Philo?"

"Philo in broke ship. Sleepy time."

"Go tell him we've got dinner," Rix said. "I bet he'll be hungry."

"Okay, Big Boss."

Sitting in his chair, Rix glanced out over the shop. Atom had done a reasonable first pass on cleaning, but there was much that was out of place. Tired as he was, Rix decided to address the issues in the morning. He opened the box of food to find a sandwich made with crusty bread and a generous slab of synthesized dark meat protein. It wasn't an unfamiliar taste, and he was hungry enough that his mouth watered at the sight. Before he could bring the sandwich to his mouth, there was a knock at the door.

"Beverly, who is it?" Rix asked, setting the sandwich back into the box.

"Skef," Beverly answered. "I can tell him you'll be open tomorrow if you'd like."

"No, I've been looking forward to this conversation," Rix said with defeat in his voice. "Is it too much to ask that I get ten minutes to eat, though?"

"It appears so," Beverly answered.

Rix opened the door. "Skef, hello," he said. "What brings you by?"

"I ... Well, I don't mean to intrude. Your friend, Kel. She said you and that new woman, Nerali, were working on a project and you've had trouble with the power outages."

Rix nodded. "She's not wrong," he said. "Can I interest you in a bottle of water? I'm afraid that's all I have to offer."

"That is not necessary," Skef said. "I can come back another time if I've inconvenienced you."

"Oh, not at all," Rix said. "Matter of fact, our project is just across this hallway. I'd love your feedback on what we've done."

"That would be grand," Skef said, following Rix across the hallway to the farm.

"My, you've been busy. I haven't seen one of these in quite some time," Skef said, admiring the hydroponics grow house from the outside.

"How'd we do?" Rix asked.

"I'd like to step inside," Skef said, his bright blue eyes darting from one feature to the next. "This is quite an interesting design. Where did you come up with it?"

"Lots of research. We blended several plans together and then made our own drawings," Rix said. "I have plans to add an atmospheric generator and a power cell to give us thirty plus days of independence."

"You have temperature control, it appears."

"Yes."

"And your room is sealed."

"Right."

"Your mix of plants is wrong for survival in the harsh conditions of Patience Station," Skef said, stepping into the hydroponics bay. "But this is quite good. You've only lost two generations."

"Two?" Rix asked.

"Yes, both of these trays are complete losses," Skef said, gesturing to the two most recent generations. "Do you have enough stock to replant? I have some variants you could add if you're amenable."

"Honestly, I'm not the primary farmer. That is Nerali and she's off station for a time," Rix said. "I was hoping you could provide some direction and maybe a little instruction. I'm at something of a loss on how to rotate these generations."

Skef smiled for the first time Rix could ever remember. "If you commit to installing an atmospheric processor and a power cell, I will visit once a day and tend to your farm. You are only a few days from the first fruits of your labor. Do you plan to expand this operation? It appears that once you are underway, you will generate enough for dozens of families. I don't believe you are to the point of financial independence, though. You would need at least six of these rooms to supply the needs of the restaurants of Patience Station, if that is in fact your objective."

"We'd thought four," Rix said. "The power cell, heater and atmospheric processor that we have in mind would be enough for six, though."

"You have sufficient space. What would the cost for such an enterprise be?"

"Give me a minute. Let me calculate that quickly," Rix said.

"Let me guess," Beverly said, appearing in a dark, pin-striped men's suit with a green shaded visor on her head. Sitting behind a desk, she punched wildly at a ten-key machine which spooled white paper tape as she did. "You would like me to run an estimate."

Rix couldn't answer without making it feel odd so he nodded agreement.

"If we salvage a power cell and atmospheric unit from one of the derelicts you've procured, the materials, including growing media, totals twelve thousand credits," Beverly said.

"Twelve thousand to bring this to six units," Rix said. "That's more than I have. I was hoping to shoestring this up by selling produce and reinvesting."

"You are dreaming, my boy," Skef said. "You've already spent twelve thousand."

"Oh, not at all," Rix said. "This is all just basic building material with a few pumps to move solution around and some baffles for cooling and heating."

"Fully self-contained micro farms," Skef said with a far-off look on his face. "This has been talked about for years amongst station growers. The cost has always been prohibitive. But you've skipped the manufactory's primary expense by designing it yourself."

"And using parts from wrecked ships. Don't forget that."

"This is more than a farm," Skef said.

"I don't understand."

"It is a roadmap to nutrition for the masses of space station dwellers, at least for those in space stations with unreliable systems," he said.

"Is that common, unreliable systems on space stations?"

"Yes and no, but there are tens of thousands of stations that could benefit from this. The good something like this could do is inestimable," Skef said. "Have you thought of packaging this for others?"

"I've toyed with the idea, but really, I needed to see it work, first," Rix said.

"That is practical. Some of your approaches are novel, others are less so. Are you open to a partnership? I would bring my considerable knowledge of biological systems. You would bring your practical engineering approach."

"Nerali is already my partner," Rix said and held up his hand as Skef started to interrupt. "How about this? Let's get two more micro farms online. We'll implement whatever changes you and I negotiate and we'll build out a business plan from there. I figure I can do that for about five thousand."

"I'd propose that I invest ten thousand credits to become a one-fifth owner in this venture. Further, I'll tend this current farm and draw up changes that I believe to be critical. Once we agree on changes, I'll make my investment and we can build the entire farm as a prototype. I'll work on securing contracts with the grocery and restaurants of Patience Station. You, of course, are responsible for the machinery."

"You're moving faster than I was expecting," Rix said.

"Perhaps, but I have invested my entire life to plant based biological systems in outer space. I am eminently qualified to know what is and isn't a good bet. This, my friend, has awakened the dreamer within. I am ready," Skef said.

28

MALFEASANCE

RIX LOOKED at the half-eaten sandwich laying on his chest. He'd been awakened by an alarm and felt the cognitive disconnect caused by too little sleep. Still hungry, he shrugged and continued eating the stale sandwich he'd passed out holding the night before.

"Rix, I hate to be a pest, but you have just enough time for a shower prior to meeting with Councilman Thudd Gaveshod."

"Right, thank you, Beverly," Rix said wearily, getting up.

"More sleep, Big Boss," Atom complained.

"I have to get up and going," Rix said. "You can sleep in, but when you get up, you need to sweep the bay again."

"Big Boss, Atom sweep good," Atom whined.

"Sorry Buddy, you made quite a mess. I need this floor clean enough for us to start repair and patching," Rix said.

"Okay, Boss. Atom start now," Atom said with a defeated tone.

Thirty minutes later, Rix was freshly shaven, showered and standing in front of the door on Level 15. *Community Council 15-005* was etched on the door.

"I'm always late for these things, too." Rix turned to Petju's familiar voice.

"You're on the council?" Rix asked.

"There are eight of us," Petju said, opening the door.

The room inside was nicely appointed with fresh paint, clean carpet and a rectangular wood-grained table sitting in the center. Several people were already present and milling around next to a table with breakfast rolls, coffee and cups of a fruity-looking drink.

"Ah, the man of the hour," Thudd said graciously crossing the room with a big smile and an outstretched hand. Over Thudd's shoulder, Rix found Quixly glaring in his direction. He decided, however, to ignore Quixly's expression, as the man often wore a scowl.

"Thudd, thank you for the invitation. Although, I'm not exactly sure how I can help," Rix said.

"We'll get to that soon enough. Load up a plate and we'll get started in a few minutes."

"I'm starving," Rix said, allowing Thudd to lead him over to the snack table.

"Goebel Marks," a Fimilint man with a dark grey trunk for a nose that hung well below his chin announced, introducing himself.

"Rix Banner."

"Oh, we all know your name, Mr. Banner," Marks said with little enthusiasm.

The man's introduction caught the attention of the only two women in the group. Rix didn't recognize either of them. Thudd also noticed the interest and stepped in. "Vergana Nor and Beva Lauge. Vergana provides legal services to station residents and is associated with the university on Caldrin-3. Beva is also an adjunct professor from Caldrin's university. I get this wrong a lot, Beva, so forgive me. I believe you study astrophysics related to ... well, heck, that's where I always get lost."

Beva gave a polite smile at Thudd's inelegance and then bowed her head to Rix. "Astrophysics is likely enough of a description to dissuade further inquiry," she said. Rix couldn't help but imagine she wanted to add – *from a simpleton like you.*

"Nice to meet you both," Rix said. It wasn't lost on him that Quixly had joined the small group so he acknowledged him. "Quixly, good to see you."

"It's time to take our chairs. You're over here, Banner," Quixly said, grabbing Rix's arm, which caused him to slosh his drink.

"Careful, Quixly, I'm not running off," Rix said.

Undeterred, Quixly led Rix around the table. "Look, don't you go making wild accusations today. Some of us must live here."

"Including me," Rix said, pulling his arm free and taking a seat at the end of the table, in front of his nametag.

"Council will come to order," Skef said, tapping a heavy glass globe against a large square plate. "Our first order of business is to welcome visitor, Rix Banner. Rix, welcome."

"Thank you," Rix answered.

"This meeting is called to discuss the events leading up to the recent recurring power failures," Skef said. "Acting Mayor Quixly, you have submitted a report. Would you summarize your findings?"

"Thank you, Council Chair," Quixly said. "For the citizens of Patience Station, this period of continued degradation of services has been a trying time. Our systems are antiquated and require significantly more funds for maintenance than our revenues allow. This is the primary cause for our power failures. Rix Banner has been helpful, but not without significant cost to Patience Station, and some would say that he has profiteered on our citizen's misfortune, requiring great sums of credits and absconding with municipal assets."

"Those are harsh words, acting Mayor Quixly. Do you have details in which to back this up?" Skef asked.

"Prior to entering the council chambers this morning, I have submitted a list of the charges on behalf of Rix Banner in the repair of this station. The totals are well into the millions of credits," Quixly said. Gasps and hard stares followed as the council turned their gazes on Rix.

"Entering acting Mayor Quixly's report to the official record," Skef said evenly.

"We should adjourn. This report is quite long," Beva Lauge said. "I had thought community sentiment was that Rix Banner is a hero. You are saying he is anything but."

Rix looked around the table, where once friendly faces had turned hard. On the table in front of him, Beverly appeared wearing a long black robe. "Quixly has tipped his hand," Beverly said.

"This is a reasonable request, Beva," Skef said. "Acting Mayor, I am disappointed that you could not provide this report prior to the start of our meeting. We have wasted the time of an already very busy council."

"I apologize, Council Chair," Quixly said with a hint of a smug grin.

"Rix, Quixly arrived at millions by using the new market value for the items in trade, including the derelict freighters. Excluding the photonic barrier devices, you were remunerated one hundred thirty credits for each hour you and your team worked. I have a report that contradicts Quixly's if you'd like to utilize it," Beverly urged.

"If there is no other business, this session is closed," Skef said.

"Council Chair, am I allowed to talk?" Rix asked.

"Do you have a rebuttal to acting Mayor Quixly's report?" Skef asked.

"I do. And by my calculations, my repairs, to include the atmospheric condensers, waste management systems and power generation systems, come to one hundred thirty credits per hour," Rix said.

"That's ridiculous," Quixly said.

"Acting Mayor, this is not the forum for interruptions. Rix Banner was invited here and will be given a chance to speak without interruption," Skef said.

"Here's a report with a rebuttal for Mayor Quixly's calculations," Rix said. "I think the most egregious is the valuation of derelict freighters that have been picked over by salvagers and were simply taking up space."

"The photonic barriers are hundreds of thousands," Quixly said.

"And they were all completely inoperable," Rix said. "Only by utilizing parts I own the manufactory rights to were they restored to full function. I repaired all the units from the municipal garage and took a pair of those units as payment. It was my labor and my parts. These units had been sitting inoperable for years. If you had wanted them fixed, you would have done so."

"Quixly, didn't you submit a request to purchase a new pair of photonic generators last year?" Vergana Nor asked.

"Yes," Quixly answered.

Vergana swiped at virtual data on her HUD. "It looks like you asked for one hundred fifty thousand credits. We didn't have the funds at that time and the issue was dismissed."

"Banner has taken two of these pairs. How is that not three hundred thousand credits?" Quixly asked.

"Seems like a win-win to me," Petju said. "We get five repaired pairs without a single credit being expended. That's good business in my books."

"I do not like this Earthling," Jesif complained. "He repaired a sewage backup in my most expensive suites. The cleanup cost was significant, and I had to pay it myself. What did you make for that?"

"Every piece of work I've done for Patience Station has a contract with it," Rix said. "This body has approved every one of those contracts. I'm not sure what the value of this conversation is, but you have both the contracts and rebuttal to Mayor Quixly's claims of malfeasance. Further, you have an issue that requires your attention."

"You are not allowed to bring new issues," Quixly snapped. "You are to answer questions."

"Acting Mayor Quixly, this is no place for a shouting match," Skef said. "If Mr. Banner believes there is an issue that warrants the attention of this council, I believe it is in our best interest to hear about it."

"The materials used to repair the power generator are inferior and will not last more than six months, twelve at the outside," Rix said. As he spoke, angry murmurs around the table grew in volume.

"Why would you install inferior materials, Mr. Banner?"

"That's the only choice we had," Rix said. "Thudd, you know our manufactory's capabilities. Could we have produced the parts I showed you?"

"No," Thudd answered simply. "It would take us six days and an emergency transport to get the radiant heat transfer cables from Grelvox. The specified alloy is very expensive. We don't have the funds. Rix, you had an idea, though, right?"

"Well, it's something of a kluge, but it's doable," Rix said. "First, moving the ice field is critical. That will extend the life of the cables we just installed. Second, there's enough room to install a second radiant transfer unit. I might need to do a bit of part design to make it all work, but it should let us use the cables we can manufacture locally. We have some time to figure that out, though. You don't have to decide to do that right this minute."

"I have a related question before closing this conversation," Vergana said. "I don't mean to interrupt a productive dialogue, though."

"I was done," Rix said.

"We've spent a considerable part of our annual budget on repairing our power generator. Is it so old that these types of failure are commonplace? Do we need to raise money for a new generator to escape these maintenance costs?" she asked.

"The system you have is good and there is no reason to replace it. Prior poor maintenance, with the installation of inferior parts, is the cause of the recent power outages. I'd recommend investigating who was involved in these installations and procurement of parts," Rix said.

"What are you saying?" Goebel Marks, who'd been quiet up to that point, asked.

"I don't think you've been getting what you're paying for," Rix said. "We have a saying on my world: buy cheap, spend twice. Although, I believe, but don't have the evidence, that you paid full price for inferior parts."

"Constable Quixly, would you open an investigation and report back to the council?" Skef asked.

"I would ...," Quixly started.

"Point of order, Council Chair?" Thudd asked.

"Of course, what is it, Thudd?"

"Constable Quixly was involved in prior repairs. Perhaps we could employ a more neutral party."

"Are you suggesting Rix Banner?"

"No, for the same reasons," Thudd said. "I believe Beva has a background in financial transactions."

"Beva, is this a task you'd be willing to take on?"

"Yes. It will take some effort to be thorough. I'm not sure what our record archival looks like."

"In the process of working on the recent repairs," Rix began. "I downloaded the last forty years of maintenance. Eight times, the system was shut down to install radiant exchange components. Six of these installations have occurred in the last eight years." And before anyone could object, he flicked the data broadly from his HUD so that anyone could look at it.

"This is ridiculous," Quixly said, fuming.

"There is nothing to worry about, old friend," Skef said. "We owe the citizens of Patience a good look at our records. We're on no witch hunt, here."

"I've had enough," Quixly said, standing suddenly. "I agreed to be part of this council so I could help. I'll not be targeted by profiteers and hucksters."

"I'll move the investigation to the top of my priorities," Beva said, looking at Quixly curiously.

"If there are no other objections, I move to adjourn," Skef said. And when no one else objected, he banged the globe onto the plate and closed the meeting.

"Rix Banner, a word, if you don't mind?" Vergana Nor called. Like before, she stood next to Beva, as two old friends would.

"Sure," Rix said, joining them. The invitation caught Skef and Thudd's attention and they too walked over.

"I believe you know more than you've said," Vergana said. "I'm good at reading people."

"You'll find that Quixly was involved in procuring the overpriced parts. It looks like there was skimming upwards of two hundred thousand credits over the last eight years," he said. "The information isn't that hard to find. I just compared the maintenance logs with the public meeting notes from the council for the same time frames."

"Hold on, here, is this right?" Beva asked, still scanning the report Beverly had produced.

"What's going on, Beva?" Thudd asked.

"Let me validate this information," Beva said, glaring at Quixly.

"I don't need to put up with this," Quixly said, starting for the door.

Rix happened to be closer to the exit and stepped into Quixly's way. "Hold on a minute," Rix said, looking at Skef for confirmation.

"Beva?" Skef deferred.

Rix held up his hands to keep Quixly from making it to the door. The men scuffled for a moment, but neither wanted to fully engage.

"Quixly, why?" Beva asked, hurt evident in her voice. "You have a good paying job. People have suffered."

Quixly sighed and shook his head. "It doesn't even matter, now," he said. "Vigno, Shixen, Jacknie – they're all gone now. We finally have a chance to kick Sable off Patience and I'm getting brought down by a semi-sentient *human*." The word *human* was said with as much disgust and vehemence as Quixly could muster.

"Sit down, Quixly. We'll talk this through like civilized people," Skef said.

Too late, Rix saw a stun wand show up in Quixly's hand. Pain and the oddest sensation of his muscles all contracting at their highest levels hit him suddenly, and he fell helplessly to the floor.

"Don't come after me," Quixly said. "There's no need for escalation."

Vergana rushed to Rix's side and lifted his head off the ground. Rix was unable to move, aside from flapping his jaw like a fish out of water.

It took a full twenty minutes before Rix's senses were fully restored. Somewhere along the line, Vergana had helped him into a chair, and between cold water and coffee, he imagined he would eventually survive.

"On behalf of the Community Council, we apologize for Mr. Quixly's behavior," Skef said. "And in light of the information Beva's been able to verify, I move that we remove Mr. Quixly from both roles, acting Mayor and Constable. Is there agreement to discuss?"

"I agree," Thudd said.

"As do I," Vergana added.

"This is pretty damning," Beva said. "At a minimum, Quixly should be removed from municipal roles that give him access to funds and resources for the time being."

"Does anyone have an opposing opinion or need further discussion?" Skef asked, waiting until he'd made eye contact with all the remaining council members. "As there is no opposition or request for discussion, please register your vote in this matter."

A short period passed as each council member made gestures, presumably tapping on a voting screen.

"The measure is passed," Skef said, banging his glass globe down. "Beva, I assume you will finish your research and make a report at the next meeting?"

"I will."

29

CLEANING UP

"Did you hear?" Kel asked, her face flush with excitement as she burst into the shop. Three days had passed since the council's fateful vote.

"All I know is it's been quiet and I've enjoyed having a minute to paint this floor," Rix said, looking at the speckled gray, freshly painted floor. It had been days of grinding, filling, sanding, rinse and repeat followed by a run with his new paint gun. "Doesn't it look great?"

"You are truly a man who enjoys simple pleasures," Kel said.

"Doesn't it look great?" Rix repeated. He couldn't imagine why she wasn't more impressed.

"Sure," Kel said, looking like she was about to burst. "Quixly is on the run!" she blurted.

"On the station?"

"No! He grabbed one of the Sable ships. Apparently, Thudd deputized a bunch of his longshoremen and they were going door-to-door on the Sable levels, rounding up petty criminals with outstanding warrants. Greasle, Marbary, Yook ... a bunch of the main Sable guys took off with Quixly. Apparently, they were headed to Sout Atal. Thudd called over to let them know what was coming their way," Kel said. "It's all anyone can talk about."

"So, not how nice my painted floor looks, then," Rix said dryly.

"No. Nobody I've talked to is talking about your shop floor. Although, if I'm honest, it looks pretty good."

"Atom worked his tail off for me," Rix said.

"The Grintok species don't have tails," Kel said.

"Not anymore," Rix added.

"You're so dumb some days. Seriously, though, isn't that great news?"

"Maybe Patience Station will have a chance now. What is it with corrupt politicians stealing people's money?" Rix asked and then rolled his eyes. "Sorry, I just realized how dumb that sounded."

"When can we start working on *Calypso*?" Kel asked.

"Help me start taking her apart?" Rix asked.

"I thought we were putting her back together."

"No, first things first, we'll pull off everything that's broken and line it up along the wall. Once we know how bad it is, we can formulate a plan to fix it," Rix said. "It's going to take some doing, but if we keep at it and get help from Philo and Atom, I bet we could get it taken apart by late tonight."

"You really like doing this, don't you?" Kel asked.

"What's there not to like?" Rix asked, handing a bag of tools to her. "I have coffee made, if you want."

"I'm going to want a nap later," Kel said.

"We'll need to take out the foam, first," Rix said. "How strong of a stomach do you have?"

"I don't understand the question."

"There might be parts of Kurth trapped by the foam," Rix said. "It's not going to be pretty."

"Oh, that. I don't love it, but I'll be fine."

"Sounds good."

It was well into the afternoon when they'd finally removed all the foam and peeled back the thin hull plating well past the damage, leaving bent structural members and ruined systems sticking out of the gaping hole. A chime at the shop's station-side door was well timed, as Rix and Kel were standing within the opening, considering what to tackle next.

"Beverly, who is it?" Rix asked.

"Thudd and Skef," Beverly answered.

"This should be interesting. Also, I need to eat something. How about we grab some food after you're done talking?" Kel suggested.

"I'd be up for that," Rix said, climbing down from *Calypso* and crossing the bay over to the door. "Thudd, Skef, come on in."

"Thank you, Mr. Banner," Skef said formally.

"Is this an official visit?" Rix asked.

"I assume you've heard about Quixly's departure," Skef said.

"Kel was telling me that he and Greasle took off, and Thudd's the new constable," Rix said, glancing at the powerful-looking man. "At least temporarily."

"That's about the shape of it," Skef said.

"How can I be of assistance?" Rix asked.

"We know you're not looking for a new job and that you like what you're doing down here," Skef said. "And I don't blame you. There's been talk of asking you to take over station maintenance for Patience. We have to ask, even though I think I know your answer."

"I'm honored, and not the least bit interested," Rix said. "Once Patience is restored to good working order, maintenance will be the job of a team, more than a single person. I know budgets are tight, but that's just how things are."

Thudd and Skef exchanged looks and Thudd cleared his throat. "The thing is, we don't know that at all," Thudd said. "As a group, the council lacks practical experience in these matters."

Rix nodded and smiled affably.

Skef chuckled. "How about we be more direct? There's a chair open for Community Council. We'd like you to take it and help manage the station. Now, before you object, you should know we only meet for a couple of hours each week. It's been more, lately, but then we've had quite a lot to deal with. Once we have a new mayor, much of the day-to-day business will be their responsibility. It's not the council's responsibility to direct work, only to review what's been done and help guide the ship."

"What happens when Patience Station needs me to fix something? Wouldn't that be a conflict of interest?" Rix asked.

"You'd be asked to abstain from voting, but your opinion would still be considered," Skef said. "What do you say? Can we put your name on the ballot?"

"Change the position to probationary for six months," Rix said. "After six months, if I love it and the remainder of the council wants me to stay, I'm in."

"Why the intermediate step?" Skef asked. "This is a paid position. Most people would jump at it."

"What kind of pay?" Kel asked excitedly. And when everyone turned to her, she quickly retracted. "Oh, sorry, I'm not here."

"It's a reasonable question, and the pay won't change your life, but it might help you sink some roots here on Patience. Currently, seats on the council pay five hundred credits each week untaxed."

"Ooh, that'd be enough to pay for a nice apartment," Kel said. "You could stop sleeping in your chair every night."

"I was working on that," Rix said. "I just hadn't gotten there."

"There is a lot of real estate available on Patience," Thudd said. "I happen to be selling some nice apartments that I'd give a friends and family discount to a new councilman."

"Buy?" Rix asked.

"Sure," Thudd said. "Let me put something together. We can look at it later this evening if you're interested."

Rix started to hem and haw, but Kel jumped in. "We'll be there," she said. "Send me the details. I'll make sure he shows up."

"I see how things work," Thudd said, smiling. "I'll send you something shortly, Ms. Warp"

"Much obliged," Kel said with a sort of curtsey.

"We'll get your name on the ballot. We'll have a vote at the beginning of next week. I doubt, given your current celebrity status, that you'll have any problem garnering enough votes to make it."

"We talked probationary," Rix said.

"A council member may resign at any point in their service without reason," Thudd said. "If it isn't for you, I'll encourage you to do just that, and I can promise there will be no hard feelings."

"Hmm," Rix said, mulling over the options. He didn't like quitting on anything, but he could see Thudd's point. "I'm going to feel like a heel if I drop out after six months."

"Your input will be invaluable, my friend," Thudd said. "Thank you for volunteering to serve Patience Station."

"Do you mind a question?"

"I can't imagine why."

"Is it true you ran off the remainder of Sable?"

"That's a complex question. I suppose with the likelihood of you joining the council, and given your history as a relative newcomer, some background is in order," Thudd said. Rix nodded thoughtfully, urging him to go on. "It's easy to think that a person is a pirate or not a pirate. Association with Sable makes you a pirate. Staying clear does not. The problem with that kind of thinking is that it's too general. Sable sucked in good, hard-working families who had no way to resist them. The boys and I took advantage of the power vacuum left behind by Vigno, Shixen, Greasle, and others leaving the station. We rounded up the most egregious thugs and presented choices: take what you want and skedaddle, or wait to be incarcerated."

"Did you get many takers?"

"Enough for us to start the process of returning ownership of real estate on Levels 10 to 13 to Patience Station."

"Return to the municipality, away from Sable," Rix clarified.

"Just so."

"What happens to that real estate? Does Patience Station collect rents, then? How will people make those payments? Do they have jobs?"

"See, this is exactly the sort of thoughtful dialogue we need in council," Thudd said. "There are no easy answers, but we need to make survival possible for those who are left behind. Jobs, like what you've done for Atom, are the key here. Next week, I'll propose that Patience moves slowly in collecting rents. I'll also propose that we create an actual police force instead of a process server, such as the constable used to be."

"I'm not sure I understand the difference," Rix said.

"The constable's office had muddy jurisdiction. Patience Station needs to combine the space control, the work Hutari is doing, with a real law enforcement branch."

"That sounds expensive."

"It is. We need to attract trade to generate taxes," Thudd said.

"A real, chicken-egg type of problem," Rix said.

"I don't think my idiomatic translator worked with that," Thudd said.

"Oh, which came first, the chicken or the egg?"

"Right, that's perfect. And it's easy to see why pirates make a municipal system fail. If more than half of the citizens of Patience Station fall outside of the taxable umbrella, we don't have the money to keep things working, which encourages those who can leave to do so," he said. "We need to make Patience attractive to traders and settlers alike. We need industry like what you're doing here. And we need to figure out how to do it without large cash outlays."

"I assume Patience is in a poor cash position then," Rix said.

"We are. As an example, we can't afford the higher quality radiative whatchamacallits you proposed," Thudd said. "We need a way to stretch out the use of those things we have."

"In that example, move the ice like we've talked. Keeping that power generator cooler should help extend the life of what we just installed," Rix said.

"You've been a big help by exchanging repairs for non-cash trades," Thudd said. "I hope we can keep finding ways to make that work."

"It's been beneficial for me," Rix said. "Used tools, junked ships and shop space are all critical to getting my business off the ground."

"Skef said you're starting a hydroponics business?"

"I am," Rix said. "My partner, Nerali, is off station currently. When she gets back, we'll really get going."

"I don't know that I've met her," Thudd said, thoughtfully. His eyes glazed over for a moment as he looked at a virtual screen. "Oh, I've seen her around."

"We'll see you later this evening, then?" Rix asked, not wanting to get into an extended conversation related to Amari with Thudd.

"Meet me on Level 21 at 1830?" Thudd offered.

"We'll be there," Kel said smiling.

With Thudd gone, the pair returned to *Calypso* where they set to the task of pulling back the last of the hull sheeting that would expose the remainder of the damaged structural members. Two hours later, they were working to remove equipment and decking from the interior. And, with a little more space to move around in, they brought both Philo and Atom aboard so that all four could get engaged.

"When you said we could get this done today, I thought you were nuts," Kel said, standing with hands on hips, looking at *Calypso's* gutted middle. They'd made several piles against the shop's wall to include: hull sheeting and equipment too ruined to be anything but sent to the reclaimer, equipment that could potentially be repaired and equipment that was in good shape but had been removed to allow access to other parts. "What's next?"

Rix checked the time. "We have thirty minutes before we're meeting Thudd. Let's get a shower in before we do that. I was thinking I'd eat meal bars once we get back. I've sent an order down to the manufactory for the replacement structural members. I'd like to try to get that installed tonight."

"Do you ever rest?" Kel asked.

"This kind of work is fun and besides, what else am I going to do? I suppose we could play cards if you want," Rix said.

"Uh, we could get a drink and socialize a little," Kel said.

"With whom?"

"Whoever's around," Kel said. "If you always lock yourself away like this, how will anyone know who you are and what you can do?"

"I suppose I'd enjoy grabbing a beer or something," Rix said.

"I want to check out Greevo's new Loose Bolt Lounge," Kel said.

"Who is Greevo?"

"Well, you might like him," Kel said. "He's a Grintok like Atom, but he used to be a parts runner for Malkin back when this place was a trade hub."

"That's a lot of new information," Rix said. "Who is Malkin?"

"He was a big-time spaceship repair guy. Did everything from engine overhauls to confidential customizations for discrete haulers. He took off about five years ago. He got pushed out by Sable. Greevo was all about parts procurement and delivery," Kel said. "I've used him to get parts for *Calypso* in the past."

"I've never heard of this place," Rix said.

"Loose Bolts Lounge is on Level 13," Kel said. "Greevo is taking advantage of the vacuum of Sable being gone."

"Dang, that was fast."

"Well, like I said, it's new and I imagine it's not exactly put together all the way," Kel said. "But, Greevo would have access to good alcohol. He's that kind of guy."

"Sounds fun. Sure, let's do it."

"Might be worth packing a pistol, though," Kel said.

"Meet me up on Level 21 with Thudd and then we'll see about your Loose Bolts Lounge," Rix said.

"Okay, and wait for me. I might be a couple of minutes late."

Rix shook his head, knowing full well Kel would be late. Crossing over to the farm, Rix was surprised to find that Skef was tending to the plants. He didn't have a lot of extra time but stuck his head in to see how Skef was faring.

"Have you given my offer any further thought?" Skef asked. "I looked at those designs you sent back. You've taken care of my objections with that last set of changes."

"Are you okay if we hire someone to do the installation? I have a lot going on. I don't mind getting someone started and checking on progress, but otherwise, I can't get to it for several days," Rix said.

"How it is built does not impact me, largely," Skef said. "I'm confident you'll manage the capital of our business effectively."

"Do you know anyone who is good with their hands?" Rix asked.

"I know just the man. Rook Hadden," Skef said. "He does some odd jobs for me from time to time. He's a hard worker."

"I'd love an introduction."

"I'll have him stop by in the morning," Skef said. "Did Thudd find you? I know he was going to stop by."

"We talked."

"I imagine he wanted to talk about his new police force and taking back the Sable levels," Skef said.

"He mentioned something along those lines," Rix said. "Mind if we catch up on that later? I need a shower and I'm meeting someone."

"I was just about done here, myself," Skef said, smiling politely.

Hurriedly, Rix showered and switched into the only change of clothing he owned, careful to put his work clothes into the simple garment cleaner he'd picked up. As he brushed his hair and finished getting ready, he smiled at his reflection in the mirror. Even with all the chaos and tension of living on a space station beleaguered by pirates and decay, he felt more alive than he had since The War.

"Rix, there's something you need to see," Beverly said, cutting into his reverie.

"What's that?"

"A request for funds to pay for transport of biological remains."

30

HONORING SACRIFICE

"WHAT KIND OF BIOLOGICAL REMAINS?" Rix asked.

"Those of Elizabeth Anne Clyde," Beverly said. "Does that make any sense to you?"

Rix stood in silence, stunned. The name was his grandmother's maiden name. It couldn't be a coincidence.

"Rix?" Beverly probed.

"How much?"

"Funds?" Beverly asked and when Rix didn't respond, she continued. "Six thousand, five hundred credits."

"Pay it."

"Rix, that will bring your accounts to nearly zero," Beverly said.

"Please. Just do it," Rix said, his throat constricting. "I recognize the name. It's Amari. She arranged to send her body back. Damn it."

"Are you going to be okay, Rix?"

For a few moments, Rix allowed the flood of fear he'd been holding back to finally break free. He'd hated leaving Amari behind, even with her special skills. It had been too much and he'd known it. Tears ran down his cheeks, and he leaned against the door to the bathroom.

"Rix? Are you coming?" Kel's voice cut in twenty minutes later.

Wiping his face with a cold, wet cloth, Rix looked at himself in the mirror and straightened his shirt by pulling at the hem. "I was delayed. I'll be right there."

With confidence he didn't feel, Rix walked purposefully to the elevators and pressed the button for Level 21. Level's whizzed by and when he got to Level 18, he found that the one side of the car which was transparent suddenly gained a view of space. Any other day, he'd have found the view inspiring. In that moment, he saw only the vast emptiness of space.

Exiting the elevator on Level 21, Rix found Thudd and Kel talking quietly. Kel's eyes narrowed slightly as she inspected his face. With a forced smile, she separated from Thudd and came over to greet Rix.

"Are you okay?" she whispered.

"Something happened. We'll talk about it later."

"Are you sure?"

Rix nodded and then moved to greet Thudd. "I apologize for being late," Rix said. "I ran into something that needed my attention."

"No concerns," Thudd said. "On this level, I have four empty apartments, two of them are furnished, the others are completely empty. Do you have any idea how much you'd like to spend on a home?"

Rix looked thoughtfully at Thudd. "Honestly, I have no idea what real estate costs are on a space station."

"With our occupancy rates, I'd say it's a buyers' market," Thudd said. "The first unit is right this way."

"Talk to me about financing," Rix said. "Who around here does that? Do I contact one of the big banks through the network?"

"You can. Although, I suspect you might not get far due to your relatively short credit history," Thudd said. "If you're amenable, I'd take a run at carrying your loan. We can discuss details if that's interesting."

"Let's see the properties, first," Kel said. "You guys can have your stuffy money conversation later."

Despite the circumstances, Rix managed a smile. "Sure."

"This first unit is empty and is eighty square meters. It has a spaceside view, but it is only two meters in width," Thudd said, holding a door open for them. "If you're looking out from the asteroid, we're far to the left, most of the unit is behind rock, therefore a very safe unit."

Entering, they found themselves in a roughly rectangular room, the wall on the far side irregularly shaped, natural stone. Directly in line with the front door was a two-meter-wide floor-to-ceiling window that looked out into the asteroid field.

"It's a clean slate and very efficient. Most folks would center the main living space on the window view, perhaps with a galley on this side," Thudd said. "One hundred sixty thousand credits is a good market value in a reasonable market. I'll do better than that if you're interested. I wouldn't focus overly on the price, though. Best to get what you want."

Rix looked around. He liked the idea of starting from scratch, but he had a lot of projects already and wasn't sure building out a house was a priority. "Are room separators expensive to manufacture?" Rix asked.

"A good question, Mr. Banner," Thudd said with a big smile. "As you might imagine, the cost of room panels is very much related to what is found within them and their overall fit and finish. Forty thousand credits would get you a modest floor plan with slightly upgraded interior surfaces, to include kitchen, two baths and two nicely sized bedrooms."

"It's more view than I had in my apartment," Kel said. "But I don't know if I'd want to own it long term."

Rix gave her a contemplative look and nodded his head. "That's kind of where I'm at," he said.

"A larger view, then?" Thudd asked. "How about the size? Can you envision the living space you need in this footprint?"

"It's tight," Rix said.

"That's good information," Thudd said. "Let's move to the next suite which is already built out and has an upgraded three meters of view over the asteroid field."

The next apartment had clearly been lived in by a large family. While debris had been removed, the walls and carpet were well-used and in need of updating. The layout of the space was also not to Rix's liking, and they moved quickly to the next.

"How about the two of you go in and take a look first?" Thudd said, standing outside the third apartment. "I have a call I need to make. I won't be but a minute."

At ninety-five square meters, the apartment was larger than the first two they'd seen and there were two windows looking out over the asteroid belt. Rectangular, the space was completely devoid of all features, which drew their eyes to the windows.

"This one is bowed out," Kel said, jogging over to one of the windows. "Can you imagine having a kitchen table here so you could look out while you're having breakfast? Or what if this was a bedroom and you had a round bed shoved up next to it? It'd be like you were sleeping in the asteroid belt."

Rix joined her in the bump out which was only about a meter at its greatest depth, even so, adding drama to the space. "Definitely an eating nook," Rix said. "No reason to limit it to just breakfast. I'd put a long table and comfy chairs here. Kitchen could be just behind a wall back toward there."

"Why not leave it open to the kitchen?" Kel asked. "Put an island between, so you can work in the kitchen and still look out."

"Isn't that weird, to be open like that?"

"I'm not sure I'm the best judge of weird. I just know I don't want to be stuck in the kitchen making food while everyone else is enjoying the view."

"Thudd didn't say how much. I bet it's expensive," Rix said.

"What do you think?" Thudd asked, joining them a moment later.

"I like it," Rix said. "You didn't mention a price. I'm guessing that's not good news."

"You're smart to think that," Thudd said. "This window feature is unusual and pushes the price. We're looking at two hundred thousand with a build-out of fifty thousand. I could back the price off some and get you to two hundred thirty thousand. But that's about the best I could do."

"You were talking about carrying a loan for me," Rix said. "And, just to be clear, this isn't even a possibility unless I win that seat on the council."

"Hmm, so, eighteen hundred credits a month would have you paid off in twenty-five years," Thudd said. "That number includes the recurring fees that Patience Station collects and a little bit of insurance for me, considering your credit history."

"How can you afford that?" Rix asked.

"I own the apartments already," Thudd said. "They're sitting empty, not one earning me credit. I have to put up fifty thousand credits for manufactory work, which I get a small piece of, and then I take your payments and apply them directly to paying off the upgrades first. Three years in, I have that money paid off and it's all gravy from that point forward. Also, presuming you don't do anything crazy, a space that's designed for living will sell better than one that's completely empty."

Rix listened to Thudd's explanation and realized he was right on. It made him wonder if Thudd's interest in him being part of the council was at all related to the transaction, but he soon let the idea go, knowing it wasn't a question that could be answered.

"Let me think on it?"

"How about we see how you do in the polls next week and we'll talk after that?" Thudd said.

"That sounds good."

"Are you still up for trying out Loose Bolt Lounge, Rix?" Kel asked. "Thudd?"

"I'd love to," Thudd said. "I haven't had a chance to see what ol' Greevo has been up to. Gutsy opening up in Sable space before the dust has even cleared. It's a good move, though. He probably has a claim on the space he's using. It's hard to tell."

"That works to his favor, I'd imagine," Rix said.

"If he pays occupancy tax and utilities, I can't imagine Patience Station will have any arguments with a business opening up in Sable territory, especially if he can provide jobs," Thudd said. "I'll meet you down there in twenty minutes?"

"Sounds good," Kel said.

Tapping Level 13 on the elevator, Rix and Kel were finally alone. "I have bad news," Rix said.

"Oh?" Kel asked.

"Sixty-five hundred credit bill for shipping biological remains for Elizabeth Anne Clyde," Rix said.

"From where?"

"Grelvox."

"I don't get it. Who is Elizabeth Anne Clyde? That name doesn't sound familiar at all," Kel said.

"It shouldn't. That's my grandmother's maiden name. It was something I discussed with only one person that I'm aware of," Rix said.

"Biological remains?" Kel asked. "Are you going to pay it?"

"I sent the money already," Rix said. "I think she's dead, Kel."

"Are you going to be okay?" Kel asked. "I don't like the sound of remains. I'm sorry, Rix."

"I knew I shouldn't have left her," Rix said, his face hardening.

"You can't do that to yourself, Rix," Kel said. "Amari is a veteran clandestine operator. She wouldn't have wanted you to sacrifice yourself."

"We should have turned around when we got control of Jacknie's ship."

"And then what?" Kel asked. "Let him go free?"

"We could have turned him over to Dravari."

"Really? And when word gets out that you did, what then? You'd have painted a target on your back the size of Patience Station. Amari was considering all of this. We talked about it and came up with this plan. It was the best option we had. Remember, she needed it to work just as much as I did. Jacknie and Vigno were after us. You were not their focus."

"You can say what you need and I can't really argue with you," Rix said. "It doesn't change that I feel like I could have done something."

"That I can understand," Kel said. "I have that feeling every day about so many things. You can let regrets drive your life or you can honor Amari's sacrifice."

Rix didn't respond other than to nod his understanding.

31

WHAT REMAINS

"CONGRATULATIONS!" Thudd said, pulling Rix into a big hug.

Five days had passed since Rix had received word of Amari's remains being shipped, and his mind was anywhere but election results. His confusion must have been evident, because Thudd prompted him, "You're officially Councilman Banner! You're going to need to make an appearance. People are asking about you."

"Oh," Rix said, registering the information.

Uninterested in taking on other projects, Rix had thrown himself into upgrading the hydroponic farms using Skef's recommendations. After locating an old atmospheric processor on one of the derelict ships, the only remaining work was to find a large enough battery to power the farms through extended outages.

"Might be time to talk about that real estate I showed you," Thudd said, looking around Rix's shop, which had suffered from inattention.

"Basically, I get two hundred credits for my council position, the other eighteen hundred go to you?" Rix asked.

"I think you're talking about the ninety-five-meter place with the bump-out window," Thudd said. "It's a nice place, and just as soon as I get a design from you, we can start with construction. You could be in there middle of next month."

"What kind of up-front money do I need?" Rix asked. "I'm not sitting on a bunch of cash."

"Can you come up with two thousand?"

"That'd about wipe me out, but having a place to live is appealing."

"Are you doing okay?"

"Why?"

"You look like the backside of a Gondarg mine rat and I can smell you from ten meters."

"Look, I got some bad news that I can't really share," Rix said.

"It's about that recovery mission when you went out to pick up Kel and *Calypso* got shot up, isn't it?"

"I can't really say."

Thudd nodded. "Get a shower and we'll get you some food. If you can manage a smile, it'd let people know you're invested in this new position. Do you think you can do that?"

"I'll get it together," Rix said. "Give me twenty minutes."

"I'll be in Loose Bolt Lounge. You need to make nice with Greevo since you blew him off last time," Thudd said.

"Sorry about that," Rix said.

"No need for apologies," Thudd said. "I'll send the contract for the apartment later today and you can send your deposit and a signature once you're in agreement."

"Thank you, Thudd."

"Thank me by showing up this time, okay?" Thudd said, clapping Rix on the shoulder and exchanging a meaningful look. Without further conversation, he exited the shop.

"What's up, Big Boss?" Atom asked, crawling out from his makeshift bed in the corner of the shop.

"I have a meeting," Rix said. "When I get back, we're going to clean this place up."

"Then work on red woman's ship?" Atom asked.

Rix glanced over at *Calypso*, which had sat for several days. Finances were his primary issue on repairs, as he needed to manufacture three thousand credits worth of ribs for the super-structure. With his bank account sitting at three hundred fifty credits, repair was a ways off, and it wasn't helpful that Thudd's apartment had eaten the last of his credits.

Stepping from the shower, Rix pulled on fresh clothing and contacted Kel. "Hey, what's going on?" she asked.

"Want to go to Loose Bolt Lounge? Apparently, I'm on the council now," Rix said.

"Congratulations?" Kel said, questioningly.

"It's a good position for me," Rix said. "I don't want to run things, but I wouldn't mind having some input."

"You'll have plenty of that," she said. "Did you get a shower? You weren't smelling too good yesterday. Are you going to be okay when that crate is delivered? That's tonight, right?"

"That's a lot of questions in a row," Rix said. "Meet me at Loose Bolt?"

Kel chuckled. "Okay, I'm heading there, now."

"You might consider using the groomer Kel left behind," Beverly said, appearing on the stainless-steel shelf beneath the mirror. "You look like a mountain man."

Rix grinned. "You saw that book about Jim Bridger on my bookshelf, didn't you?"

"I haven't seen you smile for several days. Also, *Gordinox*, the freighter carrying your crate is early, they'll arrive in sixty minutes."

"I'm surprised they'd even come out here," Rix said.

"*Gordinox* is one of the few ships that makes regular visits to Patience Station," Beverly said. "Now about that groomer."

"My razor will work just fine," Rix said, spreading foam over his beard.

"It will work on your hair. I can program it so it merely trims your hair with a similar style," Beverly said.

"I suppose I could give it a try," Rix said, pushing his long bangs away from his eyes.

Twenty minutes later, Rix found himself on Level 13, walking toward Loose Bolts Lounge. With people spilling out from the wide entrance, Rix knew he was joining a party already in progress. Even from the outside, Rix could see that the bar was decorated with all sorts of old spaceship parts, from hydraulic cylinders to power plant panels and heat dissipation fans.

"Rix Banner, people! Patience Station's newest councilman!" Thudd said even before Rix could locate him.

A cheer went up and people raised mugs and glasses, turning toward him. "Speech! Speech! Speech!"

Rix shook his head with a smile on his face, waving off the invitation to speak, but Thudd found his way over to him and placed a hand on his back, causing most of the partygoers to quiet. “What do you have to say for yourself, Councilman Banner?”

“Well, I, uh, I’m not much of a public speaker,” Rix said. “I hope I can do a good job for Patience Station.”

A cheer was followed by Thudd turning back to him again. “What will you be most focused on, Rix?”

“Council business covers a lot of ground,” Rix said, reading a script placed in front of him virtually by Beverly. “I’d say that as a focus, I’m interested in fixing infrastructure so that Patience Station is ready for the next generation. After that, I’d like to see what we can do to help stimulate small business starts.”

Thudd gave Rix an approving raised eyebrow. “Well said, Councilman! Well said!”

Rix smiled and nodded. “I don’t suppose I could get a drink?”

This comment earned him several back slaps and a trip to the bar. “First one is on the house,” an older, green-skinned Grintok said with a raspy voice.

Showing up a few minutes later, Kel joined in on the festivities and sidled up next to Rix. “Are you doing okay? We’re going to have to get that crate soon. *Gordinox* is arriving early.”

“I’m okay,” Rix said. “Give it twenty minutes and we’ll slip out of here. I think most of these folks are just looking for a reason to have another drink.”

“Well, Thudd said he was paying for the first hour,” Kel said. “That’ll keep people happy for a time.”

Smiling, Rix worked the crowd, often relying on Beverly’s scripted responses to answer questions he could barely understand, either due to poor communication or references he had no basis for. Finally, Kel caught his eye and gestured with her head toward the exit. It took

Rix a few minutes to escape, but given the level of consumption in the room, it wasn't a significant challenge.

"I'm glad to be out of there," Rix said as they walked quickly to the elevator.

"I bet," Kel said. "We'll be down on Level 5 to meet up with *Gordinox*. They have a big load, and your crate is probably one they want to have out of the way."

"Let's grab a grav pallet from the shop," Rix said.

With the short detour included, they were nonetheless to the pier where *Gordinox* would dock several minutes before its arrival. "I see it," Kel announced after some time. She pointed to where bright lights blinked in the distance. As the freighter approached, it seemed to grow until it was at least five times the size of *Calypso*.

"Big freighter," Rix said.

"Still in the same class as *Calypso*. You should see some of the big boys. They can be almost as long as Patience Station is tall."

"That'd be something to see."

"Most of those are interstellar. Nobody would bring something that big out to Surnac Belt. It's already hard enough to get here."

It took twenty minutes for the larger freighter to settle into position and for mooring clamps to be deployed. "I have contact with the *Gordinox* load master," Beverly said. "They'll offload the crate to Hatch 014A. I'm highlighting it for you."

"Thank you, Beverly," Rix said.

"Oh, is she helping?" Kel asked.

"This way," Rix said, pointing at a hatch about a third forward from the aft-most part of the ship.

By the time they arrived, the hatch was open and an older Fimilint woman pushed a two-meter-long crate on a gravity pallet out onto the pier. The deckhand looked around and when Rix waved, she nodded and waited for their arrival.

"Rix Banner?" she asked, holding out an electronic pad with a signature request already showing.

"Yes," Rix said, pressing his hand onto the pad, which caused it to glow green with acceptance.

"I have instructions to deliver this directly to your quarters," the woman said, her small nose flexing each time she moved her head.

"That's not necessary," Rix said. "I can take it from here."

"I'm afraid I can't do that. I'm required to validate delivery to Bay 807. It's an insurance thing."

Rix shrugged. "Follow me?"

"That will work."

"Tough trip out from Grelvox?" Kel asked amiably as they walked back toward the elevator.

"Wouldn't know. Load handlers stay on the lower decks and play cards," she said.

"You any good?" Kel asked.

"Good enough to double up my earnings on a trip out to Patience," the woman said.

"That right?" Kel asked.

"We're here for a couple of days. Any recommendations?"

"There's a new bar on Level 13," Kel said. "Feels like your vibe."

"I got a vibe, do I?"

"Didn't catch your name," Kel said.

Pushing the pallet from the elevator, the woman started down the hall. "Maybe I didn't toss it," the woman said over her shoulder.

"Kel, a minute?" Rix said.

"It's 807, we'll catch up," Kel called after the woman. "What's up?"

"Is this weird?"

"We're taking remains," Kel said. "Doesn't feel weird to me. She seems alright."

"How'd she know which way to turn?"

"Only left or right available," Kel said. "Probably knew we'd correct her if she got it wrong. Don't be so suspicious all the time."

"Because people haven't been trying to do us in since we got here?" Rix asked sarcastically.

"Yeah, true. Don't sweat it. I'm packing," Kel said, tapping her back where a small weapon was tucked into her belt.

"Where do you want it?" the woman asked, waiting at the door to the shop.

"You can leave it here," Rix said.

"Just need to get it through the door."

Rix opened the door with a sigh. "Put it anywhere."

"Sign here," the woman said. Rix did as asked, and the woman looked at Kel. "See you tonight?"

"Bring some money."

The Fimil woman nodded and exited without saying anything further.

"What now?" Kel asked.

"I suppose you should open it. How about I give you some privacy?" Kel said.

"She was your sister," Rix said.

"She was, but I'm not sure I'm up for this today."

"Sure, okay," Rix said, sitting on his haunches next to the crate.

"Coming up to Loose Bolt later? It might be nice to get lost in a crowd tonight."

"Maybe," Rix said, placing a hand on the crate.

Kel leaned over and gave him a quick hug. "Try," she whispered.

He couldn't answer other than to nod.

The door closed behind her, and he sat for a while, not wanting to move. Finally, grabbing a hammer, he tapped the skinny end of a crowbar beneath a lip on the top of the crate. Fasteners groaned with complaint as he levered the top off, only to discover a covering of loose packing material, which surprised him. He set the tools on the ground.

"Dammit, Amari," he whispered. "Why wouldn't you let me help?"

He pulled at the packing material and stared at the contents, shaking his head. Whatever he'd been expecting, bags of grain, packets of seeds, bottles of alcohol and random other packages wasn't it.

"What in the hell?" he asked. "Beverly? What's going on?"

"Maybe she dropped off the wrong crate," Beverly offered, appearing as she sat on the edge of the crate, looking at him with concern.

"I'll catch up with her," Rix said, turning suddenly and rushing for the door. Slapping the pad, the door slid open. Rix felt a moment of confusion as someone stood in the door. Without looking, he tried to step around. "I've got to go."

"Do you?" a woman's voice asked. Rix froze. It wasn't just anyone's voice. His head swiveled and shock registered in his system as the woman he'd thought dead stared back at him. "Did you miss me?"

"Amari? How?" he asked. "The remains."

"Is that really the conversation you want to have?" she asked, wrapping long arms around his neck. Tipping her head to the side, she leaned forward, their lips barely touching. "Or maybe you'd like to invite me in. What's it gonna be, Rix?"

But of course, that's another story entirely.

32

RAY GUNS AND LATE FEES

WHAT FOLLOWS IS a preview of the third novel in the Spaceship Mechanic series titled Ray Guns and Late fees. The full novel will be available in the second quarter of 2026.

33

HIGH WIRE

"WHEN WILL YOU BE BACK, Kasit? We need to talk," Zenith Quel looked at the boy who'd seemingly turned into a man overnight. Thin, muscular, and quick to smile, Kasit was every bit as attractive as his father had been and she worried that those attributes would put him on his father's path.

"I have a job to run for Mara Vell," Kasit said. "It's a piece of cake."

"Mara Vell is dangerous, Kasit," Zenith said. "Did you talk with Kha'rem? He has work over at Driftmarket for you. It's good money."

"I'll stop by Kha'rem's after my run," Kasit said.

"I don't like you getting in with Mara Vell," Zenith said.

"I'm not getting in with anyone," Kasit said.

Zenith looked at her son with concern. She'd been only sixteen when he'd been born and life had always been a struggle. She'd learned hard lessons recovering from bad decisions in her teen years.

"Easy money is a slippery slope, Kasit," she warned. "Everything has a cost."

Kasit's expression softened and he stepped into his mother's space, wrapping long arms around her. "I'm not Dad, Mom. I have no interest in joining a pirate crew. Vell just needs me to move something out to Black Spire."

"You shouldn't be in Black Spire. Getta are all over Black Spire."

"I won't be for very long. It's a quick drop. They need me because I can get in from the backside. I won't even see anyone," Kasit said and before she could object further, he continued. "Mom, I love you, but I need to live my life the way it makes sense to me. I promise, I'm not doing anything dangerous."

"It sounds dangerous."

"I'll bring back dinner from Driftmarket after I do whatever Kha'rem needs, okay?"

"Go, Kasit. Just be careful."

"You underestimate me, Mom. Nobody's faster on the wires than I am," Kasit said. "They won't even know I've been to Black Spire."

"It's a mother's prerogative to worry for her children. You're all I have, Kas."

"Same, Mom." Kasit kissed his mother's head and escaped through the front door to their bricked hovel that sat within the large bowl that made up Havenfall Enclave. Sliding a condenser filter into his nostrils, Kasit took off at a run.

Located within Ghostmist Nebula, Garanod Enclave consisted of five districts which occupied long separated masses from a failed planetary formation. The districts Black Spire, Drift Market, Havenfall, Chainreach and Quiet Coil had little in the way of codified laws, and each followed subtly different customs that were quietly observed by those looking to maintain the uneasy peace.

"You're late." Mara Vell's voice growled over comms. "You missed the ferry."

Kasit sprinted across Havenfall's bioluminescent landscape lit by dimly glowing, failing ancient space station 'suns' that had been pushed into place long ago.

Travel between the districts was safest by ferries which moved on their own schedules and slid along spider webs of fluxspan rails, which had haphazardly been stretched between.. If one had enough money and enough guts, private cars could be hired to race along, assuming the operator paid attention to the voluntary registry of who was using which rail and at what time. Collisions were common enough as were detached cars, careening out of control for various reason. Even so, ferries and private cars travelled considerably safer than rail dancers, like Kasit, who used a simple sling and no shortage of acrobatic skills to navigate the morass.

Kasit grinned as he watched the Havenfall to Driftmarket ferry starting its slide down the glowing blue rail. Slicing through the crowd of queued passengers who would wait another forty minutes for the ferry to return, he leapt from the platform and flung the end of his sling over the top. A satisfying crackle of energy reverberated through his body as the magnetic latch grabbed and his weight settled. Adjusting his connection, Kasit took advantage of the bow in the rail to freefall toward the distant ferry. With practiced ease, Kasit slowed his approach once he was within a hundred meters and at the last moment, he lifted his knees and landed atop the ferry.

"I just caught it," he replied to Vell.

"You take unnecessary risks," Vell said darkly.

"Just keeping my skills sharp," Kasit said. "Isn't that why you hired me?"

"We will see." Vell closed communications leaving Kasit to his thoughts as the light atmosphere of the nebula buffeted him.

"Someone took her grumpy pills this morning," Kasit quipped and then quickly checked to make sure he wasn't transmitting.

Approaching Driftmarket was always a view Kasit enjoyed. The smoothest of the planetary fragments that made up Garanod, Driftmarket had been hollowed out over the centuries and terraced into overlapping bazaars that clung to it like a sea of colorful barnacles. Navigation through Driftmarket was not for the fainthearted as urban planning had played no part of its evolution. Stairs, spiral walkways, escalators and every method of conveyance joined otherwise dysregulated streets and alleyways. Having spent his entire life on Garanod, Kasit knew the area as well or better than anyone and his unique skills as a rail dancer lent themselves to traversing the landscape.

Thirty minutes after leaving home, Kasit dropped lightly onto a cobblestone walkway. Straightening his shirt, he knocked softly on a salmon-colored door where no light shown through the opaque glass, suggesting no one was home.

The door opened a crack and a young woman peered out. Seeing that it was Kasit, she opened the door. "One of these days, you will not be so lucky. Mara requires precision in schedules. You were almost late, today," the girl scolded.

"And yet I wasn't," Kasit said, grinning broadly. "Do you have it?"

"Were you followed?"

"There aren't five people in all of Garanod who could have followed the path I took and before you ask again, I did not see any of them on top of the Driftmarket Ferry nor running across the rooftops," Kasit said confidently.

"This is no game, Kasit," Pera said.

"And yet I take great pleasure in it," Kasit said. "Do you have the package?"

Pera picked a leatherbound journal from a humble table that sat near the entryway. "Take this to a man in Black Spire. He will be wearing a red diffuser with this symbol on it," Pera said. On the table she spilled a measure of salt and drew an arc beneath which she used her finger to create two small dots. “He will be near the 132 rail and is waiting for you.”

“Red nasal diffuser with that symbol. This is supposed to be an easy job. What’s with all the intrigue?” he asked.

Pera brushed her hand across the salt. “It is an easy job. Finish it without attracting attention.”

“When do I get paid.”

“Be patient. Payment is certain, but do not come back here.”

34

RAY GUNS AND LATE FEES

WHAT FOLLOWS IS a preview of the third novel in the *Spaceship Mechanic* series titled *Ray Guns and Late fees.* The full novel will be available in the second quarter of 2026.

CHAPTER 1 – **High Wire**

"When will you be back, Kasit? We need to talk," Zenith Quel looked at the boy who'd seemingly turned into a man overnight. Thin, muscular, and quick to smile, Kasit was every bit as attractive as his father had been and she worried that those attributes would put him on his father's path.

"I have a job to run for Mara Vell," Kasit said. "It's a piece of cake."

"Mara Vell is dangerous, Kasit," Zenith said. "Did you talk with Kha'rem? He has work over at Driftmarket for you. It's good money."

"I'll stop by Kha'rem's after my run," Kasit said.

"I don't like you getting in with Mara Vell," Zenith said.

"I'm not getting in with anyone," Kasit said.

Zenith looked at her son with concern. She'd been only sixteen when he'd been born and life had always been a struggle. She'd learned hard lessons recovering from bad decisions in her teen years.

"Easy money is a slippery slope, Kasit," she warned. "Everything has a cost."

Kasit's expression softened and he stepped into his mother's space, wrapping long arms around her. "I'm not Dad, Mom. I have no interest in joining a pirate crew. Vell just needs me to move something out to Black Spire."

"You shouldn't be in Black Spire. Getta are all over Black Spire."

"I won't be for very long. It's a quick drop. They need me because I can get in from the backside. I won't even see anyone," Kasit said and before she could object further, he continued. "Mom, I love you, but I need to live my life the way it makes sense to me. I promise, I'm not doing anything dangerous."

"It sounds dangerous."

"I'll bring back dinner from Driftmarket after I do whatever Kha'rem needs, okay?"

"Go, Kasit. Just be careful."

"You underestimate me, Mom. Nobody's faster on the wires than I am," Kasit said. "They won't even know I've been to Black Spire."

"It's a mother's prerogative to worry for her children. You're all I have, Kas."

"Same, Mom." Kasit kissed his mother's head and escaped through the front door to their bricked hovel that sat within the large bowl that made up Havenfall Enclave. Sliding a condenser filter into his nostrils, Kasit took off at a run.

Located within Ghostmist Nebula, Garanod Enclave consisted of five districts which occupied long separated masses from a failed planetary formation. The districts Black Spire, Drift Market, Havenfall, Chainreach and Quiet Coil had little in the way of codified laws, and each followed subtly different customs that were quietly observed by those looking to maintain the uneasy peace.

"You're late." Mara Vell's voice growled over comms. "You missed the ferry."

Kasit sprinted across Havenfall's bioluminescent landscape lit by dimly glowing, failing ancient space station 'suns' that had been pushed into place long ago.

Travel between the districts was safest by ferries which moved on their own schedules and slid along spider webs of fluxspan rails, which had haphazardly been stretched between.. If one had enough money and enough guts, private cars could be hired to race along, assuming the operator paid attention to the voluntary registry of who was using which rail and at what time. Collisions were common enough as were detached cars, careening out of control for various reason. Even so, ferries and private cars travelled considerably safer than rail dancers, like Kasit, who used a simple sling and no shortage of acrobatic skills to navigate the morass.

Kasit grinned as he watched the Havenfall to Driftmarket ferry starting its slide down the glowing blue rail. Slicing through the crowd of queued passengers who would wait another forty minutes for the ferry to return, he leapt from the platform and flung the end of his sling over the top. A satisfying crackle of energy reverberated through his body as the magnetic latch grabbed and his weight settled. Adjusting his connection, Kasit took advantage of the bow in the rail to freefall toward the distant ferry. With practiced ease, Kasit slowed his approach once he was within a hundred meters and at the last moment, he lifted his knees and landed atop the ferry.

"I just caught it," he replied to Vell.

"You take unnecessary risks," Vell said darkly.

"Just keeping my skills sharp," Kasit said. "Isn't that why you hired me?"

"We will see." Vell closed communications leaving Kasit to his thoughts as the light atmosphere of the nebula buffeted him.

"Someone took her grumpy pills this morning," Kasit quipped and then quickly checked to make sure he wasn't transmitting.

Approaching Driftmarket was always a view Kasit enjoyed. The smoothest of the planetary fragments that made up Garanod, Driftmarket had been hollowed out over the centuries and terraced into overlapping bazaars that clung to it like a sea of colorful barnacles. Navigation through Driftmarket was not for the fainthearted as urban planning had played no part of its evolution. Stairs, spiral walkways, escalators and every method of conveyance joined otherwise dysregulated streets and alleyways. Having spent his entire life on Garanod, Kasit knew the area as well or better than anyone and his unique skills as a rail dancer lent themselves to traversing the landscape.

Thirty minutes after leaving home, Kasit dropped lightly onto a cobblestone walkway. Straightening his shirt, he knocked softly on a salmon-colored door where no light shown through the opaque glass, suggesting no one was home.

The door opened a crack and a young woman peered out. Seeing that it was Kasit, she opened the door. "One of these days, you will not be so lucky. Mara requires precision in schedules. You were almost late, today," the girl scolded.

"And yet I wasn't," Kasit said, grinning broadly. "Do you have it?"

"Were you followed?"

"There aren't five people in all of Garanod who could have followed the path I took and before you ask again, I did not see any of them on top of the Driftmarket Ferry nor running across the rooftops," Kasit said confidently.

"This is no game, Kasit," Pera said.

"And yet I take great pleasure in it," Kasit said. "Do you have the package?"

Pera picked a leatherbound journal from a humble table that sat near the entryway. "Take this to a man in Black Spire. He will be wearing a red diffuser with this symbol on it," Pera said. On the table she spilled a measure of salt and drew an arc beneath which she used her finger to create two small dots. "He will be near the 132 rail and is waiting for you."

"Red nasal diffuser with that symbol. This is supposed to be an easy job. What's with all the intrigue?" he asked.

Pera brushed her hand across the salt. "It *is* an easy job. Finish it without attracting attention."

"When do I get paid."

"Be patient. Payment is certain, but do not come back here."

ACKNOWLEDGMENTS

To Rachel Aukes and Jordan Olsen for excellence in editing and word-smithery.

To my beta readers: Carol Greenwood, Kelli Whyte, and Lyle Clingman for wonderful and thoughtful suggestions. It is a joy to work with this intelligent and considerate group of people.

Finally, to Elias Stern, cover artist extraordinaire.

ABOUT THE AUTHOR

Jamie McFarlane is the father of three and lives in Lincoln, Nebraska. An avid runner, scuba diver and hiker, Jamie enjoys the active life writing fulltime affords him.

Word-of-mouth is crucial for any author to succeed. If you enjoyed this book, please consider leaving a review, even if it's only a line or two; it would make all the difference and would be very much appreciated.

If you'd like to receive automatic email when Jamie's next book is available, please visit http://fickledragon.com. Your email address will never be shared and you can unsubscribe at any time.

For more information
www.fickledragon.com
jamie@fickledragon.com

ALSO BY JAMIE MCFARLANE

Spaceship Mechanic

1. Boltguns and Duct Tape
2. Jump Drives and Coffee Stains
3. Ray Guns and Late Fees (second quarter 2026)

Junkyard Pirate Series

1. Junkyard Pirate
2. Old Dogs, Older Tricks
3. Junkyard Spaceship
4. Junkyard Veterans
5. Junkyard Raiders
6. Junkyard Ghost Ship
7. Junkyard Commandos
8. Junkyard Mercenary
9. Junkyard Saboteur

Oldest Starfighter Series

1. The Oldest Starfighter
2. Rogue Commander

Privateer Tales Series

1. Rookie Privateer
2. Fool Me Once
3. Parley
4. Big Pete
5. Smuggler's Dilemma
6. Cutpurse
7. Out of the Tank

8. Buccaneers
9. A Matter of Honor
10. Give No Quarter
11. Blockade Runner
12. Corsair Menace
13. Pursuit of the Bold
14. Fury of the Bold
15. Judgment of the Bold
16. Privateers in Exile
17. Incursion at Elea Station
18. Freebooter's Hold
19. Black Cutlass
20. Privateer's Supremacy

Space Troopers Series

1. Rebel's Call
2. Rebel's Run
3. Rebel's Strike

Privateer Tales Universe

1. Pete, Popeye and Olive
2. Life of a Miner
3. Uncommon Bravery
4. On a Pale Ship

Henry Biggston Thrillers

1. When Justice Calls
2. Deputy in the Crosshairs
3. Manhunt at Sage Creek

Witchy World

1. Wizard in a Witchy World
2. Wicked Folk: An Urban Wizard's Tale
3. Wizard Unleashed

Guardians of Gaeland

1. Lesser Prince

www.ingramcontent.com/pod-product-compliance
Lightning Source LLC
LaVergne TN
LVHW020040110826
845155LV00029B/563
9781943792221